P R A I S E   F O R
The Duke Undone

"I loved *The Duke Undone,* and so will my readers!"   —Eloisa James,
New York Times bestselling author of *My Last Duchess*

"A beautiful blend of seductive suspense and heart-tugging romance that I could not put down. Romance fans should make room for this author on their keeper shelves!"   —Lyssa Kay Adams,
national bestselling author of *Crazy Stupid Bromance*

"Joanna Lowell's skillful storytelling and dazzling characters create one of the most exciting new voices in historical romance today."
—Julia London,
New York Times bestselling author of *A Princess by Christmas*

"A charming romance with an atypical heroine and a to-die-for (and hot!) hero in this unique tale of a duke and a struggling artist in Victorian London."
—Jennifer Ashley,
New York Times bestselling author of *The Stolen Mackenzie Bride*

"I really loved this book—in fact, I couldn't put it down. It's a fabulous feast of a story that plunges you into the Victorian era with all its levels and complications—into the art world and among aristocrats and slum-dwellers. There's tension, adventure, derring-do, a fight against corruption on several levels, a rich cast of characters, and a hero and heroine to admire and cheer for. All in all, a rich and heartwarming historical romance. Highly recommended."
—Anne Gracie,
national bestselling author of *Marry in Scarlet*

THE DUKE UNDONE

Joanna Lowell

JOVE

New York

A JOVE BOOK
Published by Berkley
An imprint of Penguin Random House LLC
penguinrandomhouse.com

Library of Congress Cataloging-in-Publication Data

Names: Lowell, Joanna, author.
Title: The duke undone / Joanna Lowell.
Description: First edition. | New York: Jove, 2021.
Identifiers: LCCN 2020042420 (print) | LCCN 2020042421 (ebook) |
ISBN 9780593198285 (trade paperback) | ISBN 9780593198292 (ebook)
Subjects: GSAFD: Love stories.
Classification: LCC PS3618.U568 D85 2021 (print) |
LCC PS3618.U568 (ebook) | DDC 813/.6—dc23
LC record available at https://lccn.loc.gov/2020042420
LC ebook record available at https://lccn.loc.gov/2020042421

First Edition: April 2021

Printed in the United States of America

1st Printing

Book design by Katy Riegel

This one is for Gail.

PROLOGUE

London
October 1881

As LUCY COOVER turned into the narrow alley, her eye caught the patch of early morning sky peeping out between the tenements. Violet, paling to softest blue. The silver moon still floating above a single rosy cloud. Her fellow students at the Painting School would never believe the slums of Shoreditch could offer such beauty. But how to capture that quality of light? She held up two fingers and focused on the span between. Still gazing upward, she took another step.

Something beneath her foot *crunched*.

Not mud, not refuse.

Dear God. There was a *hand* beneath her boot. The hand attached to a wrist, and the wrist to a forearm, the forearm to an elbow, the elbow to an upper arm, shoulder, neck, head.

She had trod on a corpse.

Lucy sprang back. The feel of fingers grinding beneath her heel made her stomach plunge. But the corpse didn't stir.

Well, a corpse wouldn't.

There he lay, stretched before her. She felt her heart pounding in her ears. She could hear the street sounds and see, between the bowing walls, a sliver of morning life. Omnibuses and donkey carts rolled along, hemmed in by the throngs. Every morning, Lucy hurried past crumbling tenements, crossed through grim, teeming courtyards, and squeezed through this passageway, a shortcut to the High Street, where she caught the omnibus to the Royal Academy of Arts. She'd stepped on her share of rotten onions and, once, a rag that squeaked and discharged a rat.

This was something new.

She steeled herself for another glance. *Ah.* Poor soul, he'd been deprived of life *and*—she swallowed—every last stitch of clothing. Shoreditch teemed with street toughs, notorious for theft and murder. Knocked him on the head, perhaps, stripped him of coin, cloth, and shoe leather. Dumped him in the passage to rot. Her skin prickled as it turned to gooseflesh. She whirled around, but no one loomed behind her. This had to be the loneliest alley in all of London. She turned back slowly.

How strange, this feeling that she and the corpse occupied their own little world, a quiet pocket in the clamorous city. The busy street was so close, but the passersby kept their eyes down or fixed straight ahead. For help she would need to send up a cry.

Murder!

And yet . . . her gaze dropped again. The corpse was beginning to strike her as remarkably vital. Surely, murder most foul never left the skin with such a ruddy glow. Or the limbs arranged with such casual, insouciant grace. The morning was uncommonly fine, and the moon still floated directly overhead. Was it her whimsy or did it lend an odd, silvered clarity to the light?

It felt wrong to stare. But she was, after all, *trained* to stare. She lowered her bag to the ground. She drew her brows together and gave the corpse a long and steady look.

One arm was bent behind his head. The other arm was flung across the broad expanse of his chest. A chest that was, almost imperceptibly, rising and falling.

He lived.

There was just enough room for her to edge around him. She circled by inches, breath catching as she took in every detail. From head to toe, he was, in a word, magnificent. A figure of geometric perfection. He could easily stand among the statues she'd sketched in the Antique School. Except he wasn't marble. Wasn't nearly so smooth, so rounded. Any bust of Achilles would look well with that straight nose and strong chin, those full but starkly shaped lips. But no sculptor would dare carve that jawline. It was too square, too harsh, contours darkened with stubble. The *maleness* overpowered and was completely wrong for classical forms. Old gods and warriors wore thick, curled beards as profuse as a maiden's locks. The young ones showed sloped cheeks that flirted with girlishness.

This man was not girlish. No. Not that. She noted the bulge of biceps in his bent arm. The width of the forearm. She moved her eyes over his torso, the masses of muscle well-defined, dusted with more of that utterly unclassical hair, then traced the diagonal lines that ran down from his hip bones.

She looked away, then back at the black curls at the base of that V of muscle. Here, then, was another deviation from classical precedent.

Canvases and statues had led her to expect something slightly more . . . cherubic from *that* part of the anatomy. Obviously, artists upheld a long tradition of minimizing male genitals for the sake of composition. Or decency. Or . . . Did this particular man exhibit some quirk of proportion?

Her suppressed giggle emerged as a snort. It didn't matter, of course, the man's particular quirks, but that he had them at all. That he was *particular*. Not an abstraction, a mathematical proposition in stone. Those cold, white statues she studied had taught her little about flesh, the tones and textures, the play of shadow and light, hard and soft. All those hours in the studios of Burlington House trying to work out how the sinews of the human form wrapped the armature of the bones . . .

She almost clapped her hands. She felt flushed, wild. Here it was, the whole mystery of creation. No wonder women were denied access to life classes, banned from drawing semidraped and undraped figures. It wasn't because the sight was corrupting. It was because the sight was illuminating.

She leaned closer and caught a whiff of him, caustic enough to cut through the alley's fug of mud and mildew. She wrinkled her nose.

Spirits were emanating from his very pores. He wasn't dead; he was dead drunk. Drank himself witless, and some of the local lads had played him for the fool he was. They could have left his *drawers*, for God's love.

She dropped down into a crouch, dust and straw puffing up around her. She knew it was madness to sit on her heels beside a naked stranger, a sot, full as a tick on forty-rod gin. Drunkards didn't often emerge from sleep in the sweetest of moods. This one was strong. His body showed strength in every line. He might leap up without warning, swinging his fists in a rage.

Her reflexes, though, were lightning quick. She could dodge a groggy blow.

"Hullo." She cleared her throat, sidled closer. *"Sir."*

She only meant to rouse him. She wasn't trying to memorize the balance of his features, the shape of his mouth, the sharp peaks of his upper lip. But somehow time was passing. She could hear the factory whistles sounding and her eyes were still wandering, sliding down to his chest and arms. She'd have to *run* from the omnibus to make her morning lesson.

She rose, crept out onto the street. On the corner, a red-faced bobby was blowing his whistle. She'd bet her right eye the police would give the man a sniff, heave him up on the wagon, and dump him in a jail. The thought disturbed her. She turned away. There, a ragpicker, painfully young, all but hidden by the bag on his back.

She gave him a smile. "What's your biggest piece of sacking?" The boy sized her up as he dug out a filthy rectangle of cloth. Bigger than a fig leaf, but not by much.

"A shilling," he pronounced.

She sighed. "Never mind." She'd sacrifice her shawl. She slipped back into the alley and covered the man's lower body with odd reluctance. It wasn't the shawl she regretted. It was losing the sight of him.

Back on the street, she found the boy waiting, more of his wares displayed for her on the pavement.

"There's a man sleeping in that alleyway," she said. "I'll give you a tanner to stand right there and keep an eye on him. If he starts to go blue, call a bobby."

The boy snatched the coin and grinned. He was missing both his front teeth. Probably he wouldn't even wait for her to climb into the omnibus before he trundled off, taking the shawl with him.

"Don't go too near," she added. "He eats little boys."

And he might, for all she knew. The man had certainly done nothing to deserve her sacrificing a shawl and spending sixpence. *And*, at this rate, missing her morning lesson.

Nonetheless, she felt protective of him.

She had to force herself to walk away.

On her way home, she took the same shortcut and hardly knew if she was happy or sad that the man was gone.

Late that evening, she found herself hunched over her sketchbook, staring at the blank page. When she shut her eyes, she could see him perfectly, see his contours and the dynamic tension latent in his resting muscles.

She inched her fingers up the pencil, hesitated. That man was someone's son. Brother. Husband. She had no right to reproduce his likeness at a whim.

But the image was there, on the insides of her eyelids.

The seeing was a kind of feeling. She was feeling her way toward something extraordinary. She could capture it, his beauty. The heat of his slumberous, living flesh.

All alone in her little room, her great-aunt Marian asleep downstairs in the dress shop, and just overhead, hidden by the slant of the roof and by the clouds, the moon, a secret accomplice, she could put down a line, and then another, and another.

The image was there, with her in the darkness. Not that man's body anymore, but her own vision. *Hers.*

She blinked her eyes open.

She pressed her pencil lead to the page.

CHAPTER ONE

London
Five months later

PERRY FORBES HAD murder on his mind. Anthony saw this at once. The red face and popping eyes gave the game away.

Also, the revolver. The deuced fool had the barrel trained on him.

Anthony sat perfectly still behind the wide walnut desk, fingertips resting on the letter he'd just lately smoothed flat, so he could struggle to read and reread the unwelcome lines.

Amazing how quickly a day could go from bad to worse. And the unexpected turns its rapid decline could take.

Perry Forbes was as notorious for his blathering as for his dodgy business ventures. He invested in companies that sold everything from patent medicines to threshing machines and bored his acquaintances cross-eyed with details about projected profits. Often, they invested too, just to silence him. Under the best of circumstances, his appearance in a man's study heralded hours of unholy tedium. Today it seemed to herald death.

"A little privacy for this tête-à-tête?" Anthony mustered a faint smile. "You look like a raving lunatic. Shut the door."

Forbes wavered on the room's threshold. His coat and cuffs gaped open, and his red face was purpling. But he groped about behind him until he grasped the brass door handle. Maybe it was harder to disobey a duke than kill one. Or maybe he agreed. Better to be discreet when lodging a bullet in the brain of an unarmed aristocrat sitting at his desk in times of peace.

The door clicked as it closed.

Anthony resisted the urge to rub a tense muscle in his neck. His problems were twofold, but at least one canceled out the other. If Forbes did succeed in shooting him dead, he wouldn't have to worry what Collins would say to Robert Yardley about this extraordinary encounter.

Where *was* Collins? It was unlike the butler to pass up an opportunity to eavesdrop. If Anthony were still a betting man, he'd wager Collins was hovering in the hall. But the man also enjoyed passing the afternoons in the kitchen, inventing new harassments for the cook. Anthony wouldn't claim the odds were good, or even decent, but there was a chance he could contain this situation before word spread through the house.

He pushed back his chair an inch at a time, sliding his fingers slowly across the desk. He kept a pistol in the top drawer. He doubted Forbes had ever looked down the barrel of a gun. Most likely, he'd stop pointing his once he'd experienced that rather singular sensation.

Almost there.

"Don't move." Forbes worked his fingers, trying to seat the revolver's grip more firmly in his palm. His arm trembled badly. "Dear God, I'll shoot you through the heart."

Anthony froze. Then he laughed, raising his hands. Perry Forbes was determined to make himself interesting at last. Well, why not? For decades, Weston Hall had acted as the lightning rod for London's most electrifying scandals. If Forbes wanted an inch in the gossip columns, he'd come to the right place.

"Is this a robbery? Old boy, don't tell me you're bankrupt. Was it the American hair-growing tonic?"

Forbes lurched forward, toppling a side table. A brass vase bounced on the Oriental carpet, then rolled into Forbes's path, nearly underfoot.

"H-how dare you," he stuttered. Then he emitted a strange sound. Anthony frowned. Christ, had the fellow *honked*? Murdered by a goose. There wasn't much dignity in it.

Forbes honked again.

"Ho," he added. "Bankrupt. That's a laugh."

Ah, so it was *mirth* he was affecting. Anthony kept his own face impassive.

"I've got deposits in banking houses all over the world. This past year my investments turned an enormous profit. Enormous." Forbes punctuated his speech by jabbing the air with the revolver.

"Wonderful," murmured Anthony. "And here I was, calculating the price of my life. Well, if you don't need the money, I'd just as well keep it."

In truth, he had no money with which to buy his life, even if he didn't judge it dear. His estate, his houses, his accounts—all controlled by Yardley, who disbursed his pitiful allowance, who made financial decisions large and small on his behalf. Forbes would never believe it. The Duke of Weston, a legal child. He could scarcely believe it himself.

"So, not a robbery," he said. He held Forbes's gaze.

Don't look down.

"A crime of passion, is it? Bit cowardly, this approach." He shook his head. "You show more courage in commerce. Go threaten a landed security, or a fat bond."

"Devil take you." Forbes took another lurching step, the toe of his boot rolling over the vase, which shot out from beneath. He flew backward, discharging a single shot. Anthony felt the heat as the bullet grazed his left biceps and swore under his breath. He'd come through howitzer bombardments unscathed in high mountain passes only to have a clodhopping businessman with a pocket pistol draw blood in Piccadilly. The irony made the wound sting all the more. Colorful curses readied themselves to roll off his tongue. Mess-tent profanity. But he bit back the words. Flicked his hand and a drop of blood fell onto the carpet, swallowed instantly by a cabbage rose. Footsteps pounded below. Servants running to and fro.

Damn. Damn. Damn.

"Weston, are you . . ." Forbes struggled to his knees. The fight had gone out of him. He sagged lower. "I didn't . . ."

Anthony rounded his desk and stepped over Forbes. He pushed the heavy door open and leaned out into the hall. As he'd feared. Collins, long, pale, eager, approaching on the double, flanked by two footmen.

"Your Grace? We heard a shot."

Anthony flirted with denial. *No shot. Peculiar thunderclap. Strange weather we've been having.* But that was preposterous, and a version of the truth could do no grievous harm.

Collins used to look at him like this when he really was a child, a naughty boy about to receive his comeuppance, most often delivered in this very study, then his father's. He'd resented it at the time, and he detested it now.

"Mr. Forbes was giving me a thorough tour of his new revolver." Anthony tried to speak lightly, angling another few degrees so the door blocked the bulk of his body. "Next time, we'll leave off the trigger."

"Shall I call for a doctor?" Collins raised his colorless brows. His gimlet eye shone. It was clear enough what he imagined. The weak-minded, volatile young duke had drilled a hole in his visitor.

"Doctor?" Anthony tugged his mouth, not quite a smile. "You're not understanding. No casualties here. The bullet hit the wall."

Collins looked inclined to argue. When Anthony's father was alive, he wouldn't have dared twitch an eyelid.

"That's all." Anthony spoke curtly and folded himself back into the study, slamming the door. For a moment, he leaned against it. Blood was rolling over his elbow.

For months, he'd been honing his performance, acting the well-behaved gelding, blinkered and biddable. Following the rules laid out in the codicil to his father's will.

No drink. No scandal.

By day, at least.

He'd be damned if he let bloody Perry Forbes jeopardize his future.

"Get up."

Forbes shuffled on his knees, goggling up at him. Perhaps the command was too complex.

"Up," he said. Then, in a few short strides, he closed the distance and hauled Forbes to his feet, injured arm burning like fire.

He took a breath through his mouth. Nonetheless, Forbes's smell flooded him. Stale tobacco. Whiskey. His mouth didn't water, but it felt . . . *awake*. Needful. Christ, he craved the heat of alcohol, the way it burned, distracting from the deeper pain. The way it blurred his thoughts.

Forbes was whimpering now with impotent rage.

"Sit," said Anthony and pushed him down into a chair. He picked up the revolver, checked the cylinder, then pocketed it. He didn't need a gun to find out what in the bloody hell was going on. Standing over Forbes, he blinked, noticing for the first time that the study was dark, with an unpleasant chill. Before, as he'd sat behind the desk squinting down at that letter, the gloom had seemed natural, an emanation from within.

What was that sentence he'd read again and again?

My babes have grown so thin, I could keep them in my pincushion.

And that was only one sentence, in one letter. He'd received a half dozen letters from tenants on his estate. They'd come bundled together in a small packet assembled by the parson.

Damn. Damn. Damn. The day's refrain.

Anthony rounded the desk. Sunlight beamed through the bullet hole in the drape. Lucky the bullet hadn't shattered a pane of glass.

He pulled open the drapes and sunlight poured in. He glanced at the splintered wood of the casing, then at Forbes, who slumped against an armrest, head in his hand. The light shone on his white scalp where the dark hair had thinned. Anthony threw himself into his chair. His arm throbbed. He reached for his handkerchief, then thought better of it.

"Give me your handkerchief," he said, and Forbes silently handed over the square of white silk. He watched dully as Anthony removed his jacket. The sight of the bloodied shirtsleeve made the color drain from Forbes's face.

That's right. Anthony felt a grim satisfaction as Forbes blanched. *You shot a duke.*

The wound was shallow. Just a scratch, really. With his right hand and his teeth, he knotted the handkerchief into a makeshift bandage. Again, the irony struck him. Field dressing a bullet wound at one of London's best addresses. He laughed and Forbes flinched. Not a complete imbecile, then. He didn't mistake the laughter for a sign of good humor.

"Start talking." Anthony's tone was mild. "Your companions usually beg you to desist, I know. Enjoy the novelty."

"How long . . ." Forbes whispered the words, head bowed.

"Can't hear you."

"How long . . ." Forbes started again, louder now. "How long have you . . . and she . . ."

He lifted his head and met Anthony's eyes squarely. The idiot was in deadly earnest. It became him. He looked almost ennobled by his sincerity.

"God almighty," Forbes said quietly. "I love her."

Comprehension dawned.

"What's this?" said Anthony, leaning forward. "Forbes, you're a greater fool than I'd imagined. I've never interfered with your wife."

He cast about in his memory for an image. If recollection served, she'd been the pretty blonde with the curls at Buxton's masquerade, the one garlanded with flowers. Ribboned crook, vulpine smile. Yes, he could picture her.

"You did. You seduced her." Forbes's voice quavered. "Maybe drugged her with some foul tincture."

Too much. Anthony's jaw hardened. He stood and Forbes rose as well, straining upward in an effort to appear taller than he was. It made no difference. Anthony topped him by several inches. He looked down his nose.

"My women are willing," he said. "Always."

"I knew Stowe, don't forget." Forbes raised his chin. "I saw the two of you together. Nothing too debased. Drugs weren't the half of it. You recall that time at the Rose and Myrtle, in the flagellation room?"

Anthony said nothing. His brother, George, the Marquess of Stowe, had been picked up by the constabulary with a saddle on his back. His flanks were bloodied from zealous grooming with a gold-handled currycomb. The gossip columnists had outdone themselves with double entendre. That spring—Anthony's first in the army— the talk was of nothing else.

"And that whore that washed up with him when he died? They said she was a child."

"Ah." Anthony stepped back to put himself out of neck-wringing range. The satisfaction he'd derive from the feel of Forbes's windpipe collapsing beneath his thumbs would be fleeting, the consequences lasting. He took three slow breaths.

That poor young woman—she hadn't been a child, but at the brothel she had often dressed in schoolgirl frocks.

He still cursed his brother for his colossal stupidity. His monumental selfishness. Had he gone to his doom laughing as though death were his last and best lark?

The *Pall Mall Gazette* had run article after article detailing the accident. So had the *Telegraph*, the *Times*, the *Illustrated London News*. The list went on. The scandal had reverberated to the ends of the earth. Even locked in the garrison jail at Kandahar, Anthony had heard the rumors before he received official notification.

Suddenly, staring into Forbes's mottled, furious face, he wanted to laugh. Trouble had a way of finding him.

"I am not my brother." He composed his own face into a mask. "A shame. Mrs. Forbes might have preferred him."

"I'll kill you," Forbes exploded.

At that moment came the knock. Anthony put his back to Forbes, casually, making his unconcern into a fresh affront. The door opened. Collins had sent a footman with a tray. Someone to check that Forbes still breathed. The footman's eyes darted to Forbes again and again as he set down the tray on the desk. He didn't look at Anthony, a stroke of good fortune. Even so, Anthony sidled to the left, hiding the bandage as best he could.

Such foolishness.

As soon as the footman had departed, he turned and lifted the bottle from the tray, filled two glasses. The liquid was thick as syrup and stank of sugar. It made Anthony's stomach revolt. His father had drunk lemonade by the gallon. Enemies in Parliament had called him the lemonade lord and made mockery of his anti-vice campaigns. He had succumbed to only one reckless passion in his life, for the woman he married, an unsuitable choice, the mad daughter of Greek immigrants. A mistake that had yielded three more mistakes.

George. Anthony. Euphemia.

You children are my ruination. How many times had he said it? Enough times to make it true.

"Lemonade?" Anthony pushed a glass into Forbes's damp hand. Forbes sniffed it sullenly, nose wrinkling.

Per the codicil to his father's will, there wasn't a drop of sherry, brandy, whiskey, rum, wine, or beer in Weston Hall. The whole house—dry from cellar to dome. If Anthony swallowed so much as a mouthful of liquor, Yardley's trusteeship would continue beyond his thirtieth birthday.

Thank you, Father, for all the trust you put in me.

With this mocking, silent toast, he tipped back his own glass and sweetness rippled down his throat. The taste of decay. He poured himself more. He could see his distorted features reflected on the curved surface of the bottle, stretched out, goblin-like.

Afghanistan had shaken his faith in heaven and hell. In that rugged, beautiful country, he'd glimpsed the heavens and also seen with his own eyes the inferno that men can make on earth.

He wished that he still believed in an afterlife. Anthony wanted his father watching when he turned thirty, shed all legal fetters, and assumed control of the dukedom. Watching when he spent one hundred thousand pounds on champagne, when he went to the Derby and hazarded the country house in Somerset on a single horse. He wanted his father watching when he hired two dozen private investigators.

Ransack the city, he'd tell them. *Find my sister. Find Effie and bring her home.*

His thirtieth birthday was only weeks away. He had to lie low, quash distractions. He had to focus. He incurred too much risk as it was, stealing out his window at night, haunting the streets of the Old Nichol, of Shoreditch, Stepney, Bethnal Green, restless, looking for Effie, or for annihilation. Forbes's crazed, inexplicable mistake was one too many.

Time to end this violent interview. Quietly.

"You're confused," he began. "I'm willing to forget—"

Forbes cut him off.

"I'm not confused," he said thickly. He returned his glass of lemonade to the tray, forcefully, so the contents sloshed. "Your Grace"—he spit the words—"I have the proof at home."

AND SO ANTHONY found himself spinning down a broad lane in the carriage of a man who'd lately shot him in the arm. The silence that pertained between them on the short journey to Forbes's town house wasn't any chillier than circumstances required.

Proof. He could not let that stand. If his name was printed in relationship to any scandal, however minor, he'd wake up on March 26 as he'd woken up on March 25, a legal child. Powerless to help his own sister, forbidden from seeing his maternal relatives, sober by fiat.

London blurred behind the window glass. Houses of spotless cream and yellow stone. Stout gentlewomen carrying fluffy dogs. Shopgirls, clerks, milkmen. Beggars, too, even here.

My babes have grown so thin . . .

Those letters from the tenants—they'd taken him by surprise. Last June, when the steamer from Bombay had docked in Southampton, he'd arrowed straight to his family's seat in Hampshire. He'd been nearly three years from England, and the stables at Stratton Grange felt more like home to him than Weston Hall. He'd needed to ride over the acres of field and forest, for days and nights on end, before he could allow his chest to open, allow himself to breathe like a free man. It wasn't the homecoming he'd imagined. George, dead. Effie, eloped and abandoned, disowned and vanished. Himself, rescued from prison, and spared public disgrace, by his furious father, to whom he was now irrevocably bonded. Still, as he galloped, spring rain streaming across his face, the raw, fresh smell of torn grass rising warm from the earth, he did feel free, if only for the duration of a few wild heartbeats.

Too soon, Yardley had been sent to collect him. They'd walked together through the village, Yardley striving to put him at ease, striking a cheerful note, pointing out the features of the new cottages, trim structures of brick and slate.

You remember they were hovels, even here in the village, and it was worse on the farms, earth and thatch. I designed these cottages to ventilate. They're sanitary, healthful buildings, a great improvement.

He'd sounded pleased. He hadn't mentioned an increase in rents and Anthony hadn't thought to ask. He'd never concerned himself with estate management, cracked his jaws yawning if conversation turned to land agents, bailiffs, auditors, or surveyors. On every visit to Stratton Grange, he'd inspect the stables from hayloft to harness room, gallop every hunter, scratch behind the ears of the carriage horses and feel their hooves for stones. Beyond that, he noticed little. Did the farmers grow wheat in the fall and corn in the spring or was it the other way around? Or did they grow hay?

Now that it was his duty to notice, he found he hadn't the habit of it. Or the power to act.

Until those letters, he hadn't known that his tenants were starving—and freezing—in their modern cottages. Earth dwellings were dank, but they held the heat.

Damn. Damn. Damn.

The carriage jerked and settled. Arrived.

He walked lockstep with Forbes up the stairs and through the entrance hall, which was hung with tapestries, smoke darkened, as though they'd been passed down through generations of Forbeses. Pity they still smelled slightly scorched. No matter how much profit a businessman turned, he couldn't buy a birthright. As they passed into the study, Anthony loosed a breath, permitting himself one moment of insane speculation. *Proof?* Did the wife herself wait by the fire in that shepherdess getup, ribboned crook already pointed in accusation? Was *he* the fool to be drawn into this maddening game?

"Well." Forbes broke the silence. "Go ahead. Tell me now you never *interfered* with my wife."

Anthony turned his head, following Forbes's gaze. At first, he didn't comprehend what he was seeing. He narrowed his eyes. *What in Christ's name . . .*

He realized his jaw was hanging open and closed his mouth, too hard. His teeth clacked together painfully. Words rushed through his head but refused to order themselves into rational statements. *A prank. A stunt. The sort of thing George . . . But George . . . But how . . .*

A painting leaned against the wainscoting, just to the left of the door. Light from the windows fell upon it. The heavy gilt frame touched by sun seemed a mass of living sparks. The canvas itself . . . Could the angle be at fault? Did the light play some trick on his eyes?

No. This was no optical illusion.

He approached, muscles tensed, as though something might leap out at him. When he was a foot away, he lowered into a crouch, leaning close enough to see the texture of the paint, the vibrant pigments richly and boldly applied. The central figure—male, nude, recumbent—dominated the scene. The figure was stretched on his back, asleep, one arm behind his head and the other outflung. The artist had given his face, and form, the warm tint of living flesh. The figure looked natural. He looked *palpable*, ruddy and real.

He looked exactly like Anthony Philby, seventh Duke of Weston.

The breath burst from his lungs. He sprang up and spun around. The very world seemed different. Off-balance. Emptied of its reality. Forbes had come up behind him.

"What a wonderful little joke." The man stuck a hand inside his coat, no doubt reaching for his handkerchief, or his pistol, before realizing he had neither. Sweat streamed down his forehead.

"Joke?" Anthony echoed the word. It was meaningless. His mind was a perfect blank. Again, the painting drew his eyes. Christ almighty, that was his *body* painted in its every detail on the canvas. He'd never thought consciously about his proportions. The width and length of his forearms, for example. But he recognized them. The jolt he felt as his eyes swept up and down the canvas was most unpleasant. His chest. His thighs.

"How you must have laughed together," Forbes said. "Where was she going to hang it? In her dressing room? Where she could simper at you in her dressing gown?"

For the love of God, his *cock*. No folds of well-positioned drapery protected the figure's modesty. Everything appeared, as in life. Totally exposed. The muscles in his neck had gone rigid.

"It *is* you, Weston. I still hoped, until I looked at you in front of it . . . there was a chance . . ."

Anthony scrubbed a hand across his face, which did nothing to disarrange it.

George, at least, had looked a proper heir. He was pale like the Philbys, with that long, thin Philby nose, the blue eyes, the fine blond hair. Anthony and Effie bore too strongly their mother's stamp. Their father could barely stand to look at them.

"I don't understand," he said, hating the admission. He'd never been much for studies. His memory was sharp, but letters had always swum around instead of lining up neatly into words. Reading felt like chasing schools of fish across the page. This sensation he had now, it reminded him of how he'd felt in school as a little boy. Irked. Baffled. Trying to blink some sense into something beyond reason. "God above, what's the meaning of this?"

But Forbes seemed not to hear him. He was gazing at the painting bitterly. "Adelaide left for Inverness day before yesterday. Her sister's lying-in, and her mother went to visit and took a bad fall on one of those cursed Scottish walks. Hit her head on a rock. You think it's all moss and heather, but there's granite beneath. She might die."

Now he looked daggers at Anthony, his lips twisted.

"Imagine my surprise when porters appeared on my doorstep with a crate. For Mrs. Forbes, they said. I'll take it, I said. Bring it here."

Anthony could hardly follow what Forbes was saying. His senses had all gathered in his eyes. His staring must soon bore a hole in the canvas. Someone had stolen his image. The idea opened up onto further impossibilities. A wild-eyed artist making a pact with the devil, who then flew him into the bedchambers of the aristocracy with an enchanted paintbrush. Madness. But maybe . . . maybe the artist hadn't needed the devil.

Perhaps *he* was all the devil it took.

The gaps in his memory accused him. Lost hours. He'd never been discovered on those nights he roamed the city, and so he'd counted himself lucky. The reporters, the solicitors, Yardley, Collins— as far as they knew, the Duke of Weston retired at half past eleven and slept like a baby.

But the artist who'd painted his naked form? What did he know?

The ache between his eyes sprouted teeth and claws. Something was *chewing* inside his skull. He drew a deep breath.

"Your wife bought this painting." He said it carefully. "From whom? Who painted it?"

"Coover, L. Coover. Look there, in the corner." Forbes stabbed at the painting with his finger and stared accusingly at him. "I went through Adelaide's letters. None from *you*."

"There wouldn't be." Anthony thumbed his eyebrow, hard. "We've never exchanged as much as a how-do-you-do."

Forbes tucked his chin and marched to his desk, snatched up a letter.

"And I found this, an introduction from that Coover. Said he showed mostly on the Continent, where the art was *daring*. He'd heard what she was looking for and he had the picture that answered to her specifications."

This clarified nothing.

"Nice way to dance around it," said Forbes bitterly. "She was looking for you."

"Give it here."

Anthony tugged the letter from Forbes's fingers and studied it. He looked up.

"He signed it 'Royal Academician, Visitor in Painting.' Visitor in Painting?"

Forbes shrugged. "Chaps who teach the classes at the Academy. But, I'd think you'd know better than I do who this man is and what he does. Or do you kick off your trousers for strangers?"

Deuced difficult to explain a scenario he couldn't fathom himself.

"This painting," Anthony began. He stopped. Began again. "This painting you see here, I don't know how or why your wife ended up with it, but it's not what you think."

Again, that infernal honking. Forbes leaned forward, pantomiming amusement by aiming a slap at his knee. He missed his leg completely.

"Oof," he said, overextending his arm with a look of surprise, staggering.

Anthony was familiar with all the forms of drunkenness, could author a taxonomy on the subject. Forbes was exhibiting the violent, the maudlin, and the hilarious tendencies. Better, perhaps, than George's perversity, his pursuit of pleasure derived from increasingly sophisticated cruelties, but still, insufferable.

Forbes righted himself. He rubbed the corner of his mouth where moisture had gathered.

"So my wife is innocent? I wrong her? Prove *that*, Your Grace."

"Innocence is harder to prove than guilt." Anthony dropped down by the canvas, tossing his remark over his shoulder. "I'll assign myself the easier task."

Grimly, he heaved the painting forward so the frame braced against his chest. If anyone saw this image—the Duke of Weston, *in puris naturalibus*—the gossips would invent their own stories. The *Pall Mall Gazette* would run those stories. He would lose his right to control his inheritance.

He pulled the knife from his boot. No, he couldn't cut it free. Something in him refused to put the blade to canvas. Instead, he used the back of his knife to lever out the nails that held it to the stretchers.

"What are you doing?"

Anthony ignored the question, working his way slowly around

the perimeter. Nail by nail. At last the canvas was loosed. He rolled
it up into a neat tube, about the length and width of a telescope barrel. Without ceremony, he rose, rolled canvas in hand.

"Thank you for the picture," he said pleasantly, reaching inside
his coat to rip off the makeshift bandage. He dangled the stained
handkerchief. Forbes's monogram was picked out in cream thread.
"And thank you for the handkerchief. Very good of you to initial the
evidence." Anthony gripped Forbes's shoulder and pulled him close.
His whisper was infused with menace. "One word about any of this,
and it's straight to Newgate."

"Adelaide . . ." began Forbes, and Anthony stepped back and
smiled.

"The easier task," he said, inclining his head. "I swear to you I
didn't touch your wife. But perhaps you should write to her sister in
Inverness and inquire after her mother's health."

Forbes's eyes were popping again.

"Are you implying . . ."

Indeed Anthony was. Forbes, despite this bout of unexpected
fire, didn't seem likely to satisfy a woman of appetite.

Anthony was no longer a betting man, but he'd become a cynic.

"I wish the fair Adelaide a merry cuckolding. Wherever she may be."

He sketched an ironic bow and let the door bang on his way out.

WHEN HE REACHED Weston Hall, head pounding, he slipped around
to the garden, to the small glasshouse in the walled-off southeast corner. Long ago, his mother used it to grow grapes, figs, and flowers. It
was empty now, had been for years and years, more than two decades.
Anthony ducked inside, crossed to the lead-lined brick tank. Once,
that tank collected rainwater. Now it held bottles of rum, gin, and
whiskey, as well as shirts, jackets, cloaks, and trousers.

Anthony unlidded it and stowed the rolled painting carefully,
wrapped in a linen shirt. He shrugged out of his coat and took a long

pull from a whiskey bottle, sitting on the edge of the tank. The sound of footsteps jerked his head around, but he relaxed when he saw the blocky figure cross the threshold. His valet, Humphreys, come to check the store of liquor. The only member of the staff he hadn't inherited with the house. He'd brought Humphreys on himself, and the youth—who couldn't clean a collar and tied a cravat as though he were haltering a horse—performed splendidly as his lookout and confederate.

They'd developed their bond in the jaws of death. Anthony counted it dear.

"The bugger. He blasted a hole in you." Humphreys was at his side in an instant. Anthony fended him off with the bottle.

"Nicked me," he said. "Once I've bathed, you can tie it up, and I'll be as good as new."

Humphreys rubbed his jaw, staring, then shrugged. "Right-ho. I'll get a bath drawn, then." His concerned look gave way and he grinned. "You won't mind when I burn that shirt."

The other day, he'd singed Anthony's linens as he tried to dry them by the fire.

Anthony glanced down at the bloodstained sleeve and laughed. "Do your worst."

But as soon as Humphreys was gone, his smile faded. With the lad's help, he could cover up this imbroglio with Forbes, but a larger problem remained.

That problem was one L. Coover.

What to do? He drummed a heel against the tank and tipped the bottle again.

Chapter Two

When Lucy had set up her easel by the classroom doorway, she had been thinking purely of the angle the position afforded her. The model sitting for the female students of the Upper School of Painting possessed an extraordinary pair of nostrils. Only three-quarter profile would do them justice.

She had *not* been thinking of the potential interruptions.

Every half hour or so, Maude rose, stretched, and drifted out of the classroom. Which meant that every half hour or so, she passed behind Lucy on her way to the door. She was approaching now.

Ignore her.

Lucy tightened her fingers on her chalk stone. She blew grit from her lines and leaned back to inspect them. Not bad. This was her second attempt at a life-sized study of the model's head. The first had been dreadful. The model was a handsome woman in the prime of life, and the head Lucy painted did look strong and splendid. It also looked, less happily, as though it belonged on the shoulders of a retired general. In fact, whiskers and a bicorn might still rescue the picture from the rubbish heap. With such modification, she could sell it to a public house as a portrait of a military hero. She'd decided to put the canvas aside for later as she attempted a better likeness.

The classroom was top lit, sunlight filtering down from fish-scale panes of glass set in the sloping ceiling. So illuminated, her under-drawing already showed promise.

She felt the air behind her stir.

"Enchanting!" Maude sounded breathless and amazed. Lucy could almost *hear* her eyelashes fluttering. Maude did *enchanting* very well. No doubt her easy raptures served her well at parties.

What an enchanting pudding! What an enchanting observation about the weather!

"The picture grows more gorgeous by the hour," Maude continued in the same breathy tone. At that, Lucy glanced up. Was Maude so weak-minded she couldn't see that Lucy had begun afresh? But Maude wasn't even looking at her easel. She was rolling her eyes at Susan, who was taking advantage of Maude's absence to add a few brushstrokes to her own picture.

"Look at Susan's painting face!" Maude's voice became conspiratorial as she tapped Lucy on the shoulder. "Isn't it fearsome?"

Defeated, Lucy let her right hand drop into her lap. Maude would linger until Lucy gave way. Best to get it over with. Lucy considered Susan for a long moment. She was handling her exquisite French paintbrush gingerly, as though it were a long-stemmed rose.

The other girls owned such beautiful brushes! Not to mention shining palette knives, japanned sketching boxes, superfine papers, and paint boxes filled with hundreds of colors, oils, and varnishes. Sometimes the sight made her heart twist. All instruction in the Academy was gratuitous, but students supplied their own materials.

Every tool Lucy used was old and plain. But so what? You couldn't *buy* technique. It didn't matter if your paintbrushes came from France.

Susan's lips were thinned into a grim line.

"Her face is not fearsome in the least," Lucy said at last. "She's *concentrating.*"

Try it sometime.

"She should concentrate like this," said Maude, her face assuming a dreamy expression. "That's nicer, isn't it?"

"Indeed." Lucy shrugged. "You could be a Visitor in the School of Painting Face."

"Laugh if you will," Maude said with a sniff. "But no one wants to commission a portrait painter who looks an absolute *ogre* at the easel."

Lucy frowned at the barb. Maude knew that she—not Susan—aspired to a career in portraiture. So, Maude saw her as an ogre, did she? Well, Maude's was one commission she wouldn't mind losing.

"There's a spot of charcoal on your collar," she rejoined, turning back to her easel and raising her chalk stone. "I do hope it comes out."

That did the trick. Maude's hands flew to her throat. She spun on her heel to attend to this sartorial disaster. As the sound of footsteps faded down the hall, Lucy absently plucked a bit of cat fur from the folds of her skirt. She sewed her dresses herself, using remnants of the rich fabrics left over from Aunt Marian's days as a theatrical costumer for the most famous actresses in London. The results were unusual but lent her an aura of eccentricity, which was ultimately preferable to the alternative: that she arrive at the Academy drably turned out in cotton ready-mades, the uniform of the lower middle class. Unthinkable. Instead, she dressed boldly and didn't bother with the white pinafores favored by girls like Maude, who attended classes in pretty, fashionable gowns. The profusion of textures and colors hid specks of paint, chalk, and charcoal, more or less. Her dear old tomcat, Mr. Malkin, shed fine gray hairs that proved more difficult to disguise. But she'd rather find herself forced to pluck hairs from her skirts than forbear from stroking her most beloved companion.

Art—and life—were messy. Let the Maudes of the world waste their time worrying about spots.

She'd nearly lost herself in her work—sweeping her brush fluidly over the chalked lines—when she sensed a new disturbance from a similar quarter. Susan had pushed back her chair. She was moving toward the door, curious, no doubt, as to Maude's whereabouts.

Drat it. This next step was crucial. Any infelicitous stroke at this stage would bear out in the finished picture. Lucy bit her lip with annoyance and kept on determinedly. If she'd arrived at the studio earlier, she would have set up her easel on the other side of the room, where the angle was just as promising and the chance of interruption minimal. But of course, Gwen Burgess had arrived first and claimed the better spot. Gwen was tall, fine boned, effortlessly elegant. Last year, she had won the Gold Medal in the Schools' landscape competition. Students and Visitors alike fawned in her presence, but she ignored their attentions. Lucy's best friend, Kate, had made repeated overtures, all rebuffed.

She's disagreeable, certainly, but she's Augustus Burgess's sister! Kate had had the good grace to appear sheepish as she answered Lucy's questioning look following a third failed attempt to entice Gwen on a sketching trip to the British Museum.

That's not the only reason I want to befriend her, she'd added hastily. *She's terribly interesting, and her brushwork is divine. But, Lucy, if we were friends with Gwen she might invite us to one of Augustus Burgess's salons. Just imagine!*

Augustus Burgess's celebrity wasn't limited to the pages of the *Art Journal*. His bold, large-scale figure paintings were invariably lauded in all the papers, touted as "the talk of the clubs." He had been the youngest artist to exhibit at the Royal Academy since J. M. W. Turner, and he'd recently been elected Academician. He hosted salons where models sat, in various draperies, for the lucky painters at his legendary studio-house, itself a marvel of aesthetic interiors. Every March, on Studio Sunday, crowds crushed into his studio to preview the pictures he planned to submit for the Summer Exhibition.

Lucy doubted Gwen Burgess would ever extend an invitation to her brother's salon. Gwen was more than disagreeable. She seemed to suffer human interaction.

At this very moment, the Visitor in Painting, Mr. Barrett, was hovering around Gwen's easel offering an energetic critique. Lucy would do almost anything for that kind of consideration, but Gwen looked grave, even pained.

Stop staring at bloody Gwen Burgess.

Gwen's face was a smooth oval, like a Renaissance Madonna. Nothing like the model's.

Lucy blinked and lowered her hand before her distraction could destroy her work. Was it lack of sleep that made it so hard to focus?

She dropped her brush into a pot of water and glanced again at Gwen. Mr. Barrett had buzzed away. Gwen was painting with quick, sure strokes, eyes darting between her canvas and the model. Everything came easily to her.

"Lucy!" It was Susan, tapping her shoulder. "How enchanting!"

Lucy stiffened. But suddenly, a reprieve was granted. Maude burst through the door, ablaze with excitement.

"You can't guess who I saw in the Gibson Gallery!"

In an instant, Lucy and her picture were forgotten. Susan all but sprang toward Maude, grasping her hands.

"Simon Poole?" She named a student in his sixth year, an architect whose height, handsome face, and long blond hair were entirely to blame for his rakish reputation. Lucy doubted he'd ever met a debutante he preferred to the Doric column.

Maude swept her head from side to side in a gesture of magnificent negation. She pulled back and spoke slowly, inserting significant pauses after every word.

"The. Duke. Of. Weston."

Susan let out a gasp, more than loud enough to invite Mr. Barrett's censure. But he was locked in discussion with Ada Jenkins, a fine cartoonist with no color sense. If he noticed the commotion, he made no sign.

"What was the Duke of Weston doing in the Gibson Gallery? What were *you* doing in the Gibson Gallery?" Susan's eyes narrowed. The Gibson Gallery was just up the stairs from the classrooms. There was no attendant posted to watch who came and went, and male and female students often climbed the steps together. To *study the statues*. The Royal Academy was filled with statues, but everyone seemed to agree that they were more educational in a private setting, with the right company.

"Arthur Creswell wanted to show me a statue," said Maude vaguely. "Something clever about a foot." Maude did not sound as though she'd found the foot clever. Lucy supposed whatever cleverness Arthur Creswell had on offer ceased to rate once a duke appeared on the scene.

"Why, he must plan to acquire a marble!" said Susan. "The one of Courage killing the serpent, do you suppose? I've always thought it the perfect statue for a war hero."

"Have you?" purred Maude. "When were *you* in the Gibson Gallery?"

Susan's cheeks pinked.

"He might prefer bronze," she said, straightening her pinafore.

"I shouldn't say this," said Maude. "You're too prim."

She glanced at Lucy to make sure she was listening before continuing in a lowered voice.

"The duke's older brother, who died, he once came to the Schools, and he commissioned William Beauclerk in the School of Sculpture for twelve foot-long marble . . ."

Her voice caught on an irrepressible giggle, and she buried her face in her hands.

"I can't," she said into her fingers.

Despite herself, Lucy found that she'd twisted to stare. Susan's eyes were saucers.

"*Dildos,*" breathed Maude.

"Those are . . ." Susan couldn't finish her sentence.

"Yes." Maude nodded. "Exactly. Twelve foot-long marble dildos for something called the Feast of Venus at a brothel he *owned*."

Susan looked aghast. Lucy stifled a groan. Maude flushed with triumph at the effect she'd produced.

"What did they *do*?" asked Susan breathlessly. "With the . . ." Her voice dropped to a whisper, but this time she was determined. *"Dildos,"* she said.

"Well, there was a banquet, of course, with courtesans dressed up like nymphs," said Maude, less certainly, eyeing Susan to gauge her reaction.

"Which means they were practically naked," Maude continued. "And they danced in that state, danced around the dildos, to which they made offerings, of fruits and flowers."

"While the men ate cutlets?" Susan's nose wrinkled.

"And watched," said Maude. "It was entirely perverse. The orchestra didn't dare to glimpse the goings-on. They played facing the wall."

Susan's mouth formed an O of nervous excitement. Lucy shook her head wryly. She'd seen enough rutting in alleyways to fill in the blanks should Susan ask Maude to elaborate further. She'd wager spectatorship didn't satisfy hungry guests at a Feast of Venus.

But Susan had hugged herself, shivering, her thoughts clearly leaping ahead.

"You don't think the duke is here to commission . . . *dildos*?" Susan asked. "I won't believe it. He's not so very wicked as his brother. He *did* get sent to the Magistrates' Court. For breaking the stained-glass window at All Saints Church. That was him, wasn't it? But he fought to defend the empire!"

Susan's father had survived bayoneting in the Crimean War, and she often expressed a deeply felt pride in the courage of the common soldier. As far as Lucy could tell, Susan's notion of *common soldier* compassed nothing lower than an officer with a barony.

"I don't care if he is wicked," said Maude. "I met him for the first time at a party months ago, and I still think he's the handsomest man I've ever seen."

"And the richest," suggested Lucy sweetly.

"That too." Maude pursed her lips. "But I'd fancy him if he hadn't a penny."

She paused.

"Or a title," she added, with a doubtful lilt. Then she scowled at Lucy.

"Shouldn't you attend to your picture?"

That she should. Lucy turned back to her canvas. The Duke of Weston sounded dreadful, even if he wasn't as wicked as his brother, who, if Lucy recalled the story correctly, had managed to kill not only himself but a female companion when he capsized a stolen yacht.

Marriage, in the best of circumstances, to the best of dukes, was bound to end a woman's art career.

The Duke of Weston was the worst of dukes. Marriage to him spelled disaster, at least for a woman who wanted to make her own mark on the world.

It was nothing to her if Maude and Susan squandered their training. Maude could fancy the Duke of Weston all she wished. Lucy preferred, though, that she do her fancying on the other side of the room where she belonged. She wanted to paint in peace.

Behind her, she could hear Maude murmuring. Susan squealed.

"No! Surely, Lady Henderson didn't *pay* him . . ."

Lucy loaded more paint on her brush, grimacing. Long break couldn't come soon enough.

When it came at last, the classroom emptied quickly, the students, the model, and Mr. Barrett streaming down the hall in search of air or refreshments. Lucy pretended to wash her brushes, waiting for the moment when she'd be alone. She didn't have a big, bright room, let alone a house, as a studio. She treasured the little intervals in the school day when she had the classroom all to herself. All that space changed the way she thought, and painted.

Kate was the last to leave. She came up to Lucy and caught her elbow, squeezing it with appreciation as she gave her picture a brief nod.

"Will you use my burnt sienna? I bought loads."

Kate was frank about her wealth, and generous. She and Lucy, fast friends since their days as probationers, had first bonded over their admiration of the Pre-Raphaelites. Lucy loved their pictures, the jewel-bright colors and detailed foregrounds. There was little in the way of flowers and foliage in Shoreditch for her to study *en plein air*, but she set herself to re-creating in paint the embroideries and frills she observed on the sleeves and bodices of her aunt's most elaborate gowns. Kate was enthralled by the lifestyle of the painters themselves, their passionate spirits and rebellious attitudes.

We should start our own circle, Kate had declared early on in their friendship. *A sisterhood!*

And they'd prepared statements filled with youthful enthusiasm, outlining exuberant, sometimes contradictory, principles they hoped to embody in their work. But until one or the other of them painted something noteworthy, it was difficult to think of themselves as a real circle. Circles, for one thing, required more than two members.

Recently, Kate had begun to focus on a series of paintings she called her *mirror pictures*, sumptuous interiors in which mirrors reflected some portion of the room, or the figure. The Grosvenor Gallery had agreed to hang three of them, and she intended to submit three others for the Summer Exhibition. Kate, at least, was destined for a brilliant future.

"Thank you, but no," said Lucy, smiling. "You gave me plenty on Monday."

In truth, she'd used almost all of it, on another false start, a scene of children taking tea out of mismatched cups at a deal table in a sweet shop. She'd wanted it dim, but the low lights resulted in unintended muddiness. Nothing to do but wipe it all away.

She couldn't bring herself to accept additional supplies from Kate so soon, not when she'd wasted what she'd just been given. She took too much as it was.

Kate opened her mouth to argue, then shrugged, letting the subject drop.

"Join me for billiards?"

"You're mad." Lucy laughed, rolling her neck on her shoulders, bending back with her hands at her hips. Lord, she felt as though she belonged in the Gibson Gallery. The muscles in her neck and back might have been hewn from stone. But her refusal had nothing to do with her stiffness. During long break, the male students smoked, played billiards, and debated on topics plucked from the latest issue of the *Art Journal* with the energy of original thinkers. *We're the real artists*, their attitudes seemed to signal. *You girls sit in the courtyard and eat your tea cakes.*

In 1860, Laura Herford became the first female to study at the Schools, receiving her acceptance before the Academicians realized what the *L.H.* on her application signified. A woman. An interloper. Two decades on, male students retained their overwhelming majority. And they received better training! They attended the Life School, for the study of drawing from the nude. The Life School, which was barred to women.

Lucy struggled hard enough to feel at home in the Academy, even among the female students. She saw no need to incur more discomfort for such a paltry prize. Control of the billiards table! Who cared about that? Let the men have their silly games. Billiards was not her field of endeavor.

Kate saw things differently. To her mind, any challenge to male dominance within the Schools furthered the cause. Most days, she marched away from the much smaller gathering of female students to mingle with the men.

Their company isn't a bit more interesting, she'd explained to Lucy. *But I must make my point.*

Kate's point, it turned out, was sharper than anyone expected. It seemed she had a knack for billiards. Not only did she play; she won more often than she lost—much to the chagrin of her opponents.

"I've written another petition." Kate grinned, smoothing her chestnut hair, cut short so it lay close to her scalp. The effect was shocking but not unattractive, emphasizing Kate's small, even features and large gray eyes. And the style went better with her jacket and trousers.

"Help me collect signatures in the canteen."

"Oh." Lucy tried for a light tone. "I wasn't thinking I'd go to the canteen. I thought I'd stay and paint."

For all the good it would do. Her new portrait—she hated to admit—was showing considerably less promise than she'd first imagined. The model's striking face looked younger and less masculine in the new portrait, but the magnificent nose was wrong, too soft and fleshy. She'd not a chance of selling this one, not even to a public house. And less of a chance of exhibiting it, even in one of the minor galleries.

She didn't feel confident in any of the pictures she'd painted of late. There wasn't a single one she could imagine submitting for the Summer Exhibition. One was all she needed, one picture hung well in the Summer Exhibition to win her the recognition of the public. Hundreds of thousands of people passed through Burlington House between May and August every year. One picture—well, one *stunner*— and commissions would follow.

One *stunner*. That was the difficult bit.

"I should really keep on," she said, in part to convince herself. Her stomach was growling. The canteen called to her. She could treat herself to a slice of cake, help Kate with the petition.

There wouldn't be any time, though, to paint later, not tonight or the next night. Aunt Marian's most loyal customer, Mrs. Fairfax, had placed a large order for the alteration of her entire wardrobe. There'd be plenty of work to fill the evening.

She made a face.

"There's catching up we have to do," she said by way of explanation. "From those days when my aunt's sewing machine was broken."

Kate understood at once. It wasn't a secret that Lucy worked in a dress shop, and that the dress shop didn't precisely cater to the higher order, but only Kate was privy to the full situation. She knew how

Lucy and her great-aunt Marian struggled, and she knew that Lucy had precious little time after classes for anything but sewing and sleeping.

And often there was less sleeping than even Kate suspected.

"They could fix it after all!" Kate beamed at her. "That's marvelous."

Lucy smiled feebly. Her aunt's ancient machine had proved beyond repair. She had resolved the crisis in the nick of time. By buying a brand-new Singer.

She couldn't mention it. Kate would want to know how she had managed, and she was not prepared to tell her.

"Yes," she said. "A very great relief."

"Well, sign the petition now, then. I can't promise I'll do as well as you at coaxing the other girls to sign, but I'll box their ears if it comes to it." Kate knelt on the stone flags and unfolded a piece of blue paper. Lucy hesitated. The very fact of her hesitation shamed her. Did she not share Kate's commitment to equity for male and female students? She believed just as strongly that women should receive the same instruction as the men, up to and including drawing and painting from life. Women would never achieve what men achieved if their education remained inferior. But sign her name *first* on a petition that an Academician would read out at the Council Meeting?

She swallowed a weak protestation. She wanted to be fearless, like Kate.

Easier to be fearless with a fortune. A little voice was cautioning her. *You need the goodwill of the Academicians. Don't challenge them. Let Kate lead the charge because she has less to lose.*

Lucy knelt beside Kate, took the pen Kate handed her, and signed with a flourish.

"Now," she said brightly, struggling to her feet in her long skirts. "Leave me to these nostrils."

"Certainly." Kate sprang up with easy grace. "When you need that burnt sienna, remember my paint box is open."

It turned out, Lucy didn't have long to forget. There was even less burnt sienna in the tube than she'd thought. Once again, she needed to accept Kate's help.

She owed so many so much. Her parents. They'd sacrificed their health, their *lives*. Lucy's mother had churned out illustrations for penny papers at breakneck speed, giving up her dreams to struggle alongside Lucy's father, whose vision was already failing from years of squinting over boxwood blocks. Aunt Marian. She did whatever she could to spare Lucy in the shop, shooing her to bed when she fell asleep at the table, thread slipping from her needle. And Kate, fiercely loyal, the sort of girl who'd split her last farthing with a friend.

How could Lucy ever repay all their kindness? All their trust?

She needed to buy her aunt more than a sewing machine. She needed to buy her *two* sewing machines and hire full-time shop assistants to work them.

She was halfway to Kate's easel when she heard the scuff of a boot on the doorsill. Someone had returned to the classroom early. She whirled around, fighting a furious blush. The girls with more money sometimes looked askance at the girls with less. Suspecting them of wanting what they didn't have enough to take what wasn't theirs.

She was no thief creeping about to filch other girls' tools. But surely her face was the picture of guilty defiance.

A man filled the doorway, tall and broad and dark. He didn't notice her flush. He didn't pay her any mind at all. He was glancing around the room, already shifting his weight to move on down the hall.

With a start, she recognized the ratio of shoulders to hips, the staggering breadth of the former accentuating the leanness of the latter. He was somehow taller even than she'd imagined. Although his height made perfect sense given his length when sprawled upon the ground, his verticality astounded her.

There could be no doubt.

"My corpse!" The words burst from her. Hysterical laughter threatened to follow and she clapped a hand over her mouth. The man whose body she'd spent months daydreaming, drawing, realizing in every detail in oil and pigment, until she'd breathed life into the form and had begun to think of it, of *him*, as her own creation. He was suddenly scant yards away.

His dark brows arched as he turned back toward her.

"My corpse." His voice had the unmistakable drawl of the best society. "I am unfamiliar with that expression."

He was looking at her as though she had sprouted two heads, with a mix of curiosity and revulsion. She saw herself, suddenly, as he would see her, short and scrawny, frizzy-haired, in a vivid dress of purple silk and black brocade. To make it, she'd wedded components of gowns her aunt had sewn for two very different productions, a music-hall melodrama and a Shakespearean tragedy. She felt her flush deepen.

Her attire was interesting but not outrageous, not by art-world standards. Kate wore trousers, and Redcliffe Davis wore an earring!

This man did not hail from the art world. His suit was plain; the wools and linens were of the highest quality. His jacket and trousers were expertly tailored. If this was his typical attire, no wonder he'd been stripped to the skin. A family could dine off the buttons alone.

She swallowed hard. She remembered the heat emanating from his body, the smell of sweat and spirits. This man was clean-shaven. He wore his hair combed back. She knew already how he would smell: perfumed. Wealthy.

Nights, when she lay down at last but couldn't sleep due to her racing mind, she'd imagined meeting her corpse again. Silly fantasies. He was always wearing rough clothes, and he always recognized her, as though from a dream. He was a farmer. A blacksmith. A gamekeeper. She'd conjured all sorts of country professions.

He was never this, never the gentleman. Imperious and disdaining. The sort of man who would always be a stranger.

She shared nothing with him. Her sense of connection had been exposed in a heartbeat as an absurd presumption. It was ridiculous, but she felt *betrayed*.

"Only students are allowed in the Schools," she said, too sharply. "Perhaps . . . you are lost?"

He brushed this suggestion away. Dismissing it. Dismissing *her*.

"I'm looking for someone." And although there was no one in the room to find except for her, he stepped across the threshold and began to prowl the room's perimeter. His stride was athletic. Lazy and sure.

She stood rooted to the spot, staring.

In her picture, she'd styled him classically, as the shepherd king Endymion, but here, in the flesh, his fluid grace made him seem predatory, a poor fit as a protector of small, defenseless creatures. He moved like a panther.

"The Visitor in Painting." He closed in on her, eyes sweeping over the uneven ring of easels, the model's chair in the center of the floor. "Do you know him?"

They were green, those eyes, green as moss, but without any of the softness. They were hard, clear. Startling. She'd never have guessed that exact shade. How to convey its brilliancy? Pale green lights added to darkest emerald.

She had looked too long. Suddenly, his gaze grew piercing.

He was staring back.

"Of course I know him," she said. Her mouth was dry. She could look at this man for a year, for a hundred years, and never grow weary. He did not feel the same way about her. His eyes slid away again easily, turning to more interesting sights. He circled an easel, Susan's, and leaned over it, peering closely at its contents, then returned his eyes to Lucy with a sniff.

"I don't see the likeness." He folded his arms at his chest. She knew how his biceps curved, how the muscle swelled. She could make a map of his veins.

Likeness? Her comprehension had lagged behind his words, but now she snapped to attention. Likeness to whom? *Her?* Ha! She tried to access her reservoir of scorn, which she could usually rely on to resource her lavishly when she interacted with arrogant men.

He *would* be the type who took a woman for an artist's model rather than an artist proper. Did he even know this was a female class? That women painted at all?

What devastating setdown could she deliver?

He strolled to the next easel.

"Ah," he said. "This one, too, has nothing of your face or expression. Mr. Coover is a poor teacher."

She choked on the phrase she'd been preparing. What had he said?

Mr. Coover?

Her heart seemed to stop completely; then it sped up, not beating, but whirring, like the mechanism in a sewing machine.

"The Visitor in Painting," she said slowly. "Mr. Coover."

Good God.

The letter to Mrs. Forbes.

In the missive, she had created the perfect persona, one calculated to appeal to the young woman's particular desires.

L. Coover was unknown in England. This point was, of course, a necessity, but also a boon. Mrs. Forbes didn't want to follow the herd.

Yet L. Coover was feted in France, the darling of the Paris salons, and had lately returned to England as a Visitor. Mrs. Forbes didn't want to appear common and needed her venturesome taste affirmed.

Lucy had felt a queer elation as she wrote. To present such a version of herself—iconoclastic, accomplished, confident—it made her shiver.

The moment Kate had introduced her to Mrs. Forbes, at the Winter Exhibition, she'd recognized the opportunity.

I adore art, but my husband knows nothing *about it. Nothing.* Mrs. Forbes had tossed her head as she spoke so her jeweled earrings twinkled and her throat extended. *Tell me . . . do you think one of these men would agree to paint me nude?*

She'd looked triumphantly at the knot of Academicians clustered beneath a massive eighteenth-century oil and then at Lucy and Kate, so transparently eager to shock them both that Lucy had felt a wave of tenderness. It was almost sweet, this round-cheeked, well-heeled young woman's determination to prove herself naughty.

Kate had grinned her irresistible grin.

I'd paint you nude, she'd said, and Mrs. Forbes's mouth had dropped open before she'd thrown her head back spontaneously to let out a peal of laughter.

Perhaps next year, she'd said. *Truly, what I want for my own chambers is a male nude, but only if he's a god. No suffering saints or martyrs. Pure masculine perfection. Something to restore the eyes and the ideals after watching one's husband gnaw a drumstick. I'm like a Frenchwoman in that respect. Life is more stimulating in France, n'est-ce pas?*

Kate had laughed about Mrs. Forbes all the following week.

I've seen her at a dozen parties. She's always like that. I've met Mr. Forbes, too, and let me tell you, he is not remotely French. How could such a wild little creature end up tethered to a weak-chinned dullard?

Kate had laughed again, more bitterly, answering her own question. *She's very pretty; he's very rich. That's what marriage is all about, n'est-ce pas?*

Lucy hadn't written to Mrs. Forbes then. Even when she finally finished her picture, in February, she'd waited a week before she could bring herself to write.

The picture was the best—and largest—she'd ever painted. She'd used the pattern of embroidered leaves on her favorite gown to create a botanical pattern that replaced the mud of the alley. The pattern curved, so that the figure appeared to lie on a hill, with a cave behind him and the moon hanging overhead, a shade less than full.

She was waxing as she fell in love.

In myth, Endymion the shepherd king was a man of such beauty the moon herself longed to shine upon him always, to keep him for her very own. She bid Zeus, her father, put him in eternal sleep. As Lucy had studied her sketches and planned her composition, she'd realized that the story was the perfect fit. The moody, romantic symbolism represented the deeper truth.

The picture turned out bright, expressive . . . charged. Maybe even indecent. The light seemed to come from all sides, showing the precise details of the sleeper.

There was a frankness to it that frightened her. The picture, evenly lit by the moon, glorying in the male form, seemed a testament to feminine desire. She'd painted it for herself alone. But she couldn't roll the canvas and keep it in the corner of her bedroom, not when it could be converted into the money she so desperately needed. A private sale had been the only answer. She'd started a dozen letters—*Dear Mrs. Forbes*—but laid down her pen without finishing.

And then the sewing machine broke. And the rent came due.

If her corpse was asking for Mr. Coover, Visitor in Painting, that meant he had talked to Mrs. Forbes. He had seen the picture. Understandably, he wanted to confront the artist. He wanted a word with *Mr. Coover*.

Cold sweat was breaking out across her brow.

"Mr. Coover," Lucy said again, groping for what came next. "It is he you hope to find?"

That green gaze fixed her again, scrambling her thoughts. Her corpse gave her an ironic smile.

"It is not a hope, but an inevitability," he said slowly, as though doubting her wit. "We have important matters to discuss."

Her panic mounted. She focused on a point above his left shoulder.

"Then I hate to bring such tragic news." What was she saying? She listened to the words issuing from her mouth, as much a spectator as the man she addressed.

"Mr. Coover is dead. Has died. Just the other day."

Another corpse. Dammit.

She didn't dare look at his face.

"Terribly sad," she continued. "Were you very dear friends? My condolences."

These sympathies—which took her completely by surprise—seemed to warrant her bestowing upon the bereaved a kind and forthright look. She risked looking up at him, lips pressed into a sad smile.

A mistake. His brows had climbed again, and his expression did not encourage further compassionating.

She glanced toward the door. "I really must be going. I'm wanted in the canteen. We are taking up a collection for the widow."

Dammit. Dammit.

"How very kind." Her corpse approached. She had no choice but to look at him, he was so large and so close.

"She will be solaced, I'm sure. It was quite unexpected?"

"Very much so." Her voice continued smoothly and she marveled at herself. Her mother used to scold her for telling tales, and it seemed she hadn't lost the knack of it.

"He was sketching in a field . . ." What were they called? With animals? She knew nothing of the countryside firsthand.

"A pasture," she said. "He was consumed with his work and didn't notice the danger until it was too late. He was trampled. By cows. And a bull. Gored and trampled."

That should finish him. She shuddered at the pathetic scene. Cows rearing on their hind legs. Blood staining the clover. Peasants in the distance, pointing. The fatal moment captured in the style of Gainsborough.

"It's a great loss for the Academy."

He was watching her closely. Too closely. How much better she had liked him when his eyes were shut!

"Now," she said briskly. "Shall I show you out? You really aren't allowed to be down here. The policy is terribly strict."

She made for the classroom door. If she could get him out of the building before he asked any questions, there was a chance that all would end well.

She looked back. He hadn't budged. She raised an eyebrow and tipped her head, smiling to encourage him. She refrained from beckoning as she would to Mr. Malkin.

Ch-ch-ch. Here, puss. Come along.

Her corpse seemed to come to some independent decision. In four strides, he'd reached the door and extended his elbow. Offering to escort *her*.

"Forgive my discourtesy," he said smoothly. "We haven't made a proper introduction."

Her response was automatic.

"Lucy," she began, and stuttered.

A proper introduction would hardly do in the present circumstances.

"Miss Lucy," she said.

She touched his sleeve, trying to keep the pressure of her fingertips so light she would feel only fabric, no hint of the flesh beneath.

"Weston," said her corpse. She yanked her fingers up as though burned. Maude's excited voice purred again in her ear.

The. Duke. Of. Weston.

Not only a gentleman; a duke, and a wicked one at that. A notorious jackanapes. So rich that nothing was precious, not even human life.

The vilest specimen of a vile species.

She tried to step back, but he anticipated her movement, letting his hand drop over hers, pinning it.

"Your Grace," she said. "The door is right this way."

Maude was hunting for the man this very moment. She *had* to eject him from the premises.

As she turned them down the hall, he swung her lightly around in a half circle, steering the opposite course.

"I believe I passed the canteen earlier," he said. "That's where you're soliciting donations for Mrs. Coover's relief? Permit me to join you."

He must have felt her flinch. The hallway, lined with casts of antique sculptures, stretched before them. She could see the canteen at the end of the hall. Never before had the sight filled her with dread. Her mind raced, trying to work out some solution. Some explanation she could provide to avert the impending disaster.

Nothing. She couldn't think her way clear.

Think, she thought wildly, *think*. Only her wits would preserve her. No idea presented itself. Instead, the canteen doors banged opened and laughing students poured out.

Long break was over.

She almost sagged against him. But, no, she had to gather herself. *This was the moment.* She took advantage of his split-second distraction to slip her hand from his. Then she darted forward, plowing into the crowd of students who flowed on down the hall, obscuring her as she made her escape.

CHAPTER THREE

ANTHONY WATCHED THE flash of purple silk as it was swallowed in a sea of white pinafores. A horde of lady artists was descending upon him. Men trailed behind them, some in fancy dress and others in shabby coats and floppy ties. Murmuring voices and the sounds of boots striking the dark flagstones rose to the vaulted ceiling. The students split off into classrooms, several sparing him curious glances.

Miss Lucy was nowhere to be seen.

He took a few steps forward, then stopped. No point in pursuing her. She either was a dramatic personality who delighted in fabrication or suffered some ailment of the brain. Even an addlepate could model, inertia being the sole requirement.

More students passed by. The hallway was emptying and he'd yet to see a man who looked old enough to shave. Clearly, the Visitors were not as punctual as their students.

He glanced into the nearest classroom. It was like a battlefield in plaster. Torsos without arms. Legs without torsos. Dozens of heads. The students were settling into their places. A few were shrugging out of their coats. He moved away from the door before his presence could be remarked.

He knew cursed little about art. Still, he could understand the appeal of painting Miss Lucy, and also why the canvases represented her so poorly. She didn't look like any woman he'd ever seen in a painting, for one thing. Firstly, she was freckled. Her eyes weren't round and limpid. They were narrow with watchfulness, the irises like sherry held to the light. Her hair didn't flow across her shoulders or fold back in a neat wave. She piled it on her head, where the wild curls could have served as a nest for blackbirds. Everything about her face and figure was mobile, expressive. She had no perfect beauty to capture. But there was something about her that fascinated. Perhaps *because* it was so difficult to pin down.

He rocked on his heels, displeased with where his thoughts were heading. As he did so, he locked eyes with a maiden sitting demurely on her marble perch, one hand resting on her draped lap. She was bland and smooth and ideally proportioned. A young Greek girl. She was one of dozens of statues and plaster casts that lined the long hallway. His mother had loved such things. Marble and bronze figures depicting mythic heroes. Pottery vases. Antiquities of all kinds, selected from her father's warehouses. Anything, really, as long as it was beautiful. Not only priceless objects, but fragile, fleeting things. She'd filled rooms with flowers that she cultivated.

The sound of a slamming door brought his head up. Stragglers. A few wild-haired young men in baggy trousers were just leaving the canteen. He recognized one of them, by family resemblance. All the Ponsonbys had that vivid, nearly crimson, red hair. The middle child, Cecil, had been a friend since boyhood. This would be the youngest. Thomas. His collar was none too clean. But his companions, they wore no collars. All of the youngsters—for they were scarcely out of their teens—looked as though they slept under open sky. Only their pale skin and expensive boots belied the raffish impression. Young men of property in the garb of paupers.

He let them pass without pressing them for information. Best not to approach queerly dressed denizens of these underground workshops. Besides, the sight of Thomas Ponsonby, last glimpsed in an

Eton suit, now grown broad through the shoulders, and grown unfamiliar with starch and a good hard bar of soap, hit him like a blow. He'd missed that transformation, missed Cecil's reaction to it, which he could well imagine: good-humored, overacted consternation. With two older sisters and two younger brothers, Cecil had always tried to provide the glue that held his siblings together, except he wouldn't say *glue*. He'd say *magnetic field*, or *horseshoe-shaped solenoid*. Whenever Anthony and Cecil used to ride or row, dine or drink, they'd talked horses and sport, to be sure, but the rest had crept in. They'd divulged secret ambitions, childhood hurts.

That was why he'd been avoiding Cecil ever since he'd returned to London. They knew each other too well, and too much had happened during their years apart. There was too much he wanted to say but couldn't. It would crack him.

Suddenly, he felt the urge to overtake Thomas. *Tell your brother, tell Cecil, that . . .*

What?

Nothing. It was easy enough to push Cecil out of his mind. He'd been doing it for months.

Stay put. Focus. Await Mr. Coover.

The trouble was . . . he was bad at waiting. Very bad indeed. He paced the short length of hall between classroom doors.

"Your Grace."

He turned to the voice, low and breathless. Two more stragglers, young women, one fair, one dark, hovered in a classroom doorway. They looked far more conventional than their male counterparts, with smooth, upswept hair, jewelry, and neat muslin dresses protected by pinafores. They looked like debutantes. Eager and dewy, conscious of their charms. His hackles rose. He'd never developed a taste for them, as George had.

Palate cleansers, George had called them, and he'd set himself to seducing one, or two, between more elaborate debauches.

He himself had no desire for morsels. Nor was marriage in his immediate purview. Forming a new family under the present conditions...
it would be a grotesquery.

The fair girl caught his eye and dropped into a flawless curtsey.

"We met at a musicale given for Miss Pitcairn. I daren't presume
that you remember."

He didn't. Despite her lack of presumption, the pause she provided plainly invited him to supply her name.

The dark-haired girl also curtseyed.

"Your Grace!" she trilled.

The provided pause lengthened uncomfortably.

Once upon a time, Anthony Philby went out of his way to put
girls at their ease, even the petted, irksome ones who pretended their
heads were stuffed with goose-feather down and fairy dust. He'd
gotten on well with girls, perhaps because he understood that they
were people, not poppets, however they were presented in mixed
company. Any man with a sister should know as much. From the
moment Effie learned to talk she'd tried to boss him, showing a
strong-mindedness that only intensified with age. Most of their misadventures in the nursery were undertaken at her initiative. After he
went off to school, she'd howl him down at holidays if he showed her
the slightest hint of condescension.

There was an obvious flaw in his theory, however. Effie's humanity had never kindled in *George* a respect for the female sex. To him,
women were disposable. But then, so were men.

None of that mattered now.

The Duke of Weston put no one at ease.

They recognized him? Fine. They would get the ducal treatment.

His expression was pure ice.

"Maude Newcombe." The fair girl smiled, a pretty smile. Determined to ignore his bad behavior. Such girls were trained to it. So
men could act all the worse. It wasn't fair, but what was?

"Susan Pickering." The dark girl curtseyed again and Miss Newcombe slanted her a furious glance before smiling at him more widely.

"What do you think of our Schools?" Miss Newcombe edged forward and Miss Pickering had no choice but to fall back a step. Miss Newcombe lowered her voice even further, drawing him into her confidence.

"It's not very cheerful belowground. I'd much prefer the classrooms moved upstairs."

"Some of the rooms are like crypts," said Miss Pickering loudly. "There's one filled with rejected paintings that's so gloomy I could cry."

She did look as if she might cry, but out of frustration. Miss Newcombe, with almost imperceptible movements of her hips, was continuing to maneuver her backward.

He frowned equally upon them both. "Is this your classroom?"

They were standing in front of the room in which he'd encountered the peculiar Miss Lucy.

Miss Newcombe pulled a face.

"Unfortunately." She sniffed. "It's horribly stuffy. And today the weather is so enchanting. Shall we walk in the park, Your Grace?"

Miss Pickering gave a tiny gasp. "Maude! Our lesson."

"Oh, hush. I finished my picture." Miss Newcombe tossed her head and stepped forward, her arm sweeping up, anticipating his proffered elbow.

"Shall we?" She was really quite lovely. No doubt in her experience the elbows she anticipated materialized posthaste.

"A tempting offer." Anthony looked at her arm but made no move to intercept it. "I'm waiting for your Visitor."

Miss Newcombe continued her arm's arc, lifting her hand to brush the shining curves of her hair, as though this had always been her intention.

"Mr. Barrett?" Miss Pickering sensed an opening. "He won't be a moment."

"Not Mr. Barrett." He kept his tone neutral. "Mr. Coover."

Miss Newcombe and Miss Pickering exchanged a look, united in puzzlement. Miss Newcombe shook her head.

"There's no Mr. Coover. Alas." She sounded a regretful note.

"There's Miss Coover," Miss Pickering chimed in. "Could you mean Miss Coover?"

"Miss Coover is not a Visitor," said Miss Newcombe tartly, "so she does not signify."

Anthony focused on Miss Pickering, who blushed deeply and let her eyes drop.

"And who is Miss Coover?" he asked.

"She's a classmate of ours," said Miss Pickering. Now that she held his attention, she faltered, cutting her eyes to Miss Newcombe, soliciting her help. Miss Newcombe was looking daggers. "She doesn't signify," Miss Pickering added hopefully.

"Her father, Mr. Coover." Anthony felt frustratingly slow. He could see pieces now, but not the grand design. "*He* is also an artist?"

"She has no parents," said Miss Pickering. "Poor Lucy." She glanced back at Miss Newcombe with apology.

The pieces were rearranging themselves.

No *Mr.* Coover at all. Lucy Coover. L. Coover. Miss Lucy.

A figure appeared between the two women. A thin, long-nosed man, all in black. He'd come swiftly and silently down the hall. He looked like the Day of Judgment.

"What is the meaning of this?" His spectacles magnified his disapproval. He blinked rapidly.

"Mr. Barrett!" Miss Newcombe spun around, flushing crimson. "Thank goodness you're here. Now we can get back to our easels. Which of course we were about to do regardless. Well."

Her smile was painfully bright. "Mr. Barrett, the Duke of Weston. Your Grace, Mr. Barrett."

She fluttered her lashes at Anthony. "We told you he'd be but a moment. So very nice to see you. I do hope we meet again soon."

With palpable reluctance, she turned toward the door. Miss Pickering hesitated.

"Perhaps you would like to see our portraits?"

"He might like to very much," said Mr. Barrett, folding his arms. "However, he will not. I, on the other hand, will be around to inspect them presently."

At this both girls took to their heels.

Now it was Anthony who bore the brunt of Mr. Barrett's scrutiny. He glanced over the man's narrow shoulder down the long hallway.

Miss Lucy—Miss Lucy *Coover*—must have turned right at the canteen. She'd taken the stairs, then, to the library or the statue gallery. Unless there was another exit, one he hadn't seen when he'd wandered the rooms of the second floor, she was still up there.

He would find her.

"You wanted to speak with me?"

With a start, Anthony met the Visitor's gaze. It was altogether too keen for his liking.

"I had a question," he said. Damned if he didn't feel like a schoolboy, caught out in some mischief. His throat tightened. He searched for something probable.

"What do you consider the best way to begin a painting?" As he spoke, his forehead prickled. He'd sweated often as a schoolboy, waiting for the switch.

"I thought I might paint." He had to clear his throat before going on. "But you see, I don't know how to start."

Each one of Mr. Barrett's blinks seemed to tick away a minute. Was he incredulous? Or simply scornful? At last, he spoke.

"If you wish to paint a landscape, put on the canvas some semblance of the landscape. If you wish to paint a dog, put on the canvas some semblance of a dog. If you wish to paint a bowl of fruit upon a table . . . Do you grasp the general principle or should I continue?"

Were his eyes twinkling? No, it was light glinting on his lenses.

"I grasp the principle perfectly."

"Good," said Mr. Barrett dryly. "Now it's only the practice you're wanting."

"I'm off to practice, then." Anthony nodded at Mr. Barrett as the man turned smartly and marched into the classroom.

He exhaled then, and jogged for the stairs.

HE FOUND HER in the library. She was sitting alone at a long table, scowling over an enormous book. Propped up, it would not have looked out of place at a siege, the kind of thing archers would crouch behind to nock their arrows. Open on the library table, it didn't do a thing to hide her. Maybe she hoped the sheer force of her attention would render her invisible. She *was* imaginative, after all. But not so lucky.

As he came alongside her, he watched her posture change. Her shoulders stiffened. Her head lifted slightly, but she did not turn to look at him. Instead, she scowled with increased ferocity down at a color plate, reaching out to turn a heavy page with a gentleness that belied her fierce expression. The book wasn't just a prop. She handled it like a sacred object.

"What luck," he said. "I feared I'd lost you in the crowd." At that, she glanced up eagerly, not at him, but at a man he'd scarcely noticed, a thin, white-haired man halfway up a ladder with a small volume in his hands, poised to return it to a high shelf. The librarian. Of course, this room of all rooms would have its sentinel.

"Mr. Naylor." She spoke softly, but her voice carried surprisingly well in the lower register. It was a deep voice for a woman, warm and velvety. "The Duke of Weston has come to see the library."

A valiant final effort.

"Eh?" Mr. Naylor was struggling to fit the book back in its place. "What's that?"

She opened her mouth to answer, but Anthony reached out and

touched her wrist. It was cool, the pulse leaping beneath the skin. She went still as stone. After a moment, she jerked her wrist back. He brought his head down to hers and lowered his voice.

"Miss Coover," he said in her ear, so close a stray curl brushed his cheek. "A word."

He had already seen her blush. Now the color leached from her face, so the freckles stood out more starkly. As did her lips. Their color was richly red. Those lips parted.

"My apologies," she said. "I must be getting back to class." She stood. The smile she gave him was unconvincing. "I'd love to talk, of course, but I'm terribly late."

She started forward. With one stride, he insinuated his body between her and the door.

"Mr. Barrett won't mind. When I left him, he was occupied with two of your classmates. Charming women."

She folded her arms tightly beneath her breasts, the scowl returning. When she spoke, though, her tone was simply curious.

"I don't know who you might mean."

"Miss Newcombe and Miss Pickering."

"Of course," she said, looking away.

Remarkable: how much her face communicated. Much more than she intended. So. The pretty debs did not meet with her approval. Perhaps she got on better with the wild-haired young men. Yet her brand of bohemianism struck him as distinctly at odds with their studied shabbiness. Her dress, strange as it was, fit her well, emphasizing her graceful proportions, her slim torso and straight shoulders. She wasn't fashionable by any standard he knew, but she had some other quality. Call it *style*.

Her slippers, he noted, were cheap, worn down at the heel.

He lifted his eyes and saw she was watching him closely.

"They assure me that there is no *Mr.* Coover, Visitor in Painting. Living or dead. And so, Miss Coover, *we* have a matter to discuss. Shall we begin?"

He hadn't raised his voice, but she winced and glanced back at the librarian, still up his ladder, now occupied in tugging a book with both hands.

"Not here," she said. "The Gibson Gallery."

She walked quickly, without any affectation, the unselfconscious strides of a woman who measured distance in miles rather than lengths of ballroom. When he overtook her to open the gallery door, she stepped back and her face transformed. Gone was the flustered girl, guilty and mutinous. She seemed to forget herself altogether. She narrowed her eyes, observing his gesture, the way he turned his body, with a knowingness that unnerved him. It was as though she could see through his clothes.

Which, in a sense, she could. After all, she'd immortalized the sight.

He frowned as he pulled the door closed behind them. She was a problem. The severity of the problem remained to be seen.

He leaned against the wall, but she kept going, heedless of the fact that he no longer followed. She stopped halfway down the room, in front of a marble Roman in helmet and sandals, as though picking an ally. When at last she turned back to face him, he saw her hunted expression.

In the library, they might have been overheard. But in the gallery, she was alone. Absolutely alone. He saw her shift restlessly as she recognized her plight. A marble ally is no ally at all.

He pushed off the wall and strolled toward her until an arm span of space remained between them. He'd thought it a reasonable distance, but from where he stood, he couldn't help but take notice of her warmth and fragrance, the subtle rise and fall of her chest. Maybe it was the contrast with the gallery's chilly throng of motionless white figures.

She smelled like roses and common gin, a faint piney scent. His thoughts blurred. What he was experiencing now felt like anticipation— two bodies responding to each other, intuiting their perfect fit.

Maybe their bodies didn't intuit. Maybe they communicated their intimate knowledge.

The final pieces slid into place.

He thought of her worn shoes, and, now that he looked more carefully, he recognized the mauve tinge to her eyelids, the delicate shadows beneath her eyes and her cheekbones, for what they were: signs of exhaustion. She'd polished her accent but she couldn't fully smooth away those round vowels. An orphan, Miss Pickering had said. Short and slight from a childhood of underfeeding.

He sucked in his breath. She wasn't a model. She was an artist—a splendid one at that. But to make ends meet, she also worked, worked in the profession most accessible to women of her class.

She was a prostitute.

An assumption that explained his intense feeling of rediscovery. He had bedded this woman, bedded her after sucking down gallons of beer and liquor, a river's worth. Some nights were like that, as though the Thames flowed over and through him, bringing oblivion. He'd bedded her and forgotten her.

The realization did him no credit.

Before the army, he'd spent more time in brothels than he cared to recall. Collecting George. He would wait, sometimes for hours, on the grimy back stairs of public houses, in vast drawing rooms hung with silk curtains, in tiny, close chambers surrounded by silver cages of white mice and yellow canaries. In the end, he would drag, or carry, his brother to the coach while he mewled, sang, vomited. Over the years, he had made the acquaintance of dozens of prostitutes, from alley-treading three-penny uprights to bejeweled courtesans attended by serving girls in French underwear.

At which brothel, on which night, had he met Miss Coover?

Lately, he had sworn to himself—and several madams—that he had no interest in transacting. And it was true. The idea horrified him, after what George had done. He visited such houses only to assure himself that Effie hadn't fallen so low.

But when his conscious mind slipped beneath that dark current . . . what then?

He stared down at the spiral curls piled messily atop Miss Coover's head. His gaze dropped, caught on the curve of her bottom lip. In reaction to his regard, she drew the lip between her teeth. Guarding it.

Had he taken the time to kiss those lips? To kiss the inside of her wrist? To nuzzle her curls until he found her earlobe and sucked it between his teeth?

Alas. Drunk men seldom did.

The shame he felt wasn't new, but the portion had increased. He might flatten beneath it.

He didn't realize his expression had changed until he saw her swallow. He took a step back.

"You're a terrible liar," he told her, with a lightness he didn't feel. "Cows aren't known for murderous rampage."

She shot him a quick, surprised look. A smile came and went on her lips, the first real smile he'd seen from her. It was fleeting, but impossibly lovely. She shrugged.

"I added a bull," she said thoughtfully. "If you could see the scene as I'd imagined it, you'd feel differently, I think. The cows had a terrifying aspect."

Dramatic, not addlepated. But he already knew that. Perhaps she was obvious about certain falsehoods out of habit—a technique deployed to distract from the greater deception. For she *was* adept at deception. He knew that now, too. Surely no one at the Royal Academy was aware of her other profession. Democratic plainness in dress did not necessarily signal broad-mindedness. They would never accept her as one of their own, if her secret came to light.

"I have yet to behold the cow that strikes terror in my heart," he said.

"But of course not, you're a war hero," she murmured. "How silly of me."

When not narrowed to slits, her eyes had a long, curved shape. Cat eyes. They mesmerized.

Did she seriously think his jest was a boast? That he was enough of a braggart to praise his own courage in the face of cows?

"It's hardly that. It's just . . . I like everything that goes on four legs." He glanced away, gazed for a moment at the statue of a huntress and her hound.

"Dogs. Cows. Horses. Elephants. Camels."

"Cats," she offered.

"Cats," he agreed, before he looked back at her and saw the mockery on her face. She *hadn't* been serious. He stopped talking, pressing his lips together. Listing four-legged animals didn't pass for conversation even in brothels.

It was the allusion to his heroism that had rattled him.

Miss Coover was waiting for him to speak with a strange expression on her face. He disgusted her. Well, of course he did. A fornicator too drunk to recall what he'd done—and no doubt too drunk to have done the thing properly—doesn't make a good impression. If she were less intriguing, would he feel less humiliated? Pointless question. He had to address the situation head-on.

"You didn't have to lie at all," he pointed out. "You could have saved yourself some trouble, if you'd presented that painting to me, instead of peddling it to Adelaide Forbes."

"Your Grace," she said, chin lifting. "I never knew your name."

"Oh." He cleared his throat, nonplussed. He should be pleased he'd had that much good sense. Even blackout drunk, he'd known better than to reveal his identity.

He wasn't pleased. He didn't like the version of himself he saw emerging.

"I was surprised when you walked through the classroom door," she said. "Do you know, I'd taken you for a farmer." She laughed, and her face passed through that strange phase of beauty before it became, once again, ordinary. The freckled face of a barmaid with a barmaid's quick, sharp eyes.

"A farmer," he echoed. He wore a coachman's cape when he ventured out at night, and a felt hat, far less fashionable, and eye-catching, than his fine long coat and topper. But whatever the ensemble suggested, it was a far cry from *farmer*. And if he'd opened his mouth . . .

Perhaps he hadn't spoken a word to her.

In the taxonomy of drunkenness, Anthony fit into several categories, combining the self-destructive, brooding, and silent tendencies. Had he pushed her down on the bed, pushed up her skirts, saying—*asking*—nothing?

Oh, embarrassment could manifest as agony.

"Yes, a farmer," she said. "But in art, shepherds are more abundant. Hence, Endymion."

The name meant nothing to him. No doubt it was written in one of the books he'd avoided during his short stint at university. He'd been a scholar of rugby football—could recite every national code and its history—and had particularly excelled at putting what he knew into practice on the field. Other subjects he'd mastered: cricket, rowing, fencing.

"Sounds Greek," he observed, and she thinned her lips.

That's right. He was a perfect boor. The world's finest education had been his to waste. How had she come by hers?

"You *did* see the picture?" she asked.

Their eyes locked, and she looked down. At first, he mistook her bowed head for a sign of chagrin. Acknowledgment that the picture was tantamount to a violation. But no. She was marshaling her forces for a spirited defense.

"It's not a portrait, you understand," she said, looking up at him intently. "It's not *you*. I based Endymion *on* you, which isn't the same thing. The subject is mythological."

Several objections sprang to mind.

"Then why wasn't Endymion the one shot for adultery?"

Her jaw dropped.

"I don't . . . Shot?"

Stupid. He needed to contain this situation, not compound it.

Too impulsive. That had been his teachers' complaint. And the generals'. When would he learn? Her presence shook his self-command. It was too unsettling, knowing he'd had her, *fucked* her, when every detail of the encounter—good or bad—had been scrubbed from his mind. How had he behaved? What kind of man was he, really, when no one was watching, when even *he* wasn't watching?

He shook his head dismissively.

"It was nothing," he said. "Never mind. Forbes holds a gun like it's a hot eel. I've lost more skin shaving."

"But he . . ." Her horror was genuine. Not a trace of her former righteousness remained.

"He intercepted the picture and recognized me." Anthony realized that he was testing his wounded arm, moving it experimentally. Her eyes followed the motion. He pressed the arm to his side.

"And feared he understood his wife's sudden interest in art."

"You must believe I had no idea of such a thing!" Her exclamation carried her a step closer. The air she displaced stroked him like a finger. He tipped his head to the side, tapping his thumb against his thigh. "Mrs. Forbes bought the painting sight unseen, based on my description alone. She wanted a nude god and that's what she received."

"Whatever I believe, whatever myth you read . . ." He leveled her with his gaze. "Make no mistake. The subject of that picture is me."

It was the truth as he saw it. Plain and simple. But it didn't sit well with her. Her eyes were slits.

"If you understood *anything* about . . ." She bit off her protestation.

"Anything about . . ." he prompted.

"Anything!" she said. She stretched out her hands. "*You* are not my subject. You are the means I used to explore a classical ideal. Every figure composition needs a model. The models aren't the point. It's the aesthetic approach that matters. If you weren't a . . . a . . . *philistine*, you'd know Endymion from the moon in the upper left corner."

"The moon, is it?" He smiled. "So Endymion was a kind of night watchman for sheep? Even a philistine knows you need to stay awake for that. And wear a tunic," he added, an afterthought.

She hissed at him. Not since he'd turned in a Latin composition on the back of a cricket scoring sheet had his failure of intellection incurred such wrath.

"*In mythology*"—she spit it out—"Endymion was a shepherd so beautiful the goddess of the moon fell in love with him and visited him while he slept. *Love. Beauty. Those* are the subjects of the painting."

She was easy to annoy. He knew better than to tell her she was magnificent in her outrage. Pink had blossomed across her cheeks. He wondered if she'd had red hair as a child, red curls that darkened to this shade of copper brown. She blushed like a redhead. Face, throat.

Had he licked her nipples and watched their rose color spread? He was a philistine for forgetting.

She was muttering something. Amending her accusation. *Conceited pig* it sounded very like. And that last was surely *idiot*.

"Idiot though I may be," he said, "I am not an artist's model. I am the Duke of Weston. And I fear I trump your Endymion in notoriety, at least in contemporary society. And so, your classical ideal is compromised by your infelicitous choice in raw material. Mr. Forbes is not the only person who will find himself unconvinced that my face belongs to a shepherd."

Miss Coover's face looked thunderous.

"Isn't he, though?" she said. "Mrs. Forbes wanted to hang the painting in her chambers. No one else will see it."

"True enough." Anthony pressed on as her indignant expression wavered. "I'm not worried about that picture. My present concern is . . . other pictures."

"There are no others." Her mouth formed a straight line. "I am sorry you were nearly killed," she added.

In the pause that followed, he realized there were two ways of interpreting the sentence. Her look challenged him to inquire as to her meaning.

"Thank you," he said with a smile.

"Well. That's that. I'll be going, then." She drew herself to her full height. There wasn't much of her, but her pile of curls added inches up the vertical axis.

"Miss Coover." He held up his hand. "If you possess studies, sketches, any material whatsoever that shows my likeness, I must ask you to turn them over. I can't—I won't—have my figure reproduced."

"Fine." She didn't look at him.

"I must also ask for your silence." The portion of shame—it grew more enormous by the moment. He had to tamp it down, ignore it.

"I *require* your silence," he clarified, putting steel in his voice. After all, he wasn't really asking. Asking wasn't good enough. Too much was at stake. He needed a guarantee.

Sleepless nights of drinking and whoring. He would not be reading of them in the *Pall Mall Gazette*.

"It is in both of our interests." He forced himself to continue, even as her eyes found his, narrowing with apprehension. "Your silence for my silence."

"On which subject, pray tell, can I expect your silence?" She licked her lips, nervous. "It was wrong to misrepresent myself to Mrs. Forbes," she conceded in a rush, then caught her breath. "Do you threaten to expose me?"

She was close enough to touch. All he had to do was raise his hand. "I will keep silent on a more serious subject."

Now her eyes looked a question. She would not make this easy for him. He forged on.

"On the subject of your employment, Miss Coover," he said, while she blinked at him. He inhaled, prepared himself. If he couldn't be delicate, at least he would be direct.

"I will tell no one that you are a prostitute."

CHAPTER FOUR

FOR A MOMENT, she held perfectly still. Then the reaction came, swift and explosive. She laughed up into his face, a great burst of disbelief.

"Is that how you divide my sex?" she asked. "Ladies and whores?"

She bent sharply, arm across her stomach, convulsed, though her laughter sounded more like exclamations of fury. She righted herself, eyes bright.

"Can you fathom that a woman may be neither? That there are some women a man like you cannot pay or marry?"

He stared at her. Her very hair seemed to crackle around her.

"But how, then . . ." He spoke stiffly. "In your picture, I am . . ."

"Stark naked, just like I found you. By the smell, I'd say you'd been rolled out of a tavern. I stepped on you, in fact. Thought you were a rat, at first. Then a dead man."

My corpse.

His eyes pricked with the memory of lacerating sunlight. He'd woken in an alleyway, aching, bare-arsed in the cold mud, a rag-picker boy jabbing the sole of his foot with a stick. When was that?

October. Shortly after his father's death.

"That was how it happened. So, you and I . . . we did not . . ." He wasn't a born orator, but before he'd met Miss Coover he'd better luck finishing his sentences.

"No, Your Grace," she said. "We did not."

Relief galloped through him. *Thank God.* He hadn't misused the woman. No. *She* had misused *him.* Anger rode in. How dare she look at him like that, all righteousness and outrage?

"You found me, you say. The victim of a crime."

"A fancy fellow like you. Coins rattling in your pockets." She sniffed. "You're lucky one of the lads didn't gut you like a fish."

She'd let her accent slip. Her vowels had broadened. She was still furious. But he detected a hint of uneasiness in her expression.

"Certainly." He gave her a cool smile. "It was of course my own fault that I was robbed and left in the mud. I'm sure I all but asked you to stop and take a good long look as well."

There. Her eyelids twitched. He'd scored a point. She was on the defensive now.

"I covered you," she said, a weak protest.

"Covered me? That's rather rich coming from the woman who put my nether parts in a picture. Miss Coover." He lowered his voice, stepped closer. "Whatever *ideals* you were exploring in your art, the fact of the matter is this: you made me your model without my consent."

They stood toe-to-toe. She stared at him. She opened her mouth to argue.

"*You,*" she said, accusation in her voice. But something shifted behind her eyes.

"*You* . . . are right," she finished. She looked as surprised as he felt.

"You're right," she repeated, more firmly. "I'm sorry."

It was his turn to stare. Confounding woman. Despite himself, he laughed.

"And how do you mean, *covered* me? I woke naked as the day I was born. I had to buy a shawl off Nick so I could hail a cab."

"Nick?" Her brow furrowed.

"A little ragpicker." He'd had to take the bright-eyed urchin with him to make good on the sale. On the ride to Weston Hall, Nick had given him an earful about his ma and da and wee sisters.

"That was my freely given shawl he sold you." She laughed. "How much?"

"He asked for a quid." The cabman had waited with Nick behind the stables while Anthony crept into the glasshouse for clothes, then up into his study for coin.

"And I paid him sixpence to watch over you." She shook her head admiringly. "Clever boy."

"I gave him back the shawl, or I'd return it to you."

"I wonder how many times he can sell it." She smiled. "It was kind of you to let him keep it."

He shrugged, uncomfortable. What was a tattered triangle of paisley-print wool to him? She was the one who'd been kind. He didn't tell her he'd slipped Nick one of his father's gold pocket watches as well, to help his sick ma. Nick had vanished from his thoughts. He'd become too aware of Miss Coover's proximity, the rise and fall of her breasts.

She was a confounding, extraordinary woman. She'd covered him with one hand and exposed him with the other.

As the pause extended, she sighed.

"I *am* sorry," she said. "I'm not just sorry you nearly died. I'm sorry for what I did. Something came over me. It's no excuse, but . . ."

She sighed again. "I pass through that alley every day. Suddenly, you were there."

Shoreditch. His mind twisted and turned through the boggling labyrinth of tenements, flophouses, bars, theaters, brothels, and workshops. She was native to that borough, where he slummed after midnight. And yet here she was, in the Royal Academy, on his side of London.

They'd made reciprocal journeys. But hers had been harder. Shame again, heavy, thick, a wellspring of sludge that never ran dry.

"It was like a miracle," she said, eyes widening slightly, the line of her lips softening.

He startled.

"A miracle?" He shook his head. "Stepping on a soused idiot?" He laughed softly.

She didn't.

"Seeing you," she said. The slight burr that gave her voice its velvety nap snagged in her throat. The words emerged as a croak. That croak was all it took. Something felt *different*. Charged. Something was kindling.

His skin prickled.

"Everything I wanted to know."

There was only a whisper of air between their bodies. He couldn't resist.

"Everything?" He drawled the word and reached out, slowly. He touched a ringlet that skimmed her temple, felt its spring, then rubbed it between his fingers. She shivered but didn't flinch away. A line appeared between her brows.

"Not everything. I couldn't see your backside," she said. "But I feared you'd wake if I tried to tip you over."

A laugh escaped him. She could be blunt, and humorous. Laughter didn't break the spell. It strengthened it. He laid his thumb on her cheekbone. Her skin was smooth, those little golden freckles without texture.

"Here I am, awoken," he said, with mock grandiosity; then he cleared his throat. "Which means it will be more challenging now, to see my bare backside. You will have to beg my permission."

He slid his thumb down her cheek, and her skin moved, the soft flesh tightening. How novel, to *feel* a woman scowling.

"Go on," he said. "I might take pity on you if you ask very nicely."

She drew back abruptly, eyes glowing. He was provoking her, but God knew she deserved it.

"So gracious of you," she said, all politeness, through gritted teeth. "But I can manage without."

"You should take advantage of a man's offer, instead of, well." He paused to frown at her. "Taking advantage."

"I *said* I was sorry." Her hands were in fists at her sides.

"You did." He acknowledged it. "I can see the signs of your sincere contrition." His voice was dry, and his eyes dropped to her fists, which she released instantly, brushing at her skirts. "As a reward, to counterbalance all that remorse"—he twitched away his smile—"I *give* you permission. You don't have to beg." He rocked once on his heels, then stood stock-still, a hand on his hip, posed. He barely moved his lips. "Do what you will with me."

She was staring at him now, the ferocity of her scowl diluted by sudden uncertainty. He'd unnerved her. Good. He'd wanted to unnerve her, as she'd unnerved him.

"You were so resourceful, when you found me *stark naked*, as you say, in that alley." He abandoned his pose, rolled his head on his shoulders, stretched his limbs, aware that she watched him narrowly. "But your faculties fail you, it seems, when you're forced to meet the gaze of your subject."

He smiled, a smug smile, he knew. He leaned forward and lowered his voice, making it silky. "You really can't think of one single thing you want to do?"

She stepped back in haste, caught herself, and looked at him, face aflame. Then she marched forward, put her hand on his neck, and gripped. She rose onto her tiptoes and kissed him.

SHE HAD MADE a miscalculation. A significant one. The realization dawned on her without illuminating a solution.

His surprise lasted no more than an instant. He rocked back once on his heels, then pressed forward, leaning into her, curving her body back like a bow. His mouth was warm and sweet, moving on hers as he licked at the seam of her lips, parting them.

What had she been thinking? That she could turn the tables? Teach him a lesson?

No. A little voice chimed in the depths of her mind. Like always, she had been more interested in her own education. She'd wanted to learn his mouth beyond its color and shape, its abstract form. She'd wanted it since the first moment she saw him.

She was learning now. His mouth . . . it was heat and moisture, and a faint honeyed taste.

Beneath her hand, she felt the movements of his throat, the friction of the tiny hairs embedded in the skin of his jaw. She let her hand slide down, slide across his shoulder, broad and hard.

She already knew his anatomy, knew the moment her palm would begin its downward slope, bump of clavicle, bunched density of deltoid and biceps. But her knowledge was changing. It felt less like mastery and more like surrender. To know wasn't to order the world, but to open to its mystery.

His arms came around her and their strength made her gasp against his mouth. He liked that. She felt his lips curve before he drew her lower lip between his teeth, suckling the plump flesh, scraping its tenderness ever so lightly. He was smiling. Not her corpse, not Endymion. The Duke of Weston. A buffoon. A selfish, conceited idiot. A man who shattered stained-glass windows and pickled himself with gin.

The subject of your picture is me, he'd said, and it was he whom she was kissing, not an idealized figure. It was madness to pretend otherwise.

But, dear God, his beauty convulsed her senses.

This was like nothing she'd experienced with boys in the borough, the few that she'd kissed, all bright, skinny lads in caps, older brothers of the girls with whom she'd once shared clothes-peg dolls. They were fervent and earnest, and in the end, she'd batted them away. They were a distraction, and she was very good at maintaining her focus.

This was different. This was a threat.

Every heightened instinct urging her to push him away was turned against her, into pure sensation. Now both her arms were wound around his neck, and his hips ground into her skirts. The swelling she felt between his thighs made her eyes fly open. He was growing larger, harder, and when she pulled back to assimilate these new dimensions, the arm around her waist kept her close, and his mouth dragged from hers and pressed hot and wet against her neck, before his teeth closed on the lobe of her ear.

She moaned, unable to stop herself, kneading his shoulders. She hadn't seen the back side of his body, how the muscles knit over his ribs, the way his buttocks jutted from the iliac crest, but maybe she could *feel* . . .

No. His jacket muffled detail. Whereas the silk of her gown scarcely protected her. She could feel the individual pads of his fingers sweep across her shoulder blades, exploring her as she longed to explore him, working their way down the knobs of her spine.

She dug with her fingers, feeling the savage desire to rend the cloth. Touch was a new frontier. She wanted more of it. Criminal that he should rub against her cased in layers of linen, silk, and wool. He found her lips again, his breathing as ragged as her own, his tongue stroking deeper.

There were hollows she hadn't even considered, negative spaces, that suddenly thrummed with feeling. He was licking into her, and she felt heaviness and heat gathering lower down in her belly, an answering ache.

Kisses before had natural ends. Two self-contained bodies touched at the lips, then separated.

How had she entered into such a complicated new arrangement? Even her breathing seemed tangled with his. She had to go still, hold her breath, to begin extrication. He gentled his lips, coaxing, teasing. He could bring a statue to life with that mouth, make Venus sway from her plinth.

She brought up her hands and pushed once, hard, against his chest. He was immovable. A solid wall. But after a moment, he stepped away.

His green eyes dazzled, hot and bright between those bone black lashes.

"Bravo," he said dryly, with unpardonable composure. "I won't forget *that* anytime soon."

He pushed back a lock of hair that had fallen forward, the gesture so graceful she felt her heart trip.

Beauty would be her doom.

She sniffed. "I should hope your mind isn't so marinated. It's midday and you smell . . ."

"Like what?"

He smelled delectable, like he'd been spiced. His scent still flooded her.

"*Not* like a barrel of gin," she said. "That is, sober."

"I am sober. I've given it up."

She repressed a snort. *She* was the terrible liar? He frowned. For some reason, it seemed to matter to him that she believe his claim.

"Congratulations," she said. "Did you leave your blue ribbon at home? It's probably for the best. Temperance badges elicit rude comments in bars and gaming houses. Brothels too, no doubt."

He gritted his teeth at her. Fine white teeth, flawless.

"You jump to conclusions about my habits based on an anomaly. I was not myself in October."

She lived in Shoreditch, not under a rock. Scandal sheets sold on street corners all over London. She did snort.

"And before? In September? When you broke the window at All Saints?"

He stretched his neck, turning his head to the side. "Sometimes anomalies come in twos." The way his nose came down straight from his forehead—the impression it gave of strength and nobility—he'd done nothing to merit such a profile.

"A sacrilegious act." She folded her arms. "It might have been a window by Burne-Jones! He is a *brilliant* painter."

In fact, one of her and Kate's favorites.

"His stained-glass designs aren't decorations only," she said. "They're masterpieces."

At that, he began to laugh. He hadn't laughed like that in her presence, boyishly. Dimples creased his cheeks.

Dimples. She was entirely undefended against dimples.

"It's not the vandalism of the church that concerns you," he said, "but the possibility that the work of Burne-Jones might have been its target."

"Of course the vandalism of the church concerns me," she snapped. "And if you'd so much as cracked a panel of a Burne-Jones window, you'd be concerned too, because you'd be going straight to hell."

"I don't suppose my innocence of this particular crime will spare me the fate you prescribe."

He didn't sound concerned. He sounded cold, matter-of-fact. His smile had vanished. He had done all manner of appalling things, things he remembered and things he'd forgotten. The papers had reported some of it. The lion's share of misadventures were no doubt unrecorded. A man like him would never change.

"No, I suppose not," she murmured. "Although I've heard you're not so wicked as your brother."

She shouldn't have said it. If he'd sounded cold before, now his voice iced over.

"Spare me your thoughts regarding my brother." He was looking down his nose at her, a look that made her want to shrivel.

"The studies you made for that painting. The sketches." He spoke in a clipped tone, all business. "I will have them."

"You won't!" God help her, he touched every nerve. He issued a command and her first instinct was to resist, with force. "They're mine." She felt her mouth pull mulishly. "I won't display them, or paint from them. But . . ." She shrugged. She had no finer phrase, so she settled on repetition for emphasis. *"They're mine."*

"You will send them to me, or I'll batter down your door and take them."

"Good luck. I don't live in a famous mansion named for my forbears. My door is harder to find than yours."

A shadow flicked across his eyes. Was he remembering what he must have seen on his carousels? The houses with windows patched over with rags and paper, the tenements listing from their decayed foundations, the teeming courts with their jumble of wooden galleries and garbage-clogged gutters?

Aunt Marian's shop occupied a tiny corner of an Elizabethan house, massive and well built but divided into several businesses and living quarters. It didn't feature in a Baedeker's guide to London.

"The Academy must record the addresses of its students." He drew his brows together, his expression dark. "I don't think you want me to speak to the Keeper. Or the president."

She had no rejoinder. If the Duke of Weston complained about her conduct, or worse, produced her letter to Mrs. Forbes, the council would strike her name from the list of students. She had impersonated a Visitor to sell a painting that dishonored a duke.

She'd be expelled at once.

"I don't want to do it either. Not when you've worked so hard to get here." His glance swept her and the gallery and seemed to roam further, to take in Burlington House, the Royal Academy itself, and all it stood for.

The words were uttered without irony. For a moment, she felt naked before him, more naked than he could ever be, with his money and power, all of it handed to him. It was a strange feeling. He recognized her ambition, recognized the sacrifices she had made to get so far. There was a note of something that sounded like admiration in his voice. But also, an unmistakable threat.

He would ruin her all the same.

"I'll send the sketches," she whispered.

"And do I also have your guarantee of silence regarding our acquaintanceship?"

She fixed her eyes on a statue, the foot of a statue, a clever foot, the foot of Hercules, no less. The heel was a thick pad of muscle pressing into the rippling mane of the Nemean lion.

"Yes?" Weston prodded.

"I'm practicing silence." She pursed her lips. Her mouth, which had sweetened with his kisses, tasted bitter. She dragged her eyes up to look at him.

He was smiling a faint smile.

"Make sure you perfect the art."

"Tell me," she said in a rush, even as a part of her—the sane part—was begging not to ask, not to be told.

"My painting. Once you explained to Mr. Forbes . . . Did he let Mrs. Forbes keep it on the wall?"

She searched his face, now a mask, beautiful and remote. Only a muscle in his jaw ticked, his jaw that was perhaps his one imperfection, a shade too square.

With deadly calm, he delivered the blow.

"I took the picture," he said. "I took it and destroyed it."

She sagged, then clenched her muscles, her teeth. Her eyes felt tight and hot. She would not cry in front of this man. She would not cry in front of anyone.

Why should the information cut like a knife? The picture was already gone. She'd sold it. Had she imagined that someday the Forbeses would donate it to a museum? That it would feature in exhibits dedicated to the early work of Lucy Coover?

Months of labor, of love. Of fantasy.

"Miss Coover." He was going to say something else, her corpse, but he wasn't her corpse, he never had been. She stepped around him and bolted for the door. Hatred gave her feet wings.

She *hated* him, the Duke of Weston. She wanted to erase him from her memory. But for her, the recourse didn't lie at the bottom of a bottle. She stumbled blindly down the hall, down the stairs, into the dark corridor of classrooms. There was no recourse.

She would go to her grave before she would forget his face.

CHAPTER FIVE

SATURDAY DAWNED WET and gray. Lucy spent the first part of the morning bustling through the shop, layering high-quality silks and muslins around rolls of cheaper fabrics to create a sumptuous display. She draped the front racks with pretty chintzes and opened drawers so shining ribbons and colorful laces peeked out. The drawers looked bountiful, packed with trimmings. No customer would guess that there was nothing behind those few visible bits of ornament.

The drawers were all but empty.

Every now and then Aunt Marian looked up from her sewing machine to smile at Lucy's progress. She was in the far back of the shop, letting out seams in one of Mrs. Fairfax's unutterably ugly day dresses. Back when she was Miss Clara Oakes, Mrs. Fairfax, a soprano who sang opera at the Lyceum Theatre and was feted by the press for her daring fashion, had been—for a season at least—as famous as the queen. Now she was stout, widowed, and somber-minded, with tastes that ran to prudish severity.

Seeing her aunt drowning in all that black and gray fabric caused Lucy physical pain. What a waste of her talent! Aunt Marian was a *genius*. Theater managers used to send her their more glamorous singers and dancers. No comic opera, no romance, no gothic or nautical drama, was complete without Aunt Marian's elaborate gowns, each with its signature flourish. At the peak of her success, she'd employed five seamstresses. She'd partnered with Dodie Thistleship, costume designer for the leading Shakespearean actresses of the day. That had been the beginning of the end. Dodie Thistleship took credit for Aunt Marian's patterns, patterns that set society trends. Slowly, Aunt Marian was edged out and forgotten.

She was lucky that *any* star continued to patronize her, even an aged star determined to sport the silhouette of an eighteenth-century dowager. The beau monde took no more notice of *Miss Stirling, Dressmaker*. The shop couldn't stay afloat on rare special orders. They eked by on rack sales and girls from the penny gaffes who wanted a bit of lace edging.

Still, the shop remained her aunt's pride and joy. Lucy wouldn't let it look like a ragpicker's cart, however depleted the stock, however meager the prospect for new sales.

She finished arranging trimmed bonnets in the counter display, then surveyed the corner of the shop where clients were once measured and fitted by the dozen behind a green velvet curtain. Now that corner was occupied by a woeful little table piled with Mrs. Fairfax's petticoats. Sighing, she pushed through a rickety door and went past the little kitchen, down the narrow hall to the back court to retrieve her latest creation. She burst into the shop carrying a bottle filled with fern fronds and moss and set it in the center of the little table.

"There," she said with satisfaction. She'd gotten the idea after a visit to Kate's house. The Holroyds had two large glazed cases on ornate tables in their drawing room containing dozens of fern species from around the world. With what glass Lucy had to hand, and one fern she'd bought from a Drury Lane root seller, she'd made a miniature version. It was simple, true, but absolutely cunning. If she did say so herself.

"What do you think?" she asked. "Never mind! Don't look until I'm done."

She walked backward to the front door and cast an eye over the shop. Gorgeous, even with the light coming feebly through the small, wavy panes. The Argand lamps gave the room a warm glow, and even her aunt, thin and drawn at her sewing machine, looked picturesque in the background.

At the sound of a knock, Lucy turned, smoothing her skirt, but it was only the wind, rattling the door against the frame. A dummy dressed in black broadcloth caught her eye. She grimaced, dragging the dummy away from the window. Aunt Marian could do better than advertising family mourning! She stripped the dummy and began to lace a gown of cheerful yellow silk around its wasp waist. It was Aunt Marian's style, but it was her own handiwork, bountifully embroidered with daisies.

"This is all very nice," said Aunt Marian. Her new sewing machine was purring along as she pumped the treadle. "But, Lucy . . ." She paused, a twinkle in her eye. "Are you expecting the queen?"

Lucy made a face and gave the gown a few final tugs.

"The queen would look well enough in one of your dresses," she said. "You've outfitted plenty of queens."

"Guinevere, Cleopatra, Cymbeline, Gertrude . . ." Aunt Marian laughed, ticking off the characters she'd costumed.

Lucy laughed too and dragged the dummy back to the front of the shop.

Perfection achieved, she could settle in for a few hours of needlework. Maybe it *was* foolish to keep the shop looking elegant, with the semblance, at least, of luxury. The women who came in off the street were by and large seeking out ready-made print frocks, something prettier than they'd find in a market stall, for a holiday or for church. They didn't have much to spend, and they paced the floor warily, on guard against their own desires.

She sank into a chair and reached into the open basket on the floor for her needle and thread.

"Go on." Her aunt made shooing noises, her hands too busy at the sewing machine for the accompanying motions. "Aren't you working on a picture of Flossie Dowling's boys?"

"It came out wrong." Lucy threaded her needle swiftly. "I whited it out. I have to start over again. So, you see, I'm not working on anything."

She shrugged as though the subject was of no import whatsoever, gathering undersleeves onto her lap that Mrs. Fairfax had allowed might do with a *bit* of decoration.

"The light's bad for painting anyway," she muttered, plucking one of Mr. Malkin's hairs from a cuff.

Now that Aunt Marian couldn't manage the precipitous stairs, Lucy slept alone in the garret, which she also used as her studio. Saturdays and Sundays she tried to paint for an hour or two when the sun was out and sew later into the night, to save on oil. But it scarcely mattered on such a gray morning.

"Whited it out!" The shop fell silent as the belts and wheels of the sewing machine stopped turning. "Without showing it to me?" Aunt Marian shook her head. The sewing machine began to hum again and she bent low over the table.

Aunt Marian was also frizz-haired, although hers was now iron gray. Lucy spoke haltingly to her mass of curls and hairpins.

"The portrait was ludicrous," she said. "The faces had the texture of overripe cheese."

Aunt Marian raised her head.

"I don't care if you doubled the size of Tom Dowling's head and painted on an extra eye. I'd have liked to see it."

Lucy forced herself to meet her aunt's gaze.

"I'll show you the next one." She tried to make the promise sound new, as though she hadn't made it before, after she'd bought the sewing machine.

My dear girl! Aunt Marian had looked between Lucy and the gleaming Singer with tears in her eyes. Then she'd blinked, scowled to conceal the hurt.

You sold a picture and this is the first I know of it?

At that moment, Lucy would have promised her anything.

It wasn't that she found her aunt's interest burdensome. As a girl, Lucy had solicited her opinions, presenting sketches with shy excitement. Aunt Marian's bright, dark eyes had a piercing quality, and her praises gratified. They always rang with truth. Aunt Marian saw, even in Lucy's scribbles, energy and emotion, the potential of a grand design. Her faith was unshakable.

Lucy had been afraid to show her *Endymion*. After a lifetime spent associating with theatrical personalities, Aunt Marian wasn't easily scandalized. But a male nude, bathed in moonlight, the personification of longing . . . Lucy didn't dare. *An experiment in classicism* was how she'd described the picture. Aunt Marian could sense her discomfort and allowed her to leave it at that.

The most recent picture, of the Dowling boys . . . it was simply a failure. Whatever flaws Aunt Marian imagined, the reality was worse.

"Truly, you'd have been disappointed," she said.

"Very well, then." Aunt Marian gave a stern nod. "What are you waiting for? Off you go. Paint something better."

Lucy looked helplessly at Mrs. Fairfax's gowns hanging along the back wall, all of them in need of letting out, of new buttons, of even dowdier collars.

"I'm paying the older Cosgrave girl to come sew with me. Now, don't say a word! I'm paying her from *your* money, so it's you who bought yourself the time. With one picture, you earned more than I made on Cymbeline and Gertrude put together, so drop that sleeve."

The one picture had taken Lucy nearly five months and she'd never have gotten such a sum if she hadn't pretended she was a man, famous on the continent and a Visitor to boot.

But that was an objection she couldn't make.

Lucy tucked away her threaded needle. For a moment, her aunt sewed in silence; then she sighed.

"I'll see it someday."

Lucy's stomach dropped.

"You won't," she said, too bitterly. She'd had nightmares of the canvas burning as she tried to pull it from a great fireplace, big as the gates of hell, and Weston leaning on the mantel, laughing. Mercifully, when he started to kiss her, the force of her anger woke her up and she lay awake, heart pounding. Saved from that particular perdition.

Aunt Marian peered at Lucy speculatively over the thread unspooling from the bobbin.

"It's just a feeling I have," she said. "I can't explain it."

Lucy managed a wan smile as the knock came at the door.

Not the wind this time.

The knock repeated.

"That'll be Megan now," said Aunt Marian, but the woman who burst into the shop wasn't the pale, timid Cosgrave girl. The woman was short, broad, and ruddy, well into her middle years.

"Mrs. Cantrell." Aunt Marian finished her seam and stood painfully. "It's a wet morning to come out."

"Miss Stirling." Mrs. Cantrell's round face was damp, with rain and with tears.

"Don't tell me it's your husband." Aunt Marian rushed to the younger woman, forgetting her stiff knees, and helped her into a chair.

Overcome, Mrs. Cantrell shook her head.

"Not one of the children?" At her aunt's look, Lucy hurried to put the kettle on the hob.

"No, no, they're fine, all in good health, thank God."

The Cantrells were a boot-making family, had been for generations. Most boot makers worked in factories now, but the Cantrells still ran the shop two doors down as a family business. They were numerous. Even the youngest Cantrell children could cut and sew and paste. Their tiny store was a manufactory in miniature.

"You haven't heard?" Mrs. Cantrell pressed a hand to her cheek and stared around the room, avoiding Aunt Marian's gaze. She seemed to notice Lucy for the first time, hovering on the threshold between the little back kitchen and the shop proper. "You look well, lass," she said, and her voice broke.

She was Irish by birth and had been a beauty in her time. The story was she won Mr. Cantrell's heart with a glance. He'd felt her green eyes pierce him like a dart as they haggled over the price of oranges. His parents tried to dissuade him—an Irish basket girl!—but he would not be moved. Her eyes *were* an extraordinary color. Lucy had only seen one pair that made their emerald seem dim by comparison. She didn't want to think of them.

Mrs. Cantrell's eyes were brimming.

"Perhaps you'll find a man at your painting school who'll give you a good home, a decent, hardworking man, like my Alvin, but not so unlucky. That's what I hope for you."

She meant well, of course. Mrs. Cantrell was bighearted, quick to anger, and quick to laugh. Sometimes, Lucy could hear her from down the street, yelling at her children or singing as she soled baby shoes. Family was everything to her.

Nonetheless, Aunt Marian snipped back.

"Stuff and nonsense. A man!"

Aunt Marian made no bones about her own hopes for Lucy, or about her belief that, when it came to realizing those hopes, a man would prove less a boon than a bane. She fixed Lucy with a fierce look before turning it on Mrs. Cantrell. Sometimes she transformed into a veritable gorgon. Her hair made a magnificent prop.

"Lucy needs a man as much as a toad needs a side pocket. She'll make a triumph with her oils, mark my words," declared Aunt Marian. "We'll all be part of a big crowd looking up at her pictures on the wall. I'm saving my legs for it."

She meant it. As painful as it was for her to move, if Lucy exhibited anywhere in England, she would run after trains, clamber in and out of cabs and omnibuses, trudge miles.

"One day, she will become a member of the Academy!"

"Is that right? Then I'm glad," murmured Mrs. Cantrell. Like all the neighbors, she humored Aunt Marian, the resident firebrand.

Aunt Marian did tend to get carried away. The Royal Academy

had never elected a female Academician. Neither were its members known for their radical ideas. Change came slowly, if at all.

Lucy was more likely to stand for Parliament.

"I just want her to be taken care of." Mrs. Cantrell's eyes were welling again, and she dried them with a handkerchief. "I don't know what we're to do."

"What is it? What's happened?"

Aunt Marian had gone unnaturally still, bracing herself.

"They've put up notices." Mrs. Cantrell balled the handkerchief in her fist. "They're all around, notices and placards. They're demolishing the house, the whole block. It's been condemned."

"Condemned?" Aunt Marian sank back into her chair. "Condemned? Our block?"

Some streets in Shoreditch were little more than open sewers. But this wasn't one of them. The Elizabethan houses that fronted onto the narrow lane had been divided into tinier and tinier sections to fit more and more families, but at street level the shops, if not prosperous, were clean and respectable.

"This house?" Aunt Marian continued. "It's solid as bedrock! It's old, but it will stand forever."

She looked dazedly about as though expecting the ceiling beams themselves to speak their confirmation.

Now Mrs. Cantrell's eyes blazed green fire. "I told the bill poster," she said, "him that was putting up the notices. I told him you couldn't find a stouter, squarer house, and families living more respectably, in any corner of England. Wasn't nothing to do with him, he said, and so I offered to let him see for himself how strong the walls were by knocking his head on them. He didn't like that, not a bit of it."

"It's nothing to do with the bill poster, that's right." Aunt Marian's voice was hoarse. "It's the vestrymen looking to make a penny. And the city . . ."

Her voice broke. On other occasions, people shushed Aunt Marian when she began to rail against local government with the passion of a pamphleteer. But today Mrs. Cantrell nodded. Aunt Marian cleared her throat and continued.

"We all know that the Board of Works is rotten as old meat."

The kettle was screaming for half a minute before Lucy shook herself and turned on her heel. She filled the teapot and put cups on the tray with trembling fingers.

She could hear her aunt talking again in that same strained voice.

"I remember Mr. Pomeroy complaining when it came time for the board to send out its inspectors to check the theaters. He had to give free tickets and I don't know what else, or they'd declare a fire hazard and close him down."

"You don't have to be telling me," said Mrs. Cantrell. "The Board of Perks, they call it. Alvin went to talk with James Purcell."

Neither woman looked at Lucy as she set the tea tray between them. Bile was rising in her throat. She retreated to the chair in the corner.

Condemned! And their only hope James Purcell! Since he'd been appointed vestry clerk, his cronies had become the parish rate collectors and sanitary inspectors. He'd improved only the streets that ran past his furniture workshops, and he'd been accused—by an irate surveyor—of taking cuts of the paving contracts to boot.

"James Purcell. We'd be fools to trust in James Purcell."

Her aunt sounded old, older than Lucy had ever heard her sound before. She *was* old. She wouldn't survive the loss of the shop. The enormity struck her like a slap. She bit back a cry, and her aunt gave a small start and glanced in her direction.

"But surely there's something to be done." Lucy stood, bumping the little table. She put a protective hand on the bottled fern as it wobbled.

Another knock. Megan Cosgrave at last. She hesitated on the doorstep, thin and stooped, clutching her sewing bag. Her eyes were huge. She, too, had seen the notices.

"Oh, Miss Stirling, it isn't fair! Your beautiful shop!"

"It's not gone yet, Meg," said Mrs. Cantrell, rising. She looked at Aunt Marian. "James Purcell can't be trusted, true, but he can't be condemning buildings willy-nilly either."

"*He* can't, that's right," said Aunt Marian, quietly. "Not alone."

"Don't stand where you'll catch your death of cold." Mrs. Cantrell turned back to Megan Cosgrave. "If you're here to sew, you'd best be sewing."

"And you, too, Mrs. Cantrell, I'm so sorry!" Megan's lips were trembling. "They haven't any right."

"What of your building?" asked Lucy. The Cosgraves lived in a sagging tenement overloaded with perilous wooden galleries, one of dozens built around a tiny court. The privies stood over cesspools. People had to fight to take their water from a common standpipe.

Under recent acts of Parliament, the vestries under the vestry boards, the district boards, and the Metropolitan Board of Works had been tasked with improving public health through housing reform. They sought out landlords whose diseased, overcrowded buildings were on the point of collapse and compensated them handsomely for the seizure of their properties. The tenants were sent scurrying like rats. New roads crisscrossed the old sites. Model dwellings went up, with fewer rooms and higher rents.

Slum clearance in one place resulted in more congestion elsewhere. No one on the boards seemed to care so long as the evictions rolled out and the money rolled in.

The inspector of nuisances had visited the Cosgraves' tenement the previous month. Mrs. Cosgrave had told Aunt Marian the news with resignation.

They'll have to knock it down around our ears. We've nowhere else to go.

Megan shook her head and came farther into the shop, lowering her worn bag. "The only notices went up here."

Aunt Marian laughed. She laughed so hard tears streamed down her cheeks. Lucy watched, stunned and helpless.

"Miss Stirling." Mrs. Cantrell hesitated, then approached Aunt Marian's chair, laying a gentle hand on her arm.

Aunt Marian hated fussing, but she didn't swat Mrs. Cantrell away. She choked off her laughter with a short sob.

"Villains," she said. "Perfect villains. I wish I could dress them for the part. Scarlet pantaloons and waistcoats. Everyone would know them for what they are."

"That'd be a sight, James Purcell in scarlet pantaloons." Mrs. Cantrell patted Aunt Marian and stepped away.

"It'd be a sea of scarlet pantaloons." Aunt Marian swiped at her eyes angrily.

"Your landlord," she said to Megan. "He's making a fortune, packing more and more people into his buildings like maggots in a nut. More than enough to pay off Purcell and the inspector of nuisances. He'll keep extracting rents until the floors are caving in; then he'll let the city take his properties at market rate."

"But here?" Lucy burst out. "No inspector of nuisance came here."

Not that she knew of, anyway. Heat mantled her cheeks as three pairs of eyes fixed on her. Weren't most of her days spent on the other side of the city? Maybe it wasn't her place to speak. Even as the thought formed, she rejected it.

This is my home.

"We're the nuisance." Aunt Marian sounded old again, old and sad. "Someone wants to lease this block for his own purposes. Someone who can bribe, or influence, Purcell, his inspectors, and the medical officer himself."

Lucy's face grew hotter.

"If he were wearing his red pantaloons, I'd go right up to him and scratch his eyes out."

Aunt Marian laughed, a real laugh this time.

"Exactly," she said. "Now bring this half-frozen girl a cup of tea before she expires."

Lucy went and fetched another cup. Mrs. Cantrell had taken her seat and was sipping her own tea. Megan sat beside her. Lucy set down the cup and filled it. The tea was strong and hot. Megan took a grateful sip, but not before turning it white with milk and adding sugar until the liquid could stand a spoon. Her best meal of the day, Lucy was willing to wager. She pulled her chair closer to the other women and sat.

With the sewing machine stilled, the sound of rain was audible.

They sat for a time in silence, listening, each lost in her thoughts.

Even when she was shivering under her blanket up in her little garret room, Lucy always felt comforted by the sound of the rain falling on the roof tiles. It reminded her that she was dry and safe, that she was fortunate.

Now she wanted to crawl up over the eaves, to protect those roof tiles with her body, to hold the house together, come what may.

The door flew open. Mr. Cantrell ducked into the shop, face livid. Megan shrank back. Her father, it was widely known, made free with his fists. The girl was never easy in male company. Lucy touched her arm to let her know there was no cause for fear.

"Alvin!" said Mrs. Cantrell. "What happened? Did you find him?"

He gave her a stark look as he snatched off his hat.

"He was at the George and Dragon," he muttered. "With a half dozen of his friends or I'd have left him bleeding."

Here was a side of Mr. Cantrell Lucy had never seen. He'd always seemed far more reserved than his fiery Irish wife, a gentle giant. But it made sense. Mrs. Cantrell would hardly have married a man without spirit.

All at once, he seemed to remember himself. To notice he and his wife were not alone. He nodded at the rest of them.

"Not the finest day," he said, slapping his hat against his leg. Tiny drops sprayed from it.

"Irreparable structural defects. That's what he said. Dangerous, and pestilential, attested to by the inspector, and Dr. Jephson signed off."

"Jephson?" asked Mrs. Cantrell.

Mr. Cantrell gave his hat a final slap. "The new medical officer for the vestry. Agrees we're a risk to public health."

"Lies!" Lucy crossed her arms and trapped her balled fists beneath her elbows, to keep them from flying at nothing.

"But Purcell knows—" began Mrs. Cantrell. Her husband cut her off.

"It's beyond Purcell. We're condemned. The Board of Works has already received an application for the leases."

Mr. Cantrell ground his teeth so hard Lucy feared they might break.

"Purcell's opening a coach-making workshop," he continued at last, loosening his jaws by tugging at his beard.

"Needs extra hands, he told me, large and small. We can have work, even the babies, if we don't fancy mending boots on the street."

Mrs. Cantrell gave a strangled cry.

"Red pantaloons in Parliament too," muttered Aunt Marian. Mr. Cantrell looked uneasy, no doubt suspecting the bad tidings had dislodged something in the old woman's brain.

"The MPs win elections giving speeches on the floor about ending misery and squalor. The Lords make their names passing improvement bills. From where they sit, it's a job well done. But from where we sit? There's more human suffering every day."

The firebrand, still sparking, faculties no more or less intact.

Mr. Cantrell looked relieved, but he shook his head.

"Some mean well enough. Do you remember the Duke of Weston's speech?"

Mercifully, Mr. Cantrell took Lucy's gasp for affirmation.

"I read it, the five inches they printed in the *Times*," he said. "He was arguing for a royal commission on housing *because* the prior remedies have increased the evil."

"Sound and fury, signifying nothing," responded Aunt Marian tartly. "These politicians all mean to trounce their opponents or line their own pockets, probably both. You won't see them righting wrongs in Shoreditch."

"The two of you are not debating on the floor of Parliament," broke in Mrs. Cantrell, her voice shaking. "In case you've forgotten, you're in a house that's about to be demolished. I don't think we've time for debates."

"Niamh," said Mr. Cantrell and opened his arms. She walked into his embrace and he held her. The tenderness of his posture contrasted with his grim expression.

Aunt Marian had laid both her hands atop her sewing machine. Lucy knew she was calculating their resources, totting up what it was all worth: their furniture, their stock, their sewing kits, their linens, their shoes.

Lucy rose slowly on rubbery legs. She felt strange, at once hot and cold. She had to do *something*.

The Duke of Weston. He'd wanted to establish a royal commission on housing. He'd wanted to address the evils caused by eviction, jobbery, and corruption.

She could race to the George and Dragon and fly in the face of James Purcell.

Or she could race to Mayfair and apply to the Duke of Weston. Both options felt absurd, pointless. She couldn't overcome James Purcell by force. Nor could she influence a duke's political agenda.

She had to try one or the other.

Before she'd thought to formulate her plan, she was running up the back stairs for her cloak.

CHAPTER SIX

THE WALK FROM the omnibus was cold and wet. When she reached Park Lane and the Duke of Weston's town house came into view, she stopped for a moment to stare. It was grand, of course, but rather ugly, the front plain, clad in Bath stone, an austere portico the only relief from flatness. A chilly-looking place.

Good. Serves him right.

A sudden cloudburst forced her to run across the forecourt. She dashed up the steps and took shelter between pediments, glaring at the enormous door. Had a more bedraggled person ever banged the knocker? She doubted it.

The butler confirmed her suspicions. His face was expressionless, its denial absolute. He cut an extraordinary figure, whippet thin, tall and straight, holding the door open at a doubtful angle. His baldness seemed to indict hair itself for mess and immoderation. Certainly, Lucy had never so felt quite so painfully self-aware of hers. She looked a fright.

She tried to sniff to recover her dignity and sneezed.

"Please advise His Grace that Miss Coover is here," she said. "The painter."

The butler's disapproval deepened. The sharp lines in his face might have been carved with a knife. She peered past him into the entrance hall, high ceilinged and brightly lit. At the end of it, a marble staircase curved toward the upper story, the handrail and newel-posts twinkling like gems. They were made of crystal.

She was so close. But that glowing interior seemed another world. Infinitely out of reach.

She should have tried the servants' entrance. Why in God's name had she marched up the front steps? She could blame the rain, but her pride was the culprit.

Probably she'd have fared no better with a footman. She might have pretended she was after a job in service, begged to see the housekeeper, then dodged down a hall and crept to Weston's study via the back stairs. But this was not a house likely to tolerate irregularities of dress or temperament in prospective maids. Front door, back door. There was no entrance that suited.

"Do you have a card, Miss Coover?" The butler's posture did not change, but the door creaked slightly, giving him away. He was already angling back inside, preparing to shut her out. Desperation forced her hand.

She couldn't turn back now.

"A card?" She hesitated. "Of course. My card."

She lowered her head, hunching over, as though preparing to rifle through her bag for the requested item. From that position, she lunged forward and ducked beneath his arm. Her wet shoes squelched on the marble floor as she darted down the hall.

LAVINIA YARDLEY WAS ignoring the commotion in the hallway, pressing determinedly on with her side of the conversation. Her side was the only side.

Anthony had spent the past quarter hour twisted uncomfortably in an overstuffed chair, trying to catch her father's eye. He'd called a meeting with Yardley to query him about the rent increases on the Hampshire estate. Somehow that request had translated into a tea party. Yardley seemed to imagine Lavinia's presence would lift Anthony's spirits. Certainly, Yardley was in good humor. He nodded frequently as his daughter spoke. Sometimes he laughed.

He was a gingery man, with the sort of broad face that positively wreathed with smiles. Throughout Anthony's boyhood, his ready warmth had provided a welcome contrast to his father's unremitting coldness. In fact, it was hard to reconcile the differences in their personalities with their decades-long friendship. But friends they'd been, grown close through the first family tragedy, and inseparable after the second. Yardley had become his father's confidant and adviser. And his go-between.

Lavinia was saying something about Parisian chocolates, and Yardley was nodding benignly. Anthony shifted in his chair. One day—soon—he'd make a bonfire of all this furniture.

That sound came again. *Squeak-squeak-squeak-squeak.*

Was an unusually large rodent tearing helter-skelter through the house?

"Papa says she has gone to the Riviera, so I won't see her, which makes me feel wretched," Lavinia whined. "It has been such a *terribly* long time. But mother is a tyrant. I'll be trapped in Paris the whole two weeks getting stuck with pins by dressmakers."

Anthony looked at Lavinia, meeting her eyes for the first time. They were round and blue, like her father's, but without his mildness of expression. Her eyes accused him. High spots of color burned on her alabaster cheeks. She was quite cognizant of his distraction, and not a little put out. She was a lively girl, dressed for more appreciative company in a gown shimmering green, fussy with lace panels. He'd known her from the cradle. As a little child, she'd been a favorite playmate of his sister. She deserved better from him, but he lacked, at least at the present moment, the capacity to worry about her feelings.

"Effie?" he asked roughly.

"Of course, Effie," said Lavinia, sulking now that she had his attention. "She's in Cassis, isn't she? I know I'd prefer Cassis to Paris, but I don't get a say in anything. I hope she's not so very ill anymore. Have you heard how she finds the resort?"

"She is enjoying the sea bathing," interjected Yardley.

Anthony drummed his fingers on the arm of the chair, ignoring Yardley's warning glance.

"I have not heard," he said. But he went no further.

This explanation of Effie's whereabouts remained universally accepted, a fact that alarmed him. She herself had kept her love affair, and subsequent elopement, a secret. Only he had known of it, and his father, who condemned it. And Yardley. But why, once she'd found herself abandoned by her husband, disowned by her family, hadn't she confided in a friend, if not Lavinia, then Rose Ponsonby or Cora Ashbee? Why hadn't she gone to someone for help? Why had she disappeared, leaving Yardley to maintain her reputation with bland lies as to her whereabouts?

Anthony had questioned everyone with whom she'd ever shared the least tie of affection. He'd broken the rules that bound him and sent Humphreys to Leicester Square with a message for his aunt Helen. The reply brought back bore out the claims of the others.

No one had had the least word from her.

"As soon as Papa gives me her address, I will write and see if she's well enough to meet me in Paris." Lavinia tapped her father's arm reprovingly.

"I keep forgetting." Yardley crossed his legs, then uncrossed them to lean forward and lift his teacup.

It came again, the squeaking. And now pounding footsteps.

Suddenly, a voice rang out in the hallway, a husky female voice, roughened further with indignation.

"Don't flap me about! I'm not a bed linen."

In an instant, Anthony had flung the door open. The sight that greeted him made his chin hit his chest. He closed his mouth with difficulty.

Miss Coover stood dripping in the hallway, looking angry as a wet cat. Her shoulders were up around her ears, and she'd tucked her chin like a boxer. She was glaring at the footmen ringed around her. By the way one of them had just leapt back, Anthony had the distinct impression she'd stamped his toes.

"Miss Coover," he said, and she turned to flash Collins a look of triumph. The butler was standing outside the ring of footmen, motionless and deadly calm. If Miss Coover thought she could provoke Collins, she was sorely mistaken. He had the composure of a clockwork automaton.

"Your Grace." As she spoke, Collins's eyes rotated until they centered on Anthony.

She had promised silence on their acquaintanceship, and yet she had turned up on his doorstep, rain soaked and mud spattered. Worse, if he read the situation right, she had charged past Collins and led the footmen on a merry chase, and, in the process, she had startled him into revealing that they had some connection.

The fact that he had fantasized about seeing her again added vinegar to the wound.

All the proofs of probity Anthony had displayed over the past months—Miss Coover's arrival had given them the lie.

He could feel Lavinia and Yardley stirring in the room behind him. How to contain the damage?

"It was good of you to come," he said, surprising her, surprising himself. "I feared the weather would dissuade you."

A puddle had formed on the marble beneath Miss Coover's feet.

She narrowed her long eyes at him, golden-brown in the gaslight. He met her gaze steadily. He didn't know what caprice had directed her thus far. Now she would follow *his* lead, or she would regret it keenly.

He hoped his own eyes made this very, very clear.

Collins reached out to accept Miss Coover's cloak and gloves. He tried to take her shoulder bag, but she gripped the strap tighter. The struggle was brief and infinitesimal, but both parties gave their all. Collins retreated without the bag.

Anthony watched him go, dragging a long breath through his nose. *Dammit.* The butler's scrutiny of his actions was bound to increase now that the house had been breached by a chit of a girl behaving for all the world as though she had some claim on his attention. When he'd mastered himself, he turned to Miss Coover. The words died on his lips.

No longer swathed in yards of dark wool, she seemed suddenly to burnish the marble hall with warmth and color. Her dress was a soft shade of brown, embroidered with red chrysanthemums, which brought out the coppery tint of her hair. The dress, although artistic as you please, wasn't—thank God—entirely without structure. A bodice of pleated silk and a heavy sash at the waist kept him from seeing the natural curves of her belly and hips through the fabric.

The footmen were looking, too, from the corners of their eyes.

His scowl matched hers as he propelled her into the sitting room.

"Miss Coover," he announced. "My painting teacher."

He felt her startled twitch, the brush of her hip against his thigh.

"Allow me to present Mr. Yardley. And this is his daughter, Miss Yardley."

Lavinia gawked at Miss Coover as she rose in greeting.

Yardley's raised eyebrows were all for Anthony.

"Is this a new passion?" he asked Anthony after he'd taken Miss Coover's hand.

"Pardon?" Anthony inched sideways, putting more distance between himself and Miss Coover, whose face was in the process of undermining his attempt to salvage the situation she'd created. Her eyes flicked from one person to the next, scrunched brows communicating her confusion.

Or maybe she'd caught a chill. The tip of her nose was bright pink. Her teeth chattered lightly until she gritted them. Whatever rictus contorted her features, it certainly didn't pass as a smile.

He'd like to station her beneath the eves of the house, under a waterspout, and let nature take its course.

"I didn't know you plied the brush." Yardley smiled with open curiosity.

Anthony smiled back. "Oh, well. Yes, I've a mind to try my hand at painting horses."

Lavinia resettled herself on the sofa, rolling her eyes. She made no move to pour out tea for the new visitor.

"Unless you mean painting *on* the horses, I don't believe you." She looked at Miss Coover. "He can't possibly make a *picture* of horses."

Anthony's smile slipped. Lavinia saw competition everywhere and did not tolerate it kindly.

Miss Coover pushed a wet lock of hair behind her ear, a wary gesture.

Wariness at such a late stage struck Anthony as nearly obscene.

"I suppose he can, if he applies himself," said Miss Coover slowly. "Just horses?" she asked Anthony. "Or do you mean to paint fox-hunts and steeplechases? Polo perhaps?"

"Just horses," said Anthony. "Please, have a seat."

"That simplifies things," said Miss Coover. Her eyes locked on his.

Could the others feel the air snap between them?

She set down her bag and perched on the sofa. Lavinia smiled a closed-lipped smile and edged away.

There *was* a communicable quality to Miss Coover's dampness. Her bag appeared as muddy and battered as her shoes.

Anthony returned to his chair, trying to think of what to say. At least Miss Coover hadn't contradicted him. He'd half expected a torrent of abuse.

When she'd exited the sculpture gallery, right after he told her he'd destroyed her picture, she'd looked as though he'd pulled her heart out with a rusty pair of fire tongs.

She did not think of him fondly. Her sketches had arrived addressed to *The Philistine*. Luckily, he had taken to having Humphreys lie in wait for the letter carriers and pluck out the important envelopes.

She wanted something from him now, wanted it enough to play along.

His fingers drummed the chair arm.

"He's never been able to stay still," said Lavinia, with a pointed look at his drumming fingers. "When we were children, he couldn't sit through a game of whist, or a little melody by Mozart, and he's no better now. *I* wouldn't want him for a painting pupil."

Now that Lavinia had managed to put both Anthony *and* Miss Coover in their places, she looked happier. Miss Coover glanced at her and then at Anthony, rather coolly. She didn't want him for a painting pupil either. Before she could say something to that effect, he sprawled in his chair, aping carelessness. Physically restless, quick-witted but slow to decipher words and sums—as a boy, he'd practiced buffoonery as self-protection. And maybe Lavinia was right. He *was* no better now.

"I can already see the horse I want to paint, so that should make the task go quicker." He shut his eyes. The sudden darkness soothed him. What a relief, to escape, however briefly, this cursed sitting room.

"Describe the scene," came Miss Coover's voice. Listening to her voice with his eyes closed . . . it felt . . . intimate.

He opened his eyes.

"A horse on a dusty plain," he said. "Midstride. A large gray Arabian charger, saddled, no rider."

He cleared his throat, reached for his teacup. He hadn't expected the words to emerge with such earnest force. He'd bought Mizoa from a horse dealer in Bombay and lost him on the road to Kandahar. Days he didn't think of that long, bloody road were days he counted lucky.

He could count those lucky days on one hand.

He felt Miss Coover's gaze on him as he blew—needlessly—across the surface of his tea. The sip he took was lukewarm.

After a moment, she nodded.

"Very good. You'll start, though, with anatomy. They use a plaster cast of a flayed horse as a teaching aid at the Royal Academy. It's a wonderful tool but for students only. You'll have to make do with drawings."

"A flayed horse!" Lavinia shuddered. "I'd rather look at anything else."

"The Antique School keeps a cast of a flayed man as well." Miss Coover considered Lavinia for a moment before continuing. "The man was first nailed to a cross, to settle a debate about the position of the crucified body."

Lavinia took this in. She looked personally aggrieved by the information.

"Are they training artists or ghouls?" she demanded.

"He was a notorious murderer in his time," said Miss Coover. The hint of a smile tilted the corners of her mouth.

Anthony frowned. She had no right to enjoy herself.

Yardley leaned forward with interest.

"You're a student in the Academy Schools? I attended the Schools myself. In my day, of course, things were very different."

Miss Coover bridled slightly. Anthony supposed she represented the chief difference, and resented it.

"The ladies make good students, I've heard." Yardley smiled as he confirmed Anthony's suspicion. "Especially the pretty ones." His wink was avuncular. "At the very least, I imagine the presence of ladies in the halls checks the unrulier impulses we men indulged from time to time, at whichever unsuspecting Visitor's expense."

He wore a fond expression, recalling some bit of youthful raillery. Miss Coover, Anthony noted, appeared less pleased.

He remembered the two very pretty young ladies he'd met in the Schools, their interest in him, their seeming ambivalence about their instruction. *Prettiness*, he was willing to guess, was not the modifier most important to Miss Coover when assessing the merits of female students. Nor would she think taming indocile males their chief function.

"Tell me," said Lavinia, giving Miss Coover a sly smile, "what do you think of Weston Hall?"

Miss Coover hesitated, puzzled.

"Weston Hall," she said. "*This* Weston Hall?"

"There's no other." Lavinia raised her thin brows.

"Should I respond as a social caller?" asked Miss Coover. "Or do you want my opinion as an artist?"

She looked at Anthony, who shook his head in warning.

"Oh, as an artist, surely," said Lavinia. "No one on a social call ever said anything interesting."

"From the outside, it looks like a warehouse," said Miss Coover promptly. "And from the inside, it looks like a gilded warehouse. All the rooms are overlarge, with fathoms of air overhead. Lifelessness on a grand scale. Of course, I'm speaking of the general impression only. I'm sure the furnishings are lovely."

She shifted dubiously on the sofa, a horror in rose damask, with cushions that made no concessions to the human form. Her self-satisfaction was almost comical. She liked hearing her own aesthetic judgments and did not restrain herself from expressing them. Anthony knew her to cleave to them.

You *are not my subject,* she'd said to him, adamant. Love. Beauty. Those *are the subjects of the painting.*

Lavinia was a minx, but Miss Coover might not have walked so blithely into her trap.

"Papa designed the house." Lavinia spoke with relish. "He studied architecture at the Royal Academy, then took a degree in structural science at University College. He's very proud of Weston Hall."

Miss Coover pressed her lips together. Yardley's face was red. His architecture career had largely focused on commercial structures, none renowned for their beauty. Long before Anthony was born, he'd been commissioned by Anthony's mother's family to design a new warehouse for their shipping firm, Rodis & Metaxas. That was how he met Anthony's mother and, eventually, his father.

His work on Weston Hall had failed conspicuously to garner him more commissions from lords with mansions to remodel. He'd returned to warehouses, and, under the aegis of the Board of Works, roads.

Unfortunate, Miss Coover's critique. But astute.

"The house was built in the era of George the Second." Yardley pressed his hands flat on his knees.

Effie always said Lavinia hadn't a malicious spirit. Rather, self-absorption made her oblivious. Watching her lips curve into an expectant smile, Anthony doubted she'd realized that the subject of Weston Hall had touched a nerve. She was waiting for her father to give Miss Coover a good setting down.

"I was charged with alterations only," said Yardley. "I amalgamated smaller rooms."

"And created the double height in the hall, the dining room, and the gallery?" asked Miss Coover.

Anthony bit his tongue. Had she surveyed the whole house at a run, footmen trailing behind like gulls after a steamer?

"It was easily done. Several of the upstairs bedrooms were outmoded, entirely superfluous."

"Ballrooms instead of bedrooms," said Miss Coover thoughtfully. "That was my point. Display is the reason for being, not day-to-day living."

Lavinia seemed to find her tone inadequately incendiary.

"Which you despise?" she proposed.

The look Miss Coover gave her boded ill, but her response was matter-of-fact.

"As a domicile, it isn't to my taste," she said. "But I was not the patron." She nodded at Yardley. "I don't doubt your design answered to his specifications."

Anthony had shoved his hand into his jacket to prevent his fingers from drumming. Now he realized they were twisting his watch chain.

"It did at that," said Yardley. He relaxed his shoulders, draped one of his arms across the back of a chair.

Anthony's father had commissioned Yardley for the alterations shortly after Anthony's mother had died. It had never occurred to Anthony until now that destroying his mother's chambers had been his father's aim.

"Miss Coover, you're still chilled." Anthony said it mechanically and rose, moving to the fireplace. He leaned on the marble mantelpiece and stirred the coals in the grate. Yardley rose, too, and joined him. He was nearly as tall as Anthony, and wider, a big, bluff man who gave the impression of being in the prime of life. Anthony's father had been only a few years his senior, but he'd seemed brittle, feeble, *old*, by the time he died.

Lavinia was leaning forward on the sofa, pouring out tea.

"Which do *you* prefer," he heard her ask Miss Coover, "Paris or the Riviera?"

"Horse painting." Yardley chuckled. His amiability seemed fully restored. "You and your horses. I heard that yesterday the grooms couldn't flush you from the stables."

Yardley never mentioned how he heard what he heard. He and everyone else around Anthony seemed to talk a great deal given how much they all prized their bloody discretion.

Anthony grunted. His visits to the stable were only in part a cover for his visits to the glasshouse. The coach horses were strong, wellfleshed, stouthearted beasts, and the saddle horses, creams and blacks, were big and splendid. He preferred their stalls any day of the week to his study, where Yardley would have him stare himself cross-eyed at his father's files. Yardley urged him to comb through blue books, records of parliamentary sessions, reports authored by the Committee on Intemperance, to prepare himself to fill his father's shoes as a statesman.

He was proving far less willing to discuss Anthony's duties as a landholder.

"For once, I don't want to talk horses." Anthony lowered his voice. This room, the smallest on the floor, was still quite large. A large sitting room offered certain affordances. For example, it accommodated concurrent conversations. Lavinia suddenly pealed with laughter at some remark of Miss Coover's. Anthony looked over. They'd drawn closer together, a mismatched pair. Lavinia's head, capped by carefully molded blond ringlets, inclined toward Miss Coover, who was securing a pin in a wind-blown mass of coarse curls that seemed to swallow it.

Why was she here? He forced his thoughts away from the mystery that was Miss Coover. This was his opportunity. He turned to Yardley. "I wanted to discuss the rent increases in Hampshire."

Yardley threw a pointed look toward the women and shook his head. "It's not the time."

"It's *never* the time." Too loud. He lowered his voice. "Etiquette be damned. I didn't ask you to bring your daughter. I asked you to bring Mr. Cruitshank's reports."

"I hardly thought the matter urgent." Yardley's brows drew together. "I would know, after all, if anything was seriously amiss with the estate."

He would at that. He'd worked directly with Cruitshank, the estate manager, on the new cottages, and since Anthony's father's death, he'd been empowered to make all the financial decisions concerning them, and everything else.

"That's part of what troubles me." Anthony searched Yardley's face, hating the worm of distrust coiling in his belly. "The letters I received from the tenants describe a situation that is, in fact, *seriously* amiss. Why haven't you acted?"

"Letters from tenants." Yardley sighed. "Tenants will always make mountains out of molehills."

"They are bearing the costs of improvements my father foisted upon them."

Yardley shook his head. "They're not. The rents are the same."

As Anthony opened his mouth to protest, Yardley made a conciliatory gesture.

"They're feeling a pinch, I don't doubt. It takes more fuel to heat a larger house, more candles to light one. Those tenants who wrote to complain—your father provided them with new homes, equipped their farms with modern machines. Now they expect that every stick of firewood and loaf of bread will be handed to them."

Anthony stared at him. "The rent was their chief concern."

"They're confused. Or else they're trying to take advantage of your—"

He broke off.

"What?" Anthony tried to speak lightly. "My what?"

Lavinia's laughter pealed again.

"Miss Coover has saved me from irremediable dullness," she called. "You must hear her latest opinion."

Yardley put her off with a raised hand, and she flung herself back on the sofa, with a whispered remark to Miss Coover.

"Trying to take advantage," said Yardley.

"I'll see for myself, then." Anthony could feel a vein in his temple throb. "I'll go to Hampshire. Per the codicil," he spit, "I must ask that you accompany me."

There it was, that sad look, half apology, half disappointment.

Yardley exhaled.

"Anthony," he said. "You know your father wanted you in London, in Parliament, taking this year to familiarize yourself with his

political legacy, to make new alliances, to find your legs as a statesman. He put the properties in trust to unburden you."

Anthony's smile was humorless.

"*You* know," he said. "You know very well, in fact, that my father
wanted to control me, not to unburden me, as you say." He shrugged,
as he'd been shrugging his whole life, as if it didn't hurt. He had
shrugged when he'd first learned of the codicil. *This can't be valid.*

The solicitors had assured him that his father's myriad require-
ments were, in fact, perfectly valid, legally speaking. *Provisions that
injure the public aren't enforceable, nor are those that require the beneficiary to take illegal or immoral action.* They'd explained it slowly, with
placid smiles. *But a testator may otherwise condition his gifts. These particular conditions are to the public good, as well as to the benefit of your
character. Moreover, they apply for short duration, only until you attain
the age of thirty. Thirty-five is actually more common. It's all properly
drafted, and also reasonable. Our advice to you is, of course, compliance.*

Anthony's smile became a grimace. "He didn't think I could control myself."

"Then control yourself," said Yardley. "Show the world that
you can."

Anthony looked down, pressing the side of his fist into the mantelpiece, hard, so he felt the cold edge of the marble dig into his skin.

His father had never asked what had happened on the retreat
from Maiwand. Anthony had never offered his side of the story. That
day in Hampshire, when he'd walked with Yardley in the village
before heading to London, he'd begun to speak of it and Yardley had
stopped him by laying a hand on his shoulder.

*You don't have to explain, to me or anyone else. We've kept it out of
the papers, so that's that. You can start fresh, do you hear me? Your father will come around.*

For Yardley's sake, Anthony had shrugged, as though in agreement. But as soon as he'd arrived in London, he'd mired himself in
the old rottenness. He went to the Rose and Myrtle and fought with

George's friends, beating them bloody because George himself was out of reach. He drank and then he drank more. His father was never going to "come around," as Yardley put it. He'd always believed the worst. He'd died believing it.

Anthony crossed his arms.

"How can I control myself?" he said. "It's not a question of self-control if I can't choose who I see, where I go, and what I bloody well drink."

Yardley glanced toward Lavinia and Miss Coover to satisfy himself that they were still battling dullness.

"Don't spite yourself to spite him," he said. "Get out of the stables. Take your seat in the House of Lords. Unlike Lavinia, I *do* recollect you sitting. And to good effect."

Anthony rocked on his heels, unable to meet Yardley's eyes. It was to Yardley he'd confessed his boyhood agony with books, how he couldn't make sense of the letters, couldn't sound them out or arrange them.

Memorize the words, then, Yardley had suggested. *You've got a good mind. Pretend they're pictures, like in Egypt.*

He'd taken Anthony to the British Museum and showed him the hieroglyphics. Anthony had pored over his books after that, committing the words to memory. He never learned to take pleasure in reading, or writing, but he could do both, without fear of ridicule. Yardley alone understood the focus that had required.

He owed the man something but could give no satisfactory response. His spite was already running its course.

"She's a ghoul, it's decided," cried Lavinia, waving to get their attention. "She claims"—Lavinia widened her eyes and clasped her hands to her breast in mock horror—"I'm dying!"

Anthony's eyes flew to Miss Coover. One minute, savior from irremediable dullness, the next minute, harbinger of death. It was evident that both appellations grated. She took a deep breath and released it.

"I never said you were dying. I said you are absorbing poison through your skin."

"What's this?" Yardley glanced at Anthony as though he should have some answer.

Anthony spread out his hands. He certainly couldn't account for what came out of Miss Coover's mouth.

"Her gown. There's arsenic in the dye," said Miss Coover. "You can tell just by looking."

"It's green, yes," said Lavinia, sniffing. "That doesn't mean it's poison."

"It's emerald green," Miss Coover snapped, her patience wearing thin. "The pigment is made with white arsenic."

"I *know* that." Lavinia smoothed her skirts. "I know about emerald green. It kills the artificial flower makers. But this gown is different. It's extremely expensive."

She smiled forgivingly at Miss Coover. Then she rounded on Anthony, who had approached with her father.

"I would never say it so baldly, but I have to make her understand *somehow* or she'll go running off to the coroner."

"Of course it's expensive; it's a Worth gown." Miss Coover crossed her arms. "The fit is excellent. I have no quarrel with Worth's tailoring or his styles. The fabric, however, is guaranteed to do you injury."

Lavinia's mouth dropped open. Miss Coover ignored her and reached for her bag. Open, it seemed larger. She was up to her elbows, fumbling inside. Wood knocked on wood, and glass clinked on glass.

What the devil did she lug about? An entire apothecary, from the sound of it.

"Don't move," she said, turning to Lavinia with a small phial in her hand.

"What is that?" Lavinia started, pressing back into the arm of the sofa.

"Ammonia." Miss Coover's hands were steady as she unscrewed

the lid. "I use it in solution to strip the varnish from my brushes. If you jostle me, I'll spill more than I intend."

"What are you doing? Are you mad? You'll ruin my dress!"

"I don't think—" Yardley started forward. But he was too slow.

"Done!" With precise movements, Miss Coover had bent, lifted the hem of Lavinia's skirt, and coaxed a single drop from the phial, which she rapidly tilted up and capped.

"Now." She nodded curtly. "See for yourselves."

Anthony and Yardley exchanged glances. As one, they knelt by the sofa.

"The arsenic in the dye is arsenite of copper," said Miss Coover. "And ammonia turns blue in the presence of copper."

"The mark is blue." Anthony whistled through his teeth, sitting back on his heels. "Arsenic."

Lavinia grabbed fistfuls of her skirt, as though to lift it away from her legs, then dropped the skirt and rubbed her hands on the cushion of the sofa.

"I feel faint," she said, drooping. "I'm dying after all."

"I'll call the doctor." Yardley's face was full of concern as he stood. "You may have to postpone your trip to Paris."

"Oh." Lavinia straightened. "I don't feel so *very* faint."

"Even so," said Yardley. "Let's get you home at once."

"She'll survive, I think," said Miss Coover, returning her phial to her bag. "But if I were you, Miss Yardley, I would bury that Worth gown in a hole. Stand up."

Anthony backed away from the sofa, stifling a laugh at Lavinia's bewildered expression. Even Effie hadn't bossed her with such aplomb. Uncertainly, Lavinia stood.

"I could sew you a gown with the same silhouette, if you like this look, with the bodice and the skirt cut in one piece," said Miss Coover, as her gaze swept Lavinia up and down. "But I'd choose blue silk. Less deadly, and more becoming with your eyes."

She glanced at Anthony.

His eyes were green, like his mother's and Effie's, darker than the green silk but not by much. The color of poison. Was that what she was thinking?

"But . . . are you a dressmaker?" Lavinia asked.

"I'm a painter," said Miss Coover briskly. "But I also work in my aunt's dress shop. She's the finest dressmaker in London, and you'll be hard-pressed to find her equal in Paris. She designed all of Celestia Jordan's gowns."

"*The* Celestia Jordan? The actress?" Lavinia frowned. "Her gowns were *divine*, but, darling, Dodie Thistleship designed them."

A storm cloud formed on Miss Coover's brow.

"Dodie Thistleship," she bit out. "The woman is a hack. And a thief."

"Never!" gasped Lavinia.

"A ham sandwich has more talent." The wet cat was back. Miss Coover had raised her shoulders, spitting mad.

Impatient, Yardley started for the door, and Anthony followed him.

"I don't think she's dying." Anthony cast a look over his shoulder at Lavinia. Lavinia and Miss Coover were nose to nose. Some people would call what they were doing *shouting*.

"No." Yardley turned to beckon. "Lavinia!" He sounded more weary than worried.

"I imagine she and Moira"—he named his wife—"will be off to the ferry tomorrow morning as planned. I'll be off too, not nearly so far as Paris, just to Putney, but I'll stay a few days. To oversee one of my ongoing projects."

He looked at Anthony, then sighed and clapped a hand on his shoulder. "When I return, we'll meet to discuss the estates, if that's what you'd like. I'll show you the annual reports. If you're not satisfied, I'll accompany you to Hampshire."

Anthony managed a faint nod, but that worm of distrust still twisted inside him. He used to believe in Robert Yardley's good intentions. Now he wasn't so sure.

But, Christ, this life his father had devised for him *bred* distrust.

The shouting tapered off, and Lavinia and Miss Coover presented themselves.

"Thank you, Miss Coover." Yardley pressed her hand. "Painter, dressmaker, chemist." He bowed. "A true Renaissance woman."

"A miracle worker as well, if he ends up painting a plausible horse." Lavinia beamed at Anthony. A good row, and her brush with death, had buoyed her spirits.

Then they were gone, the Yardleys, his dear old friends, letting themselves out. He braced himself against the doorframe, then wheeled around to face Miss Coover, who did not shrink.

"Time for my lesson," he said.

CHAPTER SEVEN

THE DUKE OF Weston gave the appearance of sauntering. Certainly, he seemed unhurried as he moved down the hall, one hand in his trouser pocket.

Lucy walked quickly to keep abreast of him, too quickly. Her bag banged her side and her heart pounded. If she must sprint to match his step, so be it.

She refused to trip along behind, like a muddy child.

Despite her efforts, Weston crested the landing in the lead. She panted as she surged up the final steps. The upstairs hall was no less grand than the one below. Weston opened the door to a study, richly, if somberly, furnished. When the door clicked shut behind them, lock turning, she jumped. Her breath sawed in and out noisily. He seemed not to notice.

"Let there be light," he said. He prowled through the room, turning up the lamps. While he did so, she walked to the semicircle of chairs drawn close to the fire and set down her bag, staring at its lumpy contours. Strange—to draw strength from an old bag! But the sight was familiar. Stabilizing. Her breathing slowed.

Suddenly, he was beside her, laying his large fingers on the stem of a lamp on the mantel. The delicacy of the gesture caused her to suck her lower lip between her teeth and bite down hard.

Good God. She'd forgotten the effect of his proximity. Down-stairs, buffered by Miss Yardley and her unctuous father, she'd achieved a kind of detachment. Gone in a heartbeat.

As the light strengthened, she looked away so she wouldn't have to watch the shadows slide into the hollows beneath his cheekbones. This would be hard enough. She could *not* allow her brain to soften.

"Now we can begin," he said. "I've given up on horses. I have a new idea for my first painting."

She looked at him and wished she hadn't. The lamplight loved the stark bones of his face. Just as she'd imagined.

"Oh," he said softly, when she failed to respond. "You're *not* here to give me a drawing lesson. Then, may I ask, what *are* you doing in my . . . gilded warehouse?"

He was smiling, an untrustworthy smile.

She should have gone to the George and Dragon. At least then she might have had the satisfaction of drawing blood. One punch square on Purcell's nose before anyone guessed her intent. It wouldn't have fixed anything. But it would have felt good, and Purcell, at least, couldn't make her life any worse.

Purcell couldn't get her expelled from the Royal Academy.

Her nerves felt as though they were being wound around a bobbin.

"You're interested in the housing question," she said.

Not what he was expecting. One eyebrow lifted.

"Painter, dressmaker, chemist. What else? Suffragist? Reformer?"

He was toying idly with something in his pocket. She caught the glimmer of gold. This was not the moment to trade appellations.

Philistine, idiot, drunkard.

She hid her frown, plowing on. "You gave a speech on the necessity of a royal commission to inquire into housing conditions, over-crowding and its remedies."

"I don't give speeches. That would have been Weston the elder. My father."

555555555

She stared at him, aghast. She could see the pulse beating steadily in his throat. Hers felt scattered all through her body, ticking at different tempos. Of course. It wasn't *this* Duke of Weston quoted at length in the *Times*. If she'd been thinking clearly, she would have realized. He observed her confusion with curiosity.

"Do you want me to review for you my father's political career?" He tipped back his head. "I never paid close attention. The life of a second son is not without advantages, geography first and foremost. The world is a large place. I spent as long as I could as far from London as I could get."

The dimple flickered in his cheek, as his odd smile stretched then faded.

"Let's see." His gaze sharpened under her scrutiny. "Weston the elder, peer of the realm. I'll do my best. He was conservative—that goes without saying. Hatred of democracy lay at the heart of his philosophy. He tried to stamp it out wherever it sprouted, the usual places, at home and abroad. He distinguished himself in the fight against extending the franchise to working-class householders, and until the day he died he worked devotedly on behalf of established values, propertied interests, and the security of the empire. Many said he would one day become prime minister, but alas, his unhappy home life drove him to an early grave."

He stopped with a twist of his mouth, amusement or disgust.

"Ah, but that was a speech," he said lightly. "Maybe I, too, will have a political career."

His cynicism betrayed him. Telegraphed his insecurity. Contempt for his father masked something deeper.

He didn't think himself capable of a political career.

The realization narrowed her eyes.

Maybe it was refreshing realism. He hardly seemed the age's guiding light. But for some reason, the desire to defend him from himself rose in her. He had a casual way of denigrating his intelligence. Truly, his behavior illustrated every error of judgment. She'd called him an idiot herself. And yet he wasn't a garden-variety dull-ard. The oafishness disguised intensity, an acuity he used to cut himself down.

It wasn't comprehension he lacked, but conviction.

He could put his wit to better purpose.

Perhaps to *her* purpose.

"You *have* a political career," she said. "You're the one in the Lords Chamber now."

"My father's bench is gathering dust." He shrugged. "I am not interested in the housing question, Miss Coover. As I told you before, I am interested in the two of us putting the past behind us and moving forward as perfect strangers. You seemed to understand that at the time. But your arrival today demonstrates a profound *lack* of understanding. Or perhaps you attach less importance to your Academic training than I'd supposed?"

A muscle ticked in his jaw. His mood was dangerous.

"My understanding is perfect," she said, her stomach knotting. "I know what I risk in coming here. Trust me, if I'd had a better option, I'd have pursued it."

His face darkened further. Male vanity! He didn't want her in his house, but he looked murderous at the notion she might have gone to any other.

She took a deep breath. "You have no interest in housing, in politics, fine. But you have influence. You have the ear of anyone you want."

"Anyone?" he drawled. "To whose ear are you referring?"

She paused. He would think her mad.

"The ear of the chairman of the Board of Works."

A startled laugh escaped him. "Lord Mabeldon's ear! More whisker than ear in truth. Mabeldon went grouse hunting with my father every August, on the Glorious Twelfth. One of the many family traditions I plan to discontinue."

"It can't wait until August!"

The blood rushed to her face. She had bungled everything. Barging through his front door, interrupting his Saturday tea, shouting in his study. Stupid, stupid. She spoke to the thick navy carpet. The mud had paled on her shoes and scaled off. Little flakes embellished the carpet's gold patterning.

"My aunt's dress shop, our home, the whole block—it has been condemned."

A change came over him. He didn't move but she sensed his tension, a new engagement of his muscles that drew her eyes up the length of him. His face, painted boldly with lights and darks, riveted her.

"Why." Not even a question. His voice was soft.

"A sanitation complaint. But it's baseless. The inspectors of nuisance answer to James Purcell, the vestry clerk. He's a *pig*."

"And this James Purcell, pig. He answers to the Board of Works?" If he wasn't *interested*, he was at least intent. His eyes glittered.

"A man named Jephson, the medical officer for the borough, signed the papers. It only remains for the board to award the lease for the land."

"Award the lease . . . to whomever bribed Purcell and Jephson, this medical officer."

Yes, there was nothing wrong with his comprehension. She sensed in him a powerful alertness, and some suppressed emotion. His eyes had hooded, but he was watching her closely. She realized her hands were fists, the knuckles white.

"Surely the chairman wouldn't let this corruption stand if he heard of it. Your father—he must have wanted to appoint a royal commission precisely to prevent these abuses of power."

She'd lost him. She knew it instantly. He stiffened, pulled back, that odd smile again twisting his lips.

"A shame my father is no longer with us."

"You must do it." She reached out and gripped the nearest chair. Otherwise she might have grabbed his coat and shaken him. "*You* talk to Lord Mabeldon.*"

"And tell him what?" He pushed a lock of hair from his brow, a careless gesture. The fire popped noisily, and he spared a glance for the leaping flames. It was much warmer in the study than the sitting room. She felt clammy sweat gathering in the hollows beneath her arms.

"Tell him to dismiss medical authorities and parish administrators on a young woman's word?" He gave a one-shouldered shrug. "Mabeldon is a sporting fellow. He likes a good laugh."

"Come to my aunt's shop." She didn't care that desperation edged her words. "*Miss Stirling, Dressmaker.* You'll see the sign just off Charlotte Road, near Mills Court. Satisfy yourself that the building was wrongly condemned and give him *your* word."

He was shaking his head. "You overestimate my influence. I'm flattered, of course." He pressed a hand to his chest. "Your good impression of me owes something, perhaps, to your study of my finer features."

Mockery. It amused him, her predicament. Everyone was right about him. He was right about himself. His finer features were all external.

He was rotten at the core.

"About those features." Surprising, that she spoke so steadily. "You received my sketches?"

His look acknowledged it. But he was warier now. Here was a vulnerability. Her painting had disturbed him enough that he'd destroyed it, had doubtless destroyed her sketches as well. He cared—a great deal—about repressing the episode.

She manufactured a smile, releasing her grip on the chair, running her fingers lightly over the upholstery.

"I forgot to include a small drawing. No mythological trappings. Just you, detailed in all your . . . fineness. I was going to bring it."

His gaze slid to her bag. His face had closed, become unreadable. She pressed on, heart pounding in her ears.

"Instead, I gave it to a lithographer who is copying it onto the surface of a stone. Do you know the technique? With that stone, there's no limit to the number of cards he can print. Mr. Teed, the lithographer, prints trade cards, mostly advertisements for smokes and soaps. This card will make a sensation. Your form, in full color, a bit of text. *Bespoke birthday suits by the tailors Gin & Dice of Shoreditch Row.* How does that strike you?"

BY GOD, SHE was unpredictable. Bizarrely, Anthony's thoughts went first to Afghanistan, the day of that final battle, the Ghazis rushing up from the ravines, his squadron's failed charge, the chaos. How different it all was from the plan they'd tried to follow. Miss Coover reminded him of that difference, the gap between strategy and the overwhelm and heat of engagement. When pressed, she fought with everything she had at her disposal.

Now, as then, he found himself taken completely by surprise.

He tried to speak steadily.

"Before you advertise my birthday suit on every corner of London, consider well."

Her shoulders were rigid. She didn't know what to expect. Well, neither did he. The map didn't exist that could guide them.

"I'd prefer if my naked image wasn't pasted into every scrapbook in London." He smiled at the understatement. If she *did* print that drawing, the cards would be more than novelty keepsakes. They'd launch a thousand gossip columns.

"And so would you." He softened his voice, slowing as he searched for the way. "Or do you want to abandon fine art to deal in dirty pictures?"

Her lips thinned. She was capable of mad, brave maneuvers. Less capable of disguising her emotions. Her eyes fixed on his. Waiting.

"That would be the extent of your career after I attached your name to your handiwork." He shrugged, making his languidness a counterpoint to her tension. "Not a painter. A hack. A sensationalist."

He paused. "A pornographer."

She flinched. He, too, wanted to recoil, from the hopelessness he glimpsed in her face.

A fine impasse, this. There had to be another way.

As the silence stretched, her hand drifted up and she rubbed her temple with two fingertips, then twisted an errant strand of hair. Nervous. She'd been nervous all along. He found the knowledge oddly affecting. She'd held her own with Lavinia, with Yardley, with *him*, and the whole time she'd been thrumming inside, frantic to save her home. Now she was considering the sacrifice of her most cherished dream.

Blast Mr. Teed.

The curl she twisted—it was just the one he would have caught between his own fingers, to test the spring of it.

"Forget your little scheme," he said, voice oddly hoarse. "Neither of us gains by that route. Let's see if we can't come to an arrangement."

The idea rose in his mind, fully formed.

"This aunt of yours," he said. "She costumes actresses?"

She blinked, thrown off by the line of questioning.

"She does," she said, then corrected herself. "She *did*. Business has slowed. She doesn't have the name recognition she deserves. Mrs. Thistleship is credited with the most famous designs, as Miss Yardley pointed out."

Her mouth curved down. She had a mobile mouth, wide and lush. She scowled to great effect. But her kisses . . . they were more effective still. They'd burned through him. They'd blurred his senses like a drug.

"I take it Mrs. Thistleship receives more credit than is her due."

"My aunt never claims so. I wouldn't know myself if I hadn't found her sketches. She'd be angry I spoke at all. I don't know why I did."

He knew. Lavinia's superiority used to provoke Effie to no end.

"Miss Yardley has a certain way about her," he said. "My sister claimed she'd goad a barefoot friar into bragging about his shoes. They were always locked in some contest."

She snorted. "I thought we'd come to blows when I dripped ammonia on her skirt." Her hand moved on her own skirt, smoothing it over her thighs. "This was adapted from a stage dress. My aunt was a *visionary*, in her day. I always wear some version of her designs." She made a face. "I don't do them any favors."

The invitation was too good to pass up. He permitted his gaze to slide down her throat to her neckline and lower, lingering on points of interest. That simple bodice didn't pad, stiffen, or constrict her upper body. He could see her diaphragm swell as she drew a breath and held it, aware of his inspection. When he found her eyes again, he noted that her cheeks had flushed.

His voice rasped. "There we disagree."

"I spot them with paint." She crossed her arms protectively beneath her breasts. The chrysanthemums embroidered on her sleeves matched the russet sash. "I wasn't after your flattery."

"But you had to expect it." He smiled, a smile that widened as her eyes dipped to his mouth.

She ignored him, squaring her shoulders as she looked up, leveled him with a glare. "What arrangement do you have in mind?"

Her tone—it challenged him to ask for something despicable. That's what she thought of him, what anyone would think of him. A man who brawled on the steps of brothels, broke stained-glass windows, flopped naked in the mud—such a man should not hesitate to demand of a woman any prurient act that answered to his desire.

Touching, how she stood bolt upright, prepared to hear some vile, degraded request. Perhaps prepared even to acquiesce.

Touching, and shattering. He felt his throat closing, locking back the nausea that swelled from the pit of his stomach.

To keep her from seeing the horror in his eyes, he turned abruptly, walked to the desk, not his father's desk anymore, *his* desk. And yet, there were no decanters on the desk, no studbooks or racing calendars, just pens, a writing pad, a lamp, the blue books he'd yet to open. His mouth felt dry as sand.

He wished he were wetting his lips in the glasshouse. Burning away this heavy, sick feeling with the remaining whiskey. Washing down the whiskey with rum.

He slipped a key from his pocket and unlocked the desk drawer.

He took from it a small oval portrait framed in gilded ormolu. Miss Coover observed him with a mixture of dread and hope.

This arrangement he'd propose—she would find it to her satisfaction. She'd run to her Mr. Teed's greasy print shop, eager to avert their mutual ruination. Hope restored by his promise of help.

But Anthony suspected that, in the end, he would fail her.

With Mabeldon, a word from him meant nothing.

Strange—he needed her to agree, and yet, at the same time, he wanted to warn her off. He went to her, held out the miniature. She walked with it at once to a lamp and held it up, turning it this way and that.

"Enamel," she murmured. "Beautifully glazed. Do you know, is this Augustus Burgess's work?"

Trust her to evaluate the miniature as an object when he wanted her to focus on the girl it depicted.

"I don't know the artist," he said. "It was a gift. I only know the sitter. Euphemia. Effie."

She had sent it to him with her last letter, posted to India.

He joined Miss Coover by the lamp. She lifted her head, registering his presence, but did not move away.

"Your sister," she said. It wasn't a question.

"You see the resemblance?"

The green eyes, the black hair, the prominent facial bones, too much cheekbone and nose—they could have been twins. *They look like foreigners.* He'd heard it said on more than one occasion.

"It's striking," she said. "You're both of you striking." She flushed, lowering the portrait. He took it from her, for no reason other than to touch her hand.

"I haven't seen her in three years. I can hardly believe it. When I left India . . ." He barked a laugh, remembering those final days before he boarded the steamer. Recently court-martialed, discharged from the army, headed home to put on mourning for a brother he cursed on sleepless nights . . .

She'd taken a step back to better study him. He made his face impassive, but his words, his tone, expressed his emotion.

"The idea that I would see her was my only solace."

He forced a smile to undercut the mawkishness. Miss Coover seemed to elicit from him displays of sentiment.

She frowned. He was coming to understand her frowns. This one didn't indicate displeasure but assessment. She was puzzling out the story.

"Why haven't you? Where is she?"

"I don't know." A throat this dry cracked and bled. He felt pain when he swallowed.

"She eloped while I was still abroad. I got the news by letter. She'd married in Scotland but she was returning to London."

He'd read that last letter over and over.

Be happy for me, it urged. *I don't require anyone's blessing but yours. You'll love Charles as I do, I'm sure of it. As for my role in the circus, I've chosen musician. How could Father mount a protest when I might have chosen lion tamer? A joke, dear brother. I have written to the dragon as well, and I expect nothing but fire. He will never approve, but I hope that you might. No, I know that you will. You've always understood me. When Charles and I return to London, I plan to do worse yet. I mean to sing upon the stage! Charles's friends Frank and Madge adore my voice and want me in their show. I can use my married name, so no one need find me out and die of horror. I'm so glad you'll be home at last. Come to Shoreditch to see me sing and I'll dedicate the first song to Anthony, my cuckoo-bird brother. I'll write with my address as soon as I have one. For now, mine is a roving life, and a merry one!*

She hadn't written with her address. She'd never written again. Or if she had, those letters had never reached him. He'd learned what happened from his father's letter, which he'd found waiting for him in Hampshire.

"By the time I debarked in England, things had changed." He rubbed his jaw. "Her husband abandoned her."

Miss Coover shook her head slightly, as though in disagreement. "But then . . . she didn't come home?"

"No." The violence rising in him tested his restraint. He edged out of the circle of lamplight. "She would have known she wasn't welcome."

He'd argued with his father, pleaded with him to look for her. *She's all Thalia's*, his father had said. *She's none of mine*.

The night of that particular fight, the urge to strike his father—already weakened by attacks of apoplexy—had risen so sharply in Anthony that he'd pressed his fist against his own mouth until his lip split and blood ran down his teeth.

He could still taste the blood.

"She eloped shortly before George died. She didn't attend his funeral, nor our father's."

Lucy looked at him. He could see the questions forming. She was the questioning type.

How to explain the twisted logic that pertained in his family?

"We have a family propensity to scandal," he said. "Breaking a church window—even a Jones-Burne—pales in comparison."

Her response was automatic.

"Burne-Jones," she muttered. "A Burne-Jones window is incomparable."

"I don't exonerate myself. I only contextualize. I'm sure you know—my brother liberated one of the commodore's racing boats from the Royal Thames Yacht Club. He managed to drown both himself and an unfortunate young woman."

George had been a fine sailor, sober. According to the Newcastle-bound steam collier he'd struck, he'd veered sharply into the collision.

Miss Coover averted her eyes, opened her mouth, then closed it. So she had heard a worse version. Why not confirm it?

"The young woman was a demimondaine."

She gave a short nod.

"And my mother—" He broke off, began again. "Well, of course, it began with my mother. After her suicide in the asylum, the reporting was . . . colorful."

Her face had gone pale. She hadn't known about his mother. He looked away from the warmth in her eyes, a trick of golden-brown irises in lamplight.

"I was only a child." His muscles had tensed. It was so easy to return to that day. He fought the memories.

"My father suffered great embarrassment on my mother's account. And later, on account of his heir. Prospective prime ministers don't typically owe members of the royal family hundreds of thousands of pounds for stolen property."

The press had made more of the debt than His Royal Highness, the commodore, who had reacted to the fiasco by tactfully ignoring it. Money mattered little between men with so much at their disposal.

"He took pains to keep Effie out of the papers. As far as the world knows, he sent her to France to recuperate from the awful shock of losing her brother."

And then she stayed on, after the second blow, the death of her beloved father. Yardley had maneuvered delicately to maintain this fiction.

"Why tell me?"

Their gazes brushed, held. He had a reason to give. There were more, none he should be indulging.

"My sister may be acting—singing—in Shoreditch."

"Not bloody likely." She clapped a hand over her mouth, blush rising. She didn't have much practice in checking her thoughts before she spoke. Well, he could appreciate bluntness.

"Oh?" he said.

"What I meant is the music halls in Shoreditch aren't the West End establishments. You know that, I'm sure. If you remember."

He did remember blurred nights spent careening in and out of smoke-filled dens and filthy galleries, a serving girl with a tray of drinks at every elbow. He'd repeated Effie's name like a chant to blank looks.

"A duke's daughter singing bawdy ditties about how *I sits among the cabbages and peas* while coster lads hurl beer mugs at drunk magicians . . ." Miss Coover trailed off, shaking her head. "She wouldn't last a minute."

"She's stubborn as a mule." Like someone else he could name.

But he could supply at least a little more of the story.

"Her theatrical connections are in Shoreditch. She met her husband there, at the circus."

She whistled. "Crikey."

The whistle, and her mild oath, made him smile despite himself.

"George, my brother, took her. There was an equestrian—a trick rider—that caught her eye."

In her letter, she'd described him as "an authentic American cowboy," the only man she'd ever met who "spoke horse" better than Anthony did. He didn't trust himself to rehearse more of what he knew.

He lowered his voice. "Miss Coover, in terms of our arrangement, all I ask is that you make inquiries. The producers, managers—I don't know—of the theater might be named Frank and Madge."

"Frank and Madge." She tapped her lips in thought, then shrugged. "Not much to go on. But . . . her whereabouts are a mystery. *Yours* are not."

She'd folded her arms again. Her narrowed eyes missed nothing.

"She'd come to you, would she not? If she wanted to be found?"

She reasoned well. Too well by his lights. Her doubt spoke to his fear. Why hadn't Effie sent any word? He could think of reasons. Infirmity. Shame. A *child*. He hardened his jaw. None of that mattered.

"Nixon is her married name," he said. "When you make inquiries, inquire after Euphemia Nixon. Tell me what you discover."

She looked prepared to pursue her point, then seemed to think better of it.

"And if I discover nothing?" she asked.

"Then you discover nothing. I don't expect a miracle."

After a pause, she nodded. "And you. You'll come to Charlotte Road. You'll assess the buildings and talk to Mabeldon."

Pain began to concentrate behind his right eye. His own nod was minimal. She frowned.

"When?"

The clock chimed, the sound reverberating inside his skull.

"This week," he said. "Monday." The sooner the better, while Yardley was in Putney and less likely to hover over him.

She agreed promptly. "Monday afternoon. I'll be home by three."

"Three, then."

The glasshouse beckoned. But after Miss Coover's little escapade, he should wait, until after dinner, until tomorrow perhaps, before he slipped out. In the meantime, he'd keep choking down cups of tea.

Tea. It didn't slake his thirst.

Miss Coover was hoisting her bag onto her shoulder. Suddenly, everything irritated. Her attempted blackmail. Their no-doubt fruitless arrangement. The whole bloody situation. Codicils. Eviction notices.

"What do you carry in that thing?" he asked, raising his hand abruptly, the gesture halfway between pointing at the bag and snatching it.

She stepped back hastily, giving a pull of her mouth.

"Sketching pad, paint box, charcoals, pencils . . ." She began to list the contents, holding it close.

The pain was drilling into his brain. He needed distraction.

He didn't want her to depart just yet.

"What of my lesson?" He motioned with the fingers of his outstretched hand. "Give me your sketching pad. I never told you what I plan to paint. I shall make a preliminary sketch."

"Don't be an ass," she said, clutching the bag tighter.

"What a snob you are." He grinned, the badinage lifting his spirits. "I can draw. Anyone can draw. Little children do it."

"If you want to make random marks, like a little child, it's not worth the paper. It's getting late." She glanced at the windows, filled with dimming gray light. "I must be off. The omnibuses aren't always regular."

"I'll send you home in my coach. That will make up the time."

"What time?" She bit out the words. Oh, it was too enjoyable to tease her. She flustered openly. That expressive, changeable face, freckled and blushing, ordinary and oddly lovely—he couldn't capture the magic of it with a pencil.

But he wouldn't focus on her face. Fair was fair.

"The time it will take me to draw you." He circled her slowly. "To realize my vision, I'm afraid you'll have to take this off."

He tapped her shoulder lightly, then rubbed the lace that edged the neckline of her gown between his fingers. She caught her breath. He leaned in, slowly, and her lids lowered as her lips parted. A rake would kiss her. His own brand of roguery had never quite fit any of the models.

He caught hold of the strap of her bag and tugged. Her eyes flew open but it was too late. She let the bag go from her, face crimson with outrage.

He set it down on a chair and folded his arms.

"Strip," he said. "You don't mind nudity, I know. Your profession calls for it."

She snorted. "The Academy doesn't offer life classes to women. We aren't permitted to draw from the nude model." She linked her hands at her waist. Did she think the decorous posture would help her keep her temper?

"You found a way around that prohibition." He smiled at her. "How fortunate for you."

"It puts us at great disadvantage," she said, ignoring his gibe. "Drawing from the nude is essential to an artist's training. When women are denied life classes, they suffer as artists."

"But decency is preserved," he said and was rewarded with a withering look.

"That argument holds no water," she said, sternly. "We are petitioning to change the curriculum."

He'd be willing to bet she was heading that initiative. She had a sweet jawline but you'd never know it, due to her pugnacious habit of clenching her teeth.

He opened her bag, sliding out the sketching pad and laying it down on the chair.

"I'm glad you have no moral objection," he said. "You'll have to take off your petticoats too, and your chemise, bloomers, everything."

"I would allow you to draw me nude," she said, with a toss of her head so vehement a hairpin arced into a potted heliotrope, "if you knew how to draw."

"Would you? Or is that a bluff?" He forgot the sketching pad.

He stepped closer, and her head snapped back.

"You're bashful!" He smiled with delight. "Why, that's the last thing I would expect from you."

"I am certainly not bashful!"

He brought up his hand and touched her cheek, thumbing the skin. It was as smooth as he remembered, the gold and brown pattern of freckles impossible to feel. His thumb slid down to the corner of her mouth, then traced its shape.

Her lips parted.

"Drawing students are often instructed to make studies of individual body parts. They don't *touch* the part in question."

"I am improving upon the method," he said, and fit his mouth to hers. He licked the seam of her lips as she pressed them together. The warm, soft taste of her mouth felt wonderfully instructive. He might not be able to draw it, but with blotches of paint—shadowy red, like the inner folds of poppies; lambent brown, like a candle flame snuffed with honey; velvet black, like the midnight mosses in a sylvan cave—he thought he might translate something of the feeling.

She held still, receiving his kiss, neither rebuffing nor encouraging. Her passivity felt . . . *evaluative*. It would either chill a man's performance or inspire him to new heights. He caught her lower lip gently with his teeth, plumping it, sucking. A moan escaped her and she opened for him, allowing his tongue to slip inside, then pressing with her own, licking back into his mouth, the kiss long and sweet.

She backed away, and he bit the inside of his cheek to quell the urge to follow.

"Tell me," she said, huskily, "is this part of the arrangement?"

Ah, *that* was chilling. He shook his head, folding his arms, pinning his hands beneath his biceps.

"No." He meant it. His mouth, moistened by hers, felt dry again.

The predictable story—the one where the woman is tricked, trapped, threatened, *forced* . . . He wanted nothing to do with it.

She had turned to pick up her sketchbook, and her bent head concealed her expression.

"Good," she said and pushed the sketchbook into his chest. "I am *not* bashful. I draw myself nude. The practice isn't particularly productive, as I don't have a long enough mirror. And my figure isn't ideally suited for it."

He made a sound of negation, but she sighed and rolled her eyes.

"It's a fine figure," she said. "I don't need your compliments. But it's not full and rounded, and neither is it androgynous. It's a *body*. A contemporary body. Entirely lacking in the capacity for rhetorical grandeur."

It was strange to hear a woman speak so, of her own appearance.

"Rhetorical grandeur," he repeated doubtfully. "Is that the only measure of the figure in art?"

She regarded him for a long moment.

He read the challenge in her gaze but was too slow to guess its import.

"Let's see, then," she said. "There's charcoal in the bag. Take whatever piece you like."

Quick as thought, she twisted around, reaching behind her back. In a moment, the brown silk of her bodice sagged away from her torso. She pushed it down over her shoulders, shrugged out of the sleeves, and twisted again, undoing the sash.

He froze. He could see her shoulders and collarbones through the thin fabric of her chemise, the curves of muscle in her bare arms. He hadn't considered this before—a woman's muscles. Maybe he'd been a poor student of anatomy, or maybe he'd been with softer women. Her muscles flexed as she worked at the back of her gown. They looked firm. She wore no corset.

She pushed the bodice down farther and he saw her breasts through the chemise, the dark pucker of the nipples. Her body wasn't ample, but the dark shadows beneath the curves of her small breasts made his breath catch. The chemise was not entirely transparent. He couldn't see if she was freckled, if she blushed.

It wasn't a drawing lesson he wanted. His body stirred. He dropped the sketchbook and was at her side in an instant, stopping her hands, tugging up her gown.

"You've made your point," he grated. "This is far too advanced."

She turned from him, bending her wrists behind her back, slender fingers doing up her buttons. A tendril of hair tangled with a button. She picked at the knot.

"Here," he said and loosened the tendril, then brushed the other loose pieces of hair over her shoulders. The curls felt smooth and springy in his hands, like live things. The portion of her nape revealed was sized for his lips.

He stepped back, ruefully.

When she faced him again, her brilliant smile confirmed her victory.

He couldn't let it stand at that. He leaned over and kissed the smile from her lips. This time she responded instantly, opening to him, their tongues tangling, hers pulling his deeper.

"Maybe I'll learn to draw after all," he said, pulling back slowly. He grinned at her. She looked dazed, fingertip touching her bottom lip.

"I'm too busy to teach you," she retorted, lowering her hand, pressing her lips together. The quick rise and fall of her chest betrayed her. She tossed her head.

"But if you learn elsewhere," she added, "I *might* make the time to sit for you. Provided, that is, you sit for me." Her face darkened. "And provided you don't obliterate the canvas."

He shrugged, noncommittal.

"Let's not get ahead of ourselves," he said. "One arrangement at a time."

"Fine," she said. "We can revisit the issue at a later date."

"Please," he said politely.

She averted her gaze and gathered her sketchbook and bag.

He wasn't in a position to make *any* arrangements. How had he let this happen? He was cursing himself while he escorted her to the front hall and called for the coach, and he cursed himself when he returned to his study and saw the mud on the carpet.

He was starting to see symbols everywhere. Mud on a carpet lacked *rhetorical grandeur* to be sure, but the meaning was clear enough.

Now that she'd gotten her foot in the door, it would be no easy task to get rid of her.

CHAPTER EIGHT

"THOSE BASTARDS!" KATE stalked back and forth, pounding her fist against her thigh. Lucy watched her cautiously. Kate's temper was the stuff of legend.

"They can't get away with it. They can't shovel people out of their homes at a whim."

A chill breeze made Lucy glance at the sky, gray as a steel engraving. Rain threatened. How quickly the weather changed in early spring. When long break had begun, the day was bright and fair, gauzy with sun and cloud. She and Kate had walked to Green Park to breathe the fresh air. They'd laughed and gasped as sporadic gusts of wind made them skip forward. Something giddy had taken hold of her, the energy of the day—it loosened her tongue. Before she knew what was happening, the whole story had come tumbling out, starting from the moment she'd stumbled over Weston in the alley. By the time they'd turned back onto Piccadilly, Kate's eyes were flashing. As soon as they'd reached the narrow roadway that fronted the Schools, she'd exploded.

"And *you*!" Kate paused, glaring, then spun around, addressing her next outburst to the sky as she marched away. "How could you keep this from me? Any of it! All of it!"

Lucy had been dreading this phase of the attack.

"I'm telling you now," she offered.

Two boys burst out of the building. Infants, really, from the Antique School. They barely grunted as they barreled toward the street.

"Larvae," muttered Kate, gazing after them. "Long break is over!" she called.

Lucy snorted, and for a second, Kate's frown seemed to slip. Then her brow furrowed.

"You didn't show me the picture! *Me*. Aren't I your best critic? Aren't we *each other's* best critic?"

Best critic. That designation meant more to Kate than *best friend*. It denoted seriousness and a degree of honesty most friendships couldn't weather. They *were* best critics. Lucy valued Kate's judgments as much as Kate valued hers, maybe more. But the painting of that picture—she'd known nothing like it. The process had felt like a protracted fever, so vertiginous, so delirious, that she'd lost her moorings. She looked at Kate miserably.

"Come here." Kate grabbed her arm and dragged her past the students' entrance. Redheaded Thomas Ponsonby and tall, lanky Redcliffe Davis were trotting back from their own long-break excursion. If those two—notorious idlers—were headed to the studios, the hour was late indeed. Lucy watched them disappear through the door, Davis throwing a curious look over his shoulder.

The sound of thunder, distant but ominous, rolled overhead. Clearly, this conversation should be postponed. Before she could suggest the obvious, Kate spoke in a low, furious tone.

"What does the Sisterhood mean to you?"

Lucy felt a stab of pain in her fingers and realized she'd clenched her hands into fists. The ache in her knuckles had come and gone all winter. Too many hours with the needle and the brush. She shook out her hands, sighing.

"Study everything. Paint thrilling pictures. Elevate women artists." She could recite the main principles in her sleep.

"Together!" Kate stamped her foot. "We didn't start a secret society so we could keep secrets from each other! I would have helped you."

Suddenly, Kate threw her arms around Lucy's neck, embracing her fiercely.

"I *hate* that you sold your picture and Forbes, the chinless simpleton, saw it instead of me, and I hate even more that that *oaf* Weston destroyed it. You know he smashed the three-light window in the nave of All Saints Church? I'd have wrung the money out of my father and bought you the sewing machine."

Kate's father was a businessman with a reputation for luck and imprudence. He'd made a fortune on ostrich feathers and continued to invest unwisely, with excellent results. Kate claimed she could talk him into anything. Given that she'd cropped her hair and wore a man's kit to the Academy, Lucy believed her. Today she was wearing a mulberry-colored suit and could pass—if she didn't open her mouth—for a pretty dandy. She dressed in silk gowns and attached combs of false curls when she went out in society, but that, she claimed, was because she picked her battles.

Lucy sighed. "Thank you. But it isn't that simple."

Kate took her by the shoulders and spun her around.

"*That* is simple. *That* was your picture's proper destination."

Kate was motioning toward the large, forbidding black door set in the brick wall just beyond the students' entrance. It was the door through which porters carried the pictures and sculptures submitted for the Summer Exhibition. Lucy had stared at it hundreds of times, imagining exactly that: her pictures passing through the portal, borne up to the committee. Never her *Endymion*, of course. A male nude, painted by an unmarried woman! She wouldn't have dared, even before the man she'd painted had manifested, complicating everything, giving the lie to her lofty claims about classical ideals.

The subject of that picture is me.

To her mortification, tears flooded her eyes. Kate *scorned* tears in conversation. No crying allowed, except on the occasions when the mind was impressed by the sublimity of art or nature.

Lucy dashed the tears away as quickly as she could, shrugging. "Whatever the merits of the painting, I couldn't have submitted it." She managed a wry smile.

"The Duke of Weston, it turns out, is easily recognized."

Kate pounded her leg again. The girl was going to come out in bruises. "If only I'd seen the picture! I would have warned you. You could have disguised him."

"Painted on a beard? Flattened his nose?" Lucy laughed as she imagined possibilities, all hopeless. The import of Kate's words struck her and she narrowed her eyes. "You know him by sight, then?"

Now it was Kate's turn to sigh. "Not all of my notebooks are for sketching. I keep a meticulous log of every lord in the British Isles. The penniless ones I avoid like the plague. They're desperate to marry me for my money and can prove dreadfully persistent. The rich ones think I'm a good bit of fun and treat me with perfect indifference, if they notice me at all. The Duke of Weston is rich as sin, so I've observed him across dance floors without fear."

"The life of an heiress," Lucy murmured.

Kate scowled. "It has its dangers. Last summer, I tripped and fell into a rosebush escaping Lord Chatterton. I nearly lost an eye, and he didn't stop proposing. I've never passed two words with Weston. He's hard to miss, though, with the women stuck all over him like burrs."

Lucy blinked at this image.

"*You* don't fancy him, of course." Kate didn't phrase it as a question. "He's not very bright. They never are, the second sons who get packed off to the colonies. I heard he got sent down from Oxford for failing *all* of his preliminary exams. But he's a hero! I can't understand it. Brunelleschi is a hero, for inventing perspective. And whoever first thought of grating carrots into a cake—*she's* a hero. Riding around on a horse and shooting at people isn't heroism. It's criminal stupidity."

Lucy felt heat flood her face. Dear God. This urge to gainsay Kate—she had to stuff it down. She'd be lumped among the hopeful duchesses in a heartbeat, never to regain Kate's favor. Of course she didn't fancy the Duke of Weston! The idea was absurd. She ducked her head to hide her blush. Kate didn't seem to notice. She seemed lost in her own thoughts.

"He's a fine subject for a painting, I'll give him that," Kate said. "His mother was an Italian, or a Greek. I think a Greek. Adelaide didn't get to see the picture? She'd have loved it, I'm sure."

Lucy seized on this opening.

"Adelaide? Are you on a first-name basis with Mrs. Forbes?"

Kate grinned. "I ran into her at the British Museum. She was with Redcliffe Davis, but she's mad to sit for me. Maybe I'll put her in the Forest of Arden. She wants something Arthurian, but there's too much comedy in her face." She shrugged. "I can't think of it until I've readied my submissions anyway. I'm so close!"

As soon as the words passed her lips, she looked stricken. The wind flattened her hair against her forehead, making her gray eyes seem larger.

"Don't you dare apologize," said Lucy, smiling. "This year will be a triumph for you. You're going to exhibit at Grosvenor *and* the Academy. You *should* be excited. I'm excited for you."

Lately, Kate had been downplaying her achievements. Lucy preferred it when she crowed. Kate's recent carefulness, born of an awareness that Lucy had less cause to celebrate, only served to draw attention to the disparity.

"No more secrets," said Lucy. "But no more kid gloves either."

Kate understood.

"It's not pity, I swear it," she said. "I know I've been awkward. *Dammit*, I just think of how much time I have at my disposal, while you . . ."

Lucy was shaking her head.

"Use your time well," she said. "Paint thrilling pictures *without apology*."

"That's good." Kate laughed. She sounded relieved. "We should add that. No apologies for our unapologetic pictures!"

Lucy laughed too. "The men certainly aren't wasting their time saying sorry."

"Some of them should be," Kate muttered. "*That* is a different story." She gave herself a little shake and glared at Lucy—not with anger; with determination. "You *will* exhibit," she said.

Lucy shivered as the wind picked up. If she could settle her thoughts, focus, put aside her fears about eviction, keep jobbing out the petticoats to Megan Cosgrave, maybe she had a chance.

Kate seemed to read her thoughts.

"No one will lay a finger on your house. Weston will talk to Lord So-and-so, whatever his name is, the chairman of the Board of Works, and that will be that." She nodded with assurance. "The jobbery is too blatant to ignore."

Her grin was back, wide and mischievous. "It was *brilliant* how you threatened Weston. Nude cards! I'm inspired by your wickedness."

Lucy cocked her brow at what she hoped was a wicked angle.

"I try," she said modestly. When she'd reached the part of her narration in which she charged Weston's town house and appalled him with imminent lithographic humiliation, Kate had interrupted her with a howl of delight that drowned out the conclusion of the episode.

It was better that Kate believe she'd routed Weston, bent him to her will. Their actual agreement had been far too friendly.

She thinned her lips. *No more secrets*, she'd said to Kate, but, surely, she could omit a few details. And the situation with Weston's sister was delicate. Euphemia's secrets were not hers to share.

ANTHONY STEPPED DOWN from the cab onto Shoreditch High Street, straightening his hat. It was scarcely two in the afternoon, an hour before he was due to meet Miss Coover. He'd allotted himself that hour to explore, and as he turned off the High Street and onto another busy thoroughfare, he realized he knew nothing of Shoreditch by the light of day. It even sounded different. The roadway that stretched before him was lined with hulking warehouses, furniture showrooms, factories, and foundries. Carts piled with rough tables and skeletal chairs creaked along on their way to the varnish makers and upholsterers. Peering down a side street, Anthony could see a massive wardrobe dangling on a hoist. A group of men strained below, trying to lift it up to or lower it down from their workshop. Indeed, such sights greeted him down every side street. Men loading and unloading furniture, and inside the workshops, more men were sawing and hammering. The streets vibrated with the din. He wasn't fool enough to romanticize sweated labor. Still, the memory of engaging his muscles to accomplish something tangible made him clench his teeth.

The daily exercises he performed were mere ploy, a means to accustom the servants to his visits to the garden. They didn't tire his muscles like grooming in the cavalry regiment, hours sweeping out stables, changing bedding, brushing the horses until their coats reflected like mirrors. Discipline as activity he enjoyed, no matter how grueling the regimen. It was discipline as passivity, as prohibition, that chafed.

On a narrower street, he was trapped, briefly, behind a knife grinder and his barrow, which groaned with the weight of the treadle and grinder. His singsong rose above the noise.

"Pots, pans, or kettles to mend? Pots, pans, or kettles to mend?"

A throng of schoolboys shoved by, flushed from a victorious day of truancy, and he pushed along behind them. *That* was his tribe, the truants, the scapegraces. He followed them into muddier lanes, where the sludge beneath his boots gave way to polluting streams. The crush of people made it hard to move. Young children, scarcely more than infants, played in the ooze at open doorways. Every misery and disease impoverishment could wreak was written on the faces and figures of the men and women slumped against walls, the men and women passing in and out of the courts with baskets and buckets, with rags and bottles, the junk from which they made their livelihoods.

Anthony pressed a coin into the sticky palm of a knee-high girl tugging his pant leg and she handed up a flower. He wanted neither to hold it nor to let it go. He stumbled on. The eyes that passed over him held little curiosity. The middle and upper classes weren't strangers any longer to these districts. Charity workers and thrill seekers alike came to gasp at the horror, hoping to spy a corpse under a railway arch or factory girls scrapping in sewage.

Before he'd left for India, enjoyment of the city depended on the invisibility of the slums. If you traveled east, for the brothels or casinos, you went at night, in a coach, windows closed against the stench.

Now the slums were calling. Everyone had a use for them. Political, social, religious, personal.

Shoreditch. Guaranteed to shock your conscience into life, or kill it off completely.

By calling for a royal commission on the housing question, his father had hoped to accelerate slum clearances in the name of public health, presenting thundered demands for the end of the urban overcrowding, the improvement of sanitation.

Anthony had spent the night reading through copies of his father's speeches. He'd also read the notes on the speeches, which surprised him less.

His father had indeed worried about the poor. He'd worried that hungry, hopeless mobs would one day succumb to animal instincts. Rise up. Swarm into the wealthy precincts with clubs and knives. Slum conditions posed a grave peril to the state. Best to scrub the diseased villages from the map.

He'd proffered himself as a champion of the very people he hoped to push out of the city entirely. He would dish the Liberals in the process, picking up working-class votes for the Conservatives. He would also scoop the *Pall Mall Gazette* reporters, who were preparing an exposé on elite indifference to the suffering in London's slums.

Brilliant. Like all his father's plans, it was cold, complex, heartless.

He reached dryer ground, a proper street, paved and drained. He could still taste the foul air in his mouth. A drink. A drink would cleanse the film from his tongue.

Every morning, Humphreys brought him a few sips of whiskey, the small metal flask stowed in the soap dish of the shaving kit.

This morning was no exception. He'd broken his fast with a burning mouthful. The salutary benefit had long worn away.

A few grinning clerks were slapping open the door of a public house on the corner. He stopped walking, rocked on his heels. Pulled forward. Leaning back.

He shouldn't. The freedom he felt knowing Yardley was occupied in Putney was deceptive. The rules were still in force, the stakes as high as ever.

But no one on this dismal street could guess who he was, not in a million years. One single drink. There was no harm in it.

He put his back to the public house, walked with his head down, was almost struck by an omnibus as the lead horses came around the corner. He jogged to the next curb. Which way to Charlotte Road? He turned a slow circle, assessing.

All at once, the smell of fried onions assaulted him. His nostrils flared.

Right in front of him: another public house, this one flanked with stalls selling sheep's trotters, eel pies, pickled whelks, hot potatoes. His stomach rumbled.

A man had to eat.

The next thing he knew he was pushing open the door. He waited on the threshold to allow his eyes time to adjust to the darkness of the passage. It was one of those dim, cavernous places where you could lose any sense of the outside world. Sweat broke out across his brow.

He heard the sound of cutlery on heavy plates, men's voices, the scraping of benches. Normal sounds. Simple pleasures.

No harm, no harm.

In the taproom, he wove between tables.

"That's what you're missing, Jack. Give it to us, won't you? There's a good fellow."

Anthony paused as heads swiveled in his direction. The table before him was packed with shopworn dandies, cheap suits cut in flash style.

"For his coat," continued the youth, waving a thin hand overburdened with rings. His lips were shining, oyster shells piled on the platter in front of him.

"It'll match that paper collar he's so fond of." The table burst into laughter, except for one man—presumably Jack—who rapped his walking stick against the skull of his neighbor.

Anthony tossed him the flower and a hoot rose to the rafters.

"A toast!"

Tankards smashed together, foam spilling down the sides. Anthony watched the movement of the bubbles. Then he started forward, angling toward the bar. A potboy banged into him, almost dropping his tray. The taproom was crowded with all sorts. Swells, workingmen, a few women in neckerchiefs, smoking cigarettes. His eyes slipped over the people and locked on the taps gleaming down the length of the bar. The bartender, a smiling giant in a striped apron, was filling glass after glass.

His head pounded. He needed to leave, to find Charlotte Road with time to spare so he could walk its length, gather evidence.

"From Jack." The beringed youth was at his elbow, holding out a tankard. His round face was humorous and he winked as he pressed the glass into Anthony's hand. Anthony froze. Then he hoisted the glass in the general direction of their table.

The decision had been made for him.

"There's a dark look," came a comment from the end of the bar.

"Now, I ask you, what sort of man is too fussy for an ale? A man in need of a stout, that's what I say. Two more."

Anthony glanced at the speaker, thin as a spindle in a great clod of a wool coat. He held a tankard half-filled with stout and tipped it back, finishing the contents in one gulp. Two of his fingers ended at the first knuckle. He noticed Anthony's gaze and held up the hand.

"Bengal Horse Artillery," he said. "Lost those on the retreat from Kabul. Coldest I've ever been in my life. Couldn't load a gun, much less pull the trigger."

Anthony eased onto the stool beside him.

"I know that cold, in those mountains," he said.

The man's wizened face cracked into a smile. His teeth were gray as his beard.

"What about the heat?" he said. He took two stouts from the bartender and passed one to Anthony.

"Francis Doolan from County Tipperary. Where do we start? With the snow or the dust?"

By the second stout, they'd discussed every extreme of Afghanistan's weather and geography. By the third, they'd compared notes on British-bred, Irish-bred, and desert-bred stallions, as well as the army's supply of draft horses, cobs, and ponies. Camp yarns carried them through the fourth and the fifth, Anthony avoiding any mention of Maiwand. By the sixth, they'd waded into politics. Nearly forty years separated the first and second British wars in Afghanistan, but they sprang from a single root.

"It's an obsession," said Doolan. "Keep India safe from the grasping Russians. I never saw a Russian, did you? Waving down from a peak in the Hindu Kush? Waste of life. And for what?"

"For the Crown." Anthony laughed suddenly, a sharp bark. *Waste of life.* Afghan life, Indian life, British life, animal life. How many thousands of horses, camels, elephants, died on those marches through the passes? He'd ridden by miles of bones. All sizes.

It made no sense, defeating and dismembering the country, if a strong Afghanistan was wanted to provide a buffer against Russian influence in the region. Illogic piled on illogic.

He cooled his forehead against his glass.

"I was young when I attested." Doolan's pale blue eyes had fixed. "What an adventure, that's how I was thinking. Now I know it for a horrible, mean, miserable business. Victorious or not, the latest war was more of the same."

He'd sunk deeper into his coat. His words emerged clearly enough.

"Politics in London means violence in Delhi, in Kabul, in Zulu-land. In Dublin."

"You're talking about Home Rule now." Anthony waved for the next round.

Rubbing elbows with an Irish nationalist. His father hadn't thought to list it among his prohibitions. Because it was unthinkable.

Doolan was drawing spirals with the nub of his index finger in a puddle of beer on the bar top.

"It's all connected," he said. "Do you see?"

Anthony watched the slow, repetitive movements of the ravaged hand.

"I see," he said, pushing over a fresh beer. "Have another."

HE WASN'T DRUNK when he left the pub. No, he wouldn't say *drunk*. His body responded beautifully to his mental commands like a horse trained to subtle pressures of leg and rein.

There he was, pausing at the corner, crossing the street, turning into the early evening crowds.

They were thick, the crowds. The factory bells had sounded. Where was Charlotte Road? The crowd swept him forward. He asked questions of this man or that, the mouths moved, and his body heeded instructions, turned to the left, to the right. This shabby commercial street, this was his destination. He began to study signs in earnest. They advertised a greengrocer, a sweet shop, a chandlery, a boot maker's establishment, a millinery. He stumbled forward, stopped short.

MISS STIRLING, the sign read in gold, surrounded by a simple fern motif. DRESSMAKER.

The elderly woman at the sewing machine didn't pause in her work as he entered. He snatched off his hat, held it in his hands.

The woman's gray curls escaped her bun, spiraling in all directions. If he'd entertained any doubts, the sight dispelled them.

"Mr. Turner, is it?" she asked. Light glinted off her spectacles as she lifted her head. "From the School of Architecture? You're two hours late. You *are* Mr. Turner?"

His stutter could have meant anything at all. She took it for assent.

"Lucy went to make a delivery. She said if you turned up, I was to keep you. I think she worried I'd run you off."

The sewing machine whirred more loudly as she finished a seam.

He heard himself laugh, a nervous laugh.

Steady there. He put a hand on his chest to quiet the convulsions. Then he willed his body to stroll deeper into the shop. *Easy does it.* He tested his voice.

"You are Miss Stirling, Miss Coover's aunt?"

"You think I look too old." She snapped a thread and her eyebrows arched up above her spectacles.

"Not at all. I . . . that is . . ."

She allowed him a moment's fumbling, then shoved fabric back through the sewing machine, the renewed whirring causing her to raise her voice.

"I was aunt to Lucy's mother, my favorite niece. I'm great-aunt to Lucy."

"Your favorite great-niece." He aimed a smile. She was twinning slightly in his field of vision, so he smiled dead center.

"My own heart," she said. "Dearer than my heart." The whirring stopped abruptly and she met his smile with an owlish look. "Thank you for looking at the building. I'll eat your hat and swallow the buckle whole if your opinion sways the Board of Works, but I suppose I'm grateful you came. Might have been better if you'd come when you said, but you're here now."

"Here I am," he agreed. "Mr. Turner." The nervous laughter moved his chest a second time. Did Miss Stirling's great fondness mean that she believed her niece's lies? She seemed far too astute, too steely, to swallow obvious falsehoods.

"Student of architecture," he said, pointing at his smile. Miss Stirling's face was darkening. He intuited that his affirmations weren't having the intended effect.

Why had Miss Coover lied? Perhaps she didn't want to raise her aunt's hopes. She'd come to the conclusion that he didn't rate very highly with government officials despite his rank. She harbored no great faith in his influence, or powers of persuasion, after all.

Well, he tended to disappoint. He'd tried to tell her as much.

"I do hope the solidity of the construction is the only thing that interests you." Miss Stirling's spectacles glinted as she bent again over her machine. He couldn't mistake her meaning.

"Of course," he said and blinked at the ceiling beams. Heavy, strong, straight.

"Shipshape," he said, backing up a step, then another, following a beam, nodding his approval. He bumped something and spun to catch it as it swayed. He held a woman's torso in his arms, her gown bunching. He started, letting go. The mannequin thudded down.

"What have you done to poor Titania?"

The shop went silent.

"She's quite all right," he said. "I'll get her up."

He bent forward, and the room moved with him. A man couldn't stay upright if the ceiling and the floor changed places. He'd no choice but to fall on his head.

CHAPTER NINE

MURDER WAS TOO good for him. Lucy scooped her aunt's abandoned teacup from the table and knelt on the floor by Weston's head.

"Get up," she commanded, flicking the cold droplets of tea in his face. His eyelids twitched, the inky wings of his lashes beating once, twice. "Can you stand?"

This was how he kept his promise. Showed up hours late to their appointment straight from a bar and passed out, taking a mannequin with him. Good thing the white and rose muslin was already well and truly crinkled by design.

She tried to free the mannequin, tugging. His arm pinned the waist. She redirected her efforts, reaching under his coat to grip his biceps. His arm was heavy, the muscle dense and hard. She flopped it across his chest.

"He'll be an authority on the ceiling, at least." Aunt Marian, for all her fire, was also a mistress of deadpan. Lucy looked at her sharply. How angry was she? It was impossible to tell.

"I don't know what to do." She shrilled a little as she spoke and scowled. She did *not* whine. But this, this was vexing in the extreme. "I can't scrape him up with a palette knife," she muttered. But could she stab him with a palette knife?

"No need." Weston raised his arm, pointing his finger upward, an aspirational gesture. "I'm all but up."

He put his palm down to brace himself and shoved hard, on Lucy's knee. His fingers closed reflexively.

"*Idiot.*" She kept her voice low and knocked his wrist, glancing back at Aunt Marian. Mercifully, she was bent over the sewing machine. "You're drunk."

He propped himself, tossing his hair back from his eyes. The whites were bloodshot. Nonetheless, he raised his brows, as though inclined to disagree.

"Not a word from you." She sat back on her heels, gnawing at her lower lip. If she had a bucket instead of a measly teacup, she would *drench* him.

To think she'd drifted to sleep last night with a bubble of elation in her chest, remembering the feel of his lips. She'd been imagining he might put it all to rights, rescue the block from perdition.

What foolishness! Saved by a tall dark knight, like in a fairy tale.

In reality, the knights were selfish, conceited, indifferent *slugs*. They could not be relied on to do anything but ooze along their own course.

"Tea," she said, standing. "Hot, black, plenty of it. That's the first step."

He felt about for his hat and climbed slowly to his feet, testing them. The results seemed to please him. His balance as he bent to lift and arrange the mannequin certainly gave no cause for alarm.

"The dizziness has passed." He smiled. At least he had the decency to appear sheepish. He turned to Aunt Marian with a formality the circumstances rendered ridiculous.

"Miss Stirling," he said, bowing, "please accept my apologies. I don't know what came over me."

"When you fell on your head, or when you decided to drink yourself silly in the first place?"

Lucy was glad *she* was not the object of that stare. Weston touched his forehead gingerly, as though just realizing he'd smacked it on the mannequin's wooden torso. Lucy could see the knot forming.

"Come along," she said, avoiding looking in her aunt's direction. She should never have invited a drunkard to the shop, much less under false pretenses. Architecture student! The Royal Academy itself had probably fallen in Aunt Marian's estimation.

She led the way to the tiny room behind the shop proper, a crowded, windowless alcove. She tried to see it as he would see it: bowed plaster walls, sooty fireplace, chipped deal table, two spindly chairs, a large armchair with a battered ottoman. Would the heaped blankets on the armchair make him guess that Aunt Marian dozed there at night instead of sleeping in a proper bed? She set the old teacup with the other dirty cups for washing and put the kettle on the hob.

"No tea for me," he said. She looked over in time to see him shrugging out of his cloak, which he tossed on the back of a chair. The bulk of his shoulders, the column of his throat rising from his jacket—they indicated strength, even violence.

"You'll drink it," she said grimly. "And you'll eat a slice of bread while you're at it, to mop up some of that liquor."

"Beer," he said absently, glancing about. "Stout, in fact. It's like bread."

One swift kick and he'd be back on the floor. She considered it.

"I was just delivering petticoats to a girl who helps us with the sewing. Her father might have been at that tavern with you. He was certainly there yesterday. Her face was green with the bruises. I hope you enjoyed yourselves."

His eyes locked on hers. His jaw was clenched.

"Hitting women, children." He shook his head. "I would never stand for such a thing."

"Ha!" Her explosion startled him. His faint sneer of surprise drew the lines down from his nose, a frame for his lips. She focused on his eyes, glassy, the red threads that unraveled from the green.

"You can't stand at all, which is my point exactly. Your word weighs *nothing* in the balance. Sit. I'm not rolling you out of the fire."

He sat, folding his long limbs into the chair she pushed toward him. This docility mollified her slightly.

With calmness came the realization that she should change her tack. He was sitting in front of her; nothing else mattered. He'd kept her waiting, yes. As she'd fretted at buttonhole after buttonhole, too distracted to turn the needle true, he'd been laughing and drinking, in a tavern, maybe even in a brothel. So what?

She still needed him to go to Mabeldon. No point in ruining her chance because he'd hurt her pride.

In the silence, they could hear the whirring of the sewing machine. Lucy opened her mouth, but before she could speak, the kettle screamed. She seized it, kept herself—barely—from slamming it down on the table.

"I was early, actually," he said. Sitting, he had to look up into her face. Interesting what simple shifts could do, in terms of perspective. In terms of power. From her vantage, she waited for him to continue, staring into the black close-set waves of hair.

"I wanted to know something more of the parish, see the factories, the terraces, so I walked up and down."

He slurred and seemed to hear it. He frowned, then continued, speaking more carefully.

"I got hungry, and then . . . I got carried away."

His gaze sharpened. "Why did you tell your aunt my name was Turner?"

She made a shushing noise. The sewing machine whirred on.

"She has the ears of a bat." She filled a teacup and placed it before him, returning the kettle to the hob. She sighed, hands fisted on her hips. A ducal visit would have required more explanation than she'd been willing to give.

"If you think she'd have been courteous if she knew your name was Weston, you're mistaken. Tell her if you want, but now might not be the best moment for the truth. A man who passes out in a coachman's cape, then awakens and declares himself a duke is usually thought insane. I will style you properly when I credit you for your role in reversing the eviction."

He held his palm over the teacup to feel the heat of the steam. She had the impression he wanted it to burn.

"When I reverse the eviction. Then, of course." He dropped his palm onto the rim of the cup. His fingertips touched the table and one began to drum the surface. He enunciated so his words were clear and clipped, but he couldn't scrub the alcohol from his voice completely. Raw edges betrayed him. "Don't worry. I'll rise to the occasion."

His tone—halfway between jeer and apology—disturbed her. She looked up from his hand, studied his face, presented to her in profile: heavy lines, dramatically masculine. She let her eyes trace the dark, knotted brow, then down the straight ridge of his nose. Her gaze skimmed the full, frowning lips, the jut of the chin.

"Because I'll go to Mr. Teed?" She'd meant it as a threat, but it came out sounding like a question. She *was* a terrible liar. The way she'd spoken—it was tantamount to an admission the lithographer did not exist.

He turned his head and she felt the full force of his beauty press the air from her lungs. His eyes sparkled . . . with tears?

"Because I can't bear the thought of your being turned out onto the street." No, his eyes didn't sparkle with tears. They sparked with something hot and dark, closer to rage than sorrow. "The world is a horrible, mean, miserable place. I've seen people walking into the snow with their villages burning behind them. There, it's armies that do it, with steel. Here it's boards, with paper. I want to do something about it."

She let this sink in. Compassion—not blackmail—his motivator. And yet . . .

"The world?" She sat slowly in the empty chair beside him. He did nothing about the world. "You sit at the bar until the world disappears."

His smile was all bitterness.

"Show me what you want to show me." He stood up, stretched, reached for the ceiling beam with his fingers and pressed into it, gauging its strength. Or maybe he was holding himself upright.

"Well made," he said.

She snorted. It felt like a provocation, his body displayed, the column of his neck lengthening as he examined the beam. He smelled like malt and smoke, cinnamon and sweat.

"Sober."

"What?"

"When you talk to Mabeldon, you will talk to him sober, God help me."

"I'm not a drunkard," he said. He lowered his arms carelessly. "George is a drunkard."

A slip of the tongue, one he didn't notice.

"George isn't anything. Your brother is dead." She couldn't gentle the words, their harsh reality. "Drinking yourself into a stupor won't change that. And you *are* a drunkard. They don't all let fly with their fists."

She thought he was going to stride out of the shop. He looked stricken, tension vibrating his limbs. He pushed his hair back with both hands, massaging his skull. Then he stuffed himself back into the chair, like a figure from a jack-in-the-box, coiled to spring. They looked at each other. She broke his gaze to look pointedly at the teacup. After a long pause, he picked it up, sipped. A little of his tension seemed to dissipate.

"You're speaking from experience," he said, watching her. It was peculiar that this man, so demonstrably lacking in the qualities she valued—taste, talent, applied intelligence, commitment, generosity, loyalty, integrity—should elicit her confidences. He had a knack for striking straight to the heart of things.

The beer had lent his eyes that high gloss, that fixity. She shouldn't assume there was genuine emotion behind that intense—intensely curious—stare. Nonetheless, she responded to it.

"My father was the gentlest man alive. He was a wood engraver, for newspapers mostly. He drank to dull the pain in his back and his fingers. Many nights my mother would finish his blocks. After she died, he had less help and all the more reason to drink. His reasons were good reasons."

Pain, grief—what better?

"But the results were . . . not good." It was hard to lay out the facts. She had never feared her father. He had wanted the best for her mother and for her. What he had brought upon them—that was a different story.

"He missed deadlines. His firm let him go. He took on piecework for other engravers but left it unfinished for a drink at the pub that turned into two, three, four. I helped him home more nights than I can count."

Weston was looking at her queerly. She stopped, unwilling to endure his pity. But it wasn't pity she saw in his face, but recognition.

"He'd begun to lose his vision." She forced herself to continue. "But that's not why he fell down the stairs, an ugly fall."

He'd lingered for weeks. He'd had time to regret many things. Regret, a useless emotion. Her father's regrets didn't change her childhood. Didn't bring her mother back.

She stood too quickly, bumping the seat of the chair with the tender backs of her knees. She grimaced, stepped around Weston to reach the meager sideboard where the bread lay wrapped like a mummy. At Weston Hall, the tea involved little sandwiches, pastries, and Madeira cake. At Miss Stirling's dress shop, it was all mummified bread that savored of chalk.

"Before George died, I didn't drink."

She made a disbelieving noise. "Are you speaking in comparative terms?"

She unwrapped the bread, positioning her body so Weston couldn't observe the process. Surreptitiously, she probed, then sniffed the loaf. Passable, barely. She half turned, reaching for the knife, and met his eyes. He took another sip of tea.

"Certainly," he said. "I don't mean that I abstained. But I always liked horses, sports, *mornings*. It didn't suit me—up all night, abed until afternoon, my head splitting. And I couldn't lose my wits. If I went to the casino, to the . . ."

He hesitated.

"Brothel?" She gestured with the knife. "Don't be shy. You thought we met at one, if I recall."

He looked rueful, began to shake his head, then shrugged.

"I went to make sure George was only neck-deep in trouble. If he went under, I pulled him up again. You could say I kept his head above water."

The metaphor was unfortunate. Weston seemed to think so. His expression became more haggard, lips thinned, cheeks hollowed. He carried the guilt of his brother's death, of his sister's disappearance. It was all there, written on his face. He looked down into his teacup.

"He liked to pick fights for me to finish, to make wagers in my name and leave me on the hook for them."

"Charming," she murmured. "And you hopped to do his bidding?"

She sawed a slice from the loaf, plated it, and carried it a step to the table.

"He was my older brother."

She dropped the plate on the table in front of him. He looked startled, at either the rough service or the fare. She flushed despite herself. What did he expect? She wasn't a serving wench, and this wasn't a restaurant. He blinked at her. Then he laughed, picking up the bread and taking an enormous bite, his teeth flashing.

"I worshipped him. When I was a child, I thought he was a god. It was a time during which my mother was . . . much discussed. I fought some boy—or several—every day, and George protected me.

Eventually, he wearied of the role. He wearied of *everything*, really. No one can save anyone, so why have a care? That was his creed, in a nutshell."

He folded the rest of the bread into his mouth. It made no sense, how beautiful he could look *chewing*.

"But not yours." She took the plate and cut him a second slice of bread. He accepted the plate, balanced it on his knee.

"I seem to care," he said. "For all the good it does. Or the harm."

He ate the second slice of bread wolfishly and rose, setting the plate on the table and brushing crumbs from his jacket.

"I was hungry," he said. "Thank you. I am restored."

Doubtful. But they couldn't wait until dark. She sighed.

"Whether you are or not, we should get started. Inspectors cite all sorts of violations to revoke a lease. None of them pertain here. Let's see. Weak rafters and walls, open privies, bad house drains, vermin, overcrowding . . ."

He cleared his throat.

"I'm impressed this house stands up as well as it does. I've been in country homes where the plaster pulls away from the lath and you're in danger of getting crushed in your bed."

She edged around him, her skirts brushing his thigh as she passed. The room was cramped but nowhere near collapse. She touched the wall between the cabinets, looking up at the corner of the ceiling speculatively.

"A few years ago, the damp got into that corner and made it bubble, but I replaced that section. It's been fine since."

"*You* . . . plastered the wall?"

She scowled. Perhaps he was restored—to his former idiocy.

"A friend—a sculptor—gave me some plaster. It's not very hard to remove a section of wall and replace it, if it's a small section. It's far easier than sculpting a bust."

"Is it?" he murmured. She heard his footfall and turned, nearly bumping him. He glanced up at the smooth plaster. "I hope he didn't feel it a waste of his talents."

"A waste of whose talents?"

"The talents of the obliging sculptor," he grated. "Your friend."

"Oh." She bit the inside of her cheek to keep from smiling. *Here* was a development. Was he jealous? Of Nelly Knotwood?

"I only asked for the plaster. I didn't require her assistance."

He rubbed his thumb roughly against his brow.

"Her," he said. She pressed her lips together. No need to sour the somewhat delicate mood with a lecture on women in the arts. He could work through his surprise on his own.

"Are these yours?" he asked suddenly, pointing lower down on the wall where two framed drawings hung on nails between pinned-up illustrations cut from the papers.

"That one is," she said, indicating the portrait. "I did it years ago. I drew Aunt Marian so much she said I had to go to the Royal Academy just for a change of heads."

"She's almost smiling," he said.

Lucy rolled her eyes. "She smiles. Try arriving on time and remaining conscious."

He ignored this and nodded at the lower picture.

"So, the other one, who did that?"

"My mother." The drawing was of a curly-headed child skipping forward to stomp in a puddle. The storefront was in the background. A sweet illustration, worthy of a calendar or a book of children's verse.

That day, when the sun had come out and shone so bright after the clouds blew over, and she'd played in the street with her mother and her father and Aunt Marian looking on—she remembered it as the last day they'd all been together. It couldn't have been. Her mother had lived for several more years. But her father was increasingly absent, if not out at a bar, withdrawn into a corner, present in the flesh but otherwise absent, doing little more than lifting a glass, while her mother's fingers flew. Drawing, carving, cooking, mending.

"She never had formal instruction." Her voice came out huskier than usual, but steady. "She learned how to draw from her father. He did illustrations for book publishers, mostly children's books, volumes of nursery rhymes and things of that sort. She worked with him and then she worked for newspapers. I loved to watch her draw. I wanted to see how she did it, but it was impossible. The pictures seemed to appear all at once on the page. She was so fast. She had to be. The deadlines were relentless."

She'd tried to meet them even on her deathbed, hers and Lucy's father's as well.

Weston shifted behind her, leaning closer to the drawing. Her throat tightened. She'd never looked at it with someone else, someone seeing it for the first time. She felt oddly vulnerable.

His voice was soft. "So much life in it. I can smell the rain."

She cleared her throat, not looking at him.

"I'll show you the back court. If you can walk."

THE SUN WAS setting, which relieved the bleakness of the scene. At least the light was good, the grime touched up with gold.

"Privies," she said, beginning her tour. Slowly, she led him around the perimeter. The court backed up against another house, also condemned. It wasn't empty—but neither was it teeming with human and animal life. Mrs. Stavely was taking in her laundry. Mr. Pritchard stood in a doorway talking with two other men, their voices tense. No doubt discussing the evictions.

She ignored the curious glances.

As she pointed out the house drains, she realized that she'd lost her audience. He'd wandered toward Mr. Chesney's old backhouse, which seemed to have crumbled dramatically in the night. Surely it hadn't looked quite so derelict yesterday, with that fallen beam and the bricks tumbled into what, in summer, was a pretty little garden. He walked a few paces to the right, then the left. Was he weaving like that out of interest? Or was it drunkenness? She sighed.

"Mr. Chesney's donkeys lived there. Noisy creatures. I don't miss them, although I do miss Mr. Chesney."

"Donkeys," he mused. "They deserve more respect."

She snorted. "You love donkeys in addition to horses?" It seemed unlikely. They weren't very gentlemanly creatures. "I suppose they have four legs," she said dubiously, recalling his main criterion for approbation.

He laughed and squatted by the fallen beam. His jacket was not quite long enough to hide his haunches. She averted her eyes and noticed Mrs. Stavely gawking. She resisted the urge to make a face.

"Nothing pestilential in that old heap, although I wish it wasn't dripping bricks and beams onto my herb patch."

He stood and came toward her.

"You were saying something about drains," he suggested.

"Look here," she said, and began again. He listened as she talked about drainage, ventilation, refuse, water, dustbins, asked questions. His thinking seemed alert, orderly, efficient. The solid bread had counteracted the liquid.

"So," she said, concluding, "if inspectors come, they may recommend repairs, but they won't find the structural and sanitary defects that spurred the order to close the house. There's adequate water. The walls are plumb. The roof tiles keep the rain out."

Where roof tiles were missing, of course, rain came in. But the roof tiles were heavy and well secured. They didn't dislodge easily. She knew from experience. She'd made a hole in the roof herself, for the light, which she covered with oilcloth. Luckily, the dark patch was invisible from this angle.

They stopped and turned toward each other.

"I will convey the information to Mabeldon," he said. "I don't know what he'll make of it."

She nodded. A gust of wind came up at her back, rushing between the houses, and she stepped into him. For a moment, too brief a moment, she hoped, for anyone to have taken note, he gripped her elbows. Then he'd set her back and was off and running, reaching out to catch a white square of cloth as it sailed through the air. A handkerchief, ripped from a line. He caught it low, just before it hit the ground.

Giggles exploded behind them.

Two of the Cantrell children, the youngest girls, each clutching a handmade doll, cloth but with clever little leather boots, courtesy of their mother.

"Hello, Beth. Hello, Mary." Lucy called out to them and they waved at her shyly, eyes glued on Weston.

He was folding the rescued handkerchief over its clothesline. As the girls stared, he removed a clothespin. Instead of pinning the handkerchief, he held the clothespin high in the air, then attached it to the tip of his nose.

"My ladies," he said, bowing deeply to the little girls, who shrieked with laughter.

He removed the clothespin from his nose and attached the handkerchief with a fluid motion. Beth and Mary clambered onto an overturned barrow, facing him with saucer-eyed eagerness, waiting to see what he'd do next. He smiled at them, with a touch of uncertainty, she thought. He looked at her then, waiting for a cue.

Since the notices had gone up, she'd seen the Cantrell children more often, playing in the court or running past the shop windows. Maybe Mrs. Cantrell wanted to give them a holiday before they all landed in the poorhouse. Today, Beth and Mary were bareheaded, bundled in matching green coats, nut-brown braids falling over their shoulders. With their dolls on their knees, they made a very pleasing composition.

If the light held for a few more minutes . . .

"Lady Beth, Lady Mary, this is Mr. Turner," she said. "Why don't you tell him what we grow in the garden?" She was already spinning to race back into the house for her sketchbook.

SHE'D ONLY BEEN gone two minutes at most, but the scene in the garden had changed completely by the time she reemerged. The girls had produced a long rope, and Mary and Weston were turning while Beth hopped about, she and Mary chirping wildly the words to some skipping song with an Irish lilt.

It sounded like babble to her, but after a moment, she realized that Weston had begun to chant along. The last rays of daylight lit his eyes as he grinned at her. In that moment, he was hopelessly charming. He was also ruining her opportunity.

"Beth, Mary," she called. "When you're done jumping would you sit again with your dolls, and I'll make a picture?"

Mary dropped her end of the rope and ran back to the barrow, where she snatched up her doll and hugged it with sufficient force to pop out a real baby's eyes.

"Will you draw a portrait of Lily and Violet?"

"I prefer to draw you all together," said Lucy. "Because you're a family."

"After I jump!" said Mary, and, with Beth and Weston turning the rope, she set herself to jumping with more determination than skill, clutching her doll in her arms.

Every time the rope bumped against her ankles, Weston let the middle length drop to the ground and counted off before swinging again, nodding with encouragement.

"Now," he said when it came around, and Mary jumped again and again, beaming.

He wasn't merely indulging these children; he was enjoying himself. Who was he really? A drunkard. An idiot. A philistine. A friend of four-legged creatures, ragpicker boys, and, it turned out, children generally. She clapped to get their attention.

"Very good, Mary." She glanced at Weston. "Shall we?"

Weston stopped the rope and coiled it neatly, using his elbow as an anchor and seating the rope in the V formed by his thumb and first finger. Given the attractions of his more obvious features, it seemed unfair that a span of his hand could also make her stomach flutter.

She wouldn't waste daylight watching the man coil a rope. The girls sat on the barrow, and she sat, awkwardly, on another one. She balanced her sketchbook on her knees and studied the tiny figures before her.

Both girls were staring at their boots, downcast faces stiff and nervous.

"You can talk," she said, pencil hovering. "Go ahead. You can play with your dolls. Don't move much, but . . ."

Don't retract into your coats like turtles.

A tread alerted her that Weston had come up beside her.

"It's a pleasure to see all four of you together," he said. "But tell me—which doll is Violet and which one is Lily?"

In a heartbeat, the girls flashed to life, their round faces glowing and animated. Lucy hardly listened to the words tumbling out of their mouths, her pencil flying over the paper. Soon, they weren't even addressing Weston. Their heads tipped together and they were speaking to each other as Violet and Lily, planning a feast of sweets for Lady Beth and Lady Mary's supper.

She hadn't her mother's lightning speed, but the fading light, the chill creeping into the air, and the limited patience of her subjects propelled her hand. When Mrs. Cantrell shouted to the girls and they leapt out of their positions, she'd already captured enough and could put her pencil behind her ear with a satisfied sigh.

Not bad. There was something to it, something in the girls' posture and their rapt focus on their dolls that made the simple, private moment open up and hint at a vast shared inner world of make-believe. Maybe, *maybe*, she could turn it into a decent canvas.

"Your Grace?" She rose, frowning, for she'd heard a thud. What was he about? He stood by the backhouse in his shirtsleeves, his discarded jacket crumpled on a barrel. This time as he bent, squatting deeply, she couldn't help but indulge in the view. His trousers revealed the taut curves of his thighs and buttocks, which flexed as he strained to stand.

He was trying to lift the fallen beam.

"Of all the pigheaded . . ." The words burst from her and she stalked toward him. Men expected to be praised for feats of strength. That dated back to Hercules. But if Weston dragged that beam through the herb patch or knocked down the rest of the wall, she could be excused from applauding.

The cords in his neck stood out and he wobbled slightly as he hoisted the beam, but then, with a groan, he heaved it over the herbs and rolled it up against the side of the main house. He turned, brushing off his hands. His chest rose and fell quickly. Simple enjoyment punched those deep dimples in his cheeks. He was grinning like mad. Jumping rope, heaving beams—these were the kinds of things that brought him happiness.

She gazed at the mangled, muddy ground and the withered, broken herbs, recently liberated from the crushing weight of the beam and the portion of the wall it had brought down.

"Where *are* the bricks? You cleared away everything."

"I stacked them by the barrel."

He picked up his jacket and shrugged into it, a carelessly coordinated motion. He was thick everywhere, wide through the chest, brawny-limbed. Shouldn't such musculature present a limiting factor, working against his agility? Heavily muscled men were often clumsy, awkward. How could he move like a song, and after an afternoon at the public house at that?

"I had to occupy myself." He fastened his buttons, then lifted his head, shaking his hair back from his brow.

"It was dig bricks from the mint, or hover at your shoulder while you sketched."

The chill in the air might, with luck, slow the rush of blood to her face.

"You couldn't disconcert me." A lie, credibly uttered. "We call our Visitor at the Academy the mosquito. He's always circling while we paint."

"And what does the mosquito see these days when he circles you?"

She closed her sketchbook and held it protectively against her chest.

"Nothing that pleases him." She'd not had an encouraging word in months. "He called my last attempt rubbish."

"Then *he* is the philistine. Even I, idiot that I am, recognized your talent."

He spoke with high spirits, giddy from his labors. He wasn't thinking of what he said.

She looked away.

"Ah," she said. "The picture you saw . . ." *and destroyed.* "That was my finest."

"Miss Coover—" It sounded like the presage to an apology. She looked back at him, interrupting.

"I'm not in despair. I have a month to paint something better. And I shall."

The apology—if apology it had been—had died on his lips. He twisted them in a wry smile.

"What happens at the end of the month?"

She sighed. The date was of paramount importance to artists but meant nothing to him. "If you hope to show a picture in the Summer Exhibition, you must submit it to the Hanging Committee at the end of March."

How had they come to be standing so very close together? Lucy became aware of the other people bustling in and out of doors, looking down from the windows above. She was making herself a spectacle.

And yet, she couldn't bring herself to step away, to break their gaze. Those pale eyes sent something hot shivering through her. *A green dart.*

"Ho," he said. "Who's that?"

She looked. Mr. Malkin was creeping along the wall, his gray fur patchy, his ears notched. A tooth stuck out, exposed by a sag in his lip. This was a recent development and gave him a fierce, not altogether sane, aspect. Dear Mr. Malkin! She had the defensive urge to bundle him away from Weston's scrutiny.

"He's an old campaigner." Weston crouched, hand outstretched.

"And not sweetened by the experience." She watched Mr. Malkin approach Weston on stiff legs. "It takes him time to get used to new people. And he always scratches men."

Before she could scoop him into her arms, Mr. Malkin had reached Weston and begun to rub against his shins, purring creakily. Weston's large hand stroked across Mr. Malkin's knobby spine.

Traitor.

She sighed.

"It's not you, it's your trousers," she said. "He likes fine fabrics. That's what happens if you raise a cat in a dress shop."

His laughter was low, in the register of Mr. Malkin's satisfied purring. His hand stroked and stroked again slowly.

A new, mortifying category of emotion: jealous of cat.

"Horses always monopolized my affections, but I admire cats. They know how to be themselves."

He stood. His last sentence hung in the air between them. *He* didn't know how to be himself; it was painfully obvious. He was trying to break out of molds made by other men. His father. His brother. What would it look like, a portrait of his inner self? Black and red, brown and amber, no figures, its essence in shades, modulation, sensation. She could barely imagine such a painting. Being in Weston's presence made her think, see, feel, new things.

All the more reason to quit his presence immediately. She knew how to be *herself* just fine. Anything extra confused things. Weston was definitely *extra*. He had no place in her life. If he kept looking at her like that, she was going to do something rash.

A drunkard, she reminded herself. Absolutely unreliable.

Mr. Malkin purred louder, pressing between Weston's legs.

"I'll deal with you later," muttered Lucy, bending close to the notched ear. But when Weston left shortly after, she only stroked Mr. Malkin thoughtfully, listening to him purr and nodding in reluctant agreement.

CHAPTER TEN

KATE STOOD WITH her arms folded, tipping her head this way and that.

"It's good," she pronounced at last. "The graduation of color. All the accessories of detail. But . . ."

This *but* was what Lucy was waiting for. Kate didn't settle for good. Lucy grinned and turned her eyes to her easel, trying to see what Kate saw. It was her first attempt working from the sketch she'd made of the Cantrell girls. She'd added Mr. Malkin in the bottom left and the handkerchief sailing away from the clothesline in the top right.

"The elements aren't working together," she ventured, and Kate scowled, weighing her next words.

They were standing shoulder to shoulder in Lucy's favorite corner of the classroom. Lucy tried to still her breathing, so Kate could think without the slightest interruption. At last Kate opened her mouth, and gasped.

"Oh," she said, nudging Lucy in the ribs. She no longer looked at Lucy's easel but across the room. Gwen Burgess stood framed in the doorway. She appeared paler than usual, even peaked. Whatever had detained her from class, it hadn't been a happy experience. Lucy shifted, suddenly ill at ease, as though, desirous of usurping Gwen's rightful place, she'd somehow willed her misfortune.

Nonsense. She had no such powers. Besides, Gwen Burgess didn't own this corner. Lucy belonged there as much as anyone. Kate glanced at Lucy and gave a short nod, gathering herself as Gwen came toward them.

"Gwen." Kate called to her in a low voice. "I've been hoping to . . ."

But Gwen's face had already assumed its characteristic blankness of expression, the remote quality that made her privacy so unassailable. Without waiting for Kate to finish speaking, without acknowledging that she'd begun, Gwen swept past, making a beeline for Mr. Barrett.

Kate watched her go.

"Dammit," she swore and bent her arm, jamming her clenched fist beneath her chin. "Did you see that? She won't exchange a word with me. Lucy, we need her to sign our petition. She's a *Burgess*. Everyone on the council knows who she is. And if she signs, the other girls will sign in a heartbeat."

Lucy, too, followed Gwen with her eyes. Would Mr. Barrett have a harsh word for his pet? No, his narrow face showed only concern as he beckoned her away from the other girls, who gawked from behind their easels.

Kate sighed. "And she's disgustingly talented."

"Humph," muttered Lucy; then she bit her tongue. It was preposterous, her one-sided rivalry with Gwen Burgess. The circle would be a circle of hell if the Sisters succumbed to such pettiness.

She did rather wish, though, that Kate had not been interrupted on the verge of a dramatic critique of her painting. Too late now to resume. She could see the wheels turning in Kate's head.

"What?" she asked.

"You get her to sign." Kate leaned forward and gripped both of Lucy's arms, staring fiercely into her eyes. "Promise me you'll try."

Lucy frowned, and Kate tightened her grip. She was devilishly strong.

"Fine!" Lucy groaned her concession, shaking Kate off. "I don't know why she'd listen to me, but of course I'll try."

"She'll listen because *you* are an indomitable force." Kate winked at her, turning back to the easel. "Singleness of aim, that's the secret."

Lucy bit her lip to keep from laughing aloud.

"To winning over Gwen Burgess?" she asked. "Or to improving this painting?"

"Both," said Kate. "The painting will take more work. Too much external composition, no definite end. Look there . . ."

As Kate pointed out the painting's myriad flaws, Lucy felt her spirits surge. The criticism stung, but it meant she and Kate were *together*, more together than they'd been in months. When Gwen walked past again, accompanied by Mr. Barrett, Lucy tried to catch her eye, preparing a smile. The smile, once it reached her lips, felt genuine. But Gwen didn't look her way.

She had another chance, though, the very next afternoon. As Lucy struck out from the Schools at the close of the day, she caught sight of Gwen walking in the same direction, a half block ahead on the opposite side of the street. Could it be? Yes, she was stopping at the cabstand in front of the Criterion Theatre. Why on earth would Gwen Burgess take a cab? A family coach dropped her off and picked her up each day in the courtyard of Burlington House.

She was going somewhere without her family's knowledge.

Lucy dodged between carts, her bag banging her hip.

"Gwen!" she called. Clearly, the girl had no idea how to acquit herself. A dozen cabmen had gathered around her, vigorously offering their services. The most aggressive among them was leading her toward his carriage as Lucy ran up, panting.

"Gwen," she repeated. Gwen didn't turn. Lucy touched her shoulder and her head snapped around. They stared at each other. Gwen's face was unreadable. Lucy became aware of her ragged breathing and sweaty forehead. She pushed back flyaway strands of hair.

"I saw you and . . ."

She broke off. Gwen's paleness belied her composure. She *had* been startled, and badly. No one on a furtive expedition liked a witness.

Lucy said, impulsively, "I couldn't let you choose this cab. The cabby's a pest."

She put her hands on her hips and glared up at the cabman, who had clambered up onto the box. He was a barrel-chested, red-nosed rascal who glared back at her. Every day she walked past the stand, she heard him deliver a bullying phrase to whatever woman on the sidewalk strayed into his range. He muttered around the tobacco packed into his mouth as Lucy tugged Gwen away.

"Go on. Walk sharp, then," he called down. "None of us want you."

But he didn't speak for his brethren. The other cabmen whistled and clapped and crowded around. Gwen's eyebrows drew together. She looked confusedly between Lucy and the throng of cabmen, many of whom were gesturing to their cabs with newspapers, pipes, whips, each extolling the virtues of his particular carriage and horse.

"Now," said Lucy. "Any of these cabs will do. Do you know the fare?" Gwen's eyes flitted back to her. Her lips parted and she shook her head slightly.

"They'll charge you double and accuse you of bilking when you pay," said Lucy. Cabmen scented timidity. Gwen, with her quiet grace, made for an easy mark.

"When he tells you the fare, say, 'You're a rogue, it's not half so much,' and pay two-thirds plus a penny. You'll come out all right, and so will he."

She smiled. It was a neat formula, one she'd worked out the hard way. Gwen had been watching her closely and now she smiled too. Fancy that. A smile from Gwen Burgess.

"I'd take that one there," said Lucy, pointing. The horse was well fed at least. At her words, the cabman, white-haired, leapt with surprising agility to his high seat and caught up the reins.

Gwen glanced up at him and nodded.

"Did your brother paint a miniature of Lady Euphemia Philby?" Lucy felt the question burst from her. Not the question she'd intended to ask. Gwen angled her head, presenting the tiny shell of her right ear, its upper curve hidden by a loop of chestnut hair. She peered at Lucy out of the corners of her eyes.

"What?" she said.

Lucy repeated herself, blushing. Gwen's oblique concentration disconcerted her.

"Lady Euphemia? They're friends." Gwen's voice was low, words slightly blunted by an almost undetectable hesitancy. Was Lucy imagining things or did her mouth twist slightly to the right when she spoke? "I believe he did paint a miniature, over a year ago."

"They are not in touch, though?" Lucy persisted. "Your brother and Lady Euphemia?"

"Effie's in France," Gwen murmured. She seemed perplexed, and Lucy smiled to show the subject was closed. She'd do better to pursue the lead Anthony had given her.

Aunt Marian didn't know of any theater managers named Frank or Madge, and neither did the chorus girl who'd come by the shop for tailoring the day before. Nor the two acrobats with the snapped elastics.

An unpromising start, but she'd hardly exhausted the pool of theatrical personages to whom she might direct her queries.

Gwen glanced again toward the cab. Lucy could see her bunching her skirt in her hand, readying herself to clamber up.

"You can ask Augustus yourself," she said, slowly. "If you were to come to one of his salons . . ."

The sentence trailed off, more a hypothetical than an invitation, but Lucy seized upon it.

"I'd love to!" she said warmly. Why, this was a most unexpected and glorious outcome! Almost as good as getting Gwen to sign the petition. The memory of the petition—and with the petition, Kate—brought her up short.

"Oh," she said. "Could Kate come too?" She winced at her own impropriety. But she couldn't go to the salon without Kate.

Again, Gwen presented her right ear, her oval face still as an icon's. In the pause that lengthened, Lucy added, "Holroyd. Kate Holroyd."

The only Kate at the Royal Academy. These long pauses . . . they were strange to say the least.

"Of course, you and Kate should both come," said Gwen at last.

So, it was that simple, was it? Lucy grinned, dazzled by her success. Gwen smiled back and began to turn away.

"Wait! One more thing. You haven't signed the petition, and I wonder . . ."

"Petition?" Gwen's eyes roamed over Lucy's face as though ferreting for clues. "What petition?"

Lucy gaped. Gwen avoided the canteen, yes, but the petition made for choice gossip in the halls and in the corners of the classrooms. Was she joking? There wasn't a hint of irony in her expression.

"The petition to grant women a life class for the study of the undraped figure. Kate wrote it. We've thirty-seven signatures so far."

Gwen's face relaxed as she nodded. "If the life class is considered essential for the success of male students, then it's equally essential for female students. We also rely on this profession for our future livelihood."

Her lips *did* twist subtly rightward.

"Kate couldn't have said it better herself." Lucy pulled her eyes up, meeting Gwen's. Gwen wasn't disagreeable, not exactly. She shunned interaction, braced herself queerly when it was forced upon her, but she didn't strike Lucy as shy either. She knew her own mind. At any rate, she supported the cause, which was all that mattered. Maybe this was the beginning of something like friendship. She and Kate might even entice Gwen to join the Sisterhood. She'd make a wonderful ally.

"You'll sign?" Lucy asked.

"Mum, d'ye mean to ride or to chaff?" The white-haired cabman, who had been tugging his whiskers impatiently, now leaned down, pulling lightly on the reins so the horse pranced a step, the cab wheels knocking on the curb.

"Powers of darkness!" Lucy let out with a shout borrowed from

Mrs. Cantrell. "She'll ride in a moment. You'll get your fare. Make sure it's the legal fare," she added as an afterthought.

Gwen jerked, turning to see whom Lucy addressed.

She hadn't heard the cabman.

Something clicked into place in Lucy's mind. She stepped back, eyes widening. As though she sensed Lucy's new awareness, Gwen blanched. She sprang up into the carriage, skirts dragging on the wheel as she settled herself in the seat and pulled shut the folding door. The cab was off in an instant.

Lucy hardly had the time to reflect on the odd conclusion to her odd encounter. She'd not walked a block when she heard a male voice salute her.

"Miss Coover."

A coach rolling slowly down the street had drawn up alongside her. Weston's coach. Massive, gilded, the coronet emblazoned on the shining black door. Her heart began to pound. He'd talked to Lord Mabeldon!

But it wasn't Weston's voice.

"Mr. Yardley," she said, hitching up her shoulders. Was it disappointment or dislike that made her stiffen? Mr. Yardley threw open the door and descended to the sidewalk, beaming.

"My daughter owes you her good health. Give me the pleasure of driving you home."

"Is Miss Yardley enjoying Paris?" She didn't move. By what right did the man ride about in Weston's coach? It seemed an undue liberty.

"Immensely." His smile broadened. "And I've been enjoying my little visit to the Royal Academy. I was just at the Keeper's House. I told him about your trick with the ammonia. He said your chemistry professor would be delighted. Know your materials, that's Mr. Church's credo. And you certainly do."

She searched Mr. Yardley's face, craggy and genial. She couldn't identify the threat in his expression, or in his speech, but it was there. She sensed it. Why was he discussing her with the Keeper?

"Mr. Church's chemistry lectures have been very helpful to me." She tried to keep her voice level.

"Get in, get in." Mr. Yardley reached out his hand. "Let's talk comfortably."

Protests formed and fractured on her tongue. She hesitated.

"Thank you," she said, "but it's a good deal out of your way."

"Off Charlotte Road, near Mills Court, in Shoreditch. I had the address from Mr. Pickersgill. Oddly enough, I know the building." He shook his head. "I'm a member of the Board of Works, city representative, in the architect's office. The lease was just reviewed at our last meeting."

He observed her for a moment. "You're shocked. So was I. Your address shocked me, I'll admit it. Come, we've much to discuss."

Lucy put her foot on the step and allowed him to help her up into the coach. She slid into her seat warily, setting her bag at her feet. After a curt word to the coachman, Mr. Yardley climbed up after her, sprawling onto the bench opposite. At once, the coach began to roll, the horses clopping over the cobblestones.

"Speaking with the Keeper made me reflect again on my days as a student." Mr. Yardley crossed his legs, flinging an arm across the back of the bench. He was the picture of ease, utterly relaxed. Meanwhile, Lucy smoothed her skirts, trying to keep her knees from bouncing. Her nerves were jangling.

"We were still at Trafalgar Square. Boys in shirtsleeves, working with high spirits under the dome of the roof. It was cramped, but invigorating. We could hear the bells of St. Martin's. You must find it dismal, descending into the earth."

She smiled a tight smile. She'd heard and read plenty of commentaries, older men—artists and critics—harkening back to the glory of yesteryear. High-spirited boys under the dome, before the invasion of the pinafores.

"It's all I've known," she said. "I can't complain."

"You appreciate what you have." Mr. Yardley nodded. "It's to be commended. *You* are to be commended. You've worked hard. I recognize ambition and I respect it. I was ambitious, as a young architect. But, like you, I lacked certain advantages. My fellow students were designing interiors for the country homes of their family friends. My father couldn't provide such connections. He was in the timber trade. He did business in Shoreditch, actually."

He gave a one-armed shrug. "I didn't want to design warehouses, but I had to establish myself somehow. Perhaps I ruined myself, from the artistic standpoint. After a while, the odor of commerce clings to everything you touch."

He was still stung by her comments about Weston Hall. The coach began a wide turn. She allowed its motion to act upon her, sliding closer to the window. She edged aside the shade, praying for an inspiration, a rush of ameliorating words carried in with the breeze. She watched a hansom cab speed past, not Gwen's. It was bright red, the driver young and dapper.

"You must be wondering why I've sought you out."

She turned her head. He looked serious. Even so, the lines fanned out from his eyes, signs of good humor. His physiognomy suggested pleasantness. Why did he make her skin crawl?

"I am responsible for His Grace," he said. "I made a promise to his father."

Responsible?

"His Grace isn't a child." As soon as she spoke the words, she wanted to retract them. Mr. Yardley drew his long upper lip down over his teeth, an exaggerated frown.

"He is a danger, Miss Coover, to himself and to others. I am tasked with protecting him from his worst self. You know, I presume, that he was not the heir. Have you heard what became of his older brother?"

She cleared her throat. "He drowned, I believe."

Mr. Yardley smiled a thin, sad smile.

"Drink was a devil for him, as it is for His Grace."

She shifted on her seat. It was remarkably comfortable. Gwen would have discovered by now that the seats of hansom cabs might as well be stuffed with rocks.

She couldn't relax into the soft leather. Her body was rigid.

"You will not feel insulted, I hope, if I say I do not trust that His Grace has employed you as his painting teacher for the right reasons." Mr. Yardley uncrossed his legs. He was so tall their knees might have brushed if she didn't angle her legs to the side.

"You should not trust it either. I say this for your sake, as a father. I understand you don't have a father of your own. The outcome I predict from these lessons, should they continue, is . . . how to put it? *Not* a picture of a horse."

Blood roared in Lucy's ears. The lids of Mr. Yardley's kindly blue eyes drooped slightly at the corners.

"I've upset you," he murmured. "But it couldn't be helped." He rapped his knuckles against the bench. Once, twice.

"I have a proposal," he said, leaning forward. "We can help each other. You were served with a thirteen-week notice of eviction. I can see to it that you are rehoused within the month."

She pressed her back harder into the seat behind her. What about the Cantrells? The Stavelys? The Pritchards?

"Thank you, but there's nothing wrong with the building. That's the rub." It came out saucier than she intended. Oh well. She leveled her gaze at him. "It's not rehousing I want. I mean to stay where I am, all of us do. Once Lord Mabeldon is made aware of the irregularity—"

She broke off. His expression of concern made her stomach lurch. She realized she was twisting her hair and locked her hands together, forcing them down onto her lap.

"His Grace told you he would intercede with Mabeldon?" Mr. Yardley's concern was for *her*. Mortification turned her to stone. The coach bumped over broken pavement, but she sat scarcely breathing, immovable.

Mr. Yardley sighed. "Perhaps he meant it. But he won't follow through. And even if he did, he's a pup. Lord Mabeldon won't heed his yapping."

His confidence devastated. Tears pricked her eyes. But she held them back.

"The buildings were condemned without inspection. Lord Mabeldon *must* listen. Someone is lying."

"If that's so, the board will discover it. But I will be the one to talk to Mabeldon. His Grace doesn't understand the first thing about government. There's a procedure with these kinds of charges. A special committee must be formed to investigate."

He crossed his legs again. His suit was well cut. He was the bulky sort of man who ran to fat in later years. If he visited a less capable tailor, he might look portly.

"My offer to rehouse you stands," he said. "Should the committee's findings support the eviction."

"They won't!"

He blinked at her vehemence, then nodded.

"Of course not," he said smoothly. "So, that's all settled. Now, you ask, how can you help me? It's simple—by helping His Grace."

She was riveted despite herself.

"His Grace does not control his fortune. I control it." Mr. Yardley brushed the lapel of his jacket absently as he spoke, as though minimizing his importance.

Don't mind me. I simply control one of the largest fortunes in England.

"Before he died, his father came to the painful conclusion that full inheritance would lead to disaster, for Anthony, for the family, the dukedom. This may sound extreme, Miss Coover, but it is not. We had to sell a small island in Scotland to settle the debts of the first son."

This *we* rang strangely in her ear. How intertwined had they been, Weston's father and Yardley?

"George's death outweighed all the debts, of course. Weston the elder couldn't survive the loss of one son and his only daughter. It was too much for him."

"But Lady Euphemia is alive."

Mr. Yardley raised a pale brow. "His Grace told you that? She may be, but she may not be. She is—was—a girl bent on self-destruction. Perhaps you know that their mother died by her own hand? Such things are terrible legacies."

She averted her face, looking out the window at the traffic, horse and pedestrian, the low brick houses. She could hop out and walk.

"I make the financial decisions. I run the household in London. I run the estates. Relieved of these responsibilities, His Grace might be attending to his moral character and learning the parliamentary process, as his father intended. Unfortunately, he is not. He could, if he followed the rules imposed upon him by the will, inherit at thirty."

Lucy turned back. Mr. Yardley raked a hand through his thick hair, gingery white. She smiled crookedly.

"But he won't inherit," she said, watching Mr. Yardley's face. "Or has he followed the rules?"

"An interesting question." He rapped again on the bench with his knuckles. "The short answer is no. But the solicitors need more to go on if we're to avoid a legal contest. And that is where you may be of help."

"Oh?" She leaned back into her seat. Perhaps she *would* hop out. The coach was slowing in heavy traffic.

"No alcohol, not a drop. His Grace's father was clear on that point. I have reason to believe His Grace has flouted that rule on any number of occasions. If not daily."

Her heart began to hammer. "What reason is that?"

"I know His Grace. I've known him since he was a boy."

She couldn't help herself. "Then you know drink was never *a devil* for him, before all of this." She waved her hand vaguely. What was *this*? Family tragedy, the burden of unexpected responsibility.

"He was in the army," she continued. "He fought in the war. He had that discipline."

Heaven help her. Next thing she knew she'd be talking about his bloody heroism. Thank God Kate couldn't hear it.

"Discipline? He's lucky he wasn't executed." Mr. Yardley's eyes bored through her. "He was jailed for drink in Afghanistan. Did he tell you that? He stole liquor from the brigadier general on the retreat from Maiwand and collapsed. They left him like a dog in the road, but he managed to crawl to Kandahar. If his father hadn't humbled himself before Her Majesty, the court-martial would have returned a different verdict."

Court-martial.

She was silent. She could feel her face flaming. Why had she tried to believe him when all the evidence was stacked against him? He was a drunkard, and he was a liar. The innocent, worshipful little brother. Her lips curled.

"That story is not whispered in London, because I did everything in my power to suppress it. His Grace doesn't thank me for my help. In fact, he thwarts my efforts at every opportunity. His first order of business when he returned was to visit the very brothel best loved by his brother. He assaulted a man on the steps. Did you see that column? I assure you his father did. He had to pay the damages. Then there was the window at All Saints."

Mr. Yardley's smile twisted.

"The will forbids scandal. One article in the gossip column recording another such incident, public drunkenness, a brawl, and I can delay His Grace's inheriting to prolong his life. He needs a heavy yoke."

The coach was pulling to the right, stopping alongside the curb on Charlotte Road.

"When he bankrupts the estates, he's not the only one who will suffer. There are tenants, Miss Coover. Farms. Schools."

She put out her hand and watched her fingers close around the door handle. She took a deep breath.

"You want me to set him up."

Mr. Yardley considered gravely, as though it were a question. "I don't want more publicity. I don't want the Weston name selling papers. But I want his behavior witnessed, by men who can testify to what they see. If he is capable of behaving with sober dependability, then, of course, he should govern himself and discharge his responsibilities. But if he isn't . . ."

He wasn't. She knew he wasn't. Why did she feel as though she were betraying him? Her betrayal was immaterial.

Weston betrayed himself.

I seem to care. That's what he'd said. He did care, she felt certain. It wasn't an act, his kindness, his easy warmth. But she knew what it was like to put her faith in a kind, warm man who cared, then disappeared into a bottle.

"This special committee," she said, trying to smooth the quaver in her voice. "The special committee to investigate the evictions, you will see that it's appointed."

"I will." Mr. Yardley sat up straighter. He was looking at her expectantly. She nodded. Here was another agreement, less friendly, more likely to bear fruit. Odd that she felt something withering inside her. She spoke in a voice she didn't recognize.

"Send your witnesses to look for him tomorrow night."

She knew how to ensure that Weston met her in public where temptation abounded. All she had to do was pick the theater and name the time.

"Ten o'clock," she said. "The Albion Theatre."

CHAPTER ELEVEN

THE CROWD CRUSHING into the Albion made it difficult to chart a course. Anthony stood to the side, letting people flow past. His heart, which had raced since he'd received Miss Coover's note, now skipped a beat.

His sister sang *here*.

The building was vast, blue smoke hanging in the gaslights. The pit was already packed with rowdy men and grinning urchins. As he scanned the galleries, the audience surged to its feet, applauding wildly. He was tall enough to see the source of their wonder. Cleopatra's barge had just appeared on the main stage in a mist of perfume. By what vaporizing mechanism was the perfume dispersed? He couldn't determine the source. The perfume rolled over the audience like a cloud, its sweetness mingled with the odors of smoke and grease. Cheers, boos, and some bottles rained down from the highest gallery.

With his field glasses, Anthony scrutinized Cleopatra, black-haired, voluptuous, but pert-nosed with a mouth like a bud. An English rose with kohl on her eyes and a wig on her head, doused in jasmine. He swung the glasses. On the other stages, chorus girls kicking, comic ballerinas mincing. No and no. Effie was not among them.

He turned, sweeping the crowd. Magnified, Lucy Coover's face filled the field of vision. She was looking toward the entrance. Looking for him. Several men in caps and shabby jackets interposed themselves between his lenses and the object of interest. Then he could see her again, the wiry strands in the locks snaking down from her high twist of hair, the red and auburn tints. Detail was revelatory. He picked out the patterns of golden and cinnamon freckles on her cheeks. A darker freckle lay near the left peak of her lip. Dear God, he'd neglected that freckle, a mistake he'd like to remedy. The field glasses were revealing his errors, his oversights. Her lips were parted, the bottom lip plumped out. He studied the faint line where the plush of it divided.

His breathing constricted.

As though she could hear his thoughts, her eyes turned and focused. The warm amber irises reduced to twin slivers.

He lowered the glasses. Miss Coover stood yards away. Detail had made him miss the larger picture. Her ruby gown was a column of pleated silk that stretched around the curves of her breasts and hips. Free of corsetry. Free even—he swallowed—of all but the bare minimum of undergarments.

A fine figure, she'd said.

Had her aunt made that dress? And let her walk out the door in it? He watched as she wove her way toward him. She had to pause again and again to let streams of people flow past, many of the men—and a few of the women—craning their necks to gawk. Even so, she made good progress. Not afraid to use her elbows.

He'd borrowed Humphreys's clothing for the occasion. No one looked twice at him. In a baggy jacket and corduroy trousers, flat cap low on his brow, he blended. A very good thing. There'd be hell to pay if he were recognized out with such a woman.

Suddenly, she was before him, as close as she'd looked through the glasses.

"By all means, use them," she said tartly. "Reconnoiter a route to open seats." She glanced toward the pit, intercepting a male gaze, hot and insolent. She stared back until the man whispered something to his companion and they both turned, laughing. She shook her head, running her fingers along the little red beads sewn up the sides of the gown. He knew what she was thinking. The men who ogled *her* missed the point. *The dress* deserved attention. She was the mannequin, displaying it. But the freedom of her movements, the boldness of her gaze, her strong, supple, *contemporary* body made the dress come alive. In short, she mesmerized. The dress was stunning, yes. But Miss Coover—with that defiant chin and animal confidence— she could start a fad for sackcloth.

Did she always take the opportunity of a night out to advertise her aunt's most daring designs?

"Give them to me, then," she said. He handed the field glasses over. They were too plain to pass as opera glasses, made of heavy, dented brass. She swept the gallery and the stage and the ornate walls of the building itself, turning in a slow circle. He glared at the men who hovered to enjoy the view. He'd be lucky if he made it out of here tonight without a riot.

"Wonderful," she said, sighing. "I'd like a pair myself."

He took them from her, dropping them in his pocket with a smile. "Your eyes are sharp enough." Too sharp, some might say.

She shrugged. "For now."

A blond man, broken-nosed and bull-necked, stopped to stare. Anthony edged close to Miss Coover, leaning over her, dropping his voice to an intimate rumble.

"Do you know the freckles on your left cheek make the Pleiades?"

She glared. "So does the spatter of mud on my left shoe. Turn your binoculars on that." But her lips twitched. From the corner of his eye, he saw the blond boxer move on.

"I can't be sure she's here." She spoke quickly, a line between her brows. "I hope I didn't promise too much. Priscilla Millard—she's a singer—she said she remembered a Nixon, a dark girl, in some of the musical acts, but . . . she might have been mistaken, or this might be an off night."

He nodded, wanting to put her at ease. She sounded defensive, as though anticipating his bad reaction to a bad outcome.

"Not to worry. Either way I've gained an evening in your company."

Despite himself, he uttered this bit of gallantry in earnest. She heard it, his sudden sincerity. If before she'd sounded defensive, now she looked . . . pained. Her throat worked as she swallowed.

"We should enjoy it," he said. He'd been disappointed so many times, constructing Effie from glimpses. Masses of rich black hair disappearing into a doorway. A bold profile passing in a hansom cab. The glimpses never materialized into the whole.

Miss Coover was here, in the flesh. He'd be mad not to appreciate every second.

He gave her a slow smile, taking her arm and steering them through the crowd. "What do you most enjoy at the theater?"

"The acrobats," she said immediately. "When they climb on one another's shoulders to make pyramids. It's amazing what they can do. It's living sculpture. Oh, and the scenery, of course. And the costumes. What about you?"

She didn't wait for him to answer.

"The horses," she said at the same time he did. They both burst into laughter. Their rib cages expanded and her arm, her breast, pushed into his side.

"I went to all the battles staged at Astley's," he said. "Any hippodrama, anywhere, I was there."

"Cut the cackle and come to the 'osses," boomed Miss Coover. "That's what Aunt Marian says whenever anyone mentions horse drama."

He grinned. "No one goes for the dialogue, it's true. Who needs lines? The band strikes up, the hooves pound, the muskets pop." He shook his head. "It was my idea of paradise."

She snorted, but the corners of her mouth still twitched with mirth.

How easy it could feel between them. How *enjoyable*, despite the inauspicious circumstances. A man and a woman flirting at the theater. The air was warm, even sticky. They stopped as a mass of men shoved by, sailors. He took the opportunity to loosen his collar. She traipsed about without a corset. Why mightn't he undo a button? As he spread the fabric, he saw her eyes slide to his throat and cling for a moment. He grinned so hard he had to bite the inside of his cheek.

But suddenly, she sobered, squaring her shoulders. Her gaze grew penetrating.

"I'll enjoy myself more fully, I'm sure," she said, "once I have your assurances that the condemned buildings have been saved. How did Lord Mabeldon receive you?"

Startled, he stepped back. For some reason, he hadn't expected she'd speak so directly, so briskly, press him so soon. But of course. She faced eviction. Her aunt, too, those little girls and their adventuresome dolls. An evening out at the theater brought her no joy, in the circumstances.

"Lord Mabeldon did not receive me." He let the words fill the sudden gulf between them. He'd set out to call, via the glasshouse, where a tipple made him maudlin. On the street, he'd spied a cab drawn by a familiar-looking horse, starved but blue-blooded, an old thoroughbred, once a favorite on the racecourse. He and Cecil used to watch him race when they were boys. He forced the cabby to take him to his license owner, from whom he'd bought the decayed creature for the change in his pocket. That's what he'd done with himself these past two days, played nursemaid to a half-dead stallion in the stable, taking breaks to fortify himself with his own medicine of choice.

But he *would* talk to Mabeldon. This was simply the preparatory stage. How to explain that to a woman who squeezed what she could from every minute?

He cleared his throat. "I'm biding my time. As I mentioned, Lord Mabeldon and I aren't on firm footing. I need to approach our meeting strategically."

The inadequacy—the sheer inanity—of this must have struck her as it struck him. Her face blurred with emotion. He distinguished hurt, disgust, anger, and then, something worse, resignation. When he took her arm again, it felt limp in his own.

Reassurances rose to his lips. He'd call on Mabeldon first thing in the morning. He'd get there even if he had to pass by rainspouts pouring pink gin, even if he had to pass by Lord Lyon, escaped from the stud farm at Shepherd's Bush. But her head was turned away, her attention elsewhere.

As they settled into their seats and the performance began, he *felt* her restlessness. Each twitch of her body passed into his. He hadn't fidgeted as much studying for his trials at Eton. Her elbow bumped him repeatedly as she twisted a strand of hair with her fingers. Finally, he caught the elbow, held it still, cupped it in his hand between their bodies. She froze at his touch. The easiness between them—the natural physical sympathy—not gone, but muffled. He had spoiled the mood. Maybe he could charm her by describing Snap, the old thoroughbred.

Funny story, he'd say. And he'd tell her how he recognized him by the white sock on his pastern. Chased down the cab. He'd present it as a tale of rescue. Leave off the part about turning around en route to Mabeldon's, neglecting his side of the bargain.

Christ but he was useless.

Cymbals crashed below. A group of home soldiers at the end of the row laughed uproariously, calling out to a pretty barmaid.

She turned to him, said something inaudible.

"What?" He tipped his head. Her lips brushed his ear. Her husky voice whispered as though inside him.

"Do you see her?"

"No." He shook his head, felt her chin against his jaw, her mouth skimming the outer edge of his ear. Air puffed from her lips, tick-ling.

The theater manufactured sensation on a large scale. But there was also this other, less spectacular excitement, the excitement to be found in the heated darkness.

Surely, the Albion had its private boxes, its velvet couches. Places where he might lay Miss Coover down, stroke away the nervous mo-tion of her limbs, spend her, make her languid. Win her back with kisses.

He focused on the main stage, where scenes from *Antony and Cleopatra* continued to unfold. The barge was gone and a Roman festival was underway. Fantastical flowers of every color were strewn over the stage and goddesses in golden togas processed upon them. In her thin dress, Miss Coover wouldn't have looked out of place among them. She adjusted her head.

"Not the one on the right?"

He didn't bother with the glasses. The black-haired goddess was too slight. Effie was short, but she inclined to plumpness. Or had these recent months harrowed her, whittled her down? His jaw clenched at the thought. He squinted. No, it wasn't her. Miss Coover felt the negation in his movement.

When Cleopatra's maids presented the baskets of figs, and their round, unfamiliar faces, he sighed.

"Time to go," he said. He wouldn't keep her out all night on what had proved to be a fool's errand.

Lucy's knees complained as she rose. Good. A reminder of Aunt Marian. She needed it, to strengthen her resolve. She'd spent the show sweating, attention divided between the stage and the galler-ies. Who in the audience had been sent by Yardley to witness Weston's undoing?

Weston had risen too. She felt him at her elbow. Risked a glance.

It was difficult to read his expression. She saw disappointment, certainly. But also solicitude, an unexpected gentleness. He worried that she was disappointed too, that she felt culpable.

She did feel culpable, but not for the reason he assumed.

God help her, she *liked* this man. She didn't want to deceive him, even though he hadn't talked to Mabeldon. Even though he was proving himself blatantly unreliable, the selfish *pup* Yardley described. But protecting him would leave her vulnerable. He was his own worst enemy. She would not allow him to become hers. Her knees twinged as she turned.

Nor her Aunt Marian's.

Two men, shabby, mouths hidden by drooping mustaches, stood at the end of the row, staring. Stomach leaping, she stared back. One nodded, almost imperceptibly. Well then. The thing was already set into motion. Weston touched her shoulder.

"Care for a drink?" he asked. She sipped the air, its sweet smokiness. *He* did this. The fault was not hers, come what may.

"If you do," she murmured and started edging toward the aisle without looking back at him.

It took some time to maneuver along the promenade to the canteen below the main stage. Weston kept her in the protective circle of his arm, and she held her body rigid, tried not to brush against him as they pushed through the crowd.

Theatergoers packed the canteen, which was lurid in its luxuriance, crystal chandeliers overhead, red silk wall coverings. They sat in red velvet chairs pulled close together, Weston draping an arm casually across his chair's curved back.

"Champagne?" His eyes glowed. The chandeliers quivered as men stomped and women laughed, scattered lights moving subtly across his face. He flung one leg over the other, boot resting on his knee, a careless pose, but she could sense his agitation.

Now he was distracted, gaze trained on the trays floating past, held high by waiters in black jackets and red waistcoats. Glasses rattled on those trays, contents glinting. Ochre, amber, umber, drag-on's blood, Tyrian purple.

A familiar, lonely little hole opened up inside her.

Weston's raised finger summoned one of those waiters to his side. Lucy looked away, glanced about the canteen. Couples laughing at round tables. Brassy-haired chorus girls. Young swells in tight suits. Those two shabby men, motionless in the sea of gaiety, still staring. Her stomach leapt again. What an incautious fool Weston was; how weakly he cleaved to his purpose. No wonder he hadn't found his sister. It was so much easier to find a waiter, potboy, barkeep.

Not her fault.

When the champagne arrived, she emptied her glass before setting it on the table. Weston made a small noise in his throat, surprise or amusement.

"Thirsty?" He handed her his glass and she took it, tipping it this way and that so the foam slid over the lip, dripped down the flute. She licked it off her fingers, and when she looked up, she saw him watching her.

"It's yours," he said, waving to the waiter. "I prefer gin."

Her father had preferred gin too. She leaned back and drank the second glass of champagne. The bubbles filled her throat and she had to work to push them down. A hard swallow, like gravel. She could feel it move into her chest.

"Let's go." She spoke without thinking, and Weston offered her a smile, not the boyish grin. A dark smile.

"You're tired," he observed, and blood rose into her cheeks. Over his shoulder, she could see those two men, twin lumps, infinitely patient. They'd grow into the furniture sooner than abandon their mission. They didn't care how long it took.

"I'll take you home," said Weston. He reached out as the waiter materialized and lifted the gin from the tray.

"Soon," he said. "I'm thirsty too." For a moment, he held the tumbler in two hands, base resting on one palm, long, beautiful fingers wrapped around it. Oddly tender. Loathing lanced through her. She remembered her father sprawled on the staircase, head bowed over a bottle, crooning to it like it was his baby. Lavishing care where it didn't belong. He'd chosen that bottle over his own wife, his own daughter.

Weston had chosen it over his fellow soldiers. Over his word, his pledge to her. Over his sister. She settled deeper into her chair. A burst of laughter traveled the room.

"How much does it take?" Her voice carried, low and harsh. "How much gin?"

He let one hand drop and held the glass higher, looking into it, as though the gin were a transparent, burning eye, looking back at him. Then he set the glass on the table, looked at her, and shrugged.

"How much gin before I fall over? Attack a Burne-Jones? Wake up naked in an alley? It depends."

He was striving for lightness, a bantering tone better suited to the merriment around them. But his free hand had flattened on his knee, the knuckles going white, and his face had set in grim lines.

"No," she said, quieter. "How much is enough? Forever. So you don't need it anymore. So that . . ."

Her throat felt roughened inside. She stopped, then began again.

"I wanted him to choose us," she said. "To choose my mother. To choose *me*. But he wouldn't."

Or couldn't. Did it matter in the end?

"There wasn't enough gin, ever." She drew a breath. Why was she saying this? Mortification didn't make her stop.

"He always wanted more," she said. "Until . . ."

She knotted her hands, pressed her lips together. At first, she didn't think he'd heard. Her words had frayed into wisps, scarcely audible, and he hadn't moved a muscle. He sat perfectly still, his face unreadable. She felt sick. All the red silk, the red velvet, the quaking light. Her chair was sticky. As she shifted, the fabric of her dress resisted, clinging to an invisible stain.

Suddenly, he raked a hand over his face, into his hair. A muscle ticked in his jaw. She realized then, in an instant, that he'd heard; he'd heard clearly. No distraction now. His green gaze was fixed on her, its intensity almost unbearable.

"We'll go now," he said. He reached into his pocket for coin, and in that moment, released from his gaze, she glanced over his shoulder. Angling through the throngs, eyes scanning the tables, a tall, pleasant-looking man, who paused now and again to permit some lady's passage.

No. She exhaled. It was Robert Yardley. He'd come himself to witness Weston's folly. He hadn't seen them yet, but he was mere yards away. The glass of gin stood on the table at Weston's elbow, accusing him. A mad impulse seized her. She would not let him be caught with it. Suddenly, the glass was in her hand and she'd tipped it back. The taste was pure poison. She spluttered, rising, thrusting the glass behind her, wedging it into the cushion. Weston froze. A shilling slipped from his fingers, clattered on the tabletop.

"What are you doing?" His gaze sharpened, slicing her. She closed her fingers on his wrist, felt the warm pulse there, pounding.

"Hurry," she gasped. He allowed her to tug him forward, but as he did so, he swiveled his head, and she felt the jolt move from his body into hers. He whipped his head around and their gazes locked.

"Why is he here." It wasn't a question. His voice was terrible with knowledge. She couldn't speak, just shook her head, tugged harder. He needed no prompting. Together they plunged into the crowd.

CHAPTER TWELVE

WHEN THEY REACHED the passage at the back of the canteen, she released his wrist, throwing a pained look over her shoulder as she sped ahead, turning down another corridor. He followed.

They were passing under the side stages. The stage machinery made curious obstacles. He watched her navigate around levers and piles of rope. The air was colder but thicker, more redolent of perfume and also horse manure. A goddess peered from a doorway, waiting for someone, not them. The sound of the orchestra deafened. She reached the stairs and climbed. He took the first few two at a time to close the distance between them. When she swayed backward, he caught her against his chest and propelled her up to the narrow landing. In the alleyway behind the theater, cabmen were waiting for the actresses, smoking pipes. His ears rang.

He steered them a ways down the street, then spun her around so she faced him.

She didn't want to face him. Her eyes darted everywhere else.

"You told Yardley where to find us." He moved closer, towering over her. "Why?"

She stood by the streetlight, in that glowing circle. The silk of her dress glowed jewel bright. Her breasts rose and fell rapidly, pushing against the lightweight fabric. He ran his eyes over her, the smooth outline of her natural form.

Slowly, things were clicking into place. She'd dressed to stand out, to draw curious eyes, to *him*.

"Next time paint the dress on your body." His mouth curled with derision. "See if that gets you *more* attention."

Her lips had parted. She was flushed—not with emotion, with drink.

"Was there ever a Mrs. Nixon at the Albion?" He laughed humorlessly. "I'm twice the fool."

She stared at the ground, the broken glass glittering by her feet.

"He didn't see you," she said. "Those men did, with the mustaches, but they've nothing to report. I'm the only one who drank."

She wrapped her arms tightly around herself and met his eyes. Suddenly, she looked vulnerable. Miserable. He forced a laugh.

"What men? Reporters?" *Christ.* What kind of trap had she orchestrated? She'd tried to blackmail him. Perhaps she'd tried to blackmail Yardley as well. Told him what she knew about Effie and his own late-night pursuits. Threatened to tip off the *Pall Mall Gazette*. Yardley was devoted to suppressing gossip, removing the tarnish from the Weston coronet. Had he come to the Albion to protect him from Miss Coover? To keep him from making a very public and irreversible mistake? Drunk and on display with a flagrant wanton. "Answer me."

Miss Coover said nothing. He could see the dizziness sweep over her.

"You're stewed." He took her arm and pulled her out of the light, into the mouth of an alleyway, where they weren't displayed to passersby.

"A smidgen stewed. But so what?" She tried to break his grip. "You're not," she said. "That's what matters. Although"—she tried to free her arm again, and he dropped it like a hot coal—"I don't know why I care. You're determined to sabotage yourself. If not tonight, some other night."

Even in the shadow, he could see her eyes snapping, the shine of bared teeth.

She drew a shuddering breath, then threw her next words in his face. "I think you're *afraid* to inherit."

They stared at each other. The silence grew brittle.

He spoke softly. "Who said anything about my inheritance?"

How could she know about the codicil? The capstone in the arch of family secrets. He let his gaze bore into her until she licked her lips, looked away.

"I misspoke." Again, she hugged her midsection, but the gesture was exaggerated, a bad performance. "I'm tired. I don't feel well. Let me pass. I'm going home."

"Accuse a man of cowardice, then run away?" He shook his head. "That's hardly sporting."

"I forgot, you're sensitive about your heroism," she sneered. "Apologies, Your Grace, you're brave as a lion."

He barred the alley with his arm, and she gave his biceps a hard push. Not hard enough. She pushed harder.

"Welcome to the lion's den." His smile was unpleasant. "Push me again, and we'll stay here all night."

It wouldn't be his first night spent in an alleyway.

She abandoned her efforts and regarded him warily.

"Yardley put you up to this." He said it slowly. "He told you about the will. He wanted to catch me out, and you let him buy your help."

He pressed his fist into the brick. The double betrayal maddened him. He wanted to stamp and snort, like a horse beset by bees.

He was as weak-minded as everyone believed.

"Blame him, blame me." She shrugged, her indifference damning. "Anyone but yourself."

Her hair was half-down, the twist she'd anchored with pins in the process of untwisting.

"You lied to me; he didn't," she said. "You said you'd talk to Mabeldon. He said you wouldn't. Tell me who I should put my trust in."

"Spare me your justifications," he muttered. He pounded his fist into the bricks, once, twice, three times, mind reeling. All Yardley's encouragement, all his prattle about self-control and the House of Lords—worthless. He expected Anthony to fail. *Wanted* him to fail.

"I don't have to justify myself." She was pallid but she didn't flinch. How had she come by this equanimity? It was dark. It was late. An infuriated male was smashing the wall of the alley in which he'd penned her. But somehow, she persisted. In other circumstances, he'd be the first to admire her mettle.

Overheated, he snatched the cap from his head and stuffed it in a pocket, rocking on his heels. His jaw felt like flint.

"I acted in my best interests, in my aunt's best interests, in the best interests of my neighbors," she said firmly. "What would you have me do? Risk the roof over my head to protect your vanity?"

"More than my vanity is at stake."

"Because you won't follow your father's rules." She shrugged. "You said you're not a drunkard. Don't drink."

"I didn't drink," he grated out. He'd pushed away his gin because of the look in her eyes.

"I don't mean tonight." She stood straighter. No, he would not be touched by that either, her small, upraised chin, her stiffened spine. "Tonight . . . I was surprised."

"Surprised? How gratifying." He smiled. "And here I thought you saw me as an open book. You seem an expert on my shortcomings. Cowardice, vanity. There are others in addition, I know. I'll defer to you. Gluttony, of course, but it turns out I can allow at least one glass of gin to slip through my fingers."

"If you can, why don't you?"

His laughter echoed blackly between the bricks. "It's not so simple. Why should I follow my father's rules? He didn't amend his will because I broke a bloody window. He wanted to break *me*. Do you understand?"

She didn't, of course. How could she? But Yardley understood it all, perfectly. Pain twisted in his chest, and he jammed the heel of his hand inside his coat. Miss Coover's eyes had widened. He could see the glassy whites through the gloom.

"My mother drank," he said, his voice emerging as a rasp. "She was unfaithful. My father packed her off to the asylum. The doctors said it was nymphomania. I didn't know the diagnosis, I didn't know the word, until I heard it in the schoolyard."

Bloody days. But he'd given as good as he'd got. With George's help.

"I look like her. I have her face, her weak mind, weak character. That's what he thought, what he *said*. Christ, I couldn't wait to get away from him."

From George, too. God forgive him.

"The army wasn't what I imagined. War wasn't a spectacle, was nothing like Waterloo played on the stage at Astley's." There was an understatement. Again, his black laughter echoed, and he had to breathe slowly through his nose before he could go on. "But for the first time, I lived my own life. *Mine*."

The ghost of an expression flitted across her face, something akin to tenderness. Then she gave a slight shake of her head.

"I know about the court-martial." She whispered it, but even so the words cut like a knife. He edged closer, until he could make out the cluster of freckles on her cheek, the Pleiades. How distant he felt from that giddy moment of discovery—the field glasses revealing an asterism of dark gold flecks.

"He told you that too." He heard himself say it, the deadly calm astonishing him. "And what did he say?"

She was too quick, too perceptive, to mistake his purring tone for velvet. Beneath, it was all claw. She licked her lips, pausing before she formed her words.

"You behaved . . . dishonorably."

"How?"

She spoke slowly, watching his face. "Conspicuous inebriation."

"Yardley said I was drunk?" His throat constricted. *You don't have to explain.* He had thought Yardley assumed the best of him, not the worst of him. "I was charged with theft and desertion. Theft of the officers' rum rations, of course. Are you satisfied?"

"You told me you didn't drink before . . ."

"Before my brother died? I didn't."

She fit her knuckle between her teeth and bit down. She *wasn't* satisfied. She wanted to believe him. The realization shook him queerly. He took another deep breath through his nose, thinking of those scorching, dust-choked days, the things he'd seen and couldn't forget, though he'd never put them into words.

"You were at the Battle of Maiwand," she ventured. "I believe . . . it was a defeat?"

A defeat.

"My God," he said. "It was a rout."

In the moment, it had seemed an apocalypse. The end of the world. Would he really talk about this now, speak of that horror for the first time, to *her*, in a reeking alley? He struggled to find his way. How to begin?

"It was . . . senseless. Dust, blood, smoke, ceaseless flashes of light. Squadrons broke in all directions. By the time the general sounded the retire, we had no formation. Men were trampled by camels, fell onto their own bayonets. Some had made it as far as the village gardens and died fighting or huddled against the wall."

"Where were you?" She barely breathed it.

"The gardens," he said. "You talked of flayed men cast for anatomical study. That day I saw bodies peeled apart, ligaments and bones laid bare."

He stopped short. Began again.

"We made our way back to Kandahar, fifty miles, harassed by the

Afghan cavalry, no food or forage. The wounded rode on the guns or in wagons, on camels, donkeys. A few of us had horses. We came to a spring on the main road, but it was dry. The infantrymen broke into the mess supplies and drank what they could, the medicine, the officers' stores of liquor."

He read the question in her eyes.

"If I'd walked those twenty miles to that dry spring, with the prospect of thirty more to go, I might have done it too. They were mad with thirst. I wasn't."

He hadn't taken a sip from the plundered bottles.

"The general ordered us to leave the ones too drunk to walk in the road. They'd have been butchered."

She gave a little nod. "You tried to wake them."

"I roused who I could. We'd hardly started after the column when we came under fire. Mizoa, my horse, was shot out from beneath me."

He exhaled. She was gnawing her knuckle again, eyes haunted.

"I hit my head, lost consciousness. One of those infantrymen dragged me behind the rocks, stayed with me while the rest scattered. When the two of us reached Kandahar at last, we were arrested."

"But you were innocent of the charges!" She uttered it with warmth. "That infantryman could have told them."

How peculiar: now she was his champion. He shook his head.

"Humphreys wasn't in any to position to speak." In addition to sharing the charges, he was nearly dead when they reached the garrison, hallucinating from dehydration. "But regardless, if I was innocent of theft, drunkenness, and desertion, my only defense was insubordination. I disobeyed direct orders to help those men."

"It's not the same." She'd pushed out her lower jaw. "You obeyed the dictates of your conscience. That's a higher order. If conscience goes unheeded, we're lost. Sometimes humanity *demands* insubordination."

Her stubbornness had the power to charm when deployed on his behalf.

"I'd like to hear you say that to a military judge," he said dryly.

"He wouldn't like it when I was through with him."

"I don't doubt it." He laughed, scrubbing a hand across his forehead. He could picture it.

In the end, the judges had barely entertained the case against him. Nothing to do with conscience. Everything to do with his father.

"In any event, I was acquitted. With honor." Perversely, the acquittal was the beginning of the nightmare.

She was staring, face shadowed, jaw tensed, brows two sable slashes, marking her forehead with a frown. She took a breath, as though to respond, then gave herself a little shake. Her last hairpin had loosened and a mass of curls fell across her shoulders. She shoved it back, peering past him at the street, almost empty.

"What time is it?"

He told her, slipping the watch back into his pocket.

She groaned. "I'll be ruined for tomorrow."

"Shall we, then?" He extended his arm. She looked at it until he sighed and took her elbow.

"You don't hold me in high esteem, I know, but you're mad if you think I'll allow you to walk these streets alone at this hour."

"I walk where and when I please," she muttered, but she didn't resist, her weight warming his side.

When they turned off Charlotte Road and stopped in front of the dress shop, she slipped free, leaning her back against the door.

"Run," she advised, closing her eyes. "If Aunt Marian wakes up and sees you, you'll wish you were at Maiwand."

But retreat wasn't an option. He waited, and Miss Coover spoke again. "I didn't sleep much last night, or the night before." She laughed. "Or the night before."

She sighed and opened her eyes. "You're still here," she observed. "Well, I'm going in. As soon as I dislodge this rock from my shoe."

He glanced down. She was rubbing one muddy slipper on the

other. When he glanced up, her eyes were closed again. "Dislodge it inside," he suggested, and swept her into his arms.

Her room was at the top of a narrow back staircase. As he maneuvered through the doorway, her elbow connected with his solar plexus and he grunted.

"Put me down," she said. He obliged her, so rapidly she clung to him to keep her balance. Her weight depending from his lapels brought his neck down. He touched the top of her head lightly with his lips, feeling the roughened silk of her curls. Did she feel it, his mouth on her hair, his breath against her scalp?

She held still a moment longer, then turned away from him and lit the lamp. Light flared up along the steeply sloped ceiling. He crossed his arms, afraid to move for the clutter. Canvases leaned facedown against the walls, in stacks of threes and fours, reducing the square of usable space. The crude shelves nailed to the walls displayed a collection of bottles filled with brilliant powders. A little table beside the easel held glasses of murky water. The floor was covered with cloth spattered with all the colors of the rainbow. The bed, small, plain, shoved along the wall, seemed an afterthought.

Sighing, she took off her shoes. She dropped them on a paint-spattered cloth, and it squeaked. The cloth rippled.

She rolled her eyes.

"Mr. Malkin was once the fiercest mouser in Britain. He's hung up his sword, sadly."

"That was a mouse?"

"Of course it was a mouse." Her voice sharpened. "We don't have rats."

"Do you make them walk the plank?" he asked. She stared at him; then she followed his gaze to the board propped against the back of a wooden chair and laughed.

"No, that board has a different purpose. I'll show you." She made to climb up onto the chair but her tight dress, and imperfect balance, prevented her.

"You do it," she said. "Slide back the cover."

Perplexed, he took the narrow board. He didn't need to climb onto the chair. He raised the board to the ceiling.

"There aren't any windows up here," she said. "So I made a skylight. Well, it's almost a skylight. It's a hole really, with a pad of oil cloth to cover it when I'm not painting."

He pushed up and over, sliding back the heavy cloth. The night air sank down through the opening in the roof, a stroke of cold, silvering the room, bewitching it.

"Oh," she said, her breath catching. "You can see the moon."

He looked. The moon filled the visible square of night sky. Shut up in an attic, Miss Coover had sawed her way to the sky. She was more than extraordinary. She was marvelous, *miraculous*.

The moon was directly overhead, high and bright, nearly full. He set down the board with a tap that seemed loud in the sudden hush.

He was in her bedroom, in the night. She hadn't precisely invited him in. He should go.

Good night. Good-bye.

There were words adequate to the task of leaving. Humans had developed ritualized language to protect individuals from the specificity of their desires. Humdrum phrases.

He cleared his throat, and she looked at him. He saw the quicksilver beauty of her face, the transformation wrought by wonder at something as simple as the moon. Her face was tilted up, hair loose around her shoulders, the jewel-bright silk of her dress muted in the moonlight and the low light of the lamp, a deeper color, closer to claret. His arms could easily span the distance between them. It would be far more difficult to walk the two steps back to the door.

How the tables had turned. It seemed *he* was now a danger to *her*.

CHAPTER THIRTEEN

"I SHOULD GO." Weston hesitated, then bowed slightly. "Sweet dreams," he said, the words a low purr.

The black sheen of his hair, touched by the moon's rays, held blue lights. Was it the alcohol that made her blood effervesce in her veins? Something else was working upon her. Her little garret room, so safe and familiar, her haven—standing in the center of it, she suddenly felt poised on a precipice. She wanted to take the step that would send her plummeting. She tried to smile and suspected the result was lopsided. But he smiled back, dimples forming in his cheeks. His irises had expanded, a band of emerald encircling celadon flecked with orpiment. Gorgeous, many-hued.

He shifted his weight, and his boot knocked against her paint box. A brush rolled off the top onto the floor.

"Don't mind that," she muttered as he crouched to pick it up. "I'm always kicking things over."

He rose. His smile had faded. There was calculation in his eyes. He glanced about and what he saw seemed to decide him.

"This room, it's certainly not lifeless," he began.

"Are you referring to the mice?" She folded her arms. That brought the smile back to his lips. She watched them curve. Despite their fullness, they weren't feminine. They were too sculpted, the upper lip sharply peaked, the lower lip almost squared off.

"I refer to your dislike for domiciles defined by empty fathoms of air."

His memory was keen. She shrugged her acceptance. There was something novel, and rather nice, about a man adopting her terms.

"That is, it's charming as a bedchamber." He noticed that this bit of condescension lit her temper and hurried on. "But as a studio it lacks the bare minimum of light and space. Come to Weston Hall to paint."

Her mouth had fallen open.

"Not to the house per se," he added. "I want to avoid complications. With Yardley, the gossipmongers. Everyone. I *do* plan to gain control of the dukedom. Even if I were *afraid* of the responsibility . . ."

She felt her cheeks warming.

"I would overcome my fear. For many reasons, not the least of which being it's the only way I can make certain my sister is provided for."

Her face flamed.

"I deceived you," she said haltingly. "Exploited your fondness for your sister . . ."

"Because I gave you no cause to trust me. Like you said." His voice hollowed, but the anger—if it was anger—didn't seem directed at her. He looked at her squarely. "I *will* talk to Mabeldon."

She swallowed some lump in her throat, those bubbles of champagne.

He glanced at her easel, at the chalking on the canvas, the Cantrell girls in outline, a boyish excitement playing over his face.

"Effie has an easel. I could set it up for you. Lucy . . ."

He didn't seem to notice he'd used her Christian name.

"Consider it. It's a small space in a private corner of the garden. A glasshouse, originally for growing flowers. You couldn't ask for more light. My mother had it built and walled off. No one accesses it from the main house. There's an entrance off the mews. I'll show it to you. You could come and go as you please."

His excitement had gripped her. She chewed her lip, daring to imagine it. A glasshouse, dazzling with light.

"The only caveat is I, too, use the space. It's my . . . retreat. You may see me there, in my shirtsleeves." He dimpled at her.

Now she did feel as though she were plummeting. A studio, close to the Royal Academy, and the prospect of seeing him, perhaps daily, in his shirtsleeves.

"You have a month, you said, to paint your picture for submission to the Hanging Committee. You've done well here."

His gaze slanted. She'd labored in this room to paint the exact tint of the skin on the tops of his thighs as it shaded toward his groin. Was his smile sardonic? She had to struggle to meet his eyes. No, his look was frankly admiring.

"But your talent merits more," he said "Better conditions. Think what you could do."

She was thinking of it. She was already agreeing. But his compliment made something flutter in her stomach. He sounded so assured of her talent. She didn't want him to see how much she needed assurance. To hide her confusion, she busied herself moving a jar of chrome pigment from the table to the shelf.

"It's decided, then." She heard the satisfaction in his voice. "And will you work on this? Beth and Mary?" He was studying the canvas again.

"I'm going to white it out. I got the dolls wrong."

"Ah." He bent closer. "Violet looks a bit droopy. She has more integrity, structurally speaking at least. She lorded it over poor Lily."

Her laughter slipped out.

"You remember the names of the dolls, too." In fact, he seemed to remember everything. It didn't square. A renowned dunce with perfect recall. When he was sober, at any rate. He saw her puzzlement and lifted his brows.

"Some of us have to store things in our minds."

This was gnomic of him. She pursed her lips. "Instead of where? Where do the rest of us store things?"

He shrugged. "Ledgers. Journals. Sketchbooks."

She didn't understand him. "But—"

He interrupted. "Would you show me the sketch of the girls? I regret that I didn't watch you make it."

"Certainly." She blinked at his tone, which told her that the previous subject was closed. "It's right here."

On the bed. She pivoted slowly, aware of his gaze. Of course, the bed had been there the whole time, just a few paces away. But now the thought of it made her heart hammer. She reached the bed and sat down slowly, sliding the sketchbook onto her lap. He didn't move, but tipped his head. Then, carefully, stepping between the chair and the easel, avoiding the paint box, he approached and sat beside her. His weight depressed the mattress. She obeyed the laws of gravity, tilted into him. The sketchbook slid off her knees and thudded on the floor. She braced herself on his legs, pushing up, and felt the muscles harden to rock. These slight bodily shifts, the tensing or stretching of muscles so wonderfully developed—how enthralling. She resettled herself beside him but couldn't break contact completely. A devil ran wild inside her.

She moved her fingers lightly over his trousers, skimming the wales of the corduroy.

"These aren't your trousers."

"No," he agreed. "Part of my brilliant disguise."

"Of course." She kept moving her fingers. "What would your tailor think?"

She sighed, mind drifting. It would be a pleasure to construct and detail a suit for such an exquisitely balanced body, broad shoulders, pitched straight, wide chest tapering to slim hips, curved buttocks, straight legs. Nothing to disguise or pad. You could focus your art on the lining, the edges, all the niceties.

He stiffened, stared straight ahead. God, that profile. It should be struck onto a coin. She moved her fingers absently, examining the line of his nose, the angles of his lips, his jaw. Gently, he laid his hand over hers, stilling it.

His voice was strangled. "Lucy—"

There it was again, her Christian name, the syllables roughened. He *should* use it. His saying her name, it acknowledged the unlikely intimacy that had sprung up between them.

When he had first discovered who she was, he had assumed they'd been more intimate still.

"What did you think we did," she whispered. "When you thought we'd . . ."

He looked at her, startled, eyes brilliant.

She licked her lips, felt a thrill as his gaze dropped to her mouth. He swallowed, then laughed softly. His thumb stroked across her knuckles.

"You want to know." There was a new timbre to his voice. "I wanted to know too. It crazed me, not knowing."

"What *would* you have done?" Her face was an inch from his. There was only so much more she could discover, looking.

He smiled faintly, shook his head. For a long moment, she thought he wouldn't answer; then . . .

"I would have started with your hair," he said. Slowly, he lifted his hand, drifted his fingers through her hair, tugging the curls apart. A few tangled strands snapped. She could never get the knots out. *A bird's nest* was what Aunt Marian called it. The Stirling women were all abundantly endowed with tangles and twists, hair that wouldn't lie flat, that repulsed combs and brushes.

He found a pin and freed it. With both hands, he swept her curls forward so they framed her face, spilled across her shoulders. She could see the fascination in his eyes, a fascination that amazed her. How could her ordinary face, her inelegant snarl of hair, fascinate a man of such perfect beauty? She was common as a wren. And he . . . he was a Pegasus.

For a moment, he stared; then he laid his forehead on hers. She felt the sweep of his lashes, felt them tangle hers.

"I would have kissed you," he said against her mouth; then abruptly he pulled back. His dimples were dark and deep, his smile wicked. "Or would you have kissed me?"

She kissed him. He was here in the flesh, solid and hot and huge, filling her bed where she'd lain at night and dreamed of him, desires beating within her, amorphous, vague. Shapeless.

She was kissing him, and then there came the precise moment when he was kissing her. The bed was narrow, and he was broad, but he managed to twist until he was beneath her, her breasts tingling as they grazed his coat, her hair curtaining their faces. Another twist, and he was above her, bracing himself. She couldn't tell any longer who was kissing whom, the kisses mingled flesh and breath. They were wet, hot, carnal, a play of tongues and teeth. He dragged her lower lip into his mouth, sucked hard, then swallowed her gasp. She pushed up his jaw, hand wrapping his chin, and nipped his throat, a strange hungry impulse that startled her. She wanted to taste him, to fill her mouth with his flesh. She bit again, harder, and felt his moan against her fingertips.

He lowered onto her, his chest pressing the air from her lungs, his lips on her eyelids, on her cheeks, on her throat. She twined her arms around the breadth of him, slid a hand up the back of his neck, grabbing a fistful of silky hair. His lower body was angled away from her and she tried to pull him toward her, the whole of him, but he was immovable.

He lifted his head, mouth shining. His chest crushed closer, his heart pounding into hers.

"I would have unbuttoned your dress, unlaced it, slid it down your body, baring you."

His finger drew a line from her clavicle, between her breasts, down to her belly. She shivered. Vague desires were taking shape, locating themselves, beginning to beat. The one heart wasn't enough. She was sprouting new hearts, throbbing everywhere he touched.

"But I confess," he said, planting kisses along her jaw, "I have no idea how to operate this particular garment."

At her push, he rolled off her and sat up, leaning back against the wall, folding his arms behind his head. Watching her as she stood, backing away from the bed.

"It's one of a kind," she said, breathless, giddied by his devouring stare. That day in his study, she'd claimed she'd allow him to draw her nude, had unfastened her dress, to shock him. If he hadn't stopped her . . .

But she'd gambled that he would, and she'd won.

What she was about to do . . . It felt different. She swallowed, brushing her fingers down her sides.

"These pleats are a state secret." She spoke lightly but her breath caught. "And it comes off . . . over the head."

She began to shimmy the dress up over her hips. She'd spoken so boldly that day. *It's a fine figure*, she'd said of her own body, with all the coolness and remove she could muster. But she'd never shown so much of her body to anyone, until now.

She'd taken in the naked sight of him, unasked. Now that she offered him the sight of herself, the dress inching up her thighs, her detachment deserted her. Heaven help her, she hadn't fully grasped it—that exposure involved such risk.

What if he didn't like what he saw? She had to steel herself to look at him.

His face held that fascination she'd detected earlier, amazement, and something else, something that made his eyes hood, his lips part.

Fear fled. Ah yes, exposure could exhilarate as well. Her vision went crimson, the silk bunching over her eyes. Then the dress was off, and she was dropping it in a puddle on the chair.

"You can't wear much under it," she explained, glancing down at herself, the uncertainty returning. Light chemise, thin cotton drawers. She couldn't meet his eyes until he spoke.

"Come here," he commanded. He had shrugged out of his jacket and was sitting on the edge of the bed. His tousled hair waved across his brow. His gaze was greedy.

She obeyed. When she reached him, he spread his legs so she could fit herself between them, her bare knees against the bed. He slid his hand beneath her chemise.

"Shut your eyes," he said.

"I like to see," she began, but as his hand slid higher, over her ribs, up the curve of her breast, she felt her eyes roll up, the lids come down.

"I know," he said. "I want you to feel."

She felt. She felt his fingers close on her nipple, hard, then his thumb as it brushed the sensitized bud. The breath whooshed out of her. His other hand slid up her back, over her shoulder, down the outside of her arm, his callused fingertips lightly rasping the skin. She felt the press of his knuckles as he bunched the chemise in his hand.

"Lift your arms," he said huskily. She lifted them, and he pulled the chemise over her head. She opened her eyes to see his dark head lowering over her. Then she felt his mouth close on her breast. She moaned, pressing into him, gripping his shoulders. Something was tightening inside her, a ribbon pulling taut, connecting the beating sensation in her breasts to the beating sensation between her legs. His hand cupped her buttock, squeezing. She wiggled against his chest, panting.

"I would have kissed your breasts," he said, releasing her nipple, lifting his head. His mouth glistened. "I would have kissed your quim. I would have made you whisper my name. I would have waited until you begged for it."

He began to wind a ringlet around his finger, tighter and tighter.

"Only then would I have taken you."

He looked into her face, eyes glittering with an expression she couldn't decipher.

"But it wouldn't have been like that," he said, releasing her, smoothing her hair down with his palms, then pulling back. "Because I was too drunk to know my arse from my elbow. It wouldn't have been what you deserve."

She swallowed, tried to steady her breathing. What he was saying—it wasn't rejection. But he had stopped. He wasn't stroking her. He'd lowered his arms.

It felt like rejection.

"But you prefer it that way." She looked down. His hands were plucking at the bedspread. Large, strong hands. *Drunk.*

"No." One of his hands rose, fingers lifting her chin. She looked into his face.

"At brothels, you don't have to kiss anything," she said. She'd heard that kisses bored men. Chatter from factory girls. She didn't doubt they knew what they were talking about. They lived and worked in cramped quarters, were always repelling advances. Men wanted one thing only.

He hadn't seemed bored, kissing.

"You enjoy brothels," she said bitterly. He *did* enjoy them. Why else would he go? He'd told her he used to drag his brother out of them. But now? His brother was gone. She didn't realize how tightly she'd clenched her jaw until his thumbs massaged the joints by her ears. She sighed as the ache intensified.

"George was involved with the Rose and Myrtle, heavily involved." His eyes held hers. "I'm sure you read the articles. It caters to wealthy men with . . . quirks."

She thought at once of the Feast of Venus, those twelve dildos made with Academy plaster.

"He procured young girls for the madam. He matched girls to those quirks."

His thumbs kneaded her jaws harder.

"He had favorites himself. One of them he kidnapped, dragged away by knifepoint in the night. I had it from the madam herself. She kept that tidbit from the reporters. She didn't want her establishment to seem utterly depraved."

He grimaced, and for the first time, she saw the fine lines that fanned from his eyes.

"He could have paid her. She might have gone willingly, but that wasn't the game he was playing. She was the wench to his pirate. He stole her, and he stole the commodore's boat."

He didn't need to rehash the finale. She suddenly doubted he could. The muscles in his face had tensed. His strong bones seemed to come forward. He looked annihilated.

"Sometimes I fear that's where Effie ended up, someplace like that, like the Rose and Myrtle. Some devil making her pay for George's sins."

"You don't believe that," she breathed.

Life came back to his eyes.

"No," he said. "But I go sometimes anyway, to brothels, and I look for her. To remind myself of what can happen to women in this city."

She said nothing. She would not soothe him. How like a man, to need such reminders. A woman lived it every day, lived under the threat of male predation.

He didn't frequent prostitutes, but he hadn't been able to rule out the possibility that she was a prostitute, and that he'd gotten so drunk he'd paid for her services. He'd let his father warp him until he didn't recognize himself. Maybe she saw him more clearly than he did.

She shifted restlessly. He pressed his thumbs into the hollows below her cheekbones. Tension she held in her face, her forehead, her scalp, started to relax. But the other tension—the beating need lower down in her body—did not release. She sat beside him and leaned to kiss the base of his throat, where the pulse beat quickly. This confirmation—that he wasn't unaffected, that he, too, felt this hunger—emboldened her. She began to undo the top buttons of his shirt. He caught her hands, brought them down to the bed. She flushed. She felt chastised. But she also felt the devil of her untutored desire running, running all through her.

"That's enough." He sighed, and there was regret in his voice. "Before . . . you were falling asleep on your feet."

"I'm awake now." More parts of her, more awake than she could remember. She leaned forward and fit her mouth to his. He kissed her back, then lifted his hands and settled them, heavy and hot, on her shoulders. He held her still as he eased out of the kiss.

"Alas." His smile was gentle. "Consciousness is necessary but not sufficient."

She searched his face and understood. But surely she hadn't had so much to drink as that! Did he think she didn't know her own mind? She frowned in protest. "*I* know my arse from my elbow."

He laughed and grabbed her wrists, lifting her arms so he could kiss her elbows, the awkward posture and the strange ticklish attention lavished on such an unprepossessing part of the body making her laugh too, laugh and squirm away.

"Prove it." His tone was jesting, but his eyes had narrowed. Suddenly, his dimples flashed, and he dove forward, reaching over the side of her bed and coming up again with her sketchbook.

"Here." He thrust it at her. "If you're capable of higher-order thinking and decision making, you should be able to . . ." He paused and considered her. Dear God, did she look as startled as she felt? She turned the sketchbook over in her hands. Oh, but he was *grinning*, that wide, devastating grinning.

"Let's see. You should be able to . . . draw a cow that strikes terror in my heart."

"What?" She laughed her disbelief, and he lifted his brows, scooting back to lean against the wall.

"You said you'd imagined the scene." He gave a one-shouldered shrug. "Cows with terrifying aspect, meting out grisly death. I ask for a single cow, no more."

That was his test of her sobriety?

"You are . . ." Words failed her.

"Asinine?" He suggested impishly. "I don't consider it an insult. We've established that I respect donkeys. Your cow, my lady. Might I advocate for fangs?"

More laughter bubbled up. He *was* asinine, absurd, and, with that self-satisfied grin, overwhelmingly, irritatingly attractive.

She crawled over the bed, feeling along the crack between mattress and wall for one of her charcoal pencils. When she'd got one, she sat beside him, setting her back to the wall, propping her sketchbook on her thighs.

She pressed the pencil to the page, then lifted it. How to begin?

He spoke airily. "Put on the page some semblance of a cow."

"Thank you for your advice," she muttered, refusing to look at him, knowing his expression: dimpled and delighted and infuriating. She made a mark, the long line of a bovine spine. *Good.* Oh, but not good. The cow should be rearing. She started again, trying a new angle, and the whole while, she was aware of him, lounging in her bed, laughing to himself.

"Quiet," she snapped, whenever she felt him take an overlarge breath.

In the end, her sketch resembled a bald, block-headed horse, tall on its hind legs, mouth open.

"Fangs," she said tersely, pointing.

"Ah." His side pressed hers as he took the sketchbook. They peered at the sketch together.

"I forgot cows don't have flowing tails," she said at last. "I haven't seen many cows firsthand."

"I could introduce you to a few." He looked at her, face so near she could count those orpiment flecks in his irises, study the curvature of his lids. "Someday, we could go to Hampshire. You'd love it, I think. The fields and hedges, and—"

He broke off. *He* loved Hampshire, it was obvious. And he wanted to show it to her. Something squeezed inside her and began to ache. She rubbed at the sketch with her thumb, blending the charcoal lines.

He cleared his throat. She hoped, for both their sakes, that he wouldn't continue in the same vein, intimating some future that wouldn't be.

"It's an abomination," he said, and the smile was back in his voice. She removed her thumb. The blending hadn't helped.

She sighed, relieved and disappointed. He was right. "Well then." One question remained. She frowned at the monstrous cow-horse, which borrowed something, too, from the realm of dogs, the jaws, if not the teeth. The teeth belonged to a wild boar. "Does it strike terror in your heart?"

A pause, then:

"Yes." The one syllable rasped in his throat.

Her eyes shot up.

"You don't know a cow from a horse," he said, voice smooth again, mocking. "But you do know your arse from your elbow. So. *Lucy.*" His eyes dared her. "What do you decide?"

He wasn't laughing any longer. His expression was hard, focused. He wanted her to say something, but his look scrambled her language. She shut her sketchbook and half rose, leaning into him, sliding over him. He'd dared her to be the one who decided, and, in deciding, she was all daring, straddling him, the wool of his trousers prickling the skin of her bare inner thighs.

She felt the hardness straining at his fly and bore down, the soft heart between her legs beating faster. He made a low noise and caught her face in his hands.

"You want more?" he asked. His eyes had narrowed, just a green shimmer between jet lashes.

He'd said it, *yes,* the word a rasp. She could say it.

"Yes." She pressed her mouth to his, pushed down on his arms, guiding his hands to her hips. He suckled her lower lip, her tongue, and tore his face away.

"Yes, *Anthony,*" he prompted, fingers digging into her hips, and that large hardness—nothing like a classical nub—ground against her. Oh God, she was well scrambled now.

She took a breath, managed: "Anthony, *yes.*"

He lifted her from him and she almost cried out in disappointment, but before she could gather her senses, he'd closed the distance between them, his weight on top of her, his fingers picking through the ribbons lacing her drawers. She bucked as his finger slipped under the fabric, parting the curls, delivering a slow stroke that pushed the air from her lungs in a low moan.

"Say it again," he said, finger rubbing in time with the beating, louder now, harder, faster.

"I can't hear you."

"Anthony," she gasped, shuddering as he pressed his whole hand against her, rolling in circles. His mouth slanted over hers, stilling her head. His tongue slid into her mouth, and his finger slid into her quim.

"Oh, oh." Her breath was stuttering in her throat. She reached again for his collar, desperate to rip his shirt open, to touch the muscles straining under the skin, but he was out of reach now, backing over the end of the bed until his knees hit the floor. He held her hips and pulled her forward, and her sudden awareness of where he'd positioned himself, of what he could see, made her press her thighs together.

"Bashful?" His voice, low and teasing, collected her wits. She thought she might laugh, but the sound she made was closer to a gasp. She found her words.

"I *told* you." She sighed at the pressure of his hands on her hips. "I'm not . . ." She gave up on speech. She *wasn't* bashful, not here, not now, and she knew how to show him. Slowly, she opened her legs, wide. Wider. She heard his intake of breath.

"Ah," he said, his tone rich with appreciation. "I remember now." He nestled closer, nudging her legs ever farther apart, bowing his head. He slid her hips another inch, and oh Lord, she was against his mouth.

At the first stroke of his tongue, she bolted upright. His hands stroked down her thighs. She saw through a haze, his wild black hair, the piercing green of his eyes, and then she fell back. He licked into her, heat and moisture concentrating, the sensation radiating out from that exquisite juncture. She'd never imagined it, that part of the body, and this one, but it made sense, a perverse, gorgeous sense. And then nothing made sense. She was mewling, coming undone, her thighs falling open, shameless, exposed, spread for him.

Take me.

"Will you . . ." she moaned. What did she want? She wanted him to *take* her, like she'd seen in alleyways, that hasty jerking up and down. Once the sight had horrified her, like the word. *Fucking.* Now it seemed imperative, his cock thrusting into her, a cruelty not to have it.

"Please," she said. "Take me."

He pushed his fingers inside her, knuckles revolving, churning her, as his mouth made the liquid fire.

"Anthony," she whimpered, and she broke, heaving, grabbing at his hair, pushing his head into her, crying out, heedless of her noises, heedless of anything. He rested his head on her thigh, stroking her hip as she shuddered.

Shame, fear, joy, surprise, and something like a laugh, like the richness of a belly laugh, bubbled inside her, warm bubbles popping. Gratification flickering in every nerve. She wanted to tell him, but as her breathing steadied and slowed, it became regular, sleep carrying her away. Cool air rushed in to fill the void he left as he rose, before he lifted her up, settling her head on her pillow, spreading the blanket over her.

HE SAW ALMOST no one on the streets. Even the rats slumbered at this hour. But the bars and dram shops were open. He didn't look back at the building he'd exited, even though he could feel the tug of her.

He walked quickly. The night was eerie in its clarity. A wind pushing away the bilious London air. The moon shone down. He was burning in its light.

A sign creaked in the wind. Before he could think, he'd pushed through a door beneath.

The men in Hogg & Shirey's leaned on the long counter, still as statues, and the proprietor, a thin man with a sulfurous complexion, was himself too listless to expel them. The gin he served was sweet and weak, as much sugar water as spirits. Anthony ordered glass after glass. Lucy was sleeping and couldn't see his shame. Was he failing her? Failing himself?

He drank and imagined his father at the bar beside him, staring with that familiar mixture of shock and rancor.

The young idiot. That had been his father's nickname for him, uttered without a trace of affection.

Christ God, he needed to fight, but not as a soldier, not anymore, not as a raging second son. He had to let those selves go.

He would learn to fight as the Duke of Weston, damn his father to hell. Damn Yardley, too, for giving up on him.

But first he had to get there. Three weeks remained. Twenty-one days until his birthday.

He shoved more pennies on the bar and cursed himself. *The young idiot*, fulfilling his destiny yet again.

He knew better. And he did worse.

When he stumbled out, the lamplighters were on the streets with their ladders, turning off the gas. By the time he stepped down from the cab in Mayfair, the sky was nearly light. The moon, faded, still floated above.

Luckily, he'd climbed up the side of Weston Hall and into his second-floor window often enough that he didn't slip.

He got into his bed but lay awake, a roaring in his ears. He wanted oblivion but he'd settle for sleep.

It was a long time coming.

CHAPTER FOURTEEN

FOR THE FIRST time in months, Anthony's days fell into a pleasing pattern. After breakfast, he would pore over the newspapers, working doggedly through the accounts of parliamentary debates. He wrote letters—shaping the words carefully—letters to Cruitshank, to Mabeldon, and tucked them himself into the bottom of the mailbag. He held a few meetings with his father's political cronies, elder statesmen he'd been putting off for months. On three occasions, Yardley called while he was thus engaged. How shocked Yardley must have been, turned away at the door, the young idiot too occupied with important business to receive him. The reversal made Anthony smile.

In the late afternoon, he would stroll to the mews, pass through the coach house, linger in the stables, and make his way into the southeastern corner of the garden. If Anthony's mother were still alive, the glasshouse would glow green, a profusion of leaves, brightly starred with new blooms, pressing the translucent walls. No trees, no plants, grew inside. But now, for first time in years, the glasshouse was filled with life, with color.

He would hallo softly from the doorway, and Lucy would acknowledge him with a word, a nod, or not at all. She worked in the center of the space, where his mother used to sit in winter. He'd lounge against the brick foundation, sitting on a shallow sill, the glazed glass rising behind him, and nurse a tumbler of whiskey. He watched Lucy at work. My God, he pitied her canvas! Trapped on its easel, nowhere to run as she approached, brush raised, face twisted in a ferocious scowl. Painting, she looked twice as alive as anyone he'd ever seen, pacing, spearing her hair with distracted fingers that left streaks of paint at her temples. Her eyes seemed lit from within, slits of gold. She circled the easel, darting and feinting, like a novice fencer sent into a frenzy by a motionless master. Or *she* was motionless, standing stock-still in the flooding light in the attitude of a saint communicating with angels. Little happened hour by hour to the canvas itself, but he could see by her face that a brushstroke had transported her into raptures or dashed her against the rocks of despair.

He was enthralled by the drama. Enthralled by her.

Sometimes they spoke as she washed brushes or stretched her back, folding forward at the waist, leaning back, in an awkward, wide-legged stance. Her frank, unselfconscious physicality delighted him, and he stretched too, striking even more ridiculous postures that made her laugh. Encouraged, one afternoon, he stood on his head, which turned her laugh into a growl.

"If you kick the easel, I will bury you."

But he was far enough from the easel, to the side of it, the crown of his head aching where it ground into the iron grating. He took a deep breath, tensing his muscles, and lifted into a handstand. If he tipped too far over, his feet would hit the lower curve of the glass dome. But he didn't tip, didn't even wobble. Blood rushed to his head. Probably good—to drain the blood from that other part of him, the one making him show off for her like a green boy.

"You are a dolt," she said as he lowered himself slowly, straight down, tucking into a crouch to prevent his legs from flailing. He grinned as he stood up, shaking the hair from his eyes. Dolt was high praise, considering her usual run of epithets.

Whenever he returned to the house from one of these too-brief idylls, he felt enlivened, as though a golden spark from her eyes had touched fire to something long dead in his chest.

ONE WEEK PASSED and the next began. No matter how packed his schedule, he couldn't avoid the confrontation forever. He knew it. He didn't startle to hear Yardley's voice, even though he'd told Collins to admit no one after his noon appointment.

"That wasn't Samuel Lawford?"

Yardley stood in the doorway to the study, briefcase in hand, looking down the hall. Despite his irritation, Anthony felt amused by his expression. Yardley looked as gobsmacked arriving as Lawford had looked leaving.

Anthony dropped the report Lawford had handed him onto the desk.

"Nice fellow," he said. "Principled."

Lawford was motivated by ideals. Unlike the other politicians Anthony had invited into his study, Lawford hadn't framed the laws he was drafting in terms of party strategy or personal gain. He hadn't referred, ominously, to favors owed and grudges earned, to votes for sale. He hadn't attempted to flatter Anthony by praising his father, or attempted to manipulate him by assuming his support for bills explained via references to the financial backing of wealthy constituents.

Refreshing. Lawford made politics seem palatable, even noble. A public service.

He should have held meetings with his father's enemies sooner.

Yardley let the door bang behind him. His ginger brows had crept so high up his forehead they seemed in danger of annexation by his hairline.

"That man was a thorn in your father's side. Did he come to threaten you? His muckraking friends in the press made a hell for this family. What did he want?"

His protective air rankled. Anthony gripped the edge of the desk. Yardley's protectiveness—it was the counterpoint to his father's disgust. He should have recognized that Yardley's kindness shared the same root—deep skepticism about his mental powers.

He forced himself to smile.

"He wanted to know why I invited him. He said he'd sooner expected an invitation from the devil."

Yardley's face was going red. "You invited him?"

Anthony nodded. "I've read the records from the last parliamentary session. His ideas interest me."

He'd labored over those blue books night after night, puzzling them out, collapsing on his bed, pain stabbing behind his right eye. But the effort had paid off. The names, the committees, the bills, were now locked in his head. He'd handled himself well with Lawford.

Reading his father's notes alongside the records, he'd begun to track the forces—internal and external—that had shaped his father's political persona. He hadn't realized what a pivotal role Yardley had managed to play, without ever setting foot in Westminster.

As an active member of the Board of Works, Yardley attended long, windy meetings—several a week—where he rubbed elbows with men prominent in the affairs of every vestry in the city: aldermen, merchants, factory owners. He promised private investment in parish infrastructure, promises on which the Duke of Weston could deliver, and in return, they got their people to stuff the ballot boxes and delivered amenable MPs.

His father hadn't resorted to bribery as far as Anthony could tell. No out-and-out corruption. But he knew how to play the game, and the game depended—heavily—on legalized graft and sinecures.

Yardley's close connection with his father had given him access to the upper echelons of society. What would he do if Anthony found him less indispensable?

He felt vaguely ill, looking at Yardley's familiar face, craggy and open. At the moment, his blue eyes were bulging slightly with the force of his amazement.

"Which of Lawford's ideas caught your interest?"

Anthony cleared his throat. "He supported the Irish Land Act. The Irish farmers deserve a fair rent."

As a topic, rent no longer bored him. That one image had caught his attention, changed his outlook.

My babes have grown so thin, I could keep them in my pincushion.

Nothing dull or abstract about it. Not at home or abroad.

Yardley sighed. "It starts with a fair rent. Next thing you know, it's the expropriation of the landlords and agricultural collapse. You've a lot to learn, my boy. Men like Lawford exist in the realm of ideas. Try to implement one of those ideas and see what havoc ensues." He sat heavily in a chair, setting his briefcase on his knees. "You should get to know your own party. Have you met with Southgate? He was one of your father's staunchest allies."

Ask Collins. They both knew the butler acted as a spy. Anthony's jaw ticked. Were they going to continue to pretend that Yardley hadn't enlisted Lucy's help to extend his legal childhood? He picked up Lawford's report.

"It seems to me that Lawford exists in the realm of action. He thought the invasion of Afghanistan cruel and unjust, and he opened the debate in the Commons on the policies that led to the war. He agitated for the independence of the Transvaal. Our government's inhumanity keeps him up at night."

Yardley's nostrils flared. "Talk to Southgate about Lawford, and don't take any of his prattle to heart. The man's a jester. He's up at night because that's when he pens his witticisms."

Anthony glanced at the report in his hand, flicked the edge with his finger.

"I'm most interested in the case he makes *here*. Against intervention in Egypt. In fact, I might throw my support behind him."

Lawford had tugged at his long gray beard for a solid minute after Anthony had made that pronouncement. He had suspected intrigue. Yardley suspected buffoonery. He narrowed his eyes. Then he threw back his head and laughed.

"You're the jester." He wagged his finger at Anthony. "I should spot your clowning by now. This is what I get for urging you out of the stable." He wiped his eyes. "Point taken. Do what you will, then. I can't stop you."

"That's right. You can't."

Yardley heard the edge in his voice. He sobered, straightened.

"You're in a strange mood," he observed. "Still upset about Hampshire? Cruitshank wrote to tell me he'd had a letter from you. I told him I'd give you the annual reports."

He opened the briefcase.

"Here they are, as promised. Three years of them. Inputs, output. It's all there. The numbers are clear enough. The tenants have no cause to bellyache."

He leaned forward, tossing the reports onto the desk.

"Read them and we'll talk if you have questions."

Anthony rose, tugged the bellpull. He put his palms on the desk, bracing himself.

"Better we talk now."

"Very well." Yardley tilted his head, studying him. As Anthony hesitated, he nodded slightly, the encouraging nod he'd given on innumerable occasions during Anthony's boyhood, when he'd failed to express himself well, stumbled on his words, flew into a passion.

Calm down. Spit it out.

Yardley had listened to him patiently. Anthony set his jaw. He wasn't that attention-starved boy anymore. He wouldn't be humored.

"In ten days, I will turn thirty," he said.

"Indeed. Have I ever forgotten your birthday?"

Anthony shut his eyes briefly. No, Yardley had never forgotten his birthday.

On his eleventh birthday, just two months after his mother died,

218 • Joanna Lowell

Yardley had taken him to see the suits of armor in the Tower of London. A few bright hours of excitement in those unremittingly dark days.

His father had requested his presence after dinner and his nurse had brought him into this very room. His father had sat behind the desk at which he now stood, staring at him coldly for what felt like a thousand years before he delivered a curt ultimatum.

Your nurse tells me you've been crying about your mother. You're a grown boy now. If I hear of your crying again, I'll have you dropped in an ice-water bath where you can sit until you learn to contain yourself.

He opened his eyes. "After this birthday, we might not have occasion to talk."

"Anthony, are you quite well?"

Yardley's face creased, looking suddenly worn with care. Anthony fixed his eyes on the lapel of Yardley's jacket, took a deep breath.

"Whether I am or not, it is my concern. In the future, you will handle your affairs, and I will handle mine."

"Your affairs *are* my affairs. For now, that's the legal reality." Yardley made a resigned motion with his hand. "After your birthday, well. You'll be thirty, fully emancipated as they say. But the bonds of affection remain. I will always endeavor to help you in any way I can. You know that."

The footman knocked, entered, placed the tray on a table, vanished. Yardley regarded the tall glasses of milk. Anthony came around the desk, leaned back against it.

"I'd offer you something stronger," he said. "But I fear you'd report me to Hamilton and Johnstone."

Yardley lifted a glass of milk with a slight grimace. "Your father took the matter a bit far." He sniffed at the milk, then sipped. "I don't deny it."

"Then why are you so hell-bent on enforcing his rules?"

Yardley returned his glass to the tray.

"Hell-bent," he said, musingly. "I worried this would happen, that you'd make me out to be a demon in this. You resent the restrictions your father placed on you. I understand that. But *you* should understand the sense of necessity that drove him to it."

He ignored this. Yardley had made the case before. But this time his quarrel wasn't with his father, but with Yardley himself.

"You knew I was going to the Albion. You hoped to catch me drinking."

Yardley tilted his head. "Miss Coover told you."

"She didn't have to tell me. I saw you."

"Ah, well." Yardley sighed. "A test. You passed with flying colors. I was pleased."

"Were you?" He searched Yardley's face.

"Of course." Yardley smiled. "I'm less pleased by your continued acquaintanceship with Miss Coover. I sincerely admire her, but the attachment can't be a happy one."

Anthony didn't like it, this sudden silkiness of tone. He looked at Yardley sharply.

"What attachment? She comes to the garden from time to time. As my painting teacher." He cleared his throat as Yardley's smile widened, crinkling his eyes. "She doesn't need your admiration. She needs justice so her house isn't knocked down."

"You were too long with Lawford." Yardley shrugged. "*Justice.* That's a bit too grandiose to serve. The gears of power are gritty little things in the vestries. Don't worry, though, *I* kept my word to Miss Coover. I raised the issue of the evictions at last night's board meeting. A special committee was formed to investigate the Charlotte Road properties. Your intervention is not required."

Hot, boyish embarrassment. It flooded him. He'd kept his word, too, but to no purpose. He'd been turned away from Mabeldon's twice and had yet to receive a reply to his letters. Yardley saw his discomfort. He always did. Slowly, the older man reached again for the glass of milk and held it up as though trying to peer through it.

The solid white cylinder blocked the center of his face. He lowered the glass.

"Anthony." He paused, thoughtfully. "I've looked the other way whenever possible, but you've been cheating so broadly, you gave me no choice. I felt compelled to arrange a little *situation* so I could honestly appraise your self-management."

"*Honestly?*" Anthony snorted. "Not the best choice of words. There was nothing honest about it."

A brief beat of silence; then Yardley continued.

"You've disrespected my intelligence," he said. "You've shown no consideration for the delicate position in which I find myself as friend to both you and your father, not to mention as trustee of the estate. I've angered you by refusing to hunt high and low for your sister, but to do so would be to break my word to your father. You *could* handle the situation with maturity and patience. Take the codicil for what it is: a temporary check on your behavior. Instead, you continue to blow everything out of proportion. You've been surly, delinquent, *hell-bent*, to borrow the term, on proving that the very safeguards you despise are in fact essential and justified."

His speech had gathered momentum, and heat. He paused, meeting Anthony's eyes. He seemed reluctant to continue.

"But you're not surprised." Anthony goaded him grimly. "I've never been up to standard."

Yardley thinned his lips.

"I would chalk your recent excesses to grief and youthful defiance, but . . ."

He shook his head.

"There is a larger, more troubling pattern."

In the silence that followed Anthony's voice cracked like a whip.

"You told me not to explain!"

Yardley had silenced him when he'd tried to speak of Maiwand, not only at their first meeting in Hampshire, but later, too, on the rare occasions he'd broached the subject. He'd implied that Anthony had no need to defend himself, that an understanding existed between them.

Anthony tensed his jaws, the muscles around his eyes. His face hardened into a mask, the mask he'd learned to present to his father, never Yardley himself.

Yardley felt the novelty of his stark expression. His eyelids drooped. He looked like a sad spaniel.

"Why make you relive such unpleasantness? You were acquitted, after all," he murmured. "It was over and done with."

"My father accepted the story they told him. I expected as much. But you? You didn't doubt it?"

Leaning on the desk, he loomed over Yardley, whose large body seemed contorted, stuffed into the chair.

"Anthony." Yardley cast his eyes up. He looked past Anthony, searching the ceiling, blinking rapidly. He gripped the arms of the chair. His gaze grew suspiciously bright. "Your father sent me to identify George's body."

Anthony jerked. But his face was adamant. He stared down at Yardley, impassive.

"I was the one who saw him." Yardley's voice sank into a whisper. "He'd spent two days in the water." His chest heaved once, mightily, but he continued. "That day, I stopped doubting, and I started fearing. I feared for you, Anthony. That story—it had the ring of truth. Or maybe it was the knell of fate. You are very much *her* child."

Her child. Son of the Hellenic harlot. The mad slut. All sorts of things had been said of her. His father had once referred to her within his hearing as a bitch in heat. On that occasion, his vision had blurred, a red wave crashing over him. He'd leapt on his father. He was still young enough to be shaken off, dragged away, locked in a room.

"I am her child," he grated. "And I don't plan on destroying myself. But I will live on *my* terms. You may not like them, I warn you."

After a long moment, Yardley nodded.

"Very well, then." He rose and picked up his briefcase. "I will be the first to wish you a happy birthday."

He leveled Anthony with his gaze.

"Obey. Stay out of the papers. On March twenty-sixth we'll have something to celebrate." A smile tugged his lips. "I'll bring the champagne for the toast." He took Anthony's shoulder in a firm grip and shook it hard. "We'll get through this," he said gruffly. "Call if you want to discuss those reports."

Anthony stared at the door after Yardley let himself out. Then he threw himself onto a chair, pressing his palms together. His head throbbed. A glass of whiskey would help. But he was growing accustomed to waiting until the later afternoon, when a visit to the glasshouse had more to offer than a pain-dulling tipple.

He couldn't bring himself to inspect the annual reports from Hampshire, to chase more swarming hieroglyphics around the page. He pressed his palms together harder, then pulled them apart and looked at the sharply etched lines.

He stood and headed to the coach house to seek out a raw board, a saw, and a plane.

A HEAVY FOOTFALL alerted Lucy to Anthony's presence. Usually he was quieter. She would feel the hairs stir on the back of her neck, and she would know that he'd arrived. Every day she waited for that moment, when the air charged around her. Every day she half hoped the moment wouldn't come.

It wasn't that she minded sharing the light with him. It was that she liked it too much.

She fixed her eyes on the canvas. Her third attempt, and Violet still *drooped*. She wanted the dolls to participate more in the scene, to repay—albeit ever so slightly—the girls' attention. They didn't need to seem alive, of course. But they needed to seem . . . quickened.

More highlights. She went to her paint box, open on top of a marble bench between two enormous planters, both upside down. Anthony had turned them over so she could use them as makeshift tables.

The furnishings are sparse, he'd said when he'd first brought her inside, watching her with a strange expression, eagerness mixed with apology.

It's a crystal palace in miniature, she'd said, rapt, and it was. The glasshouse itself was small but ornate, a beautiful curvilinear structure of sheet glass and iron. He'd set up an easel beneath the apex of the dome, put a camp chair in front of it, turned over a tall urn on which he'd placed an Argand lamp in case clouds dimmed the sun. He'd carried in a bucket of water and laid out glasses and a pitcher on the marble bench, so she could wash her brushes.

You said it has been abandoned for years? she'd murmured. *The glass is remarkably clean.*

Indeed, the panes sparkled. He'd shrugged, but the dimples flickered briefly in his cheeks, all the confirmation she needed. He'd clambered around like a monkey, washing the grime off the glass.

He'd done all of it for her.

This past week had been a dream. When she left the School of Painting, she no longer dashed to the omnibus and jostled the slow miles back to Shoreditch, where petticoats, bodices, and undersleeves waited to accuse her. Aunt Marian had hired Megan Cosgrave through the end of March, had insisted on it. *Off you go. Paint something better.* These days, Lucy walked swiftly from the Royal Academy to Weston Hall, slipped around to the mews, ducked through a door in the stone wall, and entered the garden.

In the glasshouse, they were hers, the last hours of daylight.

Well, hers and Anthony's.

There it was, her tube of zinc white. She snatched it up. Another footfall brought her head around, a tart remark forming on her lips. She didn't want any bumbling around, not when her supplies were scattered all about.

"Oh!"

It wasn't Anthony behind her. This man was his opposite, tow-haired and short-nosed, with a blocky build, his livery rumpled. He grinned with unabashed interest.

"You're harder to catch than a greased pig."

She raised her eyebrows. It took her a moment to realize he referred to her sprint through Weston Hall on that wet, desperate Saturday afternoon.

"Thank you," she said at last. She couldn't doubt he meant it as a compliment.

"The boys were sweating cobs by the end of it." He wove around the sketches she'd fanned out on the floor.

"I'd bet you in a smock race, that I would," he said, nodding.

She wrinkled her nose. If this was lewdness, it was a country variety entirely opaque to her. Up close, she noted how young he was, not more than twenty. He scratched at his bare chin, squinting at her easel. He had dirt under his fingernails.

"Are you the gardener?"

"Valet." He tossed her a wink. "To me are entrusted the socks and drawers."

"Let's leave my drawers out of it." Anthony stepped into the glass-house, jacket slung over his shoulder.

"I see you've met Humphreys," he said to Lucy with a smile.

"Hadn't gotten to introductions." Humphreys placed a hand on his heart. "We went right round the Wrekin. I dunna even know the name of the girl I'm sweet on."

"A sorry plight." Anthony folded his arms, and Humphreys slipped the hand on his chest into his jacket and produced a letter.

"Came at the last delivery," he said, handing it over. He looked between Anthony and Lucy expectantly, then sighed.

"Off I go," he said and rambled out.

Lucy stared. "That's your valet?"

"Was he bothering you?"

"It was hard to tell," she said, and Anthony laughed, an easy laugh, hanging his jacket on a bit of iron projecting from a muntin. When the glasshouse functioned as such, those brackets held the ventilators.

"He puts the Shropshire on thick for the ladies, but he's a good lad."

"Humphreys." She turned the tube of paint over in her hand, placed it carefully back in the box. "The infantryman on the retreat, who you roused and then . . ."

"Saved my life." He smiled. "After the court-martial, he didn't want to rush straight home to the farm for another round of tongue-lashings. I offered him a position. It turns out I need him more than he needs me."

He held up the letter. "When he can, he intercepts the post so Collins can't steam it open or throw it in the fire. Acts as a lookout."

A lookout. So Anthony could drink without risking discovery, no doubt. She raised an eyebrow.

"More of an accomplice than a valet."

He shrugged. "He answers to anything. We understand each other."

The sky shone dove gray, the cloudy light pouring through the glass, softening the green of his eyes. Not the green of faceted jewels. Today, his eyes were green like the leaves on the fig trees that once filled the overturned planters.

Fig trees, nectarine trees, lemon trees. She'd been spellbound by his description of the glasshouse from the days when his mother tended it. Green leaves unfurling, green vines climbing, globes of orange and purple fruits hanging overhead. The air sweet and heavy as sleep. A waking dream. His face had taken on a dreamy quality as he spoke. However cynical and self-destructive he may have become, he still possessed a capacity for wonder.

Now he broke her gaze. Whistling, he walked to the tank where he stored his liquor, rolled back the oilcloth cover, took out a bottle, and splashed whiskey into a tumbler. She knew she should bite her tongue.

"Have you considered *complying* with your father's will?" she asked. "You'd save yourself a world of trouble."

He inspected the whiskey in the glass, sipped, seemed to find it to his satisfaction. "I'll take that under advisement." Without looking at her, he leaned against the low brick wall, his customary spot, and ripped open the letter. She turned back to her canvas.

Fair enough. She wasn't here to give him counsel or draw him into conversation. She was here to paint. She picked up her brush. Put it down at the sound of ripping paper. He was shredding the letter into pieces. He caught her glance and smiled.

"Destroying the evidence," he said.

Perhaps she looked uncomprehending.

"A letter from my aunt Helen." He tucked the scraps into his pocket. "I am forbidden contact with my mother's family."

He swallowed the glass of whiskey. Here was a new wrinkle. She gnawed her lip, regarding him. Prohibiting drink was one thing. Prohibiting relatives quite another. Her mental portrait of Weston the elder continued to darken. He'd disowned one child and cut off the other from people who loved him.

"Why?" she asked.

His smile was beautiful even when bitter. "My father did not share his reasons with his unreasoning son. He despised me. We ignored each other, unless my conduct made that impossible."

He put a hand on the back of his neck, rubbing at a tensed muscle.

"In the end, his health was failing. I do wish I'd tried to talk with him. About Effie, at least. Maybe . . ." He shook off the thought. "It would have made no difference. He believed that Mediterranean blood heats too easily. My mother inclined to brain fever, which brought on the more serious diseases for which she was locked away."

Nymphomania, he'd said. She thought of the paintings she'd seen in the Winter Exhibition of nymphs bathing in rivers, of nymphs caressing Cupid, of nymphs dancing with satyrs. They were fluid, graceful figures. In those paintings, the coloring was sensual. They were scenes of pleasure.

Was pleasure the disease? She wondered about his mother, this woman who wanted lush green even in winter, who died when imprisoned between bare gray walls.

"My father was always looking for signs she'd passed her weakness on to her children."

He raised the glass to his lips before remembering he'd emptied it.

"There were plenty." He laughed, laughter as bitter as his smile. "I'm sure he thought mixing with her relations would exacerbate the condition."

"You see them anyway," she said softly. "Or correspond with them."

He shrugged. "When I can. Compliance *would* save me a world of trouble. But I cannot—I will not—accept his authority, even temporarily."

He pushed off the wall, claimed the whiskey bottle, and refilled his glass.

She opened her mouth.

Don't, she told herself.

"You reject his authority," she said. "You choose blind disobedience instead of blind obedience."

Too late to stop now.

"Which means he still controls you."

He froze, half-turned away. When he finally looked at her, he saw something in her face that made him relax his stance.

"You're right, of course. I could handle it all much better," he said wryly. "When I last paid a visit to my aunt, my cousin Sofia used a crystal ball to peer into my soul. What she saw dismayed her."

He laughed, relaxing further, easing into the recollection. "Sofia possesses a distinctive flair for the dramatic. She has Greek blood on both sides, which goes a ways toward explaining it."

"Greeks are dramatic?"

"Greeks invented drama." He gave a wry tug with his mouth and she couldn't help but grin in response.

"Sofia's father, he's from Greece?"

"No. My aunt Helen married Peter Metaxas."

He registered her blank expression.

"You don't keep up with shipping dynasties? Peter Metaxas is the London-born son of Costa Metaxas. Costa started the firm Rodis & Metaxas with my maternal grandfather. They run it together, Peter and Helen. Don't quiz my aunt on rates of freight for competing steamer lines. She has a formidable head for business. She and my mother were opposites."

He fell silent and she found that she wanted him to go on. When he slipped into this mood—earnest, unguarded—and they talked together, fell into rhythm with each other, she felt an exquisite *rightness*. Felt as though they showed each other the selves most portraits, even portrait photographs, couldn't capture. Something beneath the skin.

These moments they shared were soap-bubble moments. Perfect, impossibly colored, brief. She wanted to stay inside with him longer. Before he drank a third glass and a fourth. Before they retreated into their separate, unbridgeable lives.

"What did she say to you about your soul?" she asked. "Sofia, I mean."

He set down his whiskey glass.

"You dare to ask?" He paused for effect. "She told me I was cold, sick, and silly—a strong indictment from the other world."

Her laughter rang out.

"But that's *Jane Eyre*!"

His brows had drawn together but his lips twitched in response to her amusement.

"Your Grecian oracle," she said. "She's a good English girl who reads her Brontë. Cold, sick, and silly—it's what Mr. Rochester says to Jane when he's dressed as a fortune-teller."

Now he laughed outright.

"Too bad, really. She also said I'd meet a mysterious woman and fall desperately in love. Do I have to disregard all of it?"

He seemed peculiarly intent, waiting for her answer.

"I can't say," she said, smile fading. "*I'm* not an oracle."

Suddenly, the memories flooded her. The feel of him as he slid down the bed. The thud of his knees on the floorboards. How she'd beat against his mouth.

Her breathing constricted, and she had to turn away, seizing on a jar of brushes.

"I love *June Eyre*," she said, inspecting a brush. "But my favorite from the Brontë sisters is *The Tenant of Wildfell Hall*. Do you know it? It's marvelous. A woman escapes her corrupted, adulterous husband and supports herself as a painter. She paints all day in a decaying mansion on the moor."

Ah. She was babbling. She put aside the jar, smoothing her dress. She looked at him. Dimples.

Dammit.

"Marvelous," he agreed.

"I have borrowed it five times from the lending library."

"I don't read novels," he said. "Can't, actually." He picked up his whiskey again, and she tried not to care as he took a long sip. He slouched against the wall, studying his shirt cuff.

"I'm not illiterate." He looked irritated at himself for having started down this road. "But I've never been able to figure them out. Letters, that is."

He laughed, mocking himself. He'd likely been mocking himself his whole life. Before anyone else could. She regarded him thoughtfully.

"How do you read?" she asked. "Without understanding letters?"

"I think of the words as pictures," he said, slowly. "I remember them that way, as shapes. I can't pick them apart. My Latin teacher said I had porridge for brains and that was an insult to porridge."

"The man should be boiled in porridge," she said. "Your brain is excellent! You must have a mental compendium of thousands and thousands of words."

"Something like that," he said gruffly. He shrugged, tossed back the rest of the whiskey, set the glass on the sill. But he was grinning.

"Boiled in porridge?" He pushed off the wall and came toward her, slowly, deliberately, the smile playing across his lips. His gaze was hot.

She spun to face her canvas, redirecting his attention. "You've got a good visual sense, clearly, if you're sorting through all those word pictures. What do you think, then?"

She gestured to her canvas. She hadn't yet solicited his comments, and he hadn't offered any. He'd barely looked at the picture when he came and went. Respecting her privacy, she supposed.

She felt him close behind her.

"They're confident little creatures," he said. "Oddly contained. It's interesting . . . you've taken out the garden altogether. They're almost hanging in air."

In her first versions, she'd made the figures smaller, painted in the background, the little domestic details. The bricks in the walls, the clothesline with its handkerchiefs. In this picture, she'd enlarged the figures and painted them against a dark, abstracted background, layering color until she produced the right shadowy burgundy, evocative of secrets.

"I want attention to focus on the girls, the world they're creating," she said. She risked a glance over her shoulder. Her stomach flipped. He knew nothing about art, but he was a keen and interested observer. Talking to him about her canvas felt natural. Until she looked at him. Then her mind emptied out.

"Don't move," she said. "I want to sketch you. May I? The light . . ."

The dimming sky, layered with cloud, cast a pearly light. The dome of the glasshouse *looked* like a pearl. His black hair and brows, his strong-boned face, stood out powerfully.

"Just your head," she said breathlessly, scampering for her sketchbook and charcoals. She positioned herself a few feet away.

"Stay as you were," she said. "Don't smile."

"I've been told I have a nice smile." He tried to speak without moving his lips.

"I hadn't noticed." Her hand moved rapidly. The scratching of charcoal on paper was the only sound.

"I wouldn't have broken that church window if the light were like this," he said meditatively. He didn't tilt his head, but he rolled his eyes up, trying to peer toward the dome.

"No?" She murmured it, shifting slightly, going over her lines, filling in the waves of hair.

"No," he said. "The fog was thick that night, and the window was red, a screaming red. That's how I felt when I saw it. It *screamed* at me. Red like artillery firing, metal so hot it smokes. I had to stop it."

The bottom edges of his hair almost touched his collar. She sketched the lines of his shoulders.

"Is this what you told the magistrate?"

"The magistrate didn't waste a minute on me. No, this is the first time I've spoken of it."

"Blaming the color red," she murmured. "The idea . . ."

The neck was a cylinder rising, at a slight forward incline, from the shoulder girdle. Important not to flatten it. She shaded the notch at the base, contoured the faint bump of the Adam's apple, followed the muscles as they wrapped around the sides.

"Did it stop, the screaming?" she asked, shading with the broad face of the charcoal. "When you broke the window?"

"It did, but then the police officer started shouting." The self-mockery was there again, in his voice. "If it was peace I was after, I should have chosen a different course of action."

He rolled his shoulders, tossed the hair from his eyes. His whole posture shifted.

"Drat it," he said. "Have I spoiled it?"

But she'd finished.

"Move at will." She shut her sketchbook. A good drawing. She returned the sketchbook to the bench, brushing the charcoal from her fingers.

"It's easy to talk to you." He was grinning; she could hear it in his voice. She looked up with an eagerness she couldn't disguise. That grin. Those eyes. But she saw his back instead. He'd wandered away. She watched as he poured out another glass of whiskey, her heart deflating. He gave her a sideways look, flashing a smile no less beautiful than the one she'd imagined.

"Light's going," he observed.

It was indeed, going fast. Soon, she'd be on her way home, to sew, to sleep, to wake and begin again.

"I have the mad idea," he said, "to invite you to join me for dinner."

Amazed, she folded her arms. Protests rose to her lips. She'd smudge the tablecloth with charcoal. She'd set all the servants' tongues wagging, and someone might even challenge her to a smock race. She'd no idea what spoon one used to eat mock turtle soup.

All she said was: "Do it. Invite me."

He spun in a circle, his glee contagious.

"Do you like salmon?" he asked. "Mutton? Duck?"

He reached for her, and she went breathlessly into his arms. His mouth tasted hot, of salt and peat.

"Turbot?" he murmured. Now his lips teased the sensitive spot behind her ear, found the hollow beneath her jaw.

"Turbot." She repeated it doubtfully.

"Don't decide. I'll have Humphreys bring everything," he said, releasing her and sweeping his jacket from the hook in almost the same movement. "You can see what strikes your fancy."

She jammed her fist into her stomach, tried to keep her face expressionless, but he could see the change come over her. He shrugged into his jacket, eyebrows raised, half-inquiring, half-concerned.

"What is it?"

"Nothing." She smoothed her skirt, which was burgundy and showed no smudges. "Nothing, I . . ."

She would *not* sulk like a child denied a pretty bauble. It wasn't that she wanted to dine in Weston Hall, that cold, rather hideous house. Not at all. It was just . . .

To her horror, she found herself blinking back tears. Anthony was looking at her with something very like horror in his own eyes.

"You thought I meant dine at table," he said. "Lucy, you know that would be beyond madness. After my birthday, after I inherit, of course . . ."

"Things will be different." She interrupted him with a bright, false smile. He looked agonized and paced a few steps, back and forth.

"I didn't mean to hurt you," he said. Then he swore, lifted the whiskey bottle, and caught her gaze.

"*That* will be different, at least," she said. "You will be able to drink at your table."

Awareness prickled over her.

"Ah," she said softly. "Is that why you wanted to dine with me here?" She was looking at the bottle.

How could she make this mistake? Her mother's mistake. How could she choose him when he chose *that*?

"No." He shook his head. The glasshouse dimmed, a cloud running across the lowering sun.

"I wanted to dine here because . . . it's the only place we can be." He loosed a breath. "Jesus. Maybe that didn't come out right either."

"Regardless, it's an important reminder." She began to move briskly, tidying away her supplies, setting her brushes to soak. The days left to paint her submission were dwindling. She couldn't afford to waste them. Whereas he was simply marking time until his birthday.

"Reminder? What reminder?"

She would *not* make her mother's mistake. She would *not* allow

234 • Joanna Lowell

an affable, handsome, woefully damaged man to become the center of her life. Not when that man was a black hole into which she could pour her love, her talent, until she had nothing left. Not when she already knew what it was like, the particular hell of feeling lonely in company.

"There's nowhere *we* can be." She kept her voice level. "*You* can be here with your whiskey; *I* can be here with my painting. Let's not confuse the issue. Elsewhere, well, there's no confusion at all. You are a duke, and I am . . ." She curled her lip, baring her upper teeth.

She'd achieved nothing. Could claim nothing. Artist. Seamstress. Niece.

"Lucy." He spoke into the sudden, brittle silence. "Dine with me. Here, this evening. I'm not drunk, for Christ's sake. Don't punish me."

"Poor Anthony. Punished by all. How do you endure so much hardship? We should send the little children of Shoreditch to learn fortitude at your knee."

His face shuttered. She'd hurt him. Good, she'd intended to. Better they distance themselves from each other now. When he was thirty and could drink wine at dinner in glittering company, then sip cognac with fellow lords in a smoke-filled sitting room, he was hardly likely to remember the woman who'd provided a bit of distraction in his hideaway.

"I believe my aunt is making a stew," she said. "But thank you for the invitation."

He let her walk past, the bottle still in his hand. It wasn't dramatic, no. It was just a soap bubble bursting. Her heart gone flat.

CHAPTER FIFTEEN

LUCY AND KATE gripped each other as they stepped into the hall of Augustus Burgess's studio-house on Holland Park Road. Every surface glowed with ornament: gilt, porphyry, and glass dazzling the eye. His vast painting studio was at the end of a dark blue hallway lined with life-sized panels of dancing girls, arms upraised, dark robes flowing against the gilded background. Kate had to tug Lucy past them.

"It's Gwen," Lucy murmured, pointing to one of the painted figures, dark-haired and oval-faced. Kate bestowed only a brief, dubious glance. Lucy knew what she was thinking. The uninhibited posture hardly screamed *Gwen Burgess*. When they entered the studio and spotted her in the flesh, Lucy was tempted to think she'd been mistaken. The girl stood, stiff and unsmiling, at the edge of a rowdy, laughing crowd. She did not come forward in greeting. Instead Augustus Burgess himself broke off and welcomed them. Slight and dark, with hair falling to his shoulders and a face dominated by startlingly bright blue eyes, he looked the part of celebrated artist. When he extended his hand, Kate shook it forcefully, so Lucy followed suit, blushing furiously. *The* Augustus Burgess! He was far friendlier and more animated than his sister. His gaze strayed back to Kate and he studied her for a long moment, taking in her silk knee britches and velvet jacket, before grinning his appreciation. He ushered them into his circle of guests, among whom Lucy recognized several Academy students, including—her brow knotted with annoyance—Maude and Susan.

Kate had seen them too.

"What are *they* doing here?" she whispered, indignant. Augustus Burgess's salons were exclusive, attended by famous painters of note and rising talents. Nobody would guess that, perusing this merry little assembly. Laughter pealed. Champagne flutes tinkled. Why, it might as well be a Society soiree! Three of the girls, at least, hailed from the Lower School of Painting. Had Gwen issued invitations in mockery? Where were the models? They were here to draw, were they not?

Several easels lined the wall at the far side of the room, and two others flanked the bookcase. Two men stood arguing in front of one of them, pointing at different corners of a large canvas. Not a sheet of drawing paper or stick of charcoal was anywhere in evidence.

Kate's expression held all the perplexity Lucy felt and more.

Redcliffe Davis waved at Kate languidly. He was slouching against the ebonized mantel of the massive fireplace with Thomas Ponsonby, whose vibrant hair went perfectly with the design on the chimneypiece, a floral motif picked out in red and gold.

"I want a rematch," he called to Kate. "You've been hiding from me."

"The hell I've been hiding from you." Kate glared at him. "You owe me five quid."

Someone tittered, Maude or Susan. Lucy didn't know which, so she treated them both to her most ogreish expression.

"There was disagreement, as I recall. I maintain that your sleeve touched the ball on that last shot. Hence the rematch." Redcliffe Davis looked to Thomas Ponsonby for confirmation. Ponsonby smiled regretfully.

"There's no disagreeing with a lady," he said. "I gave the match to

Miss Holroyd." He inclined his head, nodding at Kate, who looked
ready to stab him in the eye.

"Oh, stuff it," she said. "You didn't give me the match. I won it,
and I'll win the next one. Tomorrow, Davis. Long break, and the bet
is doubled."

Augustus Burgess clapped Redcliffe Davis on the back of the
neck, pushing him toward the center of the room. "She bested you
at billiards, and now she's besting you at sparring over billiards. Stop
now while you have a shred of dignity." His eyes twinkled. "Besides,
the maidens have to dress."

He whirled, pointing to a sofa. "Robes. Instruments."

"Dress?" Kate blinked. "Are we to draw each other, then?"

"No drawing tonight." Burgess shook his head. "Tonight, we
provide artistic entertainment for London's finest."

"We're to be a tableau vivant." Maude sighed her enthusiasm.
"For the Duke of Weston!"

Lucy startled, then pressed her lips into a tight smile. Over the past
week, she and Anthony had displayed a great aptitude for avoiding
each other. In fact, they made better strangers than dinner companions. No regrets. She was happy, painting. Only . . . his absence in the
glasshouse produced an odd, almost physical irritation. An itch.

She'd hoped the salon would provide a respite, remind her of her
aspirations. Which had nothing to do with the blasted Duke of
Weston.

She studied the frieze, crimson on rose, naked boys riding dol-
phins around the top of the room. Tomorrow was Anthony's birthday. Of course he'd planned a party for the night before. A spectacle.
Even if he burned down the house, by the time the news was printed,
he would be thirty, in possession of his fortune.

"Tableau vivant of what?" asked Kate. She sounded unconsciona-
bly eager. Lucy stared at her. Good heavens, she wasn't thinking
she'd participate in this nonsense!

"Ned's painting, *The Golden Stairs*." Augustus Burgess walked over to the sofa and lifted a diaphanous silver gown from the pile. "These are the very gowns worn by his models."

"Ouch," Lucy grunted. Kate had just elbowed her hard in the kidney, face glowing. Lucy scowled to suppress her own excitement.

They were talking to a man who called Edward Burne-Jones *Ned*. A tableau vivant of *The Golden Stairs* did sound marvelous.

Lucy and Kate had seen the picture the year before at the Grosvenor Gallery. Tall and mysterious, the canvas showed robed young women with violins, cymbals, and trumpets processing barefoot down a winding stone stair. It had taken their breath away.

Ponsonby jumped in. "Lady Graham will be at the party, and Miss Howard and Miss Aitchison. They were among the original models for the painting and they're set to join you in the pose. The staircase in Weston Hall winds and the railing is crystal and perfectly ethereal. The effect will be brilliant."

To Lucy's horror, Kate nodded.

"Splendid." She announced her approval. "You can count on Lucy and myself to lend our artistic support to this party of the century."

"Kate." Lucy barked it, but Kate was enjoying the attention of the crowd.

"*I* won't pose for *The Golden Stairs*, however," she said airily. "A second tableau vivant is absolutely essential. I will do *A Huguenot*, by John Millais."

A Huguenot was one of Kate's favorite paintings. It depicted a pair of sixteenth-century lovers, entwined beside a garden wall, the gallant Huguenot refusing the white armband proffered by the woman in his embrace, an armband that might have saved him from the rampaging Catholic mob.

Lucy tried again. "Kate." No good. She was competing with Burgess. He'd fixed Kate's attention, raising his eyebrows, sauntering a few steps closer.

"Do you know that painting?" he asked.

Oh dear. Was Kate going to fight with *the* Augustus Burgess?

Kate folded her arms. "We could, if you like, see which of us could reproduce it better."

"One hundred pounds on Holroyd," hooted Redcliffe Davis. "Kate, we'll split the winnings, minus the five pounds I owe you."

Burgess laughed, throwing his hands up in surrender. "I asked because the lady in that particular picture is fair-haired and small of stature. Moreover, she wears a singular look of entreaty, a look I can't imagine on your face."

Kate rolled her eyes. Burgess might be the most talented painter of their generation, but he was bacon-brained.

"I'm the Huguenot, obviously," she said. She pointed. "Maude is the lady."

"What?" Maude frowned. "No! I want to be on the golden stair."

"Yes, but your beauty forbids it," said Kate impatiently. "You're not meant to be one of many."

"Oh." Maude smiled, then caught herself and frowned more severely. "I know better than to listen to you, Kate Holroyd."

"I wish I had knee garters," said Kate, looking down at herself. "But if I can borrow a bigger velvet jacket and a hat, I'll look well enough."

"You can wear my jacket," said Burgess. He was laughing again softly. "I'll hunt down a hat."

"And me?" Maude demanded.

"You're going to wear Lucy's dress." Kate wheeled around and seized Lucy's arm. "It's velvet at any rate, and old-fashioned. And Lucy won't need it. She's going to put on a robe and carry a trumpet or a cymbal, like everyone else."

Oh, was she? Lucy looked daggers at Kate, who was blithely ignoring her agitation.

"Well, that's settled." Burgess sprang toward the door. "To the drawing room, gentlemen. The ladies need to transform themselves."

The gentlemen—and a few larvae from the Lower Painting School—followed.

"Really, the facial expression is the most important part." Kate approached Maude, who backed up into Susan. Susan gave her a shove, a bit harder than was warranted, and Kate caught her around the neck.

"There," she said, looking down tenderly into Maude's outraged face. "I am filled with honor, love, and courage, and you, you are torn between despair and desire. You're terribly far off, Maude. More longing. Remember, I'm going off to die."

"Good." Maude stamped Kate's foot and Kate dropped her arms.

"Maybe when we're in costume." She sighed. The other girls were sorting through robes and instruments.

"Gwen, will you join the pose?" she asked.

Gwen's head was bowed and she was staring at the violin case propped on the sofa. Her expression was peculiarly intense. She didn't answer. Kate shrugged and took a flute of champagne from the tray on the table, wandering across the room to inspect the easels. Lucy circled over to the sofa, selecting two small cymbals. Gwen glanced at her. Her hand stroked the violin case.

"I love *The Golden Stairs*." Lucy smiled. "Don't you?"

"I think it's his best," said Gwen, smiling back. But her smile faded as she withdrew her hand.

Something saddened her, separated her from other people. It was as though she'd found herself trapped inside a glass bell. The sounds of the outside world reached her only faintly. Lucy looked at her, unsure how to act on what she'd guessed. As she searched for the right words, Gwen turned, grabbed a robe at random, and disappeared behind a mahogany folding screen. Lucy reached for a robe of her own, wedging herself between Maude and Anna Joines, a petite brunette who produced very large historical paintings. She did so just in time to hear Susan's loud whisper.

"*Dildos,*" said Susan.

Good Lord, she and Maude were reprising the Feast of Venus.

"Shocking." Anna shivered, tossing down a silver robe and picking up a golden one. "But I don't imagine we'll encounter anything so wicked tonight."

She sounded slightly disappointed.

"I've met the duke on several occasions," said Maude. "He's unpredictable." Her smile was mysterious. "*Anything* can happen."

"What happened?" Anna took the bait. "You mean to say . . . you and the duke?"

"Well." Maude tipped her head. "There was the time we happened to find ourselves together in the Gibson Gallery . . ."

"You were *never* together in the Gibson Gallery!" Anna gaped.

"Just in passing." Maude sighed. "It was nothing really. He remembered me, of course, from the party at Constance's."

Lucy couldn't endure another second. She darted in for a robe, ducked behind the screen, and changed quickly.

"Here," she said, emerging, thrusting her dress, a heap of brown and black silk velvet, into Maude's arms. With that, she marched out into the hall. The sound of laughter followed her.

She *couldn't* pose on the staircase in Weston Hall, stand frozen with her cymbals while Anthony roamed, flirting drunkenly. He might even brush past her, climbing the stairs, some other girl on his arm, his lips near her ear as he led her to his bedroom. What mood gripped him on the eve of his birthday, his freedom?

He was bound to behave recklessly.

She stared at the mosaic floor. Its intricacy provided distraction. She drifted down the hall. Library. Picture gallery. She hovered on the threshold of the gallery. Yellow silk brocade hung between black pilasters; ornately framed pictures were spaced evenly along the walls. She adored elaborate carvings, rich colors, patterns, textures. Suddenly, though, she found herself reckoning the countless hours of labor hidden by the dazzling surfaces. Not just the architect's and the artist's labor, but the labor of the artisans and clerks, the stonecutters and woodcutters, the miners, the stevedores, the weavers, the needlewomen. It went on and on. She was part of this web that made so much beauty and so much misery.

What mood gripped *her* tonight? The opulence attracted and repulsed her.

"Miss Coover, is it?" She jumped. Augustus Burgess was coming toward her, carrying a large hat.

"I thought your name was familiar," he said. "You're Gwen's friend. She thinks highly of your paintings."

Had her mouth fallen open? If it had, he had the tact not to mention it. Gwen talked about her? As a friend? Gwen admired her painting? Here was her chance to impress Augustus Burgess, and she was opening and closing her mouth like a fish.

"The coaches are waiting," he said, when it became clear she had no response to offer. "Will you be so kind as to tell the fair company that whenever they're ready, we'll depart?"

He handed her the hat.

"For the Huguenot," he said, grinning. He had a lively good humor. A sense of fun. She'd expected a bit more snobbery and neurasthenia from the art world's darling. She imagined future salons, sketching with her friends. Kate and Gwen. Gus and Ned.

Never again would such an invitation lead back to the Duke of Weston.

Tonight was a cruel trick, an anomalous cruel trick. She would get through it. She turned the hat in her hands. Then she sighed. *Might as well.*

"Did you paint a miniature of Lady Euphemia Philby?"

"Weston's sister?" He looked surprised. "I did. She's a dear friend. You know her?"

She hesitated. "When did you see her last?"

"It was quite some time ago." The acuity of Burgess's gaze was truly unnerving. "I heard she went to France," he said slowly.

Something in his tone gave her pause. She studied his face, intelligent and mobile rather than handsome.

He didn't believe she'd gone to France. Hope sparked within her. It was all the opening she needed.

"Please." She met his bright eyes squarely. "If you know something to the contrary, tell me."

Burgess considered her. "I'm not in the habit of betraying confidences," he said. "I've been afraid to talk to Weston. I don't know if she told him . . ."

She finished the sentence. "That she eloped. She did tell him."

"Ah." He slouched against the doorframe, thinking. He was narrow shouldered, with a slight stoop. Not an imposing physical presence, but a strangely magnetic one.

"She hadn't eloped, when last we spoke. In fact, I didn't know for sure she had." He pushed a long wing of dark hair behind his ear. "She told me that she *wanted* to elope, to America. With a cowboy, she said. The miniature I painted, it was a token for Weston, to remember her by. When I heard she went to France . . . Well, I wondered if that was the real story. But with Effie, you never know. She said all sorts of things. So, she went to America?" He laughed. "Weston covered it up, I imagine. He always hated it, *talk*. Gossip. Got enough of it early on."

"He doesn't know where she is." She looked down at the hat, but she could still feel Burgess's eyes boring into her. "No one does. I shouldn't be saying this." She glanced up. "Did she mention theaters?"

"Rafferty's Music Hall." He sighed. "She liked the singers. She tried to get me to go with her, on several occasions. I would have, but I had a commission to fulfill, and by the time I called on her, she'd gone. To *France*. I was nearly chased off the doorstep."

She could imagine it. She'd someday like to paint the butler of Weston Hall, rising out of a crypt. What must he be thinking about the party of the century?

Burgess straightened. "Is there anything I can do?"

Lucy shook her head. "I don't know. If you hear from her, tell Weston."

"I always liked the fellow." Burgess said it thoughtfully. "He was the only bigger boy who didn't knock me down for the fun of it on the playing fields. Oh, he had an evil temper. He'd charge into a thicket of fists if he thought he'd heard a word against his mother. But he wasn't a bully. Bit of a fat-wit. Effie got all the brains in that family."

Lucy smiled tightly. *The* Augustus Burgess wasn't perfectly perceptive.

He returned her smile, still lost in his thoughts.

"She's a clever girl," he murmured. "She'll be all right."

She recognized the tone of a man trying to convince himself.

"And what's your connection with all of this?" he asked her.

A fair question. How to answer?

"I am His Grace's . . . painting teacher."

Burgess spun in a circle. He stared at her, hand on his forehead. She looked back at him sourly.

"A cricket bat, a rifle, a saber, yes. But a piece of chalk or charcoal? A brush?" He shook his head. "Not Weston."

And in fact, he was a bit of a snob after all.

"Why not Weston? People are surprising," said Lucy, lips thinning.

Snob or no, Burgess missed nothing. He stepped back, gaze sharp as a burin. The look he gave her made her squirm.

"People are very surprising indeed," he said, and this time his smile was real.

THE BUTLER HAD been dismissed for the night, or perhaps he'd been swept away by the throngs surging through the front door. Or gone to sleep in his coffin. There was no sign of him.

"Best keep your shoes on for now," called Burgess as he led the way down the entrance hall. The marble floor glittered with broken glass. Soon Lucy saw why. Laughing young men were swallowing their champagne at a gulp and smashing the flutes against the wall. The party underway was so rollicking that Burgess's cortege of otherworldly maidens scarcely drew a glance. Lucy turned abruptly from the group, darting into the dining room. It swam with lights and shadows. Tall red candles flickered in the candelabra. Courtesans with brilliantly dyed hair swayed their hips to music produced in fits and starts by a drunken quartet.

Lucy stared at the banquet table. Was that a woman beneath those mounded fruits? A blond dandy leered at her as he leaned forward, plucking a cluster of grapes from the woman's belly. She pivoted, putting her back to him, and wove her way to the glass doors that stood open to the garden.

She wasn't the only one who'd had the idea. The garden teemed. Shrieks rent the air as rowdies carried a kicking courtesan toward the fountain. She spotted Kate setting lanterns on the grass, Maude beside her, arms crossed, staring back toward the blazing house. It was strange to see Maude in her dress. Her pale beauty did take on a certain historical grandeur, set off by the dark velvet.

The tableau vivant was unlikely to receive the attention it deserved. Real-life lovers twined beneath budded trees.

Did Anthony count the party a success? Certainly, it was designed to shock conservative elements. His father's blood would have curdled.

She shouldn't have come. Her feet found the path that wound away from the house. She'd never entered the back garden from this direction, but she'd seen the door in the brick wall. There was a way in, and she'd find it.

She'd wait out the party in the glasshouse.

The path led her through a colonnade of cypresses that ended at another fountain. She circled it and cut away at an angle. The noises of the party had faded and her heart beat more steadily.

That's when she saw him. She froze, then pressed back into a hedge. Tall, erect, beautiful, he was coming down the path, coming from the southeast corner of the garden. Her blood turned to ice in her veins. He'd been in the glasshouse.

He hadn't been alone.

Two courtesans clung to him, one on each arm.

Her breath stuttered out of her.

Fool. She berated herself. Did she think the glasshouse hers? *Theirs?*

One of the courtesans stumbled and Anthony caught her, lifting her bodily, then setting her back on her feet. She flung a bare arm around his neck. He laughed his deep, musical laugh, the one that caused the dimples to crease his cheeks. Lucy ran. She ran down the path, back toward Weston Hall. There wasn't any escape. The peace and protection the glasshouse had provided her, the hope—all illusion. She threw herself into the center of the swirling, noisy debauch.

"THANK YOU." ANTHONY nodded at Humphreys as he extricated himself, gently, from the twining arms of the courtesans, both Rose and Myrtle girls. Humphreys had seen them stealing into the back corner of the garden and alerted him. The lad nodded back, managing to revolve a toothpick in his mouth while grinning broadly.

Meanwhile, the girls were sizing up Humphreys, whose livery made him a bad prospect. His grin, and his wink, however, sent a different message.

"This way," said Anthony abruptly, starting down the cypress-lined path. He saw Humphreys melt back between the trees. After a moment, he looked behind him. The girls were following, skipping to catch up. Anthony slowed his pace. He wasn't trying to make them hop about. For courtesans, parties were work. He understood that. But he wouldn't have them conducting their business in his private domain. Besides, so far from the house, surrounded by brick walls, no one would hear them if they screamed.

He didn't trust the majority of his guests. For all their titles and fat accounts, they were a greedy lot, always eager to squeeze harder, to wring out another drop. More power, more money, more pleasure. Many of them were George's friends, an unwholesome assortment of swells. Wealthy debtors, scofflaws. He'd tendered invitations far and wide. He'd *wanted* to throw open his doors to unsavory elements, and he'd accomplished his aim.

As though to prove it, the house came into view, brightly clad partygoers, jeweled and feathered, passing behind the windows. More roamed the garden, including a cluster of men raining punches on each other's heads as a dripping courtesan staggered in circles. He did not interrupt the fight. He felt as though he were hovering above, at the level of the rooftops. He'd made this mess, but he wasn't a part of it. He was suspended, awaiting the stroke of midnight, the release it would bring.

His enforced abstinence, his family isolation, his impotence when it came to his finances and the estates—all over.

Thirty years old. He'd expected to celebrate this birthday on the other side of the world, in a barrack or a tent, with simple rough food and simple rough company, the stars burning in the air, Mizoa close by in the dark.

If there were stars out tonight, he couldn't see them.

Past the fountain, very near the dining room verandah, he stopped short before a pair of peculiar mannequins illuminated by lanterns. The pretty blond deb from the Schools—what was her name? Megan? Maeve? She was frozen in her pose, staring up into the face of an even prettier young man, hatted, in an overlarge velvet coat that might be supposed to resemble some Elizabethan's riding habit.

A tableau vivant, a tame one. The Rose and Myrtle had been famous for staging salacious scenes, from myths mostly. After the exposé in the *Pall Mall Gazette*, the madam had been forced to scale back, to err on the side of discretion rather than decadence.

The girls who followed Anthony now fit into the new ethos. Fallen from decent families, healthy, young but not too young. One had black hair, thick, like Effie's. She'd broken sprigs from the cherry tree, woven the pink blossoms into the braid that circled her head like a crown. They were the sort of women preferred by government ministers, the sort who mingled easily at the private parties of territorial grandees. Of course, if they were to turn up at one of the Season's daylight gatherings, half the guests would faint, and the other half would blink and scratch their heads, feigning ignorance. Total hypocrisy. Well, minus the courtesans. They were honest enough.

Anthony's anger felt hot, sustaining. It would carry him forward until the clock struck midnight. Then he would go down in the flood, drain as many bottles as he pleased, forget everything. Forget everyone he'd failed.

He blinked away Lucy's face, the desolation in her eyes.

Ten minutes to go. The evening was passing quickly. He entered the house and roamed from room to room, surveying the damage with satisfaction. Broken bottles, squashed fruits. The furniture might not come through the slaughter.

In the corner of the drawing room, he saw Cecil. He was gripping one of his brothers by the scruff of the neck, directing him toward a potted plant. Before they reached it, the lad retched, vomiting on his boots.

Anthony's knees felt locked, and his gaze as well. *Dammit.* He'd wanted to forget everyone he'd failed, and now the man he'd considered his closest friend stood directly in his line of vision. Anthony ran a hand across his face, drove his knuckles into his eyes, then turned away sharply. Prepared to flee. The stiff words he'd exchanged with Cecil at his father's funeral, the subsequent calls he'd received coldly and never repaid—he couldn't take any of it back. That warm day in February, when they'd come upon each other riding in the park, and he'd ridden on . . .

No, after such sustained ill treatment, Cecil could want nothing more to do with him. Except. Anthony remained frozen in place. Cecil was here, wasn't he? And he'd never cared much for riotous parties. Rugby, riding, rowing, wrangling his siblings, and electrical engineering—these were his preferred pastimes.

This evening, he'd come to wrangle, clearly. But perhaps he'd come, as well, to give Anthony one more chance.

Anthony spun around and started across the room, heart thudding.

"Blast it, Thomas." Cecil gave Thomas a shake as Anthony approached. "What did you smoke, you rascal?" It looked as though he were shaking a younger version of himself. Nature had only one mold for Ponsonbys.

Cecil noticed Anthony and let his brother go so abruptly the boy staggered into the potted plant stand, barked his shin, and yelped. Cecil ignored him, straightening. Anthony detected no hostility in his face, but rather, wariness. He scratched behind his ear, invisible eyebrows raised, and then, on a gusty exhalation, he smiled. A warm, familiar smile.

"Sorry about the rug," he said, shaking his head at the mess. Anthony almost laughed his relief. He took a half step closer.

"I'm the one who's sorry," he said. "Christ, I've been . . ." He cut off the flow of words, aware of their audience. The room was thronged, the courtesans hovering nearby, a pair of insufferable baronets at his elbow.

"Listen, Cecil." He shifted, uncomfortable but determined to continue. "I have a surprise for you, in the stable. You'll never believe it. I couldn't believe it myself."

He wouldn't name Snap—that would ruin the fun. He'd wait and see if Cecil's eye was as keen as his, if he, too, would know the old horse by his pastern.

"Consider me intrigued." Cecil hesitated. "So. I'll come by, then." He couldn't flatten the lilt, the question in it.

"Do," said Anthony, and felt the air rush into his lungs, sickly with smoke, cologne, vomit, liquor, but he didn't care. His chest felt wider, some tight nasty band of hurt loosening. "I want to hear about the developments in your master plan for municipal illumination." Cecil had been working for years to develop a commercial apparatus for the electric lighting of all London's streets. "And I'll tell you . . ." He coughed as his throat squeezed.

"We'll start there," said Cecil, and he gripped Anthony's arm—a strong grip that made Anthony pity Thomas, who'd felt it so lately on his neck.

"Thomas!" Cecil turned from Anthony, for the boy was retching again.

Anthony brushed aside the baronets and headed for the hallway. Someone had stood a bottle of whiskey on a side table and he caught it by the neck without missing a step.

The courtesans still followed.

In the hallway, he gestured to a wide-eyed footman.

"Put the guest rooms in the north wing at their disposal."

The footman nodded, a blush creeping up into his hairline. Anthony looked past him. What he saw had the quality of an apparition. A dozen barefoot women were arrayed on the stairs, dressed in robes that glimmered in pale metallic shades. They held musical instruments in their hands. They made a beautiful, otherworldly picture.

Another tableau vivant.

If he knew a damned thing about art, he'd no doubt recognize it. He scanned the fresh young faces, unpainted and serene. The lovely musicians seemed attuned to unheard melodies, and something inside him stirred too. It was ensorcelling, their silent, motionless performance.

At the top of the steps, a woman turned her head. Nothing serene about *her* face. It wasn't precisely her face as he'd been picturing it. Bereft, the hurt softening her chin, lashes thick with unshed tears.

Lucy stared at him. Her chin was tilted up, dry eyes narrowed into gleaming slits. Contempt was written in every line of her face. He'd always been able to read that particular expression.

He strode forward, fury lifting his heels. He heard the clock strike as he reached the stairs.

It was his birthday.

He passed between the women, climbing the steps, bottle in hand. When he reached Lucy, he paused. Their eyes met, hers a smoky gold.

Without a word, he tugged her up the final step and down the hall.

Chapter Sixteen

As soon as he shut the door to his bedchamber, he crowded her against it, planting his hand on one side of her head, the bottle on the other. She tried to turn her face from him, and as she shifted, her cheek came into contact with the glass. Her lips curled.

Ludicrous, his need for her affirmation.

"I'm a good man," he said. Laughed at himself as he said it. "Dammit, I'm not who you think I am, who my father, or Yardley, or . . ."

She cut him off.

"Who are you, then?" Tension vibrated through her limbs. The same tension had vibrated through him, for weeks now. Now he almost shook with the force of his longing, with the effort it took to restrain himself from biting her plumped lower lip. A provocation. Her lips, her body, her *being*. All of her provoked him.

You're a duke, she'd said in the glasshouse. Well, here he stood, the fully empowered Duke of Weston. An accident of birth. Not even. The result, rather, of George's accidental death. Who was he, really? Once upon a time, he'd wanted nothing more than a soldier's kit, felt most alive on a fast horse opening into a gallop under a midnight sky. And now? What did he want?

He let his hand fall to her shoulder, taking up a lock of hair, winding it around his fingers before releasing it. She caught her breath. Then she reached up, curled her arm around his. He let her force his arm down, work the bottle out of his hand. She looked at it, studied it, brow furrowed, as though she could break it down into constituent parts. Glass, liquor. Sand, barley.

"I'm not drunk," he said, detecting petulance in his tone, hating it. Legally no longer a child. Why did he sound like a sulky boy? "I haven't had a sip."

"I've heard that before," she said flatly. And she had, of course. She'd heard it from him. Heard it from her father. Heard it, no doubt, her whole life.

He'd always hated being hectored, judged, patronized. Strange— with her, he *wanted* to explain, to prove himself. To be better.

She didn't look at him. She kept staring at the bottle. Perhaps she could see her face reflected there darkly.

"This is what I'd use to peer into your soul." Now she did look up. Her eyes glittered terribly. "A bottle of whiskey, not a crystal ball. But I'm not a fortune-teller. You want to find out who you are? Here. Best of luck to you."

She thrust the bottle back at him, hard, a blow to the diaphragm that knocked loose his breath.

"Lucy," he began, fingers wrapping the neck of the bottle. He lifted it, but he could see only the finger-smeared surface of the glass. When he lowered it, he met those glittering, baleful, beautiful eyes. He wanted to see his soul there, trapped in their amber.

"I saw you in the garden," she said, and laughed. The laughter hit a false note. He realized she was trembling. She had watched him coming down the path from the back garden flanked by courtesans.

"If you must have a . . . a . . . *Feast of Venus* in the glasshouse, move my easel out of the way and mind the brushes. That is my only request, and it's only a request. You have every right, of course, to do what you want with whom you want and to drink yourself into an early grave. Your Grace."

She turned, pulling the doorknob. He pushed the door closed

with the palm of his hand. The look she slanted up at him made every muscle in his body clench.

"Oh," she said. "And happy birthday."

"Dammit." He growled, bending toward her, elbows pressed to his sides to keep himself from gathering her into his arms.

"Lucy, I wasn't with them, those women. I wasn't drinking. I was . . ."

What? He didn't want to say it.

"I was waiting." He spoke the words unwillingly. "I was waiting until the clock struck. To drink. To get drunk. To drown out . . . everything."

She was staring at him, lips parting. Her expression gave him courage. It seemed . . . open. She would listen.

"I don't know why." He shook his head, rueful. "Perhaps because I can. It's funny: it used to be because I couldn't. And it's all because of *him*."

He meant his father. He meant George.

"That's what I tell myself. Told myself."

She'd been standing rigid, back against the door. He could see her posture loosening.

"I want things to be different, not because of the will. Not because I'm obeying or disobeying my father. I want . . ."

The distance between them had closed. He moved aside locks of hair, stroking down to the gauzy edge of her robe.

"I want to find the self I'm proud to be," he said hoarsely. "It's not in this bottle." He dropped it, a dull thud.

He wanted a different intoxication, less lonely. One that would please them both.

The door was thick, the walls paneled. The sounds of the party had faded, but they both heard a crash, a shout, then shrieks of laughter.

"It's late," she said. "I should go." She didn't reach again for the doorknob. His fingers ran lightly down her sleeve, closing on her wrist. The bones were so delicate. And yet her wrists were strong, her hands capable. More than capable. Gifted.

"Should?" he said. There was no more should. Not tonight.

"What do you want?" He breathed the question.

Her eyes betrayed her. They slanted down to his lips. He pulled her into his body and kissed her.

Their teeth grated together as her arms twined around his neck. Sensation sliced through him. He was already in ribbons, flayed by desire. She had done this to him, exposed him, forced him to bear witness to his own body, his own soul. He dipped down to kiss the hollow at the base of her throat, bending her backward, arm tightened around her waist. With one arm, he lifted her, hip nudging between her thighs. She straddled him, gauze bunching, air hissing out of her. One step, two steps, three. He tossed her onto the bed, stood over her, staring.

She lay on her back, wild-eyed, hair straggling down from her bun in Medusa locks, silver gown hitched up around her bare calves, sweetly rounded. Her breasts, divided by the pale blue yoke of the robe's bodice, rose and fell with her rapid breaths, full, the peaked nipples visible through the thin layers of fabric. She lifted herself onto her elbow as he turned down the gaslight.

"Don't turn off the lights," she said with urgency.

His mouth crooked. She was mad to fear that he'd proceed in darkness. He'd dreamed of the blush that stained her breasts with seashell pink, dreamed of the freckles on her inner thighs. Fire was his accomplice.

He was already lighting candles. His hands were steady, movements precise. If he were drunk, he'd sacrifice this delicacy, which served for much more than striking matches. He held a candle aloft, studying the play of light and shadow across her face, wide across the freckled cheekbones. Her eyes shone. Their color was alchemical gold, mysterious, unstable. Shadows pooled at the corners of her mouth, beneath the plush of her bottom lip. Her beauty was a be-

witchment. He set the candle back on the table, put a knee on the
bed, and kissed her again, pushing the robe down from both shoulders, kissing the upper slopes of her breasts. He slid his hand into her
chemise and forced her left breast up roughly, catching the nipple
between his teeth. He sucked and she moaned, her hands pressing
the back of his skull. Her nails dug into his scalp, tiny crescents of
pain.

He lifted his head, rolling her nipple between his thumb and first
finger.

"What do you want?" he asked with new purpose, meeting her
eyes. They were wide-open. She wanted to see, yes, and she would
see, but sight was no disembodied gift. Eyes were flesh. Matter. He
planned to make her very eyes swell with desire. A blur over everything.

But not yet.

She pushed his chest hard and he stood back as she sat up. He
couldn't help but stare at the breast that thrust above the crumpled
chemise, the rosy nipple taunting him. So impudent. He would
teach that nipple a lesson. He would *torment* that nipple.

"Strip," she said huskily. "I want to see . . . you."

He gaped at her, surprised at his own surprise. Then he grinned,
shrugging out of his jacket, unbuttoning his shirt. As he dropped his
shirt onto the floor, he felt an unexpected shyness. He'd never
stripped in this way, on command, a woman sitting straight-backed
before him, eyes hooded. He hesitated, hands on his trouser buttons.

"Go on," she ordered. It was little more than a croak.

When he peeled off his flannels, he heard her gasp. He kicked
them away, glancing at her. She'd caught her lip between her teeth.

He was so hard it hurt.

She dropped her legs over the side of the bed and stood, laying
her fingertips on his chest. Her face was bright with triumph.

"Turn," she said.

"You like giving orders," he observed. It felt unspeakably erotic, letting her have this power over him, watching her glory in it. He turned slowly, and her fingers trailed over him, sliding around his abdomen and across the small of his back and his hip, wandering down to trace the curve of his buttocks.

If he were drunk, he'd be inside her by now, plunged to the hilt, her knees by her ears. Crass and hot and fast. His smile faded as her hand closed around his cock.

He couldn't stifle a groan. Now her look of exultation was tinged with wonder.

He would teach her what she had to exult in.

"My turn," he said. He backed her up until she fell against the bed, then settled beside her. This was no narrow cot, this enormous bed with its heavy, tethered curtains, its cool, fresh linens. He had room to maneuver. He rolled her over, pulled her up so she was on her hands and knees. He unlaced the back of the robe, lifted one arm out, then the other, slid the fabric over the swell of her hips, the fullness of her buttocks. It made a frothy pile at her knees. He palmed her buttocks, curved his body over her, reached to tease her breasts as she rocked, rubbing into him. He gritted his teeth, heaving her up, forcing her head to the side so he could lean over her shoulder and plunder her lips. His hand closed on her breast, flicking the nipple, the heel of his palm grinding the flesh in a slow circle. Unconsciously, she mimicked the motion with her buttocks, grinding against him.

He could spill his seed now. He lifted her away and she made a guttural sound of protest, turning to face him. Now he could see her, the straight line of her shoulders, the upward tilt of her breasts, the slope of her waist, the curve of her belly, the tuft of hair on her mound, glinting with red in the candlelight.

Nothing blind about this experience, this feeling. He savored his awareness.

"You've bewitched me," he told her, and she made a faint sound of negation that whooshed into a sigh as he lifted her breast, licking the crease beneath. She had faint freckles even there, in that delicate, secret place. He licked up the slope, tasting the salt of her skin. With his other hand, he gripped her hip, then pressed her quim, hard.

"You said you want to see. Is that all you want?" He stroked with his thumb, parting her. Her breathing rasped. He lifted his hand to her chin, tilted up her face, looked into her eyes, hazed with longing, her longing, his longing. He could no longer tell.

"If that's all . . . I'll stop now."

Could he? He stilled his hand, withdrew it, sitting back on his heels.

"You don't have to go further."

She shivered. Cool air had rushed between their feverish bodies. Her breathing still rasped. She lunged forward and kissed him with bruising force, lips, teeth, tongue. A fierce joy rose in him, but he broke their kiss, gripped her face in his hands, held it an inch away.

"Say it," he said. "Tell me." He kissed her throat, her cheeks, her eyelids.

"I want you, Anthony," he prodded. She made a sound deep in her throat, but her voice seemed to have caught there. The look she gave him was mutinous. She liked to boss but she didn't like to be bossed. He couldn't suppress his smile.

"You have to say it," he said. "To get . . . this." He dampened his thumb with his lips while she stared, face tense, brows drawn together. He pressed the wet pad to the small knot between her thighs, the center of her pleasure, and her jaw slackened, lips parting.

"Shall I make you beg me, then?" he asked, moving his thumb. She gasped, shuddering. She tried to speak.

"You can nod," he said. And she nodded, head falling against his shoulder.

PLEASURE WAS PULSING through her, robbing her of language, of all abstraction. But she'd never had the words to describe his beauty.

Instead she'd used her hands, to paint it, and she used her hands now. She touched a vein that snaked around his forearm, followed it, felt the hard points of his elbows, stroked up the bunched muscles in his arms. She found that by scratching her fingernails across his nipples she could make him gasp, make the muscles in his stomach ripple. But then she moved her hand lower, to where the ridged abdomen flattened below his navel, and down . . .

Suddenly she was on her back, sinking into the mattress. He'd launched himself at her, covered her with his body. She wiggled, deliciously pinned. He kissed down her arms, kissed her palms; then he was kissing the instep of her foot, kissing up her legs.

No wonder the gods were always turning into beasts. The myths relied on symbols to express the most primitive fears and desires.

She felt as though feathers were about to push out through her skin. They must. She couldn't endure this feeling much longer and remain unchanged. Her need was feathered, clawed, fanged.

"Please," she moaned, and he laughed, low and sultry.

"Red," he whispered, his mouth opening against her thigh. Then he lifted her so she slid down and felt his lips, his teeth, ah, against her, right between her thighs, that delicious juncture that she hadn't known could swell and beat and produce such miraculous sensation, until he'd shown her. The moisture was gathering, heat coursing through her, as his tongue delivered a slow, long lick. She twisted and moaned. His hands gripped her hips, steadying her.

She gasped, undulating against his mouth.

"Please," she said again, breathless. Begging.

"Please what?" he said. He rose onto his elbows, mouth glistening, jaw clenched. His green eyes burned. He bent his head and licked again so she bucked, shuddering.

"Is this what you want? My mouth?"

"Y-y-yes," she stuttered. "Yes." But she wanted more. She wanted to metamorphose into something wild, a fantastical creature composed of both of their bodies, writhing as one.

Her mind felt cored like an apple. There was a hollow where the words used to be. How to say it? She tugged under his arm, bade him position himself higher up her body. She reached between his legs and gripped him, the skin sliding smooth over the hardness.

The phallus. In painting, it was so often hidden by drapes, or the angle of the thigh, the sweet curve of a single leaf. This was no phallus. The heated length of muscle extended toward her, thick, proud. Impossibly hard. Huge. It was a cock. His cock. The word thrilled her. It didn't belong to academic discourse on art. It belonged to them.

"I want your cock," she said, appalled, delighted by her daring, and then she could say no more. He stuffed his tongue into her mouth, his lips hot and briny. He shifted over her, pelvis rubbing between her thighs, his cock sliding over the swollen flesh.

"I want . . ." she moaned, and that was all, that was everything. She *wanted*. Her legs fell open wider, and then she felt seared as he slid inside her, stretching her, filling her, driving deeper. She clawed his buttocks, the burning transforming from pain into radiance, the air bursting from her lungs. He fisted his hand in her hair, pulling her head back.

"You wanted to see." He grated the words. "Look. Look at me."

She hadn't realized her eyes had closed. She forced her lids up and looked into his face, his expression hard and concentrated. His gaze locked on hers as he flexed and thrust deeper still. He clasped her hand, fingers spreading hers as they twined. Even that sensation, her fingers stretching around his, mirrored this delicious stretching inside her. She gasped, gasped again. He was galloping her now, and she was surging to meet him. There was nowhere to go but out of her body, bursting the skin. There was no line, no form, just smears of color, of feeling. Black, green, ochre, red.

"Lucy," he growled. His lips twisted. His strokes slowed but the angle changed, and she couldn't speak, could only moan, holding his back, cupping the tense curve of his flexing buttocks. His eyes filled her vision, needful. Green dominated. The world was green, a green plundered from dragons' scales. He riveted her. He filled every bit of her, until she overflowed herself. He cried out, jerking his hips, and her cries mingled with his.

"Oh, oh." She broke, seizing against him as he thrust again, again, his tongue deep in her mouth so the words he groaned were also deep inside her, felt rather than heard.

I love you.

He rolled off her, spilling his seed onto the sheets with a harsh moan. Her body still quaked with aftershocks of pleasure, warm, tingling. He pulled her against his chest. Had he said it? The vibration was fading.

I love you.

Safe and sated in his arms, she was drifting into sleep, the darkness itself velvety and carnal, a soft burgundy blooming behind her closing lids.

HIS HEAD WASN'T pounding when he woke up. His eyelids didn't cut like glass when he blinked at the bed's canopy. A sweet, warm weight pressed his shoulder, his thigh.

She lay on her side, one leg thrown across him, breath easing through her parted lips, curls spread across the pillow. He removed his arm gently, sliding it free, untangling a lock of hair that wrapped him like a vine.

Sleeping Beauty and the briar wall in one.

He dressed quietly, hurriedly, in the clothing he'd discarded the night before. No sign that Humphreys had appeared. Passed out, no doubt, under a rosebush. Just as well.

He stood at the side of the bed for a moment, looking down at her, wonder loosening his muscles, expanding his chest. She had felt like magic beneath him. The first choice he'd made on this, the day of his birth, was the right choice. Certainty glowed within like a pearl.

He would carry that glow to the solicitors' office.

As he descended the staircase, he noticed a silver trumpet standing on a step, abandoned by a pretty musician. He swept it up. He wanted to announce the day, to signal his happiness to the quiet house. He blew the first note of reveille. Ridiculous impulse. Laughing at himself, he hooked the trumpet on the finial on the newelpost at the base of the stairs and passed from the house.

He was whistling as the clerk led him through the lobby of the firm of Hamilton, Johnstone, and Giles. Fifteen minutes later, the song had died in his throat. He was sitting in a wingback chair, staring at Yardley and at Hamilton and Johnstone. The solicitors were exchanging looks of their own. Hamilton was a thin, bald, wrinkled man in spectacles. Johnstone was rounder, with copious hair slicked back, but he, too, was advanced in years. They'd both represented Anthony's father for decades.

"I don't understand," Anthony said at last. He crossed his legs, trying to contain his anger.

The ignoramus, blinking up at the learned, long-suffering men given charge of him. God, he wearied of the role.

He continued carefully. "You agree I have satisfied my father's conditions. I see no reason I shouldn't assume full control of my affairs this very day."

A champagne bottle popped. Yardley filled a flute and handed it to him. He took it numbly.

"It's a special day," said Yardley, passing champagne to the solicitors. He was dressed in an exquisite gray suit elegantly offset by the rich leather of his chair. He smiled.

"Your father would have been proud," he said.

"Spare me." Anthony took a swallow of champagne, to rinse the bitterness from his mouth, and set the glass aside.

Hamilton shuffled papers, produced one, and handed it to him in silence. The print swam before Anthony's eyes. His rage knew no bounds.

"What's the meaning of this?"

The solicitors hesitated until Yardley spoke into the silence.

"Your father wanted to exert a positive influence on your life, not merely impose prohibitions. A respectable home life will provide you with the strong and stable foundation you need to continue to make responsible decisions. None of us knew he'd written a second codicil to that effect until last week. I was organizing his financial papers, to help with the transition, and I discovered it. Of course, I brought it here straightaway, so Mr. Hamilton and Mr. Johnstone could ascertain if it was operative. Which—I defer to you, gentlemen"—he tipped his head toward the solicitors—"it does seem to be. Dated, signed, witnessed."

Anthony couldn't look at him. He leapt to his feet, addressing himself to Hamilton.

"This paper," he said, shaking it so hard the edge tore, "continues the trusteeship of Mr. Yardley."

"Until you marry, yes," said Hamilton, sighing. "Do sit down, Your Grace."

Anthony stabbed at the paper with his finger. "Not just marry. Marry a woman of *unimpeachable moral character and good breeding.*"

Johnstone smiled patiently. "Marriage is sacred, of course, and limitations placed on the right to marry aren't always enforceable. But the court does uphold provisions that *facilitate* a prosperous and sober union, particularly if the delimited category of potential spouses contains a reasonable number of options. That's the case here. No one would argue there aren't many fine women of *unimpeachable moral character and good breeding* for you to choose among."

Anthony's laughter sounded unraveled, even to his own ears. "Do I decide if the woman fits the criteria?"

"No." Hamilton cut his eyes at Yardley. "The consent of a neutral designee of excellent reputation is required. If you finish reading, you'll see that your father specified Lord Southgate."

"Neutral." Anthony shook his head. "Southgate was my father's crony and is now *his* crony." He turned to Yardley and his voice rose. "How many votes have you wrangled for Southgate? What favors does he owe you?"

Yardley looked blandly at the solicitors.

"You see how he needs a tempering influence," he murmured.

"I'm sorry this comes as such an unpleasant surprise." Johnstone leaned over his desk. "Perhaps you'll come to see it differently, as an opportunity to build the best possible future, starting now, on your birthday."

Not a bit of it. Slowly, Anthony ripped the document into pieces, letting them shower onto the carpet. Consummate professionals, neither solicitor raised an eyebrow.

"A copy, of course." Hamilton sighed again. "Smythson will have to draw up another."

"I'll contest this." Anthony swallowed bile. "Perhaps the condition itself is legal, but that codicil is dated only days before my father died. Apoplexy had ravaged his mind."

Johnstone lit his pipe. "You would need to produce evidence that the testator, your father, was not in possession of testamentary capacity."

"A preponderance of evidence," added Hamilton. "Given that the codicil is rational, of regular form and judicious disposition, without any suspicious marks or alterations. The burden of proof rests with the contestant."

More bile rose into Anthony's throat. His father *hadn't* seemed altogether sane at the end; all the old grievances intensified, wracking him. But what proof could he produce?

He dropped back into his chair so he could look Yardley straight in the eyes.

"You knew about this second codicil all along," he said quietly. "You knew, and you waited. Did you come up with it together? Who wanted it more? Him? Or you?"

"I'll find Smythson now," said Hamilton, rising. "Unless Your Grace has further questions."

"We'll give you a moment." Johnstone followed Hamilton to the door. Pipe smoke lingered in the room. The air was still. Such a tasteful, well-appointed office. Anthony's heart was beating as though enemy cannons were trained upon him.

"Let me guess." He leaned forward. "To build the best possible future, Southgate shall determine that I should marry Lavinia."

Yardley didn't have the decency to look chagrined. Instead, he smiled.

"The two of you are well suited," he said, nodding. Anthony smiled back. Then he turned and punched the back of his chair. This explosion of violence relieved nothing.

His chest heaved. Over the past months, he'd become increasingly disillusioned, but he realized his trust in Yardley hadn't died, not completely. He realized because it was dying now, and *he* was inflicted with the death throes.

Once upon a time, this man's good opinion had meant the world to him. It was the spar to which he'd clung as a boy in hostile seas.

The spar had snapped.

"I will never marry Lavinia," he said. For the first time, Yardley's mild expression hardened.

"Stop yourself before you say something about my daughter she doesn't deserve. You're angry at me. Don't take it out on her. She adores you."

"I take nothing out on her." Anthony drilled a knuckle into his temple. Christ, the waves of rage beating against the inside of his skull were going to crack it open. "It's none of our fault, who we're born to."

Once upon a time, he'd wished he was born to Robert Yardley.

"You will marry Lavinia," said Yardley softly. "Your brother threw away his life. Your sister threw away her life. Your father and I have constructed a life for you and bound you to it. As lives go, it's a good one. You should be grateful."

He felt no gratitude. He stood, put his hands in his pockets.

"I will not marry Lavinia," he said. "I will marry Lucy Coover."

"You're baiting me. Don't," Yardley warned. "Let's start well today. Miss Coover is a laughable match. I can tell you now that Southgate will agree. George had several passing infatuations with women of her ilk, all of them angling for annuities. Miss Coover has proven herself a practical, rather self-interested young woman. As soon as she sees the benefit, she agrees to the terms. Remember the Albion. You don't *marry* a Miss Coover, Anthony. The answer is absolutely no, and someday you *will* understand, and thank me."

The disingenuousness of it took his breath away. Yardley accused Lucy for falling prey to his own persuasion, based on lies and appealing to her deepest fears. But—he hated himself for it—an ugly ripple passed over him, sullying the wonderment he'd felt upon awaking. This was the real world, and there wasn't a place for them, for him and Lucy, to *be* together without reality flooding in.

Anthony couldn't bear to look at Yardley a moment longer. He looked out the window at the tree-lined street. He'd been schooled, many times, in defeat. Was learning to excel at it.

He cleared his throat. "The committee investigating the Charlotte Road properties." A squirrel was dancing from branch to branch, fearless. "Have they returned with any findings?"

He heard Yardley shift in his chair. After a pause, he responded.

"In fact, the committee met the other night. The evictions will proceed."

"Also for the best, I'm sure," said Anthony. His chest was tight, muscles like springs in his arms and legs.

"As a matter of fact . . ." began Yardley, but the tempest in Anthony's skull lashed, drowning out his words. He was exiting the lobby before he heard the clerk calling his name. More business needed attending to. Anthony scarcely slowed.

"Talk to Mr. Yardley," he said. "He handles my affairs."

HIS FEET PROPELLED him through the mews and into the back garden, down the camellia walk to the glasshouse. Habit, habit could be relied on. Lucy would have left his room by now, gone to the Royal Academy, where her own habits positioned her behind her easel.

They were led in different directions, to different ends.

He beelined for the tank, dug deep inside, searching for a full bottle. His fingers brushed a smaller, more flexible cylinder, wrapped in linen. He blew air through his nose. Lucy's painting. Not what he needed. His fingers closed around a bottle, heavy with dark rum. Good.

He was done with everyone and everything. He took a hard swallow and then another.

SHE HULLOED SOFTLY on the threshold.

"I thought I might find you here," she said. She could see him sitting on the sill, feet propped on the tank, head tilted back against the glass.

"I can hear Mr. Barrett buzzing." She came slowly into the glasshouse. Inexcusable, really, to skive off her lessons. She didn't care.

"I wanted to see you, to say happy birthday, properly."

Aside from the low buzzing—a fly bumping high in the glass dome, *not* Mr. Barrett—her footsteps made the only sounds. The light fell thickly, warm and muffling. A strange timidity made her tiptoe.

"Anthony?"

At last, he rolled his head on his neck and looked at her. A smear of blood tracked across his forehead.

"What . . ." She ran to him, but he held up his hand, stopped her.

"It's nothing. I hit my head on that bloody bracket."

She slowed, took in the bottle balanced on his knee. He slugged from it, then placed it behind him on the sill, out of her sightline. A strange mix of boldness and slyness. He didn't seem himself, or rather, he seemed the self she knew least.

A bleakness started to unroll within her, a long, blank scroll.

Swiftly, she walked to the marble bench, picked up the newspaper-wrapped package tied with green ribbon.

"For you," she said. "Happy birthday."

His face changed. It wasn't anticipation. It was closer to dread. She pushed the present into his hands. He tore the newspaper clumsily, and her stomach sank. He looked at the miniature; then his gaze shifted to her. His eyes looked empty.

"I know you might not want a portrait of yourself," she said hastily. "It's for you to give to Effie, when you find her."

She'd felt foolish, working on it during their week of silence, but she'd persisted. She'd thought, at certain moments, that the miniature might function as an exorcism, ridding her of her obsession. In the end, she'd seen it as something else entirely, something she had to give him no matter what.

A talisman for his sister's return.

He stared at the portrait, at his own painted eyes. Then he propped it on the sill by the bottle and looked away.

After the storm of tenderness she'd experienced the night before, it was odd to feel suddenly so flattened. She'd imagined that on this day, of all days, he'd grin, caper, dance, do a bloody headstand.

He must have met first thing with his solicitors. The visit hadn't gone well. She opened her mouth to ask, but he spoke first.

"Let's run away." His voice was so low she doubted the words.

"Run away?" she said. "Are you mad?"

"Mad," he said, and suddenly his voice was wild, and he stood, enfolding her in a brutal embrace. He was damp with sweat, radiating heat. She could smell the alcohol. Instinctively, she stepped back, and he let his arms drop.

"Let's get married madly in Scotland," he said. "Let's live in a cottage, or something even more picturesque, a gorse mill, and eat bannocks of oats. I'll break horses and you'll paint lairds in their drafty castles."

She blinked. The dimples didn't flutter in his cheeks. His face was stark.

"What are you saying?" Her eyes found the bottle on the sill, measured the level of the dark, sun-struck liquid. How much had it contained when he'd started?

He swiped at the blood on his forehead. He looked pale.

"I gained nothing. No, it's worse. I lost everything."

"You did not inherit?" Now she understood his wildness. But not yet how it came to be. She glanced at the floor, at the ripped newspaper, a penny rag that spilled ink on all the day's scandals, large and small, real and invented.

"Was it . . ." She hesitated. "The drinking?"

He laughed, a chilling laugh. It froze her blood to hear him so mirthless. He spun around, swept up the bottle, and slugged from it again, like a parched man might slug from a canteen of water.

"No." He shook his head. "It turns out there's another proviso." He returned the bottle to the sill, perhaps to avoid her eyes.

"I have to marry," he said. Now he scratched at his forehead, and the blood freshened, began to slide toward his brow.

"I have to marry a well-bred, unimpeachable woman approved by my father's friends." He took a quick breath. "They've gone ahead and selected one. I have to marry Lavinia."

She could not look at him, so she looked at the miniature. She wasn't Augustus Burgess, but she understood Anthony's face, the planes, the colors. The portrait was compelling, lively, unsmiling but full of humor. Only she could see the dimple waiting to flex in his cheek, because she was the one who darkened the color ever so slightly, hinting at a quirk in the muscle.

"But that's not so bad, is it?" she heard herself say. "She's lovely. Who else were you going to marry? Properly, not madly."

She risked a look at him. A mistake. Color was leaching from his face, the smear of blood, by contrast, taking on a freakish brightness.

Walk away. Walk out into the garden. You're late for class. This is not your life.

Was it her mother's voice she heard?

This man had the power to hurt her beyond her wildest imaginings. Waking up in his bed, padding around his room, she'd allowed herself to imagine a *proper* togetherness. One that meant they didn't hide from the world, or from each other. She'd allowed herself to luxuriate, believing him, believing in him. She'd thought, last night, when he'd dropped the bottle, that he was inviting her to see through a different glass, to see a different future.

She could not move. Her heart had stopped.

"No one," he said. "I'm not meant for proper marriage. Let's go. *Now.*"

"To Scotland?" Her laughter was shrill. Did he even hear himself, hear how little he offered her? "I don't know that I'd want even a reformed rake." She spit it out. "Let alone one who won't so much as pretend to offer constancy."

"Constancy?" His teeth flashed. "You mean my money? I'd be giving it up, all of it, for you. But perhaps it's my money that attracts you."

Bastard. She almost choked on her rage.

"Don't deceive yourself. You don't give up anything for *me*. You want to hide in Scotland with a bottle. Sit pitying yourself in some hovel. Spoiled *drunkard*."

She whirled but he caught her wrist. She tugged, head lowered stubbornly.

"You could stay here," she said to his shining boots. Expensive.

Kept in high polish by someone else's labor. "You don't need to run away from London to give it all up. You could work as a horse trainer and rent a cabbage-smelling flat and live a bloody decent life."

He made a noise in his throat, something like a laugh, that only incensed her further.

"Scotland sounds more exciting, more romantic, because it's a fantasy," she said. "Hand in hand, tramping through the heather. Moonlight. Sea mist. It's a silly, *selfish* dream."

She'd be throwing away years of artistic training, all her ambition. And he'd be abandoning his sister, his responsibilities, every last shred of self-respect.

"Marry Lavinia," she bid his boots. "Do the thing *properly*."

He dropped her wrist. At last, she looked up at him, unprepared for the intensity of his gaze.

"Last night," she said, and his eyes burned hotter. "Last night, I talked with Augustus Burgess. He knew of a theater where your sister might . . ."

The light in his eyes extinguished. He slumped, jaw oddly slack.

"Another theater," he said, with only a hint of mockery. His voice sounded . . . exhausted. "If I marry Lavinia, I won't have to skulk around theaters. I will control my fortune. I'll pay Scotland Yard to turn over every paving stone." He straightened, demeanor shifting slightly, a subtle physical response to the power at his fingertips.

"Effie will be found." He folded his arms, looked down his nose at her. "Without your help, such as it is."

Her mouth was dry. He wanted to make her pay, now, for her deception at the Albion. Alcohol brought out his edges, made him more willing to cut.

"*If* you marry Lavinia . . ." She stiffened her back. Clearly, there wasn't an *if*. "Well. It's what you have to do, isn't it? Settled. Simple even."

Nausea swept over her. She felt dizzied. Counted the steps to the door in her head, wondered if she could cover the distance.

Walk away. Walk away.

"I won't hold you to all your promises." She tried to smile. "You don't have to invite me to dinner."

He flinched. His green gaze skewered her.

"But . . ." she continued, a trifle unsteadily. She couldn't leave before she assured herself he would keep the promise that mattered most. "You must have talked to Mr. Yardley when you saw the lawyers. Did you ask him about the investigation? Into the evictions?"

His eyes didn't leave hers.

"The investigation has concluded," he said, with a slight shake of his head that told her everything.

The dizziness transformed into trembling.

"You *will* proceed," she said. "Independently, with Mabeldon."

Her knees shook. She wanted to cry, but not here, not while he looked at her, with bright, drunk eyes, hollowed cheeks. Beautiful. Absolutely undependable.

"Lucy," he said, "if I marry Lavinia . . ."

That *if* again.

He took her hand, thumb pressing her wrist.

"I can buy the leases. I can buy the whole bloody street."

Denial sprang to the tip of her tongue. *I don't need your help.* She wanted to say it to him. But it wasn't true. She needed his help desperately. Or . . . not *his* help precisely. Not Anthony's.

"My thanks to the Duke of Weston," she said. "Your money, at least, is worth something."

His face crumpled, then smoothed so quickly she doubted her perception. He reached behind him. She didn't want to watch him lift the bottle again. She turned, gathering up her brushes, the scattered sketches. She began to walk to the door, the scent of budding lilac from the garden and sweet hay from the mews drifting toward her. She heard the voice again.

That's my brave, good girl.

It would be the last time, light spilling down on the two of them in this crystal hideaway. She spoke over her shoulder.

"You'll send the canvas to Charlotte Road?"

He jogged around her, blocked the way, a frantic gleam in his eye.

"Of course," he said. "But this space is . . ."

She shook her head. Better to make a clean break. He opened his mouth, shut it, leaned closer.

"If there wasn't a will," he said urgently, a throb in his voice. "If there weren't these *rules* . . ."

She knew what he was asking. The lump in her throat kept her from speaking.

"You and I," he said. "We'd . . ."

"No." The answer emerged, surprisingly mellow. No snap to it. There wasn't a *we*. She would not hold her heart hostage for something that might never arrive.

Good girl, brave girl. Walk away now. Go on.

Her mother's voice, goading her. And so she walked around him, out into the garden, and away.

CHAPTER SEVENTEEN

LUCY WAS SOBBING facedown on her bed when she heard a creak on the stairs.

"You can't help, Mr. Malkin!" she muttered. "You loved him too, you jingle-brain."

"Loved who?" Aunt Marian's voice was reedy with exertion.

"Oh!" Lucy sat bolt upright. "You shouldn't have! Your poor knees."

"My knees aren't so bad as you'd like to make out." Aunt Marian's slow, painful progress across the room told a different story. But Stirling women admitted no weakness.

Lucy was a miserable example of the breed.

"I make no plans to punt on the Thames, but I can climb a flight of stairs." Aunt Marian set a loaded tray on the side table. "Have the Holroyds ruined you for my pea soup with their veal roast and fruit pies?"

Dear God. What time was it? The hours had run together.

"Of course not," murmured Lucy. She'd told her aunt she might stay at Kate's after the salon, as she sometimes did when an opening or lecture ended late. Usually, though, she arrived home the next day filled with stories.

Today she'd raced upstairs with barely a word—well before afternoon lessons concluded—and hadn't come down for dinner. No wonder Aunt Marian was giving her that quizzical look.

"I was busy painting is all." She smiled. "I lost track of time."

Aunt Marian glanced at her empty easel. Lucy had been doing the bulk of her painting in the glasshouse for weeks. She'd described the gorgeous makeshift studio to her aunt faithfully, with only one crucial deviation from truth.

She'd placed it in the corner of the Holroyds' garden.

Her tiny lies and omissions were catching up to her.

All at once, her smile wobbled. Aunt Marian's expression shaded into concern and she lowered herself gingerly onto the bed. Her weight, unlike Anthony's, barely shifted the mattress.

"I wasn't painting." Lucy flung herself onto her aunt's lap as a new storm of weeping overtook her. She used to cry often into her aunt's scratchy apron as an awkward, half-grown girl mourning the loss of her parents, and later, as an intense, overly impassioned young woman, licking smaller wounds, rejections, disappointments. It had been years since she'd done so.

Now, as then, she felt a light pressure: fingers moving slowly through her hair. Aunt Marian had always had the way of it, stroking without catching on tangles. Lucy curled into her. She could feel a thimble dig into her cheek through an apron pocket.

"I was sniveling, crying my eyes out over a man. I've let you down."

"Nonsense," said Aunt Marian firmly, pressing her palm to Lucy's forehead. "You haven't let me down. You're my pride and joy."

Lucy choked on a sob. Her aunt had done everything she could to further her education. "I'm supposed to be *beyond* all this." Winning medals. Showing in galleries. *Those* were the pursuits and accomplishments that rated. "But I went and fell in love regardless."

"Did you?" Aunt Marian's voice was mild and her fingers worked again at Lucy's hair, picking apart knots without snapping a strand.

"You want me to follow a path different than my mother's," Lucy whispered. "I'm making the same mistake she did."

"You're rusting my thimble is what you're doing," said Aunt Marian. "Here. Take this."

She shifted, and Lucy lifted her hot, wet face, sitting up and accepting a handkerchief. She twisted it so hard her knuckles ached.

"Now, what's this about your mother?" Aunt Marian adjusted her spectacles.

Lucy squirmed under her aunt's gaze, afraid to continue but unable to stop herself.

"If she hadn't fallen in love with my father, she'd still be alive," she said.

There, that was the crux of it. It hurt to utter the words aloud.

"Perhaps." Aunt Marian tilted her head. "And you wouldn't be. Your mother wanted children. She didn't regret having you, not for a minute."

Despite her best effort, Lucy's lips trembled. Her aunt sighed.

"She loved your father, but it wasn't love of him that killed her. It was a host of things, chance included. Women's lives are never easy. In love, out of love, married, unmarried—there's no formula that guarantees happiness."

She cleared her throat. "I don't oppose love on principle. But it's rarely principled in practice, by men, at any rate. You've a great talent to pursue. I want you to trust in *that* first."

Lucy lowered her eyes. Talent, intelligence, will—they sprang from, were embedded in, the body. And her body was different now. What would that mean for her?

"Do you know . . ." Aunt Marian spoke with crisp casualness. "I was in love once."

Lucy's eyes flew up. "What? You weren't!"

Aunt Marian raised a thin brow. "Hadn't love been invented yet? It's true, I'm a dizzy age."

"It's not your age," protested Lucy. "It's your nature. You're so . . ." Words bounced around inside her head. *"Impervious."*

"Hmm. Is that my nature?" She seemed to mull it over. "Well

then, he found the chink in my armor. He was absolutely dashing. I was a fool for him."

Aunt Marian spoony over a dashing young man! Impossible. Lucy could only stare. Aunt Marian pursed her lips.

"And then," she continued, "I discovered he was using me to make another woman jealous. An actress."

"He was an actor?" breathed Lucy, trying to picture the man who could have turned Marian's head.

"No, an earl." Aunt Marian smiled wryly. "Which means I might have known better. And so might she have. But I was besotted, and Celestia was an egoist."

"Celestia Jordan?" Lucy heard fabric tear. Dear Lord, she'd ripped the handkerchief. But truly, Aunt Marian vying for a nob with *Celestia Jordan*? It boggled the mind.

Aunt Marian laughed at Lucy's shock.

"He was bankrupt to boot, engaged to a Welsh heiress. When Dodie Thistleship learned of our connection, she threatened to tell the heiress. It was a proper mess."

Lucy bounced on the bed, sputtering her indignation.

"Blackmail! *That's* how Dodie Thistleship came to take the credit for your designs? You were protecting a *dashing* earl?"

"His creditors were vicious." She lifted one shoulder in a stiff shrug. "I feared for his life. Of course, the fiancée broke the engagement anyway."

"Over you?"

"Over Celestia." Aunt Marian resettled a pin in her hair. "If she were robbing the crown jewels, she'd still have demanded a spotlight."

Remarkable. Lucy blinked. "And was the earl slain for his debts?"

"He married an American whose father owned a railroad. Your soup is getting cold."

Lucy took the bowl. The soup was tepid but rich. *Heavenly*. It felt as though a decade had passed since her last meal. She slurped greedily. Aunt Marian watched her with satisfaction.

"Sniveling, but not starving yourself," she observed, standing creakily. "I predict a full recovery."

Lucy put the bowl on the tray and clasped her hands.

"I'm in love with a duke," she confessed. Aunt Marian froze. The lamplight turned her spectacles into two shining discs. Divine judgment. Lucy looked up at her.

"And is he in love with you?" came the voice on high.

She refused to entertain the question. What did it matter?

"There's nothing between us," she muttered.

"Good," retorted Aunt Marian, moving her head so that her eyes showed again through her lenses, dark and penetrating. "Heartache now means a world of troubles avoided down the road. A duke!" She folded her arms. "And I thought the worst I had to fear was that you'd taken a fancy to that goon of an architect, the handsome Mr. Turner who fell on his head."

Frowning, she turned and made her way slowly to the door.

Lucy flopped back on the bed, put her pillow over her face, and punched it slowly, over and over again.

DRESSED ALL IN black, the professor of perspective was delivering a cheerless lecture on the history of techniques for drawing cubes and circular shapes. Assistants stood beside him holding three-foot diagrams. Lucy sat far back from the raised platform. After two days of missed lessons, she had chosen to make her reappearance at the lecture, hoping to blend with the crowd. But as the lecture stumbled along, the professor shuffling notes and mumbling to his assistants, she felt a tap on her shoulder.

"How do you know the Duke of Weston?" Maude whispered, leaning forward from the bench behind. Jealousy was stamped on her face. Lucy might have laughed if the situation wasn't so unfortunate.

"I give him art lessons," she whispered back. Maude's eyes flashed disbelief.

"At midnight?"

The audience began to clap. Lucy untwisted in time to see an assistant displaying a particularly striking illustration of a reflection in a polished globe. She brought her hands together automatically, clapping as the applause faded. From the row ahead, Constance Pitcairn turned at the sound, caught her eye, and blushed scarlet.

Staggered, Lucy stared at the sketchbook on her knee.

Her worst fears, confirmed.

The story was on everyone's lips. The Duke of Weston had plucked her from the tableau vivant and whisked her down the hall. To his bedchamber.

Gossip, she told herself. Who could vouch for what happened between whom at a party such as that?

Rumors, though, had propulsive force and gathered strength as they traveled. What if Miss Yardley caught wind that Anthony had a lover and rejected his suit? He wouldn't inherit, would have no means to acquire the lease on the buildings. She'd have lost him, and gained a scandalous reputation, for nothing. She and Aunt Marian would seek housing in a jerry-built suburb, find something they could afford if they were lucky. If not, they'd look further afield. She might end up in Scotland after all.

Even the professor's soporific consideration of the rendering of the architectural orders couldn't settle her pitching mind. Unique among the lecture-goers, she remained for the duration on the edge of her seat.

She stood as soon as it ended, prepared to dash for the door, but Maude was up too, waving to get her attention.

"Where's Kate?" Maude demanded. She was wearing a blue satin dress with ribbon bows on the shoulders and a skirt foaming with lace flounces. Given the lecture, Lucy couldn't help but note her elaborate coiffure's architectural aspect. She looked every inch an impatient debutante. Nothing like a sixteenth-century Huguenot's imploring lady.

"What do you want with her?" She sighed. It was generally considered rude—answering a question with a question. Lucy gave a close-lipped smile in case there was any doubt.

"We want to sign the petition!" Lucy's gaze shifted as Susan popped up out of nowhere and stood hovering at Maude's elbow. There was no censure in her eyes. More a species of awe. Perhaps she now uttered *Lucy* and *dildo* in the same titillated undertone.

Lucy rubbed her temples. "Wonderful news."

"Is it the one Gwen signed?" asked Maude suspiciously.

"It's the petition for the life class." Lucy waited for their faces to register the information. Nothing. Susan was staring, fiddling with the tip of her braid.

"Yes, Gwen signed it," Lucy said, sighing. The Gwen Burgess effect. It was what she and Kate were counting on. Nonetheless, she felt let down by Maude and Susan's evident disinterest in the issue itself. "Signing tomorrow would be better," she added, glancing around the room.

Visitors, Academicians, art critics, students, ticket-holding members of the public—people milled about in every corner. But Maude shook her head.

"I want to sign before Agnes signs."

"There she is!" Susan dove forward, leading the way toward the stage. Kate was standing by the empty lectern, locked in a heated exchange with Simon Poole. Lucy's eyes met Maude's, and before she could help it, they'd exchanged identical smirks.

Kate and Simon had understood enough of the professor's inaudible points to *disagree* about them? Incredible.

"Perspective must *color* architecture. It's *atmosphere*. Light and shadow. The *sensory*." Kate had begun to bellow, flinging out her arms.

"Practicability is the issue." Simon Poole was tapping his foot with irritation. "A building must stand first and foremost."

"Mathematics!" Kate ejected the word with disgust. "Forget your numbers and *perceive*. How do you *experience* space? That's the first question for the artist *and* the architect."

"Of all the fanciful . . ."

The two were separated, by Maude, only with some difficulty. Kate's disappointment at an argument ended too soon gave way quickly to delight as she collected new signatures.

"You missed my victory over Davis." Kate looked at Lucy sidelong as they navigated away from Maude and Susan, who'd turned to greet Constance Pitcairn. "Where have you been?"

"Home." Lucy cleared her throat. The word felt tender in her mouth. *Home.* Everything in her future was uncertain. How had it come to this?

"I've moved my studio back to the garret. Anthony—" She hesitated.

"It's true, then?" Kate interrupted, gripping her arm. She looked poleaxed. "You? And Weston?"

Lucy could see her thoughts churning, could read the expressions as they flitted across her face. A tryst was shocking, but Lucy had gone about it boldly, unapologetically. In a way, it was marvelous, very well done indeed. Kate groped toward acceptance when another thought hit.

"Lucy." Kate's eyes were huge and her grip tightened. "Do you *love* him?"

Lucy hesitated. The Pre-Raphaelite *brothers* were always falling in love with their models, women whose faces and bodies haunted them, showing up in canvas after canvas. True muses. The Pre-Raphaelite sisters hadn't much considered the possibility.

To admit her love for Anthony was to hazard her friendship with Kate. She didn't know how Kate would react. It was one thing to tryst, to seize knowledge. It was another thing to lose her heart, to cede herself. Would Kate see it as weakness?

Kate wanted the truth.

"Yes," said Lucy simply.

After a long moment, Kate nodded.

"If there's more to him than meets the eye, that's well and good. And what meets the eye is superb." She clapped her hands. "I approve!"

The relief Lucy experienced was as keen as it was pointless. There was nothing for Kate to approve.

"Thank you," she said. "But he's marrying someone else. Quite soon, I believe."

"What?" Kate gasped. "The *bastard*. How does he dare?"

Lucy broke Kate's first rule of engagement by bursting into tears.

THE DAYS AND nights that followed offered new, dizzying lessons in perspective. Time seemed both stretched and compressed. Lucy ignored the pointed looks and whispers of her classmates, aided by Kate, who took pleasure in breaking up their hushed conferences. As the porters began to walk the hallway, carrying the first submitted pictures up to the large room in which the Hanging Committee would soon meet to pass judgment, a powerful excitement took hold in the Schools. Conversation returned to its seasonal rhythm. What would characterize this year's Summer Exhibition? Which genres and artists would the critics hail? What controversies would attend the placement of the pictures?

Now or never. Lucy threw herself into her painting, passing sleepless nights at her easel, burning through pounds of candles and lamp oil, forcing herself to put the cost out of her mind. *Concentrate.* She used a knife to pile on color, her nose an inch from her canvas, which Anthony had returned to her promptly, as promised. Electrified and exhausted, she let her composition occupy her every thought. She could almost forget he existed. When Maude approached her in the canteen at the end of the week, thrusting the engagement announcement into her hand, she didn't show a flicker of emotion.

The moment she put the final touch on her picture—late in the night, the lamp turned up, candles burning—her body drooped. *She* drooped, but Violet did not. The picture was high-toned, arresting, dreamy without the softened edges of dream.

A scant few days remained to submit, but submit she would. She had finished in time.

She allowed herself to lie abed the next morning and made her way down the stairs much later than was her wont, even on a Saturday.

Surely her mind was still sluggish from its surfeit of sleep. Dream clogged her ears. She wasn't really hearing his voice.

She burst into the shop. Aunt Marian was not at her worktable, gone to the privy perhaps. Anthony stood just inside the front door, a pained smile on his lips, and Miss Yardley, *Miss Yardley*, was coming toward her in a princess gown of geranium silk, gloved hands extended.

"Bonjour, chérie, comment allez-vous?" Miss Yardley gripped her fingers, kissing the air with rosebud lips. "Do you approve of my dress? Or was it dyed with deadly nightshade?"

She laughed gaily, squeezing harder, until Lucy felt the hard ridge of a ring straining the soft leather of her glove. She extricated her hands, trying to repress the violence of her response.

"It appears safe enough," she said. Her voice sounded colorless to her own ears. She couldn't look at Anthony. How did he dare to come here, with *her*? He *was* depraved.

"That's all I need to hear. I trust you with my life!" Miss Yardley smiled a dazzling smile, gaze flitting over the display case to the darker corners of the room, where petticoats piled on the worktables, glowing damningly in the gloom.

"It's a bit unassuming, isn't it?" she said, creases of concern bracketing her rosy mouth, but then she shrugged, laughing. "But that's the charm, I suppose. Lucy—I may call you Lucy?—after what you did for me, I feel I must repay the favor. Come to our wedding!"

She misunderstood Lucy's look of horror.

"I plan to be a *modern* duchess. You won't feel out of place. I've invited my old governess, too, and Nancy, who sells me the perfume I so like at the department store. Anthony, tell her you want her to come."

Lucy stared at the floorboards. A nail was coming up. She wanted to hammer it, hard.

"You're a perfect boor," said Miss Yardley after a long pause. "Very well. The truth will out. I had to force him to take me here. He's embarrassed to face you."

Lucy looked up.

"Because he still can't draw a horse!" Miss Yardley laughed again. "Let's ignore him. I have another reason for my visit."

Lucy blinked rapidly. Miss Yardley's radiance was painful to behold.

"I want your aunt to make my wedding dress!"

The silence thundered. Finally, Anthony spoke, warningly.

"We discussed this, Lavinia."

"And I told you the decision is mine." Miss Yardley tossed her head. "A groom mustn't meddle."

"I meddle in nothing," said Anthony flatly. "Your *mother* gave me to understand that your London dressmaker is already at work."

Lucy kept her eyes fixed on Miss Yardley, who was beginning to pout.

"She's always at work because she makes *everyone's* wedding dress. And they're horrid dresses! I might as well pay a common laborer to pave me with seed pearls. I want something original, something that Celestia Jordan would have worn."

Lucy felt a muscle in her eyelid twitch. If only she could travel back in time and sew her lips together before she'd said a word to Miss Yardley about Celestia Jordan!

Don't scream. Reason.

"Aunt Marian would love to make your dress." She resisted the urge to still her eyelid with the pad of her finger, tried to open her eyes instead, making them as round and sincere as possible. "But we don't have the right satin in stock, or the lace. We'd have to order it, and that would take time, too much time. It could delay the wedding. You wouldn't want that."

"No," said Anthony, his voice like smoke. "We wouldn't want that."

Despite herself, she let her glance stray. His beauty stopped her breath.

He'd visited his tailor, and his barber. His suit molded to his broad shoulders, his narrow waist, his long, muscled legs. The black waves of his hair had been cut close to the scalp, accentuating the boldness of his features, the strong nose and chiseled mouth. The light straggling through the windows lit his pale eyes between their fringe of lashes. His gaze was hot, bright. The force of it pierced her.

The green dart.

Her face warmed. She had devised this perfect torture. It was all her own doing.

"Miss Stirling!" Miss Yardley rushed to Aunt Marian, who had entered the shop from the back hall, a deep line of perplexity drawn between her brows.

"I'm Lavinia Yardley, soon-to-be Duchess of Weston. Your dear niece Lucy told me *you* designed Celestia Jordan's gown in *She Stoops to Conquer*, my absolute favorite. My grandmother had a scrapbook where she kept clippings of all the sketches of Celestia's gowns they published in the Ladies Column of the *Illustrated News*. I adore every one of them. I want diamond trim and shoulder straps on my wedding dress, like on the gown in *A Royal Necklace*."

Aunt Marian stared at her. Anthony came a few steps forward.

"Miss Stirling," he said and bowed.

Aunt Marian's knees could excuse her negligible curtsey.

"So, you're the Duke of Weston, are you?" she said, eyeing him with considerable suspicion. "I should have known. And you"—she rounded on Miss Yardley—"are in want of a wedding dress in which to marry him."

Miss Yardley beamed. Aunt Marian jammed her spectacles up the bridge of her nose, shaking her head.

286 • Joanna Lowell

Another proper mess. Lucy could all but hear her thoughts.

"Well," said Aunt Marian at last. "I can't help you with your wedding dress, or with your taste in husbands, but I do have the sketches from *A Royal Necklace*, as well as the lace evening gown with the rose sequins from *The Degenerates* packed away, if you'd like to see them."

Miss Yardley's face registered shock, disappointment, and excitement in comically quick succession.

"Come along, then." With a glance at Lucy, Aunt Marian shooed Miss Yardley toward a chair.

Her aunt was giving her the opportunity to make an exit. Silently, Lucy thanked her for it, and yet she failed to take advantage of the moment. Her feet felt rooted to the spot. She looked down at them. Anthony's boots moved into view.

He'd come closer.

"Congratulations," she murmured and forced herself to turn away. His hand shot out and closed on her wrist, his thumb warm against her pulse. She froze. Her eyes flew to Miss Yardley, perched on a chair, head tilted to see better what Aunt Marian was pulling from her trunk.

"It is I who should congratulate you," he said.

She looked up, scanning his face for irony. His look was ragged with intensity, but sincere.

"I assume you've submitted your picture."

"I will. Monday." She smiled briefly. His thumb moved and the blood in her wrist beat against it. She took a breath through her nose. He smelled different, the scent of his skin masked by an expensive cologne. Had he been drinking? She wouldn't know. And she shouldn't. She'd given up her right to know such things about him.

"You must be happy," he said quietly. He was leaning toward her, and she realized her weight was on her toes, that she'd tipped forward. She jerked, a full-body flinch. She thought she might see triumph in his eyes, superiority, some hint that he reveled in his power over her, her helpless attraction.

What she saw was raw need. Pain.

"Lucy." Her name rumbled in his chest.

"Very happy," she said, tugging her arm. His grip tightened. Behind her, she could hear Miss Yardley oohing and aahing.

They were perfect together, Lavinia and Anthony. A fair, feminine beauty paired with a dark, masculine one. They'd look well anywhere. In Weston Hall. At the queen's table. Not Guinevere's or Cymbeline's—Victoria's.

"And you?" she asked.

"Most happy. Exceedingly happy." His lashes swept down so black and thick she might have used them for brushes. They'd *felt* like brushes when his face pressed against her, painting detailed sensation on her skin with each flutter. When they lifted, his eyes, green as dragons' scales, burned her with dragons' fire. "Jolly even."

"Don't," she whispered. "Don't make it harder. You wouldn't be *jollier* in Scotland."

"Not Scotland," he said harshly, voice suddenly too loud. "That's not what I—"

"What are you two discussing?" called Miss Yardley. "Anthony, look at this gown. Wouldn't it be marvelous for Italy?"

Anthony dropped her arm and was at Miss Yardley's side in a moment. Aunt Marian was holding up a confection of silk and lace, and Miss Yardley pointed out the gown's four underskirts, silver, cream, and two deep shades of pink moiré, laying a careless, confident hand on Anthony's forearm. After a moment, he covered it with his own.

Perfect together.

No one looked at Lucy as she left the room.

"What?"

Anthony blinked at Lavinia, fingers drumming against the coach's window shade. Is that what lay in store for them? A lifetime of his not listening, her repeating.

He ground his molars together to keep himself from saying something unforgivable.

The coach swayed and Lavinia pressed into him, sighing, with irritation, not ardor. She began again, on the subject of their honeymoon in Italy, something to do with the merits of visiting Venice before Rome. His thoughts drifted. An alternative honeymoon played out in his head. He and Lucy on the steamer to Dieppe, leaning on the railing, the wind lifting her curls. She'd be unbelievably vibrant, body too small for the force of life it contained, and so he would press against her, a scaffold for that excess vitality. She'd be lecturing him on the light in Turner's seascapes, and he'd see something new in the common sunbeams, feel the beams from her eyes light something new within him. And when they reached Paris . . .

The small jerk of the coach as it stopped brought him to his senses. They'd arrived at the Yardleys' residence at Chesterton Gardens.

He frowned. Tried to relax his jaw before he cracked his teeth into pieces. Lavinia was looking at him.

"You're hopeless," she muttered. She threw open the door in a huff.

"Well," she said. "Aren't you coming in? Mother wanted to talk to you about the guest list."

"Another time." It sounded curt, but he was beyond caring.

He had other designs for his Saturday afternoon.

ALFRED THEWES, FIRST Baron Mabeldon, sucked his cigar with appetite, then studied its glowing coal before smiling at Anthony with large, square teeth. He was horse-faced but this chance resemblance only served to underscore Anthony's distaste.

"You arrived in the nick of time," Mabeldon said. "I was about to head out the door. I'm meeting Archibald at the club."

Mabeldon wasn't dressed for going out. He lounged in his smoking jacket, loosened cravat limp against his chest. Anthony inclined his head at the tinniness of the excuse. They both knew it was claptrap.

"What luck," he said. He should have been bolder. Done this weeks ago, barged in on a Saturday, when the element of surprise was on his side.

"Scotch?" Mabeldon reached behind him, lifted a decanter. Anthony stared at the amber winking through cut crystal, like mocking eyes.

One drink, five drinks, one hundred. *How much is enough. Forever.* When Lucy had said those words to him in the canteen, he'd put aside the gin. Maybe it was then he'd had his first inkling of the forever he wanted more. Too bad he was such a slow learner.

He shrugged. "I don't have the taste for it."

Mabeldon sucked his teeth, plunking the decanter back down.

"Starting to take after your father. Archie won't believe it. You know, he always asks after you. This year, we'll have you both on the hunt. Usually, he goes to Inverness with his college chums, and they waste whole days on the golf links. The promise of your company— a little friendly competition—will lure him back into the heather, I guarantee it. And you're almost a college chum, aren't you?"

Mabeldon's son Archibald had taken all firsts at Oxford the same year that Anthony was sent down. Mabeldon still enjoyed referencing Anthony's failure, poking the old wound. With some surprise, Anthony realized that the wound had healed over. *The young idiot.* He smiled briefly.

"We're colleagues now, at any rate." Parliament was hardly the heather, but he and Archibald would meet there before long, as Anthony tried to flush political opponents. Archibald, a Conservative MP for Bath, had been one of his father's disciples. He'd take aim at him soon enough, as he worked through the list.

"You've taken your father's seat?" Mabeldon looked surprised. "Bored of knocking about and raising hell, are you? Good, good, but there's technique to it. Your letters . . ." He broke off, shook his head, and sighed, as though he'd ignored them out of tact.

Yes, Anthony knew he wrote in a messy hand, that his style lacked finesse. But he'd made his concerns, and his demands, clear.

"Weren't the characters legible?" he asked. "I can summarize the content. The Board of Works acquired a large site on Charlotte Road, containing several buildings that do not seem to conform to the description given by the inspectors of nuisance and confirmed by Dr. Jephson. I'm prepared to hire a surveyor and bring in the medical officer of the Privy Council to issue an independent report on those properties, which could prove more than an embarrassment, for the vestry and for the board itself. The board is on the thinnest ice with the public, and the dailies want but a whiff of fresh corruption to raise the cry."

Anthony folded his arms, leaning back in his chair. His eyes flitted over the sheaves of paper on Mabeldon's desk.

"You mounted your own investigation. Show me the committee's findings."

Mabeldon's eyes skittered and he stuck the cigar back into his mouth, puffing slowly. *Was* there ever a committee? Despite his best effort, he couldn't subdue his reaction, swift and violent, his whole body bracing for a bloody contest. The energy it took to hold himself still made the sweat break out across his brow.

Every time he thought he'd come to the bottom of Yardley's duplicity, he discovered a false bottom, a deeper level yawning beneath. He called up a smile.

"I see," he said. "All the more reason for me to task myself with unearthing the malfeasance. Rumors are already circulating, as you know, that there is an inner ring within the board, members allied with certain brokers, speculators, contractors, builders, and architects, all peddling influence and services to dispose of surplus lands."

Through his morning reading regimen, he'd discovered that the *Financial News* had gone so far as to levy charges of general corruption, calling the board a "den of thieves." Criticism for the board's secretive procedures had scarcely been higher at any point in its thirty-year history. Mabeldon was in a weakened position.

If he'd imagined Anthony was too much the fool to be aware of it, he was disabused now. His long face had turned a sickly color. Anthony's smile felt less forced as he continued.

"I could localize my efforts and resolve, with your help, the misdeeds on Charlotte Road. Or I could, for the good of the metropolis, set my sights higher, and use the evidence of wrongdoing to make a case for a larger investigation. I'll move in the House for a select committee to investigate *all* of the board's affairs."

Mabeldon stared, his eyes lusterless. "You're making a mistake," he said at last.

Anthony raised his brows, made a dismissive gesture with his hand. "*You're* making the mistake with those evictions," he said. "That is, if you don't want your board dissolved by an act of Parliament."

Mabeldon stubbed out the cigar. "So. You plan to denounce Jephson? *That* story will sell papers. Far more than any story about alleged sharp dealing in Shoreditch."

He bared his teeth and quite a bit of darkened gum.

A vein in Anthony's temple throbbed as he tried to make sense of this. He kept his face neutral, but he had that panicked feeling again, the feeling of a trap closing around him. Why did Mabeldon say *Jephson* in that peculiar tone of voice?

He didn't like how Mabeldon was looking at him, like he was a plate of *salade de grouse à la Soyer.*

"*Michael* Jephson." Mabeldon waited, and when Anthony said nothing he frowned. "Don't be coy," he said. "He's the superintendent of the Putney Asylum. Before that, he was the superintendent of Normand Park."

Anthony's jaw slackened.

"The Duke of Weston," Mabeldon said, raising an arm like a

newspaper seller. "Mounting a campaign that targets the doctor who committed his mother! Read all about it!"

He dropped his arm, shaking his head.

Anthony felt a fullness in his chest, redness surging in from the corners of his eyes. Mabeldon pressed his advantage.

"Think, Your Grace," he said. "It would be painful, that history circulating again, not to mention damaging to your credibility. I owed your father tremendously, and so I'm happy to advise you now. You're better off leaving this alone."

Despite the wave of emotion crashing over him, Anthony's mouth quirked sardonically. His father had played an instrumental role in elevating Mabeldon to the peerage. In exchange for what, he didn't dare to guess.

He took a deep breath. He wouldn't let the mention of his mother divert him from his course.

"Who applied for the lease?" He leveled the question, which at first Mabeldon pretended not to hear as he fetched his watch from his pocket and made a show of noting the time.

"I'm late," he said.

"The lease," repeated Anthony.

"Joseph Statham tendered for the site. He built the Albany Road estate in Camberwell, a fine fellow," said Mabeldon impatiently, rising. "Archie will get dull waiting."

Joseph Statham. The name meant nothing to Anthony, but then again, neither had the name Jephson. He'd never considered the man who diagnosed his mother. In his mind, he'd been nameless, faceless, part of the edifice that had swallowed his mother whole. The diagnosis—defending his mother from it with his fists—was what had consumed him. Certainly, his father had never spoken to him of the doctor involved.

He'd only known his mother died at Normand Park because the schoolchildren mentioned it in one of their vicious rhymes.

Mabeldon's face looked even longer and more equine from this angle. He wouldn't allow the man to see through his exterior, to glimpse the welter beneath.

Christ, he was a mess of wounds.

He stood smoothly. "Don't let Archie get dull," he said with a laugh, picking invisible lint from his shirtsleeve.

Archibald, *dull*. He'd never been one to let moss grow under his feet. Too busy trying to climb to the top of every pile. Grasping bastard.

"We'll walk out together. I'm late, too, to meet with Samuel Lawford."

"Lawford!" Mabeldon gaped and Anthony hid his smile. He'd been choosing his friends wisely.

"Yes, Lawford," he said airily. "He agrees it's high time that a committee form to investigate board practices. How does this strike you? *Lawford* will be the one to move in the House. The press won't find a story there. Lawford has no axe to grind with Jephson. Glad that's settled. And I thank you for the advice. My advice to you? Deal with Charlotte Road."

He tipped his head. "And don't be long about it."

Mabeldon blinked rapidly. Anthony relished the look on his face. Surprise. Dawning terror.

He had just realized the young idiot was a formidable adversary.

Anthony shook Mabeldon by the shoulder as they parted ways.

"I'm looking forward to seeing more of you, and of Archie. Send him my warmest regards."

Back in the coach, he flung his limbs angrily, struggling to master his breathing. The lancing pain stabbed again, behind his right eye. He could count on liquor to dull this feeling, but he was realizing there was utility in his discomfort. The pain and need *honed* him. He was alert, restless, all corners.

The day wasn't over. He would visit Lawford. He would go by the frame maker's studio to see if he'd finished his job on schedule. Later, the veterinarian was coming to the stables to check Snap's fetlocks, to ensure the sesamoid bones were still whole. Afterward, Anthony would still have time to work in the glasshouse, sanding the oval he'd planed from the board, rubbing it with linseed oil. And Cecil might call.

He could fill a life even without Lucy Coover.

Because of Lucy Coover, something inside him whispered. Her determination, industriousness, audacity—a lesson. A goad.

If he wasn't running, he was going to fight.

CHAPTER EIGHTEEN

THE SATURDAY NIGHT crowd in Rafferty's Music Hall was roaring with laughter at a verse of doggerel *Hamlet* as Lucy maneuvered between tables toward the orchestra pit. She tried to make herself as small as possible, lest a manager spot her as she slipped backstage.

She needn't have worried. No one paid her any mind. She pushed through the stage door into pandemonium. Singers trilled scales as magicians leapt about, swinging their chimney-pot hats at a pair of escaped doves. She found herself pressed to the wall where a comic duo ran their lines. She screwed up her nerve and interrupted their patter.

"I'm looking for Mrs. Nixon," she said, and the henpecked husband turned. Before he could answer, the wife, played by a far larger man in bonnet and apron, menaced him with a rolling pin. That was that. Lucy moved on. A dapper fellow in bright check trousers and a frock coat crouched in a corner, fastening an Elizabethan ruff around the neck of a poodle that sat with an uncanny air of long-suffering patience.

"Pardon," she began, but man and dog both looked at her as though she had interrupted the toilette of the queen. She retreated and questioned a comedian who'd never heard of Mrs. Nixon but was effusive regarding his ignorance on the subject. She had no luck with the pantomime dame, and less with the musical clown who responded to her question by shrilling on his tin whistle then capering over to a juggling troupe to summon them to the front of the house.

Another wasted effort.

One of the leaping magicians trampled her toes, and she gasped, turning smack into another poodle, her yelp mingling with the dog's.

Her face felt hot, as much from humiliation as from the close, rancid air. *She* was the real comedian here, a clown burlesquing as a savior. Why was she still doing all she could for Anthony? To what end? She hadn't chosen him. She'd recognized the trap when he'd begged her to run away. But here she was, at Rafferty's, like a fool in love.

He was going to marry Lavinia. Take solace—take *pleasure*—in her arms.

She'd told him to do it. She needed him to do it. And yet, she couldn't endure the thought.

Her ungenerosity of spirit accused her.

She fought her way to the back door.

On the street, she heard the door bang again, the sound of hurried footsteps. Her heart skipped a beat. Someone was following. She spun around on a breath to confront him.

A young woman in a cloak stopped just short of a collision, surprised by Lucy's sudden reversal.

"Oh!" she gasped. Her head was bare, the strident red of her dyed hair emphasized by a sparkling headpiece plumed with purple feathers. The feathers wobbled dangerously.

"You was asking for Effie Nixon." Her accent was nasal. American.

Lucy's throat tightened. It was too soon for hope, though. She coached herself against it, gave a cautious nod. The young woman nodded back. The heavy greasepaint on her face exaggerated her features. Her eyes looked unnaturally wide as her red lips frowned.

"And what's she to you?" she asked.

"She's a friend's sister," said Lucy with barely a breath of hesitation.

Now the girl looked disappointed. "*You?* A friend of the family? She told me she had all grandees for relations, earls and princes. I should have known it for bunkum."

Lucy folded her lips, souring slightly despite herself. She'd tarnished Effie's image by association. Even an American could recognize that she wasn't cut from the same cloth as the earls and the princes.

As she'd stared at Lucy, the girl had risen onto her toes. She sighed, slowly settling her slippered feet back on the cobbles; then she rose again onto her toes. A singular habit.

"I'd hoped it was her family," she said, as though to herself. "Come to take her home."

Lucy felt the hair rising on the back of her neck.

"What do you mean?" She took an involuntary step forward. "What happened?"

The girl dropped her heels abruptly, flinging out her arm.

"There." She pointed. "We were leaving after the show, and the carriage was right there, at the end of the street. A big, fancy one. Two men grabbed her and forced her into it."

"When?"

"October," said the girl, shivering. "Late October. It was a cold night."

Lucy looked down the street, imagining the scene, the gilded coach materializing in the moonlight, the coronet winking on the door. But it wouldn't have been the coach she knew, Anthony's coach. Effie's family hadn't taken her home. Her whereabouts were a family mystery.

Unless . . . Her whole body was prickling now. Unless they weren't a mystery at all.

Had Weston the elder abducted his daughter, taken her, not home, somewhere else?

"I ain't seen her since that night," the girl continued, up again on her toes. "I wrote to Charlie about it. He started life as my humble cousin, but he's gotten too high for his nut."

She made a face, dropped her heels down hard.

"Charlie . . . Nixon?" Lucy asked.

The girl rolled her eyes. "Of course Charlie Nixon, the *great* Charlie Nixon. He's in California by now. If he ever got my letter, he didn't deign to write back. He was fit to spit when I threw in with the Flying Zamoras. Cursed me silly. I was the best wire walker in the act."

The girl rose to her toes, twirling an invisible umbrella over her shoulder, smile wide and dazzling.

"*Indispensable,* he said. Ha!" She dropped again with a burst of laughter. "Ain't nothing indispensable to Charlie. Anyways, I like it here better. It's more civilized."

She shrugged when Lucy didn't smile her confirmation. It was impossible to smile. She felt dazed.

"He's apt to be wrathy." The girl sighed. "It don't bother me. But he could have had a care for his wife. Don't think I didn't warn her off him. I know *my* relations ain't princes."

Lucy wondered briefly about the great Charlie Nixon, *wrathy* cowboy and callous husband. Had he hoped, through Effie, to wedge his hands into the Weston family coffers? Had he menaced and mistreated her before he left her to her fate?

The man was certainly a villain, but there were others, more dangerous, nearer to hand.

"Effie *is* a lady," she said, looking urgently at the garish canvas of the girl's face, all white powder and red rouge. "Whoever forced her into that carriage against her will is going to pay dearly. Think, I beg you. Is there anything else you can tell me?"

The girl nodded. "One of the men called out to the other, called him Jeffers, or Jephson." At Lucy's startled movement, she raised her brows.

"You know him?"

Lucy bit her lip hard, arms folded against her chest, steadying herself. She would get to the bottom of this, however low and dark. She met the girl's wide-eyed gaze.

"No," she said. "Not yet."

A HALF HOUR later, she was pushing open the door of the George and Dragon. The public house was doing a brisk business. The main room was crammed with patrons, mechanics and tradesmen mostly, and the waiters worked at a dash. Lucy pushed her way forward. For a moment, she felt like a young girl again, at sea in a crowd of boisterous men, hoping to spot her father, and hoping she wouldn't— hoping against hope that he was already on his way home, walking under his own power. For that moment, the feelings crowded her, made her feel bruised and fragile. But she forced them aside.

She wasn't that young girl anymore. She knew how to make space for herself. She pressed on, sweeping the tables with her gaze.

There he was, sitting at the end of a crowded table. He wasn't dressed in red pantaloons, but she'd know him anywhere, even without the signature gold-topped walking stick he flashed when strutting about the borough.

"Mr. Purcell," she said loudly. His nose was buried in the foam that topped his tankard, but he raised his head and squinted.

"If you're the one looking," he leered.

"You're lucky I'm not looking for you tonight," she snapped. This was greeted with appreciative hoots. She ignored them.

"I'm looking for Dr. Jephson."

"Come to me, asking for another man." Purcell heaved an exaggerated sigh, wiped a mock tear from his eye with an index finger weighted with a thick gold ring set with a large red stone.

"You're not a man. You're a *toad*." She bit off the words. In her fantasies, she'd followed up a tirade with a punch. She put her fisted hand on her hip. "You know the other toads," she said sweetly. "Where can I find him?"

"One of your ladies, Purcell?" A silver-haired, wolfish man was grinning at Lucy over Purcell's shoulder. "Loved her and left her?"

"More like one of Jephson's lunatics." This shout came from the other end of the table. Another man piped up.

"I'd let her escape, if I were a guard," he drawled. "If she was very, very good."

More hoots.

Lucy didn't flinch from the sallies of coarse language and the hot laughter that followed. But sweat beaded on her brow as she stared at the half-dozen male faces tipped toward her, male faces that seemed to make up a single male face, all red-rimmed eyes and gaping maw.

Lunatics. Jephson ran a madhouse. Dear God, Effie had been locked away.

"Where—" Lucy began, but something caught in her throat and she had to start again. "Where is it?" She tried to block out the other men, to stop seeing the monster they made when she allowed their faces to merge. "Where's the asylum?"

"You want to go back?" Purcell laid his index finger on the ball of his nose, so his lips touched the gold band of the ring. "Well, it's a harsh world out here, unless you've a man to look after you."

His tongue brushed the metal as he spoke. The wave of revulsion cresting inside her nearly carried her fist forward. It would feel good, splitting his lip with his own ring. But she had her knuckles to consider, her fingers. They were worth more than that fleeting satisfaction.

Purcell took a swig of beer, eyes tracking a massive woman as she made her way to the bar. She was like a ship with a figurehead: broad beamed but tapering to an exquisitely modeled head crowned with heavy locks of butter yellow pulled loosely back to fall between her shoulders. He slammed down his tankard and rose to follow her.

With the appearance of this new target, his interest in Lucy had waned completely. But Lucy wasn't finished with *him*. She stepped into his path, conjuring her most ogre-like expression, with a walloping dose of Aunt Marian thrown in for good measure. Aunt Marian could turn men to stone.

Purcell didn't turn to stone, but neither did he plow through her. He stopped, nonplussed.

"You *are* a little lunatic," he said. "If it's Jephson you're attached to, you'll have come from the new one, his pride and joy, the Putney Asylum."

He sneered down at her.

"You're wrong there." She didn't punch, but she stropped her voice with her anger, sharpening every word. "I came from Charlotte Road, and I can tell you none of us are leaving quietly. In fact, we don't mean to leave at all."

The audience of men hooted their enjoyment. She ignored them.

"I have friends in high places, Mr. Purcell," she said loudly, cutting through the George and Dragon's ambient clamor. His eyes widened, just a fraction. He wasn't alarmed, but he was listening.

"You think you're above the law." She glared into his face. "But you're a tiny, slimy thing. Go ahead and laugh. I know what's coming for you and you won't be laughing then."

He didn't laugh. His eyes tracked *her* as she crossed the room. Not as satisfying as a blow to the nose, but Mrs. Cantrell would be proud.

LUCY AND KATE clambered into a cab at the train station in Putney, Kate giving her skirts a vindictive tug as she settled herself on the seat. Lucy had pounced on her as she arrived home from church, and she'd come away at once, without risking a trip inside to change into her preferred attire.

Lucy was grateful—she couldn't have borne facing Anthony, not before she knew she had something definitive to tell him—but Kate was clearly regretting the choice. She looked out the window, fiddling with a lopsided hair comb from between the teeth of which artificial curls burst out in a pretty cluster. It was strange to see her in a gown, with the semblance of long tresses.

"Let me do it," said Lucy, sliding over to her, fixing the comb more solidly in place.

"Ouch," muttered Kate. She was still turned to the window. As her fingers plucked and smoothed, Lucy gazed out the window too. They weren't far from London, but it felt like another world. The cab was spinning along the heath, which looked wild, wild and desolate.

And then the asylum came into view.

It had to be the asylum, gray and hulking, up on a hill, the grounds surrounded by a stone wall. How could a building such as this be anyone's pride and joy?

Joy died here.

The porter in the gatehouse was young, pimpled, and easily dazzled. He couldn't bring himself to speak to Kate directly, but his eyes kept drifting to her as he addressed Lucy.

"Are you here to see the human dog?" he asked. "He's not a dog, of course, but he barks like a dog. He's a main attraction."

"Main attraction!" Kate was indignant. "Do you mean that people come to gawk at the patients?"

"Only the hard cases," said the porter to Lucy, glancing at Kate from the corners of his eyes. "Not everything's worth the trip. Melancholia, for instance, is dull as ditchwater. Lots of staring and sighing. Puts you to sleep."

Kate snorted, and the porter blushed, lowering his head defensively.

"I thought I'd warn you that the human dog isn't on the grounds, is all. He's getting a treatment. I wouldn't want you to feel disappointed."

This time Kate caught him looking, and he snapped his gaze back to Lucy.

"The wild girl might be out. She's very popular. Mr. Wilkes can give you the tour, if you like. He's one of the alienists."

"We don't want Mr. Wilkes." Kate tossed her head and one of her hair combs slid alarmingly, undoing Lucy's handiwork. The curls were still pretty, but the effect was less realistic.

"*You* can show us the grounds."

"Oh, I can't." The porter appealed to Lucy. "I stay right here and collect a shilling each from the paying guests."

"Suit yourself," said Kate cheerfully, walking past him. Lucy hurried after, and the porter followed. Kate put her hand over her mouth, turning her head so only Lucy could see her lips.

Larva, she mouthed. Lucy shrugged. They were everywhere, underwhelming young men, mostly in the way, sometimes of use.

The outbuildings were one-story bunkers arranged in rows, the effect bleak, even frightful. Muddy patches abounded where grasses had been trampled away. Lucy couldn't help but imagine that each raw slash of earth was the mark of a struggle.

"Criminals there," said the porter, indicating with a jerk of his head. "Pauper men there, pauper women there."

Beyond the bunkers, the space opened up. Women of all ages walked in the airing courts. Most of their backs were hunched, faces turned to the ground.

Lucy's stomach clenched. She heard the horror in Kate's voice as she rounded on the porter.

"Why are they here?"

The boy hesitated, picking at a blemish on his chin. "Mr. Wilkes could tell you. All sorts of reasons. Idiocy, epilepsy, mania, hysteria, dementia, novel reading . . ."

"Novel reading!" Kate gave a strangled cry and strode ahead of them. The heathland rose in a mild hill and the structures built around it resembled cottages. Wealthier patients were housed here. Dense stands of holly provided the illusion of privacy. From the main building atop the hill, the guards could see everything.

"Do you know of a Mrs. Nixon?" Lucy asked, and the boy brightened.

"Moral insanity," he said wisely, evidently pleased with the phrase. "She was admitted shortly after I started here and made all sorts of trouble. A difficult case."

He was quoting someone, Mr. Wilkes perhaps. Lucy smiled encouragingly.

"And she was admitted by her father?"

"That's right. Nice fellow, heartbroken. She was in a very bad way." The boy sighed, leading them onto a path edged with primroses that wound toward the hill. "He still visits from time to time, to meet with the superintendent."

Lucy's smile froze, and she missed a step.

"Still visits?" She laughed with disbelief. "But . . . her father is dead."

"I don't know about that. He looked alive the other day." The boy shrugged. "Of course, I'm not a doctor," he added with diplomacy.

"What does he look like? Her father?" Lucy stopped, and he stopped as well.

"He's a big man," he said. "Ginger-haired. He creases up smiling when he comes through the gate and asks me about my sweetheart, which is a bit of a joke, as I haven't got a sweetheart."

He was gazing off. Heart pounding, Lucy turned to follow his gaze. Kate was marching back to them, skirts gathered too high for propriety. The porter was getting an eyeful of her stockings.

"The woman in the chair, under that big tree." She was out of breath. "She's sketching, and it's shockingly good."

The boy worried his chin again with a ragged nail, turning to Lucy.

"*That* is Miss Fox," he said. "She killed her mother and her father."

Lucy looked for the big tree. There she sat, Miss Fox, bent over her drawing. Just beyond the tree, a woman was walking. A woman with black hair.

Before she knew it, Lucy was running down the path and veering off, flying over the grass.

Slow down, she told herself. *Don't barrel into her.*

She managed to close the final distance at a reasonable pace. The black-haired woman froze, arms stiff at her sides.

"Effie!" It burst from her. "Effie! It's you."

Disconcerting, to behold Anthony's beauty in female form. The black hair twisted into a thick braid was the same color and texture as his, and she had his heavy brows. She must have been accustomed to plucking them thin, as was the fashion, but during her long incarceration, they'd grown back. They made the look of the pale green eyes set deeply beneath even more familiar.

"Your brother sent me," Lucy panted. "Anthony."

Now those pale green eyes glowed with anguish.

"He knows I'm here?" Effie's voice was rich and fluting, but its music was terrible, rising wildly in pitch. Anguish was giving way to fury. "Where is he, then? Why hasn't he come?" She twisted her hands together, fingers bending at alarming angles.

"How could he leave me here?" She keened the question. In that haunting sound, Lucy heard the trace of her despair, the terror, rage, and degradation that had been her only companions in these lonely months.

"Shhhhhh." Lucy made a soothing noise, glancing over her shoulder. Guards and nurses were scattered about, none, as yet, observing their meeting. The sun emerged from behind a cloud and the green of the grounds intensified, barred with jet-black shadow. "He doesn't know," she said, softly, stepping closer. "He's been looking for you. He never gave up. We're going to get you out of here. I'm Lucy." She grabbed Effie's hand, trying to still her restless movements, to communicate strength. Effie's fingers were ice-cold, but she gripped back hard and, all at once, she calmed.

"I'm a friend," said Lucy, and Effie seemed to accept this without judgment.

"We should walk," she said. "Don't look at me when you talk. They think conversation will excite my nerves."

She had the same cadence as Anthony, the same elite drawl and easy, dark irony. Her mouth turned down at the corner with disgust.

"They're watching," she whispered. "I don't want them to restrain me. I can't bear that, not again."

Lucy found it difficult to look away from that fascinating face. The features were harder and more pronounced than in the Burgess miniature, as though the eyes, cheekbones, nose, lips, chin, had been outlined in ink.

She matched Effie's shuffling steps, staring at the ground, like the lunatic women who paced the airing courts. How many of those women were mad and how many were simply trapped, coping with an insane predicament? Was there a difference? Lucy shuddered, even though the sun had warmed the air.

"How did you find me?" Effie's voice reached her, and she lifted her head, just slightly, looking off over the heath. They were high enough that she could see over the wall, see the yellow of spring flowers intermixed with the green, and the woodlands, the ancient trees newly in leaf.

"A wire walker," she said. "I met her at Rafferty's Music Hall. She watched them drag you away."

"Hetty. I lived with her in the boardinghouse after—" The words cut off abruptly.

Lucy hesitated. She didn't know Effie after all. But it was easy to talk this way, the two of them side by side, speaking as though to their shoes, or the clouds.

"Anthony told me about your husband," she said.

"Husband." Effie laughed quietly. "Was he my husband? Hetty warned me he'd leave without me, that he never had any intention of staying, or of bringing me along. He already has a wife in New York, and maybe another in California."

Lucy was glad Effie couldn't see her face. Her cheeks were burning on the other woman's behalf.

The great Charlie Nixon indeed.

They were approaching Miss Fox, still bent over her drawing, and Effie doubled back, walking the way they'd come, but not before Lucy took the young artist in, the slight frame, the pale hair and narrow face. This tiny girl had murdered her parents?

"I don't regret it," Effie said, reclaiming her attention.

Lucy watched the shadows move on the grass, slowly, as the clouds shifted, waiting for her to continue.

"I felt free for the first time," she said. "Traveling with him through the countryside, and even afterward, when it was over and I was alone in London. I *liked* living on my own, singing. It was always my dream to sing. The only thing I regret is going back home. *That* was true madness. I had so little money in my new life for necessities, and the closets and drawers of my old bedroom were overflowing with treasures. Gowns, jewelry, my good hairbrush. I dreamed about that hairbrush at night. I wanted to take just a few things, to make my way easier."

She'd sped up in her agitation, and Lucy touched the sleeve of her plaid stuff dress to slow her. They'd almost reached the stone wall.

"You went home?" she murmured. "I thought—"

"I knew Collins would turn me away at the door, so I went through the garden and climbed through the nursery window, just like Cuckoo and I used to do for fun. Part of me hoped I would find him there, not in the nursery, somewhere in the house. He'd been back for months at that point, without answering a single one of my letters. That has been the worst of it . . . wondering if he knew, if he *agreed* to this—"

"No!" Lucy turned to her, interrupting, and their eyes met. Despite the odd nickname, there could be no doubt as to whom Effie meant.

"Anthony would *never* have agreed to it."

Effie heard the conviction in her voice, and perhaps something more. Her eyes roamed Lucy's face before she dropped her gaze again, turning so they shuffled once more toward the big tree and Miss Fox.

Her body was habituated to this course, back and forth, back and forth, scant yards between the stone wall and the plane tree. How many times had she walked it?

"A maid heard me in my bedroom. She summoned Collins, who took me down the hall to my father, who condemned me as a thief. I'd taken my own earrings, my own brushes, my own stockings, but he said they belonged to his daughter who died."

Her laughter was harsh as a sob.

"He looked unwell. His hands were shaking, and he raved. He said he was being drugged, that he trusted no one. He wanted me to taste his lemonade. *You'll find it bitter.* He kept saying it. *Blast your lemonade*, I said. *You need a doctor.* But he wouldn't listen. He was always stubborn and cold, but this was different. It was . . . unhinged. When I asked him where Anthony had taken lodging, he shook his head so violently I thought his neck would snap. He said he'd written a new will leaving the estate to Daphne, his favorite setter, the only creature on earth who'd never disappointed him." She took a ragged breath. "Daphne has been dead for ten years."

"What did you do?" Lucy saw the guards corralling Miss Fox, who'd risen from her chair, hustling her back toward the cottages. More nurses and guards were marching alongside patients on the path. Time for tea, perhaps, or treatment. A picture came to her, Miss Fox screaming, plunged into an ice-water bath. She shivered.

Effie was watching the progress of staff and patients across the lawn. She glanced at Lucy. "What did I do?" she repeated. "I didn't know what to do. I went to my father's dearest friend, Robert Yardley, and told him everything my father had said and that I feared he had taken leave of his senses. He agreed the situation was serious and said he'd send for a doctor. I gave him the address of the boarding-house, and he said he'd come with Anthony."

A smile ghosted her lips, suggested that her cheeks, too, held dimples in potential, ready to flex on a merrier occasion.

"I was almost happy. It was horrible to witness my father in that state, but I felt relieved, seeing Robert, knowing I was finally going to see Anthony. And I had my hairbrush."

The smile widened until it reversed into a frown, then vanished.

"The coach came that very night. My father acted faster than I'd imagined possible. I don't know how he found me at Rafferty's . . ."

She cast her eyes down, trailing off.

Lucy stared, aghast. Didn't she know? Couldn't she guess? She'd given Yardley the address of the boardinghouse. He'd had her followed. He'd sent his conspirators to Rafferty's. *Yardley* had committed her, not her father. He'd committed her because she knew that her father wasn't in his right mind, had written some kind of document that proved it.

Because she knew her father feared poison.

Her thoughts skipped in all directions. Had Yardley *drugged* the duke, to disorient and manipulate him?

It was too much, too much to comprehend and too much to convey to Effie. Weston the elder had raised his children with loathing, and they'd learned to loathe him in return. With their enemy looming so large, so close, they couldn't see the harm done to them in his shadow.

Lucy said only, with more ferocity than before, "We're going to get you out of here."

"My father will find a way to stop you." Effie's face rounded with vulnerability, and she looked younger, looked, briefly, like the girl in the miniature.

Lucy felt as though the air had turned to tiny pins. Her mouth dried until it was hard to swallow.

No one had told Effie that her father was dead, had died shortly after the night they dragged her away. She'd been locked up, isolated, instructed, perhaps, that her claims about herself, her identity and sanity, were dangerous delusions. She wasn't Lady Euphemia Philby. She was Euphemia Nixon. Useful, that a married name could erase the traces of who a woman had been.

Lucy shook her head, trying to think of what to do next, and saw Kate out of the corner of her eyes. She was waving from the path, then bounding toward them, the porter trailing. As she reached them, a bloodcurdling scream rent the air.

Miss Fox, surrounded by guards, had managed to break free and was off like a shot across the grounds. Shouts rose, and whistles blew. Nurses and guards gave chase. Miss Fox had no hope of escape. She was running a random pattern, wailing and beating at the air.

But *they* had hope of escape. The porter had abandoned the gatehouse, and the staff was distracted.

It only took half a second. Kate looked at Lucy, who looked at Effie. Then they were running too, the three of them, running as fast as their legs could carry them, breaths tearing at their lungs, running down the slope toward the pauper bunkers and across the long stretch to the gate in the wall. Kate pulled ahead, legs flashing, skirt tugged up to her hips.

A cry formed in Lucy's throat as she watched a guard coming out of the men's bunker cross the lawn on the perpendicular and tackle Kate around the waist. She went down screaming and kicking, and then Lucy was past her, chest and legs on fire. Her breath and Effie's breath sawed in her ears.

She'd get Effie out and go back for Kate.

That was her last conscious thought. The impact came from behind and sent the air from her lungs, wiped her mind. The only thing that mattered was her next breath and how long it was taking to arrive.

Dimly, she understood she was on the ground, that a great weight pressed on top of her, that she was screaming soundlessly, and that the darkness she saw, edged with red, was filling in, red and deeper red, and the scream would not become sound, because there was no air to carry it.

Suddenly, it broke. Air rushed in, but through a cloth, wet with a penetrating smell, like a sweet and strong spirit, and she was gone.

Floating. Over eons, across vast distances, she struggled to return to her body, to surface until she wore her own skin, looked out of her own eyes.

Sometimes she heard noises. Sometimes she saw shadows shift, and faces formed above her. Once she saw green and felt a longing so deep she couldn't remember the source, and then she submerged again.

CHAPTER NINETEEN

WHEN ANTHONY WAS a small child, his mother sometimes crept into the nursery at night to rock him in her arms, singing lullabies. One of those melodies came back to him as he walked behind Mr. Wilkes across the grounds of the Putney Asylum, a haunting melody, in a minor key.

"We're very proud of our facility," Mr. Wilkes was saying. "It's not a holding pen, Your Grace, but a hospital in every sense of the word. Our staff is dedicated to curing the patients, that is, those in whom there yet exists some normal function that can be influenced."

Mr. Wilkes was young, bald, and harried, with a quick, roving eye. As they passed near a huddle of well-heeled visitors, he gestured sharply to a nurse standing in a doorway. She came forward at once, whistle between her lips, and scattered the little party as the object of their interest—a patchy-haired boy on his hands and knees—snapped and growled at the air.

"An Irish vagrant," said Mr. Wilkes, walking quickly down the path. "He doesn't think he's a dog, by the way, but rather Cú Chulainn, the Irish hero. You've heard the myth? Ireland's greatest warrior. He slayed a guard dog as a boy and took its place in recompense, so they called him the Hound of Ulster."

Anthony glanced over his shoulder at the boy, now in a crouch, rubbing his ear against his bony shoulder.

"Men tend not to debase themselves in their delusions," said Mr. Wilkes. "Kings or gods every one. This way, please. We do everything we can, of course, for the pauper patients, but the Poor Law officials have all but overwhelmed us with chronic cases, a hundred from the workhouses and the country asylum in the past year alone. The private patients are far fewer in number. Some of them have rooms in the central building and the rest are lodged in the cottages. Ah, there are a few of the women on the knoll. Healthy amusements form the better part of their treatment. Good afternoon, Mrs. Blizard, Miss Laurence, Mrs. Hinson, Lady Vigers."

Three women raised their rackets in acknowledgment while the fourth stood frozen.

Anthony glanced at them, ordinary, orderly specimens, hats shielding their faces from the afternoon sun. In their walking dresses, they looked like any other Londoners of the leisure class, out to enjoy a bright day on the heath, no different from the visitors gasping at the antics of that poor deluded boy.

The discrepancy between appearance and reality chilled him.

These women couldn't return home when the shadows lengthened. They'd been separated from their families, torn from their lives. Their rooms, however comfortable, were cells.

As he watched, they began a game of badminton.

"The majority of them will reintegrate into society after treatment," said Mr. Wilkes, clapping his hands to separate a guard and a nurse who'd drifted under a stand of holly to exchange some confidence.

"Our therapies have proven most effective. The medical superintendent will be delighted to discuss our philosophy in greater depth. Your timing couldn't have been better. He has just now returned from a week in London."

They turned off the path onto a wider avenue that led up the hill.

There it was again, the silvered notes of his mother's song, floating toward him on the breeze. He pivoted, but of course he couldn't find the source of the melody. No woman crooned to her infant on the grounds. The faint tune played inside his head.

Yesterday, still thinking about his discussion with Mabeldon, he'd driven to Islington, to Normand Park, only to discover the mansion had burned to the ground. He'd never see the asylum where his mother spent her final days, the room where she'd been found, hanged, the music crushed forever from her throat.

He turned back to Mr. Wilkes.

"Your Grace?" The alienist had stopped a few feet higher on the hill, sun glistening on his bald pate. "Yes, we've broken ground for the cannery. Is that what caught your eye? Behind the kitchens there. Not much to see as yet, but we've every expectation the construction will move rapidly. I would have shown you, but I'm sure Dr. Jephson wants that pleasure."

"Cannery?" Anthony looked blankly in the direction Wilkes pointed.

"It will give us the means to achieve total food self-sufficiency and to provide steady employment to several of our male incurables as well. We're most indebted to your generosity."

Mr. Wilkes started again up the hill.

"I funded this cannery?" Anthony strode beside him, confusion curdling into anger. "I think you mean my father."

Wilkes frowned slightly. "Perhaps you were following your father's wishes, Your Grace, but we secured the funds after the New Year, from you. Your dedication to improving care for the mentally and morally diseased does you credit."

Anthony smiled, an effortful smile, his teeth like knives in his mouth. He had to hold his lips just so or he'd taste blood.

Mr. Wilkes seemed competent to his tasks, brisk and dispassionate. Maybe the Putney Asylum was a model institution, a place where the patients' surroundings had been adjusted to provide the most healthful influences, so that dangerous behaviors resolved themselves and defective brains modified their disorder, becoming rational. Maybe the Putney Asylum was deserving of support.

Even so, his father's noblesse oblige, extended by Yardley, might have found a different target. England had hundreds of asylums. If Weston the elder felt compelled to improve care for the insane, there were ways to do so without pumping money into the projects of the man who'd presided over his wife's suicide. But, of course, he had always placed the blame squarely on *her*. His financial commitments confirmed it.

"So, I'm building a cannery." Anthony laughed, a musical, maniacal laugh. He imagined his mother laughing like that, at the nurses, at the alienists, at Jephson himself. Defiant. "What else?"

Mr. Wilkes's frown had leveled off. He was a professional, adept at masking his unease with volatile subjects. But he'd accelerated. A shorter man would have had to trot to keep the pace.

"The operating theater," he said, looking at Anthony out of the corner of his eye. "There are no procedures scheduled today, so if you like, a tour can be arranged."

"What kind of procedures?" Anthony asked on a hard breath.

"We're very good with female ailments," said Mr. Wilkes. "The results have been impressive. Dr. Jephson is among the leading proponents of gynecological surgeries. His techniques are studied by surgeons across the world."

There was no mistaking his sincerity. Bile rose in Anthony's throat.

Twenty years ago, had Jephson wanted to test one of his procedures on a nymphomaniac? Was it fear of a forced surgery that had strained his mother to the breaking point?

Death had seemed to her the only recovery. He wished he could believe she'd sunk into soothing darkness and woken, healed, in a better place.

He closed his eyes briefly, shutting out the world, the last shreds of that faint melody drifting into silence. He let his body carry him forward up the hill to Jephson's office.

MICHAEL JEPHSON HAD a disarming face, even-featured and intelligent, the brows still dark beneath a thick wave of silver hair. He came around his desk smiling. The books that lined the office walls struck Anthony as smug in their abundance, hundreds of fat volumes, the bulk of them pressed into Jephson's service, an alibi for his learnedness and unerring discernment. He had to be taken aback by Anthony's arrival, but he gave no sign. He was handsome as an actor, and he played his part smoothly.

The respected doctor and administrator. His trim figure, clear complexion, and bright eyes seemed further proof of his respectability. No secret vices bloated, stained, or clouded his aspect.

"What a pleasant surprise," Jephson exclaimed, nodding at Wilkes, who vanished with a touch more haste than dignity.

"Far too long in coming, wouldn't you agree?" Anthony ignored the leather chair and strolled the perimeter of the room, inspecting it with a proprietary air. How large had his contributions been? Had he paid for these books, these furnishings? Jephson's smile had not slipped.

"Too long indeed," Jephson murmured. "I heard a great deal about you over the years, from your father. He did more for lunatics in this country than the lord chancellor and the entire Lunacy Commission."

"My mother might disagree had she not died under your supervision at Normand Park."

Jephson looked grave. His solemnity became him. He seemed even more incontrovertible, the picture of medical authority.

"An unparalleled tragedy," he said. He circled back behind his desk, sitting and gesturing to Anthony to be seated himself.

He remained standing, fingers twisting the watch chain in his pocket. He twitched his hand free when he saw that Jephson observed him with an air of clinical curiosity.

"The Duchess of Weston suffered an acute malady." Jephson's voice was heavy with sadness. "The symptoms were various and severe, but none of the doctors who consulted ever imagined she would harm herself. At the time, I suspected a somatic cause."

More Greek.

Anthony sat, accepted the glass Jephson offered, an excellent scotch, meant to be savored. He swallowed it without tasting.

"An infection?"

"Perhaps. Something physiological. Her brain tissue was healthy, no lesions. Now we understand that the reproductive organs are most often involved in these extreme cases. I wish I'd known then what I know now. I might have helped her."

Anthony pressed the rim of the empty glass to his mouth, mashing his lips against his teeth, to choke the noise that threatened to erupt.

Her brain tissue. Jephson had performed an autopsy. Why had this never before occurred to him, that his mother had been carved up, her very organs brought to account? She was buried, at least, under her maiden name in Norwood, in the Metaxas sarcophagus at the Greek Orthodox necropolis at the South Metropolitan Cemetery. Returned to her first—and happier—family. What had always been touted as a disgrace now seemed to him a mercy.

Jephson sighed.

"Today, the prognosis for a woman with your mother's condition is much better. That's a professional balm that I know can only provide so much comfort to those with personal griefs."

"I've no need of balms."

Not from you.

Anthony allowed Jephson to refill his glass. Nothing would bring his mother back. He had to live *now*, to fight *now* for what he loved. That would honor his mother's memory more than obsessive vengeance or self-destruction.

"Let's discuss a timelier topic," he said, clearing his throat. "You've recently been employed as medical officer by the vestry of Shoreditch. That's very civic of you, taking on such thankless work in addition to your responsibilities here."

"Thank you." Jephson sipped his own scotch. "Overcrowded and insanitary buildings are ruinous to the public health. I do my part to goad the vestry into prosecuting the necessary improvements."

"Hmm." Anthony swallowed the second glass of scotch. It warmed his chest. If he stopped there, two glasses, that golden warmth would be an asset.

"You think to improve public health by endorsing the destruction of properties?"

"If they're nests of infectious diseases, certainly. There are one hundred eighty-five people per acre in Shoreditch, most living in the lowest circumstances."

"But there's no statute for the reconstruction of the houses." Anthony sniffed at his empty glass. A *very* fine year. He locked eyes with Jephson. "Surely, public health suffers when families sleep in liquid filth under bridges. The medical officers in St. Pancras and Marylebone have been pushing for repair rather than demolition, *because* there's no provision for the displaced population."

All that laborious reading . . . his father's notes on the Cross Act of 1875 . . . Dr. Rendel's and Dr. Stephenson's quarterly reports to the Sanitary Committee . . . it came in handy now. Jephson's silky manner couldn't smooth away the facts.

With one fingertip, Jephson touched his temple, tipping his head slightly, like a man hearing the whine of a circling insect.

"In certain instances, repair is, of course, advisable."

"But not on Charlotte Road? And why exactly is that, Dr. Jephson?"

Jephson seemed to notice that Anthony's glass was empty. He raised the decanter questioningly, then leaned forward.

Stalling.

A tap came on the door at the same moment it swung open. A

gaunt alienist walked in, all nose and Adam's apple, looking up from a document as he entered. He saw Anthony and startled, backing away apologetically.

"I'm sorry, Dr. Jephson. I didn't realize you were occupied."

As he turned to go, Jephson held out his hand for the document, and in that moment, as the alienist came forward again, Anthony saw something irreconcilable with reality.

Two women, nurses, in starched white aprons and high white collars, passed the open doorway, a smaller woman stumbling between them. Anthony was on his feet before the woman began to flail, wild hair snarling all around her, before he could be sure.

"I can walk, dammit. Get your pettifogging hands off of me!" The familiar voice, throaty and desperate, gave his feet wings. It was the work of a moment to push aside the nurses—as gently as he could manage—and close his hand around Lucy's shoulder, the tendon so tight it jumped against his palm. Her rolling eye caught his and she convulsed with recognition, clamping her arms around him with bruising force.

It felt like an act of providence, awesome and terrible, that she should be here, delivered into his arms, shaking as though she would come apart.

God above, he would keep her together. He would hold her until the end of time if need be.

He flattened the springy curls against her head, looked, uncomprehending, at Jephson, who'd come out into the hall. His face was white as paper, but he spoke with undiminished authority.

"Release the patient at once."

"I'm not a patient." Lucy ripped free and turned, pressing her back against Anthony's chest, the way a soldier making a desperate last stand might press his back to a wall.

"You're a patient until we've thoroughly established your sanity, at which point, if your faculties are intact, I will be forced to contact the police." Jephson signaled to the nurses.

"And what was this woman's crime?" asked Anthony softly, stopping the forward progress of the nurses with a glance.

"I understand it was a violent episode, involving a patient. I've yet to interview the concerned parties." Jephson's eyes slid away. "We take such breaches seriously. The serenity and safety of our patients is paramount. But these incidents are vanishingly rare and needn't worry you." He smiled, signaling again to the nurses.

"Have you seen the site for the cannery? Come, let's continue our discussion outside."

Lucy faced him, and he saw the green and yellow bruise ripening on her cheek, obscuring the constellation of freckles. Her lashes were gummy, the whites of her eyes rheumy and pink.

"Effie." She breathed it. He had to lower his head.

"Effie," she said. "She's here."

He didn't move, but something tore inside him. There could only be a physiological explanation for this feeling: his organs were sliding out of their casings.

He looked at Jephson and saw the fear on his face. Not the fear of a man whose career has suddenly careened off track, who comprehends the abstraction of a reputation and a livelihood gone to ashes—animal fear. The fear of a lamb that scents a wolf in the fold.

He realized his teeth were bared, his hands in fists. Lucy placed a palm against his chest, as though she knew only the gentlest pressure could hold him back.

He relaxed his hands, touched her fingers, breathing through his nose until he could look at Jephson without lunging.

"Take me to my sister," he said. *He* would give the orders now. *Don't let it be too late.*

Moments later, as the door to her room swung open, he could envision it, the sight he'd never beheld, replicated, his sister hanging from the bedpost. Imagination was a blessing and a curse.

He found her sitting at the window. She was singing to herself, quietly in a minor key, his mother's haunting melody. Could he have heard her from such a distance, walking across the grounds? Or had the same memory visited both of them? What did you call such a visitation?

Looking at his sister, alive, frail but whole, as she turned from the window to look at him, he knew he was seeing a ghost, the ghost of his love for his mother, seeing it made flesh. It wasn't too late to love, to live *now*.

And then she was hurtling toward him, and he was wrapping her in his arms. He kept an arm around her as they walked down the hall, Lucy clinging to his other hand. The hall had filled with nurses, orderlies, and alienists, but as he glared they parted to let him pass. As well they should.

Goddamn it, he was the Duke of Weston. His money funded this blasted place.

He was leaving, with whomever he chose to take with him.

He paused when he reached Jephson. "Don't worry about contacting the police. There are several breaches *I* want to investigate. I'll contact the police myself."

"Not now," murmured Effie.

"Where's Kate?" Lucy demanded of the gaunt alienist.

Anthony let his sister tug him forward.

"You'll be hearing from them," he promised Jephson. "And from me."

But Effie was right. First, he needed to pluck her out of this hell.

And so they walked on, the alienist scurrying to show them the way to Kate's cell, and then they were stepping out of the asylum, all four of them walking down the hill in the afternoon sun.

WHEN THE TORRENT of words slowed and Anthony and Effie paused for breath on the leather settee in Uncle Peter's study, both of their faces were wet with tears. She'd sworn she wasn't crying for their father, and Anthony believed her. Lucy had told them in the coach that he wasn't the one who'd had her taken to Putney, but this realization, and the realization that Robert Yardley had exerted a powerful influence on his behavior at the end of his life—perhaps even hastened that end—didn't unknot his twisted legacy. The hurt they felt was too warped for the conventional releases—sobs or speeches. They'd have to sit with it, not just today, but for years of days, before they came to the end of it. At least now they'd sit with it together.

Anthony kissed Effie's brow, chucked her beneath the chin, which made her screw up her face with annoyance, just as he'd hoped. God, he'd missed that expression. Her voice had begun to scratch, and his throat was raw, but there was still so much left to say. About George, about Charlie Nixon, about the long road from Maiwand to Kandahar, about the Putney Asylum. About Lucy. But they would have time, decades, a whole lifetime. All the time they needed to rebuild their family, and make new families.

They walked together into the parlor, which smelled of honey, cinnamon, and powdered sugar. Sofia leapt up to tug Effie down onto the sofa beside her. The resemblance between them was not so marked, not anymore. Effie's face and figure had changed, seasoned into a different, darker loveliness.

"Your favorite." Aunt Helen put a honey-dipped cookie on a plate and handed it to her.

"I could eat a thousand of these." Effie smiled, a breathtaking smile, but even that smile seemed a dazzling surface ripple that left some fathomless well within untouched.

Aunt Helen noticed it. She looked at Anthony, an assuring look. *Patience*, that look seemed to urge. Too much had happened, too much had changed, to compass all at once.

"I've eaten at least a dozen," declared Lucy, dusting powdered sugar from her dress, lifting her head. "Although I can't say they're my favorite because I haven't tried the others."

"Those are good," said Sofia, pointing to another biscuit. "But you have to dip them in your tea for fifteen minutes or they'll break your teeth. That's how Yiayia broke her tooth, our grandmother."

"It is not," Effie said, laughing. "She told you that to make you slow down so there'd be cookies left for her."

"How *did* Yiayia break her tooth?" Sofia asked her mother, and Aunt Helen began to tell the story of Yiayia as a young woman in Pylos biting an ancient Greek coin she took for a lead-plugged counterfeit.

Anthony had heard it before, but he liked hearing it again. He liked watching Lucy listen, her eyes wide, a smile hovering on her lips. She fit in easily with his lively relatives. There was something comforting, and comfortable, about her presence in the room. A rare bird among rarities. He wove between tables and vases, choosing the blue-and-white brocade chair and pulling it close to her. They'd dropped her friend Kate at home—the route to Leicester Square passed near to her house—but it had made no sense to take Lucy to Shoreditch before getting Effie settled. That's what he'd said, at any rate. The truth was he wanted her here, with him, with his family. Her eyes wandered the room as Aunt Helen spoke, lighting and sometimes lingering on the objects that had fascinated him from childhood. The large pear-shaped vases with stirrup handles. The black lacquer cabinets with gold meanders. Finally, her eyes met his and held, her flush almost disguising the discoloration on her cheekbone.

Laughter and the tinkling of spoons brought his attention back to Aunt Helen. The story had ended, as it always did, triumphantly, with Yiayia losing a tooth to make a priceless discovery.

"Maria will come at once to see you," Aunt Helen was saying to Effie, naming her older daughter. "You won't believe how much little Peter has grown."

"And Uncle Peter?" Effie asked. Uncle Peter traveled often for business, sometimes as far as Greece, sometimes to meet with clients at closer ports.

"He'll be back within two weeks." Aunt Helen beamed, imagining, no doubt, his happy return, the surprise that awaited him. It was more than Effie's return—they'd finally effected a reunion, a closing of the distance that had separated the branches of the family. No more sneaking. Their father's long reach had at last fallen short.

Aunt Helen poured tea from the smaller pot into her cup, the kind she liked, thick with honey and cinnamon syrup. Her enjoyment as she inhaled the steam was so apparent that Anthony poured himself a cup and winced through a single swallow before setting it aside.

Some things never changed.

"I can't wait to see him." Effie shook her head slightly, tears shining again in her eyes. Her voice cracked, and she locked her hands, bracing her body as though she might at any moment find herself shaken awake, ripped from a reality she didn't yet dare to accept.

"I still can't believe I'm here."

"I knew you'd be back! I knew we'd see you soon," said Sofia warmly, seizing Effie's wrist, separating her hands so she could cradle the left against her heart.

Effie made a choking noise.

"I did not know. In fact—I thought—I was convinced that I would die in there," she whispered.

The room grew quiet. For several moments, they listened to the tick of the clock.

"Sofia." Aunt Helen leaned over the scrolled arm of her chair to touch her daughter's elbow. "I will speak with my niece and nephew in private."

Lucy stirred, but Anthony touched the back of her hand, bidding her to stay. Sofia rose slowly, frowning, every line of her body communicating reluctance.

"Go on, koukla." Aunt Helen laughed at her outrage. "You can have Effie all to yourself afterward."

"Koukla," murmured Effie as Sofia dragged from the room.

"Koukla mou. My little doll, my honey." Aunt Helen added sugar to her syrupy concoction, sipped, then added another spoonful. "Your mother called you koukla too. And you used to call Anthony koukla and make us all laugh. You don't remember. Well, you were little more than a baby."

Effie sank back in her chair.

"Cuckoo," she whispered, blinking at Anthony, at the echo of maternal love they'd just discovered in that silly nomination. How much they'd forgotten!

Lucy smiled, her hand shifting beneath his fingers, lifting to trap his pinky between its pad and her forefinger. The promise of that slight pressure heated his chest. The golden warmth produced by the scotch in Jephson's office was a counterfeit. *This* was true gold, what he felt now in the center of his being.

He had the strength to continue.

"Our mother," he said and waited, giving Aunt Helen the opening to speak.

Tell us about her, about what happened.

Aunt Helen hesitated, glancing at Lucy. She knew that Lucy had been instrumental in Effie's rescue, but she was still a stranger. Then her eyes found Anthony and his face decided her.

"Thalia," she said, musingly, eyes suddenly unfocused, staring at a distant point.

"She provoked me terribly."

She laughed. It was odd, to hear their mother's name uttered aloud. It felt like a taboo had been broken, the lid of a locked box lifted. Effie's eyes shone.

"I was twice as serious, so she was four times as free. But we loved each other for all our differences. She was filled with love. Do you remember that she ate a vegetable diet? No? One year, when we were children, she met the Easter lamb before he was introduced to the spit. That finished it for her. No one could talk sense into her head once her feelings were engaged. And she infected other people with her passions. I gave up lamb myself, for a season."

Aunt Helen's smile faded, and her olive skin looked suddenly waxen.

"I didn't know what your father had done. When she stopped answering my letters, I felt that something was wrong, but I waited too long to act on my intuition. The company was changing then, from sail to steam, and the prize of our fleet, a steamship built to order, had sunk earlier that spring in the Black Sea. Peter and his father had gone to Odessa to negotiate with the insurers, a trip that lasted months. I had my hands full running the household, organizing company correspondence, keeping up a family presence at the docks, acting as Peter's eyes and ears."

She sat very straight, shoulders thrown back, exposing herself for their castigation.

"When she missed Maria's birthday, I couldn't ignore it any longer. I went to Weston Hall, and your father received me."

Anthony sensed Lucy's eyes upon him and straightened his own shoulders.

"He told me that your mother had become unmanageable. That her wanton behavior, her flirting and singing, had precipitated a crisis. He described an increased fondness for drink, the application of heavy perfumes, general derangement and immodesty, called her a strumpet, an embarrassment. It struck me as a cruel misinterpretation of my sister's loving spirit and vivacity and I said so. That's when he told me she was having an affair . . . with my husband, with Peter."

Anthony started, and Lucy's hand turned, gripping his.

"He showed me a fragment of a love letter written in her hand." Bleakness moved across Aunt Helen's face, stripping the color from her lips.

"No names. But he said it had been found the month before, in Peter's office at the docks, in the fireplace. Peter had been careless burning the evidence. I walked out. I walked out blindly. I didn't ask where Thalia had gone. I learned of it in the paper, like everyone else, when it was too late. I regret every day that I didn't fight for her."

"But she . . . and Uncle Peter . . ." Effie yanked at her braid, try-ing to contain her emotion.

"Nothing passed between them," said Aunt Helen firmly. "The more I reflected, the more certain I became. The timing showed too much calculation. Why make the accusation then, when Peter was thousands of miles away? Besides, if Peter and Thalia were lovers, they would have corresponded in Greek."

A rather cold defense to be mounted by a woman whose husband had been accused of adultery with her sister. But Helen was logical above all else.

"And, of course, when Peter arrived back to England, we had it out. *Nothing* passed between them but the love of brother for sister, sister for brother. I suspect the letter was a forgery." Aunt Helen's gaze flickered. "Your father had decided on his course of action and wanted more evidence of her supposed hysteria, while at the same time forcing our families apart."

The warmth was gone. Numbness replaced it. Anthony hunched, slid his hand from Lucy's, and thrust it into his pocket, where he twisted his watch chain savagely.

It had the hallmark of one of his father's schemes. The tactical efficiency would have appealed to him. And yet . . . his father would never have falsified a document that humiliated his pride. Nor would he have needed to do so, with the right doctor in his pay.

Effie heaved a noisy breath, eyes fixed on the plate in her lap. For her, their father's death was fresh, and their mother's suffering had a vivid corollary in her own experience.

No more of this discussion.

Aunt Helen seemed to agree. She glanced at Anthony, took in his slouch, the hand in his pocket, and changed the subject.

"I almost forgot," she said, her tone lighter. "I have a present for you, a bit late for your birthday, but . . ."

She put aside her cup and went to a cabinet.

"Papou's worry beads," she said, smiling down at him. "You played with them once upon a time."

"I remember," he said hoarsely, although he hadn't until this moment, looking down at the amber beads strung alongside gold, the rich silk tassel. He let the beads drop through his fingers, twirled them so they dropped again. The movement, the rhythm, aligned him. He felt a tiny burst of wonder as he made the gesture his grandfather had made, and his grandfather's father, and his. Restlessness, harnessed in this way, could produce a kind of peace.

He rose and kissed his Aunt Helen's cheek. Lucy rose too. *Her* aunt had to be worried sick.

"Thank you for the tea and cookies," she murmured as Aunt Helen turned to her. "I should be getting home."

"You'll come back soon, though," said Effie. She seemed to shake off her pall, rising to wrap Lucy in a fierce embrace.

"Of course." Lucy's response was a bit breathless, perhaps due to the rib-cracking pressure. Her eyes brushed Anthony's as she came away from Effie, their glow unreadable.

"I'll call the coach," he said.

CHAPTER TWENTY

THE FIRST STREET passed, and the second, and they said nothing. Darkness had fallen and intermittent light from the swinging side lamp caught the green of his eyes, gave her the color and contour of his face, again and again. In the moments between, the shadows devoured everything. It was hypnotizing, his beauty revealed with startling clarity, then swept away.

Clouds of chloroform vapor still scudded in her brain, periodically blanking her thoughts. Lucy could dimly remember the seemingly interminable cycles of stupor and sudden shocked clarity, how she'd fought to hold her breath when the damp sponge descended until something hard and hot detonated in her lungs, and she inhaled and was lost.

"Thank you," he said at last, his heated voice emerging like a caress. "I cannot tell you how much." He shook his head, studying her face, which doubtless flickered as his did. Shadow swallowed his expression.

"If it weren't for you, I might have walked the grounds, stared square into Jephson's eyes, and come away again, not knowing my own sister was right under my nose."

She knew she should remain on guard against the intimacy threatening to reestablish itself between them. But there it was. She couldn't.

He leaned forward and she let him take her hand, twining their fingers together. He'd touched her hand, too, in that marvelous parlor, where she'd sat among the women he loved and felt welcomed into their circle.

Now, as then, her response to his touch was instinctual, intuitive. Her rational self, sounding alarms, stumbled far behind.

"I wish you hadn't gone alone," he said. His palm cupped her cheek, so gently she felt it only as warmth against the bruised skin.

"I didn't go alone." She exhaled, turning her face away from his hand. "Kate came with me."

"Of course. Kate. I owe her my thanks as well." His hand fell and found hers again, gripping her fingers more tightly than before. "I meant something else. I wish—I wish that you had counted on me. That you could count on me." He laughed ruefully. "What I mean is, I want to be counted on, and to count for something because of that. Christ."

The light that slid now across his face as he smiled left his dimples black as jet.

"And then?" She leaned back into the bench to counteract the force tugging her forward. This was the conversation that she had intended to avoid in the hopes that they could both escape the drive with their hearts intact. "You're engaged," she reminded him.

"I'm breaking my engagement." The smile was gone. His throat contracted, the shadow bobbing. "I won't be their puppet, not my father's, not Yardley's. Charlotte Road will be safe regardless, Lucy, I guarantee it. *Count* on me."

She pressed a fist to the window, realized she had given an imperceptible shake of her head.

"You'd rather I marry Lavinia," he said flatly. "It's simpler." He leaned back on the bench, his muscular body seeming too large, suddenly, for the small compartment. The chilled evening air electrified.

"I'm not going with you to Scotland."

"Forget Scotland. I was behaving like a spoiled drunkard. You were right. I'd rather cut out my heart than make you watch me drain bottle after bottle in a . . . what did you call it?"

"Hovel," she said.

"In a hovel," he continued. "I don't want the fantasy. I want the reality. With you. Here. Even if it's harder and more complicated."

She could slide toward him on the bench, bump her thigh, her hip, against his, fold into him. But she held herself straight and still.

"How will you save Charlotte Road without money to buy the leases?"

The light struck a green spark from his irises. His smile turned ironic, those fine lines fanning out around his eyes. She flushed.

"Don't worry," he said, sarcastically. "I wasn't asking you to accept me penniless."

"That's not fair. It's not your money I'm after, it's just . . ."

"My money is worth something," he quoted her, still smiling that ironic smile. "And I, sadly, am not."

She took her fist from the window, pressed it into her stomach, a wave of the familiar misery she could feel in his company cresting over.

"I want to count on you," she whispered. "But I'm afraid."

He leaned toward her, expression softening, and he drew her fist away from her stomach, kissing the knuckles.

"I'm afraid of loving you," she said, staring out the window as the coach rolled from his side of London to hers. "I'm afraid of my love emptying into you, emptying me out, because you've made yourself a bottomless pit. Alcohol can't fill it. I can't fill it. But you'll take and take, and I won't be able to stop myself from giving. Because I love you. That much. I'm afraid of being destroyed by it. If my father hadn't died . . ."

She strangled on a sob.

"I wouldn't have gone to the Royal Academy. I wouldn't have been willing to leave him. I would have sacrificed everything, like my mother did. I can't put myself in that position again, ever, Anthony. I can't."

He lifted her and held her tight to him, and she spoke into the curve of his jaw, just below his ear, barely sounding the words, shaping them against his skin.

"I've wondered if my father was . . . careless . . . on the stairs that night, because he wanted to release me. He wanted to die *for* me. I need someone who wants to *live*. *With* me. Fully. I need . . ."

He tilted up her head. The look in his eyes unlaced her.

"Reality isn't perfect," he said, his voice raw. "But I will work every day to fill my own holes so I'm not a sieve for your love. So it can flow back to you, along with my own. Lucy, marry me."

She could feel the smile spreading over her face.

"You're really breaking your engagement?"

"I'll do it now if you think it best. Should I redirect the coachman?" He lunged forward, and she flung out her arm to stop him.

"I have to get home," she said, laughing, dashing away tears.

"It's just as well." His voice hardened. "I don't want you within a mile of Robert Yardley."

She thought she knew all of his faces, but this one was new, cruel and frightening. She feared for him, feared what he might do during the inevitable encounter, feared what it might do to him.

He blinked several times, dispelling the shadow.

"I *will* inherit," he said. "I suspect it will take more than a fortune to endear me to your aunt. Perhaps she'll be interested to know that I'm working in the House to appoint a select committee. The committee will mount an independent investigation into the Board of Works."

"Oh, well done!" It burst from her. She thought he might bridle at her enthusiasm, not wholly untinged by surprise, but he tossed the hair from his eyes and grinned.

"I might as well be hanged for a sheep as a lamb," he said. "I'm coauthoring a bill that proposes to reform metropolitan government

altogether. Do away with the Board of Works and its crooked ap-
pointees. Replace it with a city council of *elected* men."

"Has it any hope?" She couldn't help but grin back at him. Hadn't
he boasted of the cobwebs on his bench in the House of Lords? More
than his declarations, these proofs of purpose spoke to the change
the weeks had worked on him.

"Wiser heads than mine say not a shred of hope, but supposedly
that's where the fun begins." His eyebrow quirked. He wasn't quite
so transformed as to accept whole hog the notion that drumming up
parliamentary support for a bill reforming city government could be
fun. But she could see in his eyes that he was up for the challenge.
She blinked.

"Lucy." His voice altered, the words slow and stretched. "I love you
and I know who you are and what that means. A *proper* marriage to
you would be madness, the sweetest madness I could imagine."

He hooked her hair behind her ear, so he could peer into her eyes.
Her heart swelled, and she sipped his scent, the musk of his skin,
which seemed magnetized to hers, drawing their limbs together,
their lips. The kiss was tender but searing, and the words stuck in her
throat. For a moment, she eased into him, marveling anew at his
hard dimensions.

Excitement sent lightning bolts through her, clearing the vapors
in her skull. She was *awake*. She was hurtling toward the future,
their future, a great and glorious one.

"Tomorrow." She buried her face in his throat. "Tomorrow I will
submit my picture for the Summer Exhibition. And after that . . ."

She sighed, not daring to hope aloud. She drew back far enough
to see his face, to shock herself again with his beauty.

"I'd meant to submit today, but no matter. Submissions are accepted until Tuesday." She smiled. "I feel like a mother hen, fretting
about her chick. The pictures all go into a great wooden pound in
the center of a room, stacked six feet deep. I waited so long maybe
mine will be on top and less likely to get a hole punched in it."

He didn't return her smile. Something about his expression warned her. She could see his eyelids contract, the black lashes sweep a pained angle. She cleared her throat, fighting the sudden panic.

"Funny," she said, with studied casualness. "I don't know, actually, how long I lay in that room." She brushed her fingertips nervously across her nostrils. How many times had she inhaled the chloroform? How many cycles?

"Anthony." She looked at him but kept speaking, refusing to accept the answer she saw on his face. "What day is today?"

He didn't want to speak. An eternity passed.

"Tuesday," he said. The muscles clenched along his jaw, and his cheeks hollowed starkly, before the shadow swept again across his face.

"Ah." She pushed off his chest, twisted from him, sagging at the waist. She rubbed her forehead against the window glass. She could barely speak.

"Longer than I thought." She managed to gasp the words. "Longer than either of us thought." Kate had been as dazed as she on the drive back to London. But surely only one night had passed. It was Monday, and tomorrow she could bring her picture to the door beside the students' entrance, watch the porters carry it through.

"Is it really Tuesday?" Her voice strained, broke. "Don't lie to me. Is it?"

He was silent.

"No." She shook her head.

She'd lain on her back, insensible, while the sun crossed from east to west, and the world turned and turned again. And the deadline had come and gone.

His lips moved from her knuckles to her wrists. She twined her arms around his neck, bending his head toward hers with brutal force. She was kissing him like a strangler. She couldn't tell if the salt on her lips came from her tears or their blood as their teeth clashed. The hunger was savage. She tore at the buttons of his shirt, then pushed it up, raking her hands down his ridged torso, the rib and muscle. She didn't need to unclothe him. She was done with revelation, with awe. She wanted the darker sublime, terrifying and destroying. The tears clung thick to her eyes, wetting his ear as she bit the lobe, *hard*, making him growl with a sound near to anger. *Good.* She slapped away his hands as they moved to unfasten her dress.

"No," she grated. "Now." He understood, surged with the same obliterative urgency. He seized her buttocks and jerked her onto his hips, bending her legs sharply, pushing up her skirts. She needed *this*, this violence and immediacy. It could draw blood. It could break bones.

The coach rattled over broken cobbles, the axles tipping, and she jammed her right knee into the bench, her thighs sliding up his, the flesh between grinding against the bulge of his erection. He twisted his arm up under her skirt, fingers plucking at the slit in her drawers, and then rolling over the swelling knot that made her release a sob, of pleasure, of pain, she no longer knew. She scrabbled at his trousers, pulling him free, that thick muscle springing into her hand, and then he was lifting her, seating himself inside. She bore down and he cried out, groping her breast crudely, the fabric of her dress harassing the nipple, his other hand gripping her hip. The vibration of the coach moved through them, making her teeth chatter until he forced her jaws apart, his tongue filling her mouth as he torqued his hips. The angle he struck made her buck against him and scream the scream that she had tried to force out for days, guttural and desperate. It startled him. He stilled his hips and ripped his mouth away. She saw his hooded eyes, the tight intensity of his expression. Even in the throes of this brutalizing passion, he could halt, could hold himself back—quaking—to safeguard her pleasure. He would hurt her, dominate her body, but only if and as she wished.

"Do you want me to stop?" he panted, mouth twisting, hard thighs leaping beneath her.

Slowly, she rolled her hips against him in answer, the expulsed scream opening into a sigh that became quick, panting breaths. *She* could set the rhythm, direct this torture for both of them. She wiggled, adjusting herself, driving him deeper, until there was no room for anything else, and she began to move quicker.

The coach tilted precariously in a pothole and the lamp winked out. They coupled in total darkness now, mouths fused. He strained up to meet her, hips pumping, and what she felt was better than light, more jagged and more grasping, and then the feeling tightened, curled her into a molten spring.

She exploded with the force of her climax, heaving and shuddering against him, and he stroked inside her in time with the contractions until his whole body went rigid and he lifted her away, muffling his cry against her dress.

Their breathing normalized slowly. Clothing was tugged and straightened. Their bodies, detached, solidified within their individual membranes, bounded and separate. The coach rolled on through the city. After a moment, he took her hand.

"We'll fix all of this," he said. "Count on me."

She wiped condensation from the window. There was Shoreditch, laid out in crooked misery.

"I believe I proposed somewhere along the way," he said. "Maybe I didn't phrase it as a question. You didn't answer. Look at me. Lucy. Miss Coover, will . . ."

She turned and put her damp fingers to his lips. Suddenly, it all felt too raw, too fast. Everything in her life had been upended and upended. She'd lost an entire day, the most important day of her artistic career to date. He'd still to break his engagement. To confront Mr. Yardley. Would he still want her to count on him after that?

"One thing at a time," she said. And after, when he tried to speak, eyes burning: "Shhhh."

Her head was filling again with vapor. As she stepped out of the coach, the future seemed as murky as the night.

CHAPTER TWENTY-ONE

"ANTHONY! WAS IT you making that racket?"

Lavinia poked her head out of the morning room.

"How romantic," she said testily, hurrying down the hall to intercept him as he stalked toward her, the Yardleys' butler, whose slow arrival at the front door had precipitated Anthony's wild pounding, trotting a few timorous paces behind.

"I believe you're meant to compare me to the sun at dawn, not storm into the house at dawn looking like . . ."

She searched his face, her own face draining of color.

"Anthony. Is something wrong?"

He'd rarely heard that anxious note sound in her voice. What did she see etched on his features? Bottomless sorrow? Ravening fury? He'd barely slept, had woken with the sky ink black and paced his room like an animal, dressing when the clock struck seven without ringing for Humphreys or checking his appearance in the mirror.

He stared at her, at her round eyes as blue as bells of heather. It wasn't in his power to assuage her concern.

"Where is your father?"

Her reply lagged too long. *Everything* lagged today. And to think, he'd prided himself on newfound patience. He strode past her into the morning room.

It was a pleasant scene. The curtains were pulled back; the east-facing windows shone with morning light. Yardley sat reading the newspaper in a wingback chair, a rolled blueprint propped against the arm. Enjoying half an hour of domestic tranquility before departing for the hustle and bustle of the office, where his attention would be divided among dozens of tasks. Overseeing clerks, advising district surveyors, consulting on walls and roads, drafting plans.

Covering up crimes.

His wife, Moira, sat nearer the windows, bent over her needlepoint. A copy of the *Queen* lay on the chair Lavinia had lately abandoned, open to a colorful fashion plate. Breakfast was still spread out on the sideboard.

Moira looked up, flustered by Anthony's abrupt entrance.

"Good heavens," she said. "I'd have told Cook if I'd known we were having you to breakfast."

She cast her eyes despairingly over the sideboard.

"Today of all days she crisped the bacon. But it's easily remedied. We'll send for ham and poached eggs. You do like poached eggs? I *wish* someone had mentioned this sooner."

This last was aimed at Lavinia, who had edged around Anthony to stand beside her father's chair.

"She didn't expect me. But he did." Anthony nodded at Yardley, who leaned back, shaking out his paper and folding it on his knee.

The last mail delivery of the day came at half past seven in the evening, the first of the day at half past seven in the morning.

Yardley would have received a letter from Jephson, if not yesterday then just now.

"I expected you," said Yardley evenly. "But somewhat later in the day, at the office." He sounded mildly reproving.

"Why the office?" A squall kicked up in Anthony's breast, where the rage had been circling for hours, gathering force. "This is a family matter, after all. Your wife and daughter have every right to hear of it."

"Hear what?" Lavinia frowned. "What are you talking about?"

"It turns out Effie was not enjoying sea baths on the French Riviera these many months." Anthony looked hard at Yardley. "She was wearing leather mitts and howling, locked in a room at the Putney Asylum."

Lavinia gasped, and Yardley stood, snapping the paper against his thigh.

"Have you no decency?"

That was enough to stun Anthony into silence. So. *He* was the fiend, for giving the delicately nurtured a glimpse of the inferno.

But what of him who had tended the flames?

"I don't understand." Lavinia squeezed her hands together.

"You don't understand, because you were shielded from a truth that would have pained you to no purpose. Until yesterday, the situation was well under control." Yardley shot his wife a dark look, and she rose hastily, gathering her canvas and thread.

Moira had always seemed a pettish, ill-satisfied woman, forever fussing and finding fault, with servants, with Lavinia. But Anthony had never known her to contravene her husband.

"Let's take a walk in the garden," she murmured.

Lavinia shook her head. She was looking at her father with horror, flinched when he put a hand on her shoulder.

"Euphemia was receiving the care that her condition requires," he said to her, warm and reasonable. "She suffered the onset of a severe and very dangerous hysteria, which unleashed her tendencies to exhibitionism and . . . sensuality." He cleared his throat. "In the throes of this disturbance, she formed an unwholesome attachment, and she ran off, but the man she called her husband soon tired of her. By the time she was taken to Putney, she had fallen into circumstances too degraded to recount. She was in desperate need of treatment."

"No. She didn't need treatment." Anthony felt the snarl twist his mouth. She'd needed support, acceptance, an open door. "You wanted her out of the way, because she'd realized that our father was in medical danger, a state of vulnerability that suited your interests."

He took a breath, hurling the allegation. "You were preying on his weakness."

Yardley tipped his head, oddly expressionless. "Meanwhile," he said, "you yourself were turning a blind eye to your father's debility." He released Lavinia's shoulder, tossed his paper onto the wingback chair. "Why was your runaway sister the one to realize? Hmm? You were back in town and just down the lane. Did you come to your father when he suffered his fits? Did you consult with his doctors? No, you did nothing, you said nothing. You had no concern for him then. Now that he's gone, you accuse me of predation. I wouldn't be surprised if you claimed next I *caused* his fits with poison, like a wicked Italian in a Gothic romance. You need a villain, Anthony, you need one badly, so you do not have to look at yourself. I've willingly been many things to you, but I choose not to be your scapegoat."

It was happening again, Yardley turning the tables, reframing the story, making it the familiar one, the one that had worn its grooves in his life until it seemed he had no option but to keep spinning along its track.

He opened his mouth, but Yardley wasn't finished.

"When you visited the Putney Asylum, did you ask to see the admissions register? Did you look over Euphemia's committal forms? If you had, it would have punctured your fantasy. I didn't creep through the shadows to order your sister's confinement. Your father signed the papers."

Shame prickled through him, as it always did when he was confronted with his glaring errors of judgment, his foolhardy hardihood. He wouldn't show it, wouldn't bow his head. He glared at Yardley, whose gaze was mellowing as he sensed himself gaining the upper hand.

"You were in too much of a rush, like always," said Yardley, shaking his head. "You didn't even discharge her legally. You took her and paraded out, with two additional women besides, her accomplices from a failed escape bid, in front of dozens of people—doctors, nurses, tourists. I am *shocked* to find no mention of it in the paper. I assume the editors are saving their ink today for three-inch headlines tomorrow. I won't be scrutinized, but *she* will be, and your family will be discussed again *publicly* in the vilest terms."

"Lavinia." Moira's voice rang out, surprisingly sharp. "*Now.* In the garden."

She marched from the room, Lavinia drifting slowly after, looking back at them.

Anthony clenched his fist on his thigh. Ah yes, the wagging tongues, the titillated stares. He was meant to fear such uproar, and rail against it, expending his energy on attempts to undermine, deny, retaliate.

He wouldn't. He had a clear sense for the first time in his life of which opinions mattered. He and Effie would dig in and weather the storm, three-inch headlines be damned. Perhaps he would inspire different headlines soon, when he defected from the Conservative Party, setting his sights on previously unthinkable political targets.

DUKE OF WESTON CROSSES THE FLOOR.

He managed a smile and was rewarded. Unease rippled across Yardley's face, drawing his lip down, puckering his chin.

"You say my father signed the committal form?" He shrugged, conceding the possibility. Perhaps it had been his father's last act before he died, closing the circle of harm—disguised as protection— he'd drawn around the women in his family. Yardley had initiated a process; his father had authorized it.

He could imagine another possibility.

Yardley was a talented draftsman, had known his father's hand well, and his mother's.

"I think, rather, you forged my father's name . . . like you forged the letter that convinced him of my mother's adultery."

Yardley's shoulders sagged. Anthony looked at him, the smiling giant of his youth, deflated. Smaller than he'd ever been.

"My father had in his possession a letter, a scrap of one, that my mother wrote to a lover."

There was no stopping now. The ordinariness of the morning light, the smell of buttered toast, contributed to the feeling of unreality. He took a deep breath.

"Aunt Helen said it was believed to have been found in Peter's office at the docks. My father did not make visits there his habit. But *you* held the contracts for all the company's warehouses. You were often at the docks on business. You were the one who claimed to have discovered that letter, who gave it to my father."

Yardley made no sound or gesture of denial.

"You forged it. You wanted him to think my mother unfaithful, but she was innocent. Nothing passed between my mother and Peter."

It felt good to echo Aunt Helen, to hear her conviction in his voice. But as he spoke, he heard, too, a willed naivete, painfully unconvincing. He was repeating a story crafted for children, a story in which innocence existed, in which the heroes and villains were clearly defined.

The certainty thudded in his chest, even before Yardley drew a shuddering breath and turned to face the windows, his hands linked behind his back, fingers twisting.

There was no forgery. The letter was real.

"She wrote it to you." *Christ God.* His mother had had an affair with Yardley.

"I was nobody." Yardley raised his chin, addressing a slant of light, his voice muted. Anthony had to strain to hear, grateful for the effort, which kept his body tensed. Otherwise he might have exploded, raining blows.

"A young architect without spectacular prospects—a family employee—I was beneath consideration. And he—he swept her off her feet, a duke with a glorious political career rolling out in front of him. But he didn't appreciate her. The things that dazzled him during their courtship—her exuberance, her love of song and dance, wine and flowers, gay company, the theater—grated once they were married. Flirtation and frivolity didn't become the wife of a statesman. They made each other miserable."

"And you were there."

Yardley turned. He had insinuated himself into Anthony's parents' lives for motives too complex to tease apart: desire, jealousy, greed, envy, love, hate. They'd knotted up, rotted together, a festering mass that had infected Anthony's life too.

"I made her happy," Yardley said softly. "For a time."

"Made her happy? You killed her." Anthony's voice cracked like a whip. "You betrayed her to my father, whom *you* had made a cuckold. Then you had your friend Michael Jephson diagnose her with nymphomania."

"I wasn't her only lover!" Yardley shouted. "*She* made your father a cuckold a dozen times over. She was laughing at all of us. If she didn't sleep with Peter, then he was the only man in London."

Never had Anthony let a comment such as that go unchallenged. His knuckles were still crooked from all the collisions with tooth and bone. It took impossible strength to relax his hands. He looked at his palms, the senseless lines.

Yardley's voice was soft again, frayed with desperation.

"I swear to God I thought only to stop her, for her sake as well as mine. The way she behaved—brazen, shameless—it *was* a form of madness."

Distortion. Yardley was a master of it. Maybe he believed his own stories. But his actions disproved them.

"You thought only to stop her," said Anthony. "And yet you were very careful to cover your own tracks, to preserve your relationship with my father, to play into his prejudices, to leverage his humiliation—and later his illness."

No, *wounded lover* didn't begin to account for Yardley's webs of deception, by which he'd gained so much.

Anthony pushed his hair back from his forehead with both hands. The muscles of his brow were knotted painfully.

"Whether or not you're a literal poisoner, you've poisoned every well, for what?" he said. "Revenge? Prestige? Enrichment? There is no one in your life you haven't deceived. *That* is a form of madness."

Yardley took a lurching step forward, stumbling into the wing-back chair. The blueprint propped against it toppled, bounced, and rolled, stopping short of Anthony's boots. Yardley's eyes bulged, and he stooped to pick it up.

Anthony was faster.

"A new project?" He walked around Yardley to the window with the blueprint, spread it open in the light. A detailed drawing showing the north, south, east, and west elevations of an Italianate building with huge windows, the facade elaborated with molded brick courses. The decorative elements didn't detract from the elegance. Yardley was still experimenting with proportion and pattern, attempting to reference architectural traditions, to establish himself as an artist rather than an engineer. The dignity and charm of this design showed him to have come closer than ever before. It would be a success, this building, with the Academy as well as the city.

The writing in the top left corner drew Anthony's eye.

Statham's Emporium.

He checked his abrupt violent motion and let the blueprint curl itself up. Yardley had designed the building for Joseph Statham, the developer who had applied for the Charlotte Road lease.

Anthony's smile was acid, eating away at his face. After this encounter, he might wear a death's head on his shoulders for the rest of his days. He wheeled about, grip on the blueprint hardening to iron.

"What a profitable arrangement you all have," he said. "You, Jephson, Purcell, and whatever developers want to pay for your favors. Exploiting a position on the Board of Works to win commissions as an architect is frowned on in professional circles. What will the president of the Royal Institute of British Architects have to say, I wonder?"

He tucked the blueprint under his arm, walking back across the room toward the door. He paused by Yardley.

"I will ensure that a bill of particulars is brought against you."

Yardley straightened, swallowed hard.

"I will resign," he said, composing himself. "The Board of Works itself has little future."

"*Your* future should concern you more. I won't stop with your misconduct on the bloody board." His mouth felt sandy, but he continued. "That's the tip of the iceberg. You colluded with what was worst in my father to rob me of a mother."

That had been the origin, the blow that shattered the family, shattered something in George, in him, in Effie.

Maybe their mother hadn't been an innocent, but she hadn't deserved her fate. She'd been stripped of light and color, motion, song, her children, her freedom. She hadn't possessed the strength to survive such catastrophic losses.

"And you robbed money as well. Fortunately, that kind of robbery is far easier to prove. I'm not a purist. I feel no driving need to connect you with what happened to my mother, or to Effie. I don't give a damn which of the charges stick, as long as you go to prison for a very long time."

He pushed past, but Yardley reached out, catching him across the chest, a gesture halfway between restraint and embrace. Anthony's right shoulder pressed against Yardley's left.

"Anthony." Yardley spoke hoarsely. "You're like a son to me."

There wasn't only fear in his voice, but tenderness.

Anthony's breath stopped. What was the value of truth if its substance was lies?

"I looked up to you," he said. Their faces were inches apart. He didn't need to look up now. He could look Yardley squarely in the eye.

"I was desperate for someone to see me as more than an *idiot*, and so you told me you did. You told me I had a good mind. You made me apply myself. You *believed* in me."

He laughed, and a smile twitched Yardley's lips in response.

"You were the only one. God above, I would have walked across hot coals for you, and you knew it. You always knew it. You played me like the idiot I was."

The hippodramas. The birthdays. The confidences. Decades of memories. The love between them was real, and it was also rotten to the core.

He closed his eyes briefly, and when he opened them again Yardley's were moist. The smile was gone. The very smile lines in his face had collapsed.

"I can believe in myself without you now," said Anthony. "My father is dead."

LAVINIA STUMBLED BACKWARD when Anthony opened the door.

"How much did you overhear?" he asked, shutting the door carefully behind him.

"Enough." Her gaze was feverish, and the color was back in her cheeks, too much color, blotches of hectic red.

"The engagement . . ." he began, and she dashed a furious tear from her eye.

"Do you think I care about a broken engagement? When you're threatening my father with imprisonment?"

He stared down at her, jaws grinding. His family had been torn apart. Now he would be the agent of *her* family's destruction.

Apology was inadequate. She was right: a broken engagement was the least of the ills about to befall her.

"Handle it however you will," he said, as though she hadn't mentioned her father. On that issue, he had nothing whatsoever to offer. "I won't dispute any reason you give to break the banns."

He bowed to her, no sorrow or fury on his face now. No, he felt his old mask sliding into place.

She clutched his sleeve as he started past.

"How is she?" she asked. "How is Effie?"

The question surprised him. Selfish, spoiled Lavinia Yardley— her care wasn't only for herself.

The blue of her eyes looked darker, the lids smudged.

"I don't know," he said, and his honesty surprised him more than her question. "Her experiences have marked her deeply."

Lavinia glanced away, nodded once, thinking, perhaps, of the role her father had played in producing those internal scars.

"You'll help her," she said at last. "You'll help each other. I used to envy the two of you, the world you shared."

He snorted. Lavinia had entered into their nursery games, imperially, a foreign queen demanding to be received in state.

Lavinia's cheeks hollowed.

"You never wanted to marry me," she said softly. His instinct was to protest, but the finality in her voice offered no room for it. "My father wanted it," she said, and exhaled as the silence lengthened. The tears in her eyes looked hot, as though they'd burn more splotches on her cheeks if they fell. They didn't.

"Is there someone else?" she asked.

He wanted to spare her this next humiliation. But she was studying him, her posture erect. She merited honesty.

"Yes," he said.

She was ready for it. She stretched her elegant neck, inclining her head in faint acknowledgment, just shy of a congratulations. "You weren't my first choice either." She put her hand on the doorknob. "Wait until the summer, at least, to marry her."

A small concession, and in the circumstances, easily granted.

"She's in no rush," he said wryly.

Lavinia was staring at the door, and he knew the tumult of emotions on her face didn't begin or end with him.

"You don't have to go to him," he said.

Her smile was terrible.

"I think your business in this house is finished," she said. "Please, be so kind as to show yourself out."

As he left, he heard her opening and closing the door.

HE LOOKED OUT the window as the coach rolled along to Leicester Square. The day was still young.

Lucy would be on her way to the Royal Academy, perhaps cutting through the very alley where she'd stumbled upon him. He wondered if she regretted it, if she'd spent the night weeping bitterly for lost opportunities.

Aunt Helen was already gone to inspect a ship that had docked in the night, but he found Effie and Sofia lounging over their breakfast, planning a day at the shops.

Effie was in need of a new wardrobe, feminine armor that would help her withstand the notoriety bound to attend her return to Society. She understood better than he did what lay in store; she'd been in London when the *Pall Mall Gazette* published its series on aristocratic seducers following George's death. Her elopement, her tenure at Putney, perhaps even her brief career at Rafferty's—it was only a matter of time before the whole story went to press. She spoke of the inevitable, tapping her spoon agitatedly against her cup. But when he muttered something about his failure to spirit her away in secrecy, she harrumphed.

"Rubbish," she said. "I'd rather everyone know. It's better than cringing around worrying about who will find out. And my *circus* friends won't cut me."

At the mention of circus friends, Sofia's eyes began to shine.

Effie still intended to sing. That, too, would make for a future conversation.

Anthony left them to their talk and their arrangements. Someday soon, when he'd expunged the last traces of Yardley's influence from the house, he'd bring Effie home to Weston Hall. He'd already placed Lucy's miniature on her writing desk. In fact, he'd taken it into Effie's bedchamber more than a week ago, the evening of that terrible day, when he'd turned thirty, gaining and losing so much in so few hours. Hope had ebbed from him, and he'd needed something else. Magic. An enchanted object with the power to manifest his sister's safe return. Sofia would have understood his manner, how he'd touched the miniature with closed eyes, channeling *something*, the power of the moon.

He felt tired when he returned to Park Lane, tired and strangely empty, out of rhythm with the world. He stood looking at the front door.

It wasn't Yardley he was mourning, or George, or his mother, or his father, but someone who had never existed, the person each of them might have been if life had unfolded differently.

Nothing could solace this kind of hurt. Certainly not a drink. But a bottle, a bottle could wash it all away. His throat itched, but then he swallowed hard and headed for the stables. Inside, the light was richer, slanting in golden beams, and the scent of hay and horse flooded him. He felt calmer walking between the stalls. Not a straw out of place. He eased into Snap's stall. He looked more like Anthony remembered him, lean but not gaunt, chest broad, head set proudly on his long neck.

He waved away a groom, saddled Snap himself, and rode for Hyde Park. It never quite satisfied, riding in London. Too many people, even in the parks. He couldn't give his horse its head and gallop flat out, like he did in Hampshire, like he'd done in Afghanistan, crossing the long plateau on Mizoa, the closest he'd ever come to flying.

It was a special agony, remembering Mizoa stretched out in his blood on the road. On a morning like this one, the English spring unfurling its green banner, the air so cool and fresh, all that had transpired in Afghanistan seemed a bad dream.

He needed to remember that it wasn't, that the peace that attended him here, in this gorgeous green corner of London, coexisted with every horror, even, to some extent, depended on horrors. He needed to remember if he was ever to succeed in effecting change.

He couldn't live inside his wounds, not without destroying himself. But he would bear his scars proudly, and learn from them, and not forget, not ever.

When they reached the park, Snap's stiff gait began to smooth and lengthen. Not the speed he craved, but there was a steadiness, a confidence, that came up through Snap's legs into his. He cantered a wide loop, riding until his mind felt patterned by hoof beats. The regularity put his thoughts in order. There was darkness in the world, but there wasn't only darkness. Love, trust, affection. They pounded up from below, governing his connection with the horse, the earth. The life he wanted to live, the better world he wanted to build, it started with this connection. He wanted to tell Lucy how it felt, tell her that she was part of it, this new reality he could finally imagine. But he needed to *do* more first. One thing at a time, she'd said.

At some point he became aware of the moon, pale and luminous above the trees, visible in broad daylight. He leaned back so it could shine full on his face, and he felt somehow that he could distinguish its silvered, mysterious rays from the blaring broad beams of the sun.

He didn't hesitate before his front door on the return. He walked inside and fired Collins on the spot, with wages for the month in lieu of notice. He jogged to his study, Snap's canter organizing his movements as well as his thoughts. For a moment, he assessed the books and papers; then he summoned Humphreys.

"Tear apart the house," he commanded. "Shake out every book and check inside every cushion. Don't worry about ripping the upholstery."

Humphreys grinned, reaching into his pocket and pulling out a knife.

"Not worried," he said. "What are we aiming to find?"

"It turns out my father's preferred heir is a long-dead English setter." Anthony took a book from the shelf and flipped the pages roughly. "We're aiming to find his last will and testament."

CHAPTER TWENTY-TWO

A PAPER DOLL couldn't have squeezed into the Schools through the throng. Students clustered in the roadway, talking excitedly. Lucy's hand tightened on the strap of her bag, and she almost pivoted, ready to run for Piccadilly. Then she chided herself as a twit and a spoilsport.

This was Kate's day. Nothing would sully it. If the wave of excitement crashing through her churned up darker feelings—envy, self-pity—she would simply wait until that sediment settled.

She stood, searching the crowd. Red-faced larvae wiggled into knots of older boys, eager for inside information. The pinafores made their own groupings, throwing hopeful glances over their shoulders. Redcliffe Davis and Thomas Ponsonby held languorous court by the entrance, puffing cigars, Davis's sapphire earring twinkling through the smoke.

It was always like this, confusing and exhilarating, when the first rumors concerning the Hanging Committee's decisions broke. She'd known it was coming, if not today, tomorrow. The Hanging Committee took only five days to go through the oils, another five for the watercolors.

Where was Kate? Lucy felt a clear bubble of hope rising in her chest. No need to wait any longer. If the news was good, she could share her friend's happiness without a particle of reservation.

She saw larvae ripple and scatter, and then she saw Kate, shoving through them, grinning so hard it seemed her face would crack as she ran to Lucy, almost bowling her over. Her fierce hug held her upright.

"Tell me!" Lucy gasped then laughed at the impact. "You had a picture accepted?"

"Two." Kate let her go to spin in a circle, arms upraised. "And so did Gwen, although we don't know yet where they'll be hung. But, Lucy"—she swept one of her arms out, a capacious gesture, taking in the whole chattering assembly—"everyone is talking about *you*."

As if on cue, Lucy felt a tap on her shoulder. A curly-haired blond man of about forty had come up behind her and stood with a little pad of paper. His smile was toothy and ingratiating.

"You're Lucy Coover, I take it?" he said, pencil already scratching.

"No interviews!" Kate crowed. "Unless . . . are you with the *Art Journal*?"

"The *Herald*." The man did a double take, eyes darting from Kate's gray fedora down to her fawn-colored trousers. Kate made a face, steering Lucy away.

"Don't waste yourself on *him*. We'll hold out for a *real* critic, like Alan De'Ath. Wouldn't that be cracking? An essay by De'Ath!" She took off her hat, screamed into it, then replaced it on her head at a jauntier angle.

"Cracking," Lucy agreed without comprehending. She glanced over Kate's shoulder, then to the left, to the right.

People were staring. Not at Kate. At her.

When the articles about Lady Euphemia had appeared in the papers, Lucy had feared that she and Kate would be mentioned as well, but she'd since put those worries aside. The asylum staff had drugged them both too heavily for preliminary questioning, and

Jephson had never gotten the chance to conduct his investigation. No one had learned their names.

But perhaps some new information had come to light? Or—her next thought made her face flame—was some bit of gossip going the rounds, linking her to Anthony's broken engagement?

Miss Yardley had broken it, so the story went. After the latest scandal, she'd thought better of connecting herself to a family so thoroughly besmirched.

Maude's version—which she'd recited to Susan and Constance loudly, the three of them in a huddle behind Lucy's easel—was, predictably, more shocking, including a new marriage proposal, from an impoverished Welshman, which Miss Yardley had secretly accepted.

If it were true—a very big *if*—Lucy supposed Miss Yardley was either following a wild impulse of the heart, as Maude implied, or heeding the call for self-preservation. She knew that *her* family name would soon be blotted with an indelible stain of its own. Escaping to Wales with a husband, however humble, was perhaps her best option.

"Spill it," Lucy said to Kate tersely. "What are they saying about me?"

"Saying?" Kate capered. "They're saying you're a genius, but *I* say you're a damn liar. I should dissolve the Sisterhood on principle, but I can't, not now, when we've *done it*, Lucy. We've done it!"

"This isn't about me and Anthony?" Her blush, which had subsided, fired her cheeks anew at the phrase.

Me and Anthony. He hadn't renewed his proposal since that night in the coach. Giving her time, she supposed. Or changing his mind.

In any event, he'd been occupied settling his legal affairs, traveling between London and Hampshire, and they'd only seen each other briefly.

The effectiveness of his statecraft, however, was very much in evidence. A medical inspector had come last week to Charlotte Road, a young, rail-thin doctor, Dr. Penn, who'd crawled over every inch of the properties before hopping onto a barrel in the back court to denounce, roundly, the city's swindlers and the vestry's pothouse factions to a crowd of tenants who made the air rattle with their cheers. At one point, he'd yelled out that sanitary improvement, until reformed, could be nothing but the *car of juggernaut,* a phrase Aunt Marian had repeated admiringly for days afterward.

A few of the older Cantrell children, along with a few borough lads always up for mischief, had ripped down the notices, and no bill poster had appeared to stick them up again.

The buildings were saved.

"You and Anthony," repeated Kate musingly. "It will be, in part, about Weston, yes, and *that* will be very interesting indeed." She managed to keep still as she answered, still grinning. "But the Hanging Committee didn't notice. They were too walloped! Imagine them—bored to tears, lulled half to sleep under their lap rugs by the seven hundredth piteous picture of a Yorkshire seaport. And then, behold! Endymion!"

Lucy heard her own heartbeat in her ears.

Kate clapped her hands. "I heard from Davis, who heard from a porter that there was *applause* when the foreman brought it out. The *president* said it's as good as the best myth painting by Burne-Jones."

Later, she would remember this moment—she would always remember it—how the world reorganized itself around her, the roadway changing, the Schools, the galleries, everything glowing with possibility.

"You swore to me that he destroyed it!" Kate hugged her again. "What am I going to do with you? You're a *monster,* but I love you, and your picture is going to *hang on the line!*"

She shouted at the sky. Anyone who *hadn't* been looking was looking now.

"Do you know why else I can't dissolve the Sisterhood?"

Kate swept off her hat and fanned herself with it, waiting for Lucy's reply. But Lucy could only blink at her.

"Because we're a proper Circle now. As soon as I heard we were all exhibiting, I marched right up to Gwen and laid it all out, gave her no quarter. *You need us, and we need you*, I told her, and she agreed! We *must* write a better manifesto. That's the first order of business. Something to goad the critics. Gwen will help enormously, don't you think? Where is she?"

She scanned the dense crowd.

"I told her I was going to look for you and that she should come find us. Oh well. She probably ran off to hide in the library. I suppose that's fine. I'll be the radical. You'll be the romantic. And she'll be *the obscure*. We'll make it work for us. Still, I *wish* I could figure her out."

Lucy shrugged, as if in agreement, although she'd already figured out two things. One, that Gwen had lost at least some portion of her hearing, and two, that Gwen wasn't yet ready to share that fact.

"Give her time," she said, suddenly pensive; then she scowled at Kate. "And what's this about *the romantic* and *the obscure*? Each Sister determines her own character, thank you very much."

The romantic. Indeed. But, actually, maybe . . . it fit. Heavens above, all of her passions had arrived.

She knocked Kate's hat out of her hands, unable to restrain herself. She felt as giddy as a child, laughing as Kate tried to catch the hat and batted it instead, so it bounced off of a passing larva.

She couldn't focus on Gwen, on the Sisterhood, on anything but the electrified field immediately surrounding her body, that strange glow of realized potential, of the future arriving.

She was going to show in the Summer Exhibition, show her very best, her most daring and obsessive picture, painted at the very limit of her technique.

Anthony hadn't destroyed it. He'd preserved it, framed it, submitted it on her behalf. He'd trusted her talent. He'd tried, since she'd known him, to do the right thing, and failed, and tried again. He'd kept his promises.

He'd asked her to marry him, and she hadn't said yes.

"Now where are *you* going?" called Kate, rising, slapping her hat against her trousers to knock the dust off.

But Lucy had hiked her skirts to speed her pace and she was already turning onto Piccadilly.

ANTHONY WAS STANDING in the back garden, pausing to drop his watch back into his pocket, when an unexpected sight met his eyes: Lucy, running full tilt down the camellia walk.

She threw down her bag, then bent over sharply, one hand on her hip, the other arm under her ribs. It took a moment for her to unfold. Her hair was a windblown halo. And yet, the wind didn't gust. The day was exceedingly still.

How far had she run at that speed to produce such disorder?

Anthony took a step closer. "Is there a fire?"

Her face was flushed with color, cheeks rosy beneath the constellations of freckles. Sweaty curls stuck to her temples. Her lilac dress was hopelessly rumpled. She looked ravishing.

"You could have come to the front door," he said. "I have a new butler, and the footmen, as you know, like to race."

"I'm used to coming this way," she panted. "My feet carried me. What—what are you doing here?"

She straightened up, the slightest shadow of apprehension dimming her expression.

"I was in the stables mixing ale into an elderly thoroughbred's water trough." He grinned. "He needs the fortification." The only alcohol in the back garden these days went to Snap. "I have a meeting soon, though, with Mr. Purinton, my solicitor." Finally, he'd hired a lawyer of his own. A young man with level brows, right-minded and methodical, who, best of all, had never met his father or Robert Yardley. "He lodged the caveat against the validity of both my father's codicils in the court. He wants to discuss news—good news, I believe—about the proceedings."

358 • Joanna Lowell

She looked a question. He felt as though he'd never seen her eyes before. Lit by the sun, they were the color of some fantastical liquor, a mixture of malted lilies, bulrushes, and gorse.

"You found it, then. The alternate will." She hesitated. "The one in which your father made an heir of a hunting dog."

"Humphreys found it," he said. "Stuffed in the ottoman. Not a valid document, of course. Signed without witnesses. But dated, and clearly demonstrating that my father suffered delusions at the time he amended his legal will."

It hadn't been a pleasant read, that single sheet of paper, the angular script going jagged in numerous places, words crossed out, sentences begun and abandoned. Their father referred to Effie only once, as *my daughter who died shortly after my son and heir*, and to Anthony twice, once as *the young idiot* and once as *that young idiot and coward*.

He drew strength from Lucy's brilliant eyes, and he continued.

"The larger paragraph is devoted to incoherent accusations." He shook his head.

You children are my ruination. His father's words no longer struck him as a prophecy, but as the pitiable invective of a bitter man who had lashed out instead of looking inward. Neither his father nor his mother determined his destiny. He didn't bear the blame for their shattered lives. But *his* life, his commitments, his choices, his love— he fashioned these himself, bit by bit, every day.

The morning sun shone brighter, warm rays caressing his neck. Lucy was looking at him with peculiar understanding, as though she could read his thoughts.

He wanted to fashion his life with her. Live *with* her, fully.

"He'd come to fear Yardley." He said it softly. "Mr. Purinton is confident that we'll win at trial, pleading undue influence and suspicious circumstances. Neither codicil will stand. My father's solicitors will turn on Yardley to protect their own reputations."

His inheritance would be finalized. Due to George's decease, he was his father's principal beneficiary, all of the real estate devised to him, and the money as well, excepting Effie's annuity, and a few small bequests to assorted pecuniary legatees and charities.

No trust. No conditions.

She kept watching him. He *liked* it, the feeling that she could see all of him, even the dark spots.

"There will be a scramble," he said. "Everyone trying to exonerate himself and point the finger elsewhere. But for Yardley . . ." He shook his head. "There's no way out. Undue influence is the least of it."

He'd gone to Hampshire—a long journey for two nights, but he'd needed to interrogate the estate manager in person. Just as he'd suspected, the figures in Cruitshank's ledgers didn't match the figures Yardley had presented him. The rents in the village *had* gone up; Yardley was skimming the difference off the top.

"I'm charging him with embezzlement." He smiled briefly. The freedom he'd won was public and ugly, and not without losses, but worth it all the same. He waved his hand, a gesture that took in the glasshouse, the back garden. His purgatory. "It's over."

Even in the brightening day, her face darkened.

"Over?" She tried to smile, an unfathomable hurt lurking in her eyes. Suddenly, he fathomed it. Lord, he was still a fool.

"I'm beginning again," he said. "I want you with me. Not just there." He glanced at the glasshouse. "Everywhere."

He caught her hands and she grasped them, her fingers slippery with sweat. Suddenly, her smile was real. Huge. Heart-stopping.

"You didn't destroy it," she said. "You submitted it, my picture."

Ah. Could it be? The Hanging Committee had made their decision, and it had been favorable. His breath caught.

"I couldn't." He laughed, the sound startling him. Surely, he hadn't made a sound like that since he was a boy, a sound of unadulterated joy. "I'd already shattered a stained-glass window. I couldn't put a blade or a flame to that canvas. Some talents are so great even boors and philistines can see them for what they are."

"Anthony." Her eyes searched his. "People will recognize your face."

"My *face*?" he said wryly. He would never weary of her blushes. The way the blood rose to the surface of her skin, staining her cheeks, her throat, her breasts—that delicate movement captured his attention fully. Held it. "After the Summer Exhibition, all of London will recognize a good deal more than that."

"You'll be in the papers." She looked uneasy.

"Good," he said. "I hope I'm in every paper. Because *you* are getting the attention you deserve as an artist."

"There will be talk . . ." She twined her fingers more tightly around his. "About . . ." She hesitated. "*Us.*"

"Us?" He repeated it, delighted. "I suppose so. Scandalous talk."

She was staring at him, waiting for something. The pressure she exerted on his fingers was becoming painful. He raised his eyebrows.

"*Count on me.*" She cleared her throat. "That's what you said. You said *count on me.* I wasn't sure if I could. It felt *dangerous.* I didn't want to lose myself . . ."

"Get sucked down into the bottomless pit? Understandable." He exhaled. "You have a precious self. I will lift her up. As high as the moon." He smiled. "Maybe I shouldn't have said *count on me.*"

Her lips parted, a line forming between her brows.

"Count on us," he said, pulling her closer. "Count on what we can do together."

She smiled, wiggled her hand free, and stepped back, combing at her hair. The effort changed nothing. She still looked wild. Lovely. Rare. His heart hurt, it felt so full. She linked her fingers, and again, he had the impression that she was waiting.

He rocked on his heels, uncertain. A bird twittered in the cherry tree. Her smile was becoming a grimace.

"Idiot," she muttered, and he blinked.

"*Ask* me," she hissed. "I ran all this way to answer. I got six stitches in my side so I could be here as quickly as I possibly could to say *yes, you imbecile. Yes.*"

"Oh, well then." He could take a hint. If it was put to him very, very clearly. He stepped forward and swept her up into his arms.

She felt his lips in her hair, his arms tight around her. She rocked with him as he walked.

She felt a blast of heated air. He'd carried her into the glasshouse.

"Lucy Coover," he said, setting her on the marble bench so she stood above him.

She heard the new note in his voice, and her own throat closed.

"Will you marry me?" he asked.

She'd run all this way to answer, and now she couldn't speak. She tried—it was futile—to push the lump down. The pause lengthened. He scratched his neck, heaved a sigh.

"You *don't* make this easy," he told her. She worked her throat again. God above. She pressed her hands to her neck to signal that she was too filled up—with emotion, with love—to force out a single word. But he'd linked his hands behind his back and was searching the shining glass dome for inspiration.

"I won't rush you," he said. "If you've decided you need more time to answer, I'll ask again, next week. Next month. Next year. *When* we marry, if I don't presume too much . . ."

At that she managed a giddy sound, not very ladylike, akin to a grunt. He glanced at her, a corner of his mouth lifting.

"When we marry, we'll go first thing to Hampshire. During my recent visit, I assessed every room in Stratton Grange. The morning room will be your studio. There's a whole wall of east-facing windows, and the light streams in across the meadow. Hampshire is abundant with cows, but I will protect you. As you know, I fear no cow on earth."

Laughter loosened her throat.

"Aye, you're a bold one," she said. His grin was widening.

"The country air will do Mr. Malkin good. Revivify his fighting spirit. Your aunt needs no such revivifying. But I think she'll like Stratton Grange."

"Aunt Marian!" Lucy clapped her hands. "She doesn't know yet! God save me, I've got to tell her at once."

"About your picture showing in the Summer Exhibition? Or about our wedding?" He caught her waist, swung her in a circle. She slid down his chest, heels hitting the floor. His voice was teasing in her ear.

"You *didn't* answer," he said. "Or you did, before, but it was all out of order. One more time? Lucy Coover . . ."

She stepped back and looked into his face.

"Will you marry me?" he asked, eyes glowing.

"Yes," she said instantly. And then she said it again, *yes*, but their mouths merged and *yes* mingled with the rushing of her quickened blood. He broke the kiss.

"I have something for you," he said, almost skipping to the marble bench. "I made it before I had the money to buy you all I want to buy you. Easels, canvases, canvas supports, pigments, oils, varnishes, a paint box, a traveling chest . . ."

She shook her head, mind reeling. Did he still think money was her motivation? But he was grinning with boyish excitement as he turned.

"Here," he said and handed her something plain, dark. A wooden oval, smooth and oiled, the curves graceful, a little circle cut out for her thumb.

"A palette?" She took it, fit it to her hand and arm. She ran her fingers over the sanded edge. Her stomach was fluttering.

"I needed something to do with my hands," he said. "Those were . . . *difficult* . . . days."

She nodded slowly, heat pricking behind her eyes. Difficult days he'd struggled with drink, that devil that he was learning to keep at bay.

Their story—his and hers—it would not be her parents' story. They'd write their own story. It wouldn't be a perfect fairy tale, pure happiness and light. It would be hard, complicated, real.

Now the tears were running down her cheeks. She had to do *something* with all this feeling. She turned on her heel and ran from the glasshouse. She heard him shout her name, confused, but she was back in a flash, bag braced against her hip. She lowered it to the ground, set the palette beside it, that most humble and heartfelt of gifts. She could already picture it smeared with every color of the rainbow.

"Take off your clothes," she said. "A reclining nude is well and good, but I have a new idea. I want you upright."

Her corpse, not a corpse at all. A living, breathing man, standing mere feet away, looking at her, eyes wide-open, green and filled with life. His life and her life too.

He lowered his head, fingers busy with buttons. Her breath caught as he opened his shirt, and he heard it, looked up, and grinned as he kicked out of his trousers. His watch had fallen from his pocket, and they both saw it wink in the light. They glanced at each other in agreement.

Everything else could wait.

She pulled her sketchbook from her bag, turned the pencil around and around in her fingers. Where to start? She loved *all* of him. Every line, every curve. She smiled, thinking of the time that stretched before them. She'd start here today, there tomorrow.

She pressed her pencil lead to the page.

AUTHOR'S NOTE

I GREW UP reading and loving Victorian novels. At the age of ten, I set my first "novel" in London's gothic fog: hundreds of composition book pages about the misadventures of orphaned Oliver Twistish mice. The fog served a dual purpose. It was atmospheric, *and* it obscured much of the city, so I didn't have to worry about details. (The fact that all of the characters were rodents also helped explain the geographical vagueness.) I traveled to England for the first time decades later, when I started writing *The Duke Undone*. There are a few mice in *The Duke Undone*, but they aren't the main characters. To do justice to my human Victorians, I committed myself to collecting the details that would enable me to evoke the setting and time period.

Lucy was the character who came to me first. I grew up reading Victorian novels, and I also liked to look at prints of broody, mysterious paintings by Pre-Raphaelite artists. I had the idea to write a romance that followed an artist in Victorian London. Anecdotes about the Pre-Raphaelites tend to focus on the dynamic between male geniuses and their female models. I knew I wanted to flip the expected genders of the artist and the muse, and that Lucy would be a painter.

This meant I had to learn about art education in late nineteenth century London, particularly as it pertained to women. I decided to make Lucy a student at the Royal Academy Schools. In the late eighteenth century and early nineteenth century, the Royal Academy of Arts in London was the defining force in English art. The most well-regarded English artists trained at the Royal Academy Schools, showed in the Summer Exhibitions, and became Academicians, receiving privileges that helped them further consolidate their reputations and the academic tradition.

By the 1880s, the Royal Academy didn't completely dominate the scene, and many artists were bored by its aesthetic; venues such as the Grosvenor Gallery provided artists with alternatives. But the Royal Academy retained its influence, and a painting hung "on the line" could make an artist's career. Lucy dreams of becoming another Elizabeth Thompson, Lady Butler, who became famous overnight after showing *The Roll Call* in the Summer Exhibition in 1874.

Women were admitted to the Schools in 1860, but even in the 1880s they didn't receive equal instruction. In *The Duke Undone*, Kate and Lucy are petitioning for life classes. Female students did petition (repeatedly) for permission to draw from the partially draped model. They didn't receive it until 1893. Robert Yardley's patronizing attitude toward female students wouldn't have been uncommon. To portray Yardley's condescension, I relied heavily on G. D. Leslie's book *The Inner Life of the Royal Academy*, which I read while researching at the Royal Academy of Arts' library. Leslie, writing in the early twentieth century, claimed that pretty girls make the best students (and he called the admission of women an "invasion"). His descriptions of the Royal Academy are very informative and often very pithy. I borrowed a line of his and put it in Kate's mouth; Leslie is the one who disparaged the bulk of submissions to the Summer Exhibition as "piteous pictures of Yorkshire seaports."

While I was at the library, I also had the opportunity to read through the archives, where I saw original petitions and a copy of the school laws from 1882. I got a chance to roam the basement hallways of Burlington House and to stand in the classroom where Lucy meets Anthony (when he's conscious). All of which was immensely helpful as I visualized and dramatized daily life at the Schools.

To develop the plot surrounding Lucy's eviction and Anthony's inheritance, I consulted books and articles on the municipal politics of late nineteenth century slum clearances and Victorian estate law. I found *The Government of Victorian London, 1855-1889: The Metropolitan Board of Works, the Vestries, and the City Corporation* by David Edward Owen particularly useful, as well as *The Bitter Cry of Outcast London* by Andrew Mearns and William C. Preston. I wanted to get the social and legal history "right," or right enough that nothing I wrote was strictly impossible or anachronistic.

Along the way, I fell into plenty of research rabbit holes. Every now and then, a writing day would be swallowed up by a bottomless new fascination; for example, corpulent cattle art. In the early nineteenth century, wealthy farmers commissioned portraits to celebrate and advertise their biggest, girthiest ox and heifers. Some of these portraits—such as John Boultbee's painting of the Durham Ox— circulated widely as engravings, and on decorative ceramics. Of course, Lucy's talents as an artist lie elsewhere. But drawing cows might have been a good plan B.

ACKNOWLEDGMENTS

THIS BOOK WAS a collaborative effort, and I have so many people to thank, I can't possibly do all or adequate thanking here. This is just a preliminary sketch of my gratitude! Thanks to my unflinching, unstinting agent, Tara Gelsomino, for the honesty, support, and vision. Thanks to my editor, Kate Seaver, for reading so sharply and so generously, and for asking the right questions, and thanks, too, to the whole team at Berkley.

I'm grateful to Wake Forest University for funding my research trip to the Royal Academy of Arts in London, and to Jessica Richard and the entire English department: faculty, staff, and students. You inspire my thinking and my writing practice. And answer so many of my questions about nineteenth century history and literature! Thanks in particular to Amy Catanzano and Eric Wilson, and the rest of Team CRW.

Thanks to Mark Pomeroy for orienting me to the relevant archives in the Royal Academy of Arts Library.

Thanks to Yaddo for the most magical winter ever. I didn't work on this book in the snowy woods, but I talked about it with my co-residents at dinner and their enthusiasm recommitted me to the project.

Thanks to my first readers, Joanna and John—onward to the island! And to my dramaturges, Julia, Robert, Marina, Cat, and Sarah E. Without them I would still be pronouncing the "s" in viscount. And doing who knows what else. Thanks to Anand for listening to me talk about law in Victorian England and telling me I wasn't making sense. Thanks to the friends who've turned Winston-Salem into home: Sarah H., Matt, Frankie, Marcia, Saylor, and Rian. Thanks to the girl gang for dialogue and Double Dutch. Thanks to my Providence community and its diaspora. Thanks to Hana and Miriam (much more than two) for sharing their strength. Thanks to Christine for crystallinity. Thanks to Lamar for the gift of the list. Thanks to Brad and Dona for forming the Sandgate artist posse and keeping me saner. Thanks to Art for reminding me of our work and why we do it. Thanks to Brian Conn for being Brian Conn. Meows to Kitty MaKat, aunt of feline magic. Stiv forever. Thanks to the friends with whom and for whom I build new versions of the world: Nico, Chemlawn, Corinne, Radhika, and Joanna. Thanks to Mir, whose love language is acts of service (and all the other ones). And thanks to my parents and my brother, whose love has always meant everything.

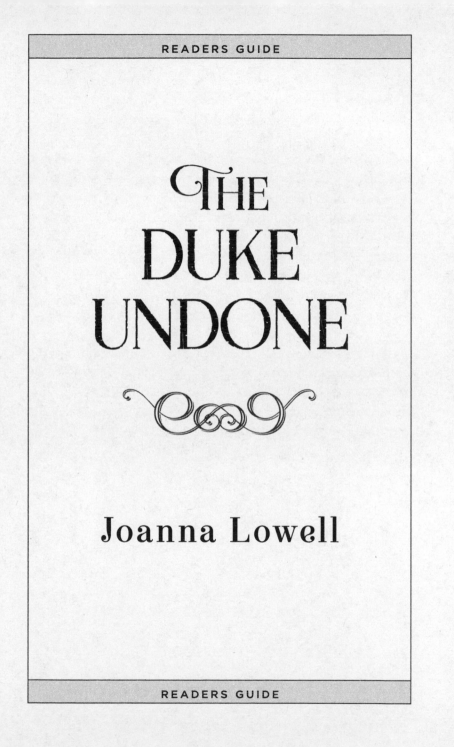

THE
DUKE
UNDONE

Joanna Lowell

Questions for Discussion

1. Lucy feels like an outsider at the Royal Academy for multiple reasons. In what contexts have you felt like an outsider and how did you react to the experience?

2. Lucy and Kate are working on behalf of equal education for women at the Academy Schools. Nonetheless, they're critical of many of the female students. Are they reinscribing sexist assumptions even as they work for equality? How should we grapple with this kind of contradiction?

3. Why does Anthony have such a hard time freeing himself from Robert Yardley's control? If Anthony hadn't met Lucy, would he have let Yardley manipulate him into marrying Lavinia?

4. Like her mother before her, Effie is put in an asylum without her consent and under false pretenses. We can blame Robert Yardley's machinations, but their confinement is made possible by the larger society, which links female sexuality to hysteria and considers women particularly vulnerable to psychological disorder. How is "madness" understood by the different characters? In what ways have attitudes toward

mental health changed since the nineteenth century? In what ways haven't they?

5. Anthony behaves self-destructively, at least in part, because of various traumas, including his family losses and his experiences in the army. What are some of the signs that he has begun to heal? Is there a particular moment you think marks a shift for him?

6. Do you feel any sympathy for Robert Yardley? What about for Lavinia? What do you think will happen to her as a result of her father's disgrace?

7. What are the challenges to Lucy and Anthony's happily ever after? What one piece of advice would you give each of them at their wedding?

8. If an artist were going to immortalize *you* in a portrait, what pose would you strike? How would you want to be depicted? Describe your portrait! Where would it hang?

Photo by Mir Yarfitz

Joanna Lowell lives among the fig trees in North Carolina, where she teaches in the English department at Wake Forest University. When she's not writing historical romance, she writes other things as Joanna Ruocco. Those books include *Dan*, *Another Governess / The Least Blacksmith*, *The Week*, and *Field Glass*, coauthored with Joanna Howard.

Ready to find
your next great read?

Let us help.

Visit prh.com/nextread

Penguin
Random
House